WRATH
OF THE
TALON

WRATH OF THE TALON

SOPHIE KIM

Westhampton Free Library
7 Library Avenue
Westhampton Beach, NY 11978

This book is a work of fiction. Names, characters, places, and incidents are the product of the author's imagination or are used fictitiously. Any resemblance to actual events, locales, or persons, living or dead, is coincidental.

Copyright © 2024 by Sophie Kim. All rights reserved, including the right to reproduce, distribute, or transmit in any form or by any means. For information regarding subsidiary rights, please contact the Publisher.

Entangled Publishing, LLC
644 Shrewsbury Commons Ave., STE 181
Shrewsbury, PA 17361
rights@entangledpublishing.com

Entangled Teen is an imprint of Entangled Publishing, LLC.

Visit our website at www.entangledpublishing.com.

Edited by Stacy Abrams
Cover illustration and design by Elizabeth Turner Stokes
Interior design by Toni Kerr

Trade Paperback ISBN 978-1-64937-399-1
Hardcover ISBN 978-1-64937-721-0
Ebook ISBN 978-1-64937-425-7

Manufactured in the United States of America

First Printing April 2024

10 9 8 7 6 5 4 3 2 1

ALSO BY SOPHIE KIM

TALONS SERIES
Last of the Talons
Wrath of the Talon

For the angry girls.

At Entangled, we want our readers to be well-informed. If you would like to know if this book contains any elements that might be of concern for you, please check the back of the book for details.

Dear Reader,

I am so excited to welcome you to the dark, romantic sequel of the Talon trilogy. This book is steeped in angst, revenge, and — of course — Korean mythology.

As I have stated before in the previous installment, retellings keep mythologies alive. They anchor them to the modern world and stave off the ever-present threat of obscurity.

Wrath of the Talon is categorized as such a retelling, and I therefore feel obliged to gently remind the audience that it is not intended to be a guide to traditional Korean mythology. This book in particular focuses heavily on the creature known as the Imugi, and for the purpose of Lina and Rui's story, their portrayal in *Wrath of the Talon* does depart from their original representation.

If you are interested in diving into the rich and fascinating folklore of Korea in its traditional context, I recommend purchasing a copy of *Korean Myths and Legends* by Hwang Pae-gang and translated by Han Young-hie. You may also visit folkency.nfm.go.kr, where a variety of resources relating to both Korean mythology and culture may be found.

It brings me great joy to introduce *Wrath of the Talon*, a book that I hold very close to my heart. It is a love letter to the stories of my heritage, to readers searching for representation, and of course the angry girls, to which Shin Lina herself belongs.

A world of hidden realms, assassins, emperors, dark truths, lies, and love awaits your return.

Happy reading,

Sophie Kim

PRELUDE

An assassin and a Dokkaebi emerge from a corridor of wavering darkness onto a night-blackened street. Shadows dance around the pair as they stand on the uneven cobblestones, staring out at the decrepit kingdom before them. The air is thick with summer heat. It smells of sweat and grime and of spoiled, rotten things that the assassin knows far too well.

The Dokkaebi wrinkles his nose in distaste.

"Well," he says, and his voice is silky smooth, lilting and harmonious, much like the melody of the flute he carries in his slender, ringed hands. "This is where I leave you."

The assassin is silent, her gaze trained on a point far in the distance. Her jaw is set and her mouth is tight. There is a haunted look to her, for her face has paled—but not with fear, not with grief.

With anger.

Pure, blistering *anger*.

The Dokkaebi watches her carefully, the sharp lines of his face gentling. Slowly, he coaxes a ring off one of his fingers—a simple silver ring, matching the argon of his eyes, with an engraving on the underside of the metal where it rests upon skin.

Call to me, it reads in the Old Language, *and I will come.*

"Here," says the Dokkaebi softly, passing the ring to his companion. "I had it made in the palace forge and enchanted by Kang before we departed. Press it to your lips and I will come to you, no matter the time, no matter the distance, no matter the circumstance."

The assassin takes the ring. It fits her fourth finger perfectly. The metal is surprisingly warm against her skin. She turns her dark eyes onto the Dokkaebi. "Rui," she says, very quietly, as if tasting his name on her tongue. She almost smiles.

Almost.

The Dokkaebi becomes very still—still as only an immortal can become—as the assassin stands on her tiptoes and lightly presses her lips against his. It is a butterfly's kiss, sweet and warm and fleeting. The assassin draws away, and once again her face is grim and wan.

"Keep Eunbi safe," she whispers. "Keep her happy. Keep her away from this kingdom."

"I will do as you bid me, Shin Lina." He takes her hand in his. "She will want for nothing."

Satisfied, the assassin nods. Turns back to the city. Curls her hands into fists.

The Dokkaebi watches as moonlight cuts white flame upon the dark green scales emerging onto the assassin's skin—at the razor-sharp scales protruding from the backs of her hands, deadly blades of sparkling teal.

The assassin does not see the flash of uncertainty that crosses the Dokkaebi's face. Does not see his jaw tighten—in concern, in sorrow, in dread.

In something almost like fear.

She sees only the road before her, paved with revenge. "Goodbye, Rui," she says quietly.

Silver eyes glitter with a dark amusement that is centuries old. "Farewell, little thief," he murmurs. "I await your calling. Most eagerly."

The assassin smiles.

An hour later, Shin Lina stands in a puddle of Unima Hisao's blood.

The storm has begun.

PART ONE

FROM DUST AND SHADOW

CHAPTER ONE

Starting a particularly bloody brawl in a tavern is by no means difficult. *Anonymously* starting a particularly bloody brawl in a tavern, however, is a completely different sort of game. It requires stealth, it requires a sleight of hand, and above all—it requires patience.

Sitting in the corner of the Moonlit Hare, Sunpo's dingiest jumak, sweat slides down my back and dampens the heavy material of my cloak. My skin sticks to the dark fabric, and underneath the rim of my black gat, my forehead is shiny with sweat, the silk headband stuck uncomfortably to my skin.

Even though the heat of summer lays over Sunpo's streets, festering and feeding upon the dilapidated kingdom and seeping into the jumak through its thatched roof, I refuse to remove the cloak concealing my black stealth suit from view.

It is similar to the one I wore with the Talons. Sleek and black, skintight but sturdy, and easy to move in. Rui wanted to add facets that no mortal tailor could have accomplished—a fabric that could stop even the deadliest of blades, hidden tools that, when uncapped, release blankets of smoke, a cooling contraption to fight against the Sunpo summer—but I declined, having no need for such things when I can summon my scales. I don't even need the jikdo I secured to the sheath at my waist, but the weight of it comforts me. Relaxes me. Yet I take care to keep my posture stiff, masculine.

I must keep the guise of a man, one who sits idly in a crevice, blending into the shadows as he traces the rim of his earthenware cup, nothing visible of his face underneath the hat save for his thin lips and the faintest outline of a white tear-streak that is a scar.

The jumak is small, filthy, and cramped. The wooden floor on which I sit is half rotten and uneven, the flimsy pillow underneath me doing little to cushion my backside. Across the tavern, men sit and drink makgeolli with sun-chapped lips, guzzling the sweet alcohol in pursuit of the cool aftertaste. The air is thick with humidity and chatter, which a month ago would have masked the stifled moans coming from the lodging rooms surrounding the jumak's tavern — but my keen ears pick up the ecstatic groaning of men, the gasps of women, and the creaking of their beds. Somewhere, a cockroach scuttles over bedsheets, dodging tangled limbs. I hear the scrape of its legs against the stiff fabric, the whispering of its antennae as they rub together in wariness.

My mouth curls in disgust and I do my best to block all other sounds save for those in the tavern. It is incredibly hard to tunnel my focus like this, to narrow my new, Imugi senses.

Those senses now strain to be unleashed and sometimes break free, subjecting me to an influx of debilitating sensation. My mind grows heavy with the effort, but I no longer hear the scuttling roach, nor the rhythmic thumping of sweat-drenched bodies, thank the gods.

A tall teenage boy with a strong brow and rumpled black hair weaves through the cluster of customers, carrying wooden trays of miyeok-guk for whomever was fool enough to order a bowl of steaming seaweed soup in this heat. The men glower acerbically at him as he walks past, but he ignores them, setting his jaw against the sneers. One of them, with a nasty smile, sticks out a foot to trip him. I narrow my eyes, but the boy nimbly dodges it and picks his way over to a slight, slender man dressed in a thin cotton hanbok.

The man is hollow with hunger, his face all angular bones. As the tray clatters before him on the low table he shares with some five other men, he falls upon the food like a stray dog who has not eaten in weeks. I watch flecks of hot soup dribble down his skinny neck with a hollow feeling in the pit of my own full stomach. Even from my spot some twenty feet away, my sharp eyesight can spot the pale-yellow liquid glisten atop sallow skin.

He drinks, he chews on the slick seaweed, he drains the bowl to dregs.

Gwan Doyun.

My target of the night.

The soup is cheap; that is why he ordered it. Gwan Doyun, once a prolific artisan, has fallen on hard times ever since the Blackbloods took over the kingdom.

Ever since eleven months ago, when the Blackbloods dispatched their Reaper to the door of his giwajip.

Doyun, an old ally of the Talons, did not pay the ludicrously expensive monthly tribute to Sunpo's new crime lord—Konrarnd Kalmin. The price that Kalmin demanded in retribution was the life of Doyun's wife.

And the Reaper had no choice but to make him pay it.

She slit the woman's throat and disappeared into the night, leaving no evidence behind, a wraith in the darkness. The next week, Doyun sent over his check. And has continued to do so ever since. He is loyal only out of fear. Out of weakness.

A fear and weakness that I shoved upon him. Gnawing on my bottom lip hard enough for a bead of blood to well up and wet my tongue, I shove down the memory of that night. What has passed, has passed. I cannot undo the slip of my dagger against the woman's throat. I cannot stop her skin from splitting, nor can I stop the red from spilling. I cannot give Gwan Doyun his wife back. I can, however, give him something else.

But first—first, I must take something.

He still wears his wedding ring. Still rubs it from time to time, a look of deep mourning crossing his face. That ring is all he has left. I do not want to take it from him, but I must.

In the end, I tell myself, he might thank me for this manipulation. I cling to that thought as the door of the jumak creaks open, letting in a blast of thick night air sticky with heat.

I slowly stand from my spot in the corner and melt into the shadows, invisible save for the flash of my white teeth as I allow myself a grim smile.

Right on time.

The Blackblood patrol I have been watching these past few days steps into the jumak, as they always do, at half past midnight. The Moonlit Hare is their favorite haunt, an establishment that once belonged to the Talons but now belongs to their gang. There are three of them, all Claws, all wearing the simple gray hanboks signifying their rank.

From their swagger, one might think them to be Feathers or Bills in the Blackblood gang, high in the hierarchy that starts at a crane's claws and works its way up to its crest. The Crown, of course, is Konrarnd Kalmin. The Crest, Kalmin's right-hand woman, Asina. I was once part of the Bills, trained killers who dirty their hands in Sunpo's blood for the godsdamned Crown, although that didn't stop Kalmin from using me as a Feather—a heistman—when he sent me to steal the tapestry from the Temple of Ruin. Legs are the ones who recruit and arrange street deals, the ones who manage the slavering Claws.

Claws. They're expendables, bottom-feeders, the lowest of the low. Kalmin finds them in the darkest, grimiest places, choosing them for their subordinance, their loyalty to the one who feeds them. They eat out of the palm of his hand. They worship the ground he walks on. They would lick his boots, if he gave them the chance. And I'm looking at three of them right now.

One of them I know.

Not the one who is short and squat with a patch of thinning black hair and a wobbling jowl. Not the one who is small and reedy with teeth like a rat. No, it's the brutish one with bruises dappling his rough skin whom I know.

Sometimes, when a Claw has been especially prolific in their drug-shuttling and weapon-dealings, Kalmin will give them a reward.

Sometimes, he will allow them to torture insubordinates.

Man Jisu used to beat me on the orders of Konrarnd Kalmin. There had always been a feverish, fervent look in his eyes. He'd enjoyed it. It was his reward.

His death will come soon enough.

Swallowing hard, I breathe in through my nose, willing my pulse to steady. I can smell the short one's breath. It stinks of cheap halji and even cheaper wine. Once, the smell of halji would have sent my throat itching for an inhale of that ashy smoke. Now I feel only a mild craving—one that I shove down, determined not to allow myself the longing pangs of withdrawal. It is becoming easier to ignore them. Perhaps one day I will not feel them at all.

Promise me that you will stop before it takes you, Sang had pleaded as we stood together in Jeoseung. I close my eyes, breathing past the grief that squeezes my heart at the memory of him—of how he pleaded for me to live. Truly *live*, away from the influence of halji.

It is difficult, but I am trying my best. Swallowing hard, I reopen my eyes and force myself to focus.

The Blackbloods are seated by the boy a table away from Doyun. They lower themselves onto the lumpy cushions, their beady eyes cutting into him in a way that makes my head cock analytically. There is a tenuous sort of violence in the air. It is subtle and nonurgent, yet still thick enough that I can taste it in the back of my throat. Perhaps the boy owes the Blackbloods a debt, or perhaps he has slighted them in some way.

Either way, the Claws' distaste toward him is palpable. I watch as the boy takes their harsh orders coolly, calmly, before leaving. His shoulders are stiff as he disappears, and his mouth is a tight line, but other than that he is unfazed—even as leers follow him through the jumak and as the same man again attempts to trip him. This is a daily occurrence, then. One that, although concerning, doesn't require my intervention, at least at the moment.

I turn my attention back to the table, where the men drum their fingers impatiently.

The brand of the Blackbloods—that black crane captured mid-landing—is marked on the back of their hands and is visible to all.

And Doyun has seen them. The man is staring at them, his face drained of all blood, his long soup spoon trembling in his hand. The silver shakes. Sweat dribbles down his crooked nose. His hand reaches for the small dagger at his waist. His pupils are dilated, and his mouth is a tight white line.

Guilt stabs into my side, bitter and dark. He is scared, but I need him to be angry. Fear is not enough to want to take a stand, to join my side, but fury is. And although I hate myself for it, I can push Doyun that final step.

I move along the wall, careful to keep to the shadows, where I am unseen. It is one of the many new tricks that I have learned—how to slither through the night unnoticed, as sly and as silent as a snake. It is still an effort to do so, though. These past few weeks I have been inconsistent in my agility, sometimes fast and lethal, other times like a fawn learning to walk. I am still learning how to navigate this new body of mine. This form that is both Imugi and human.

The ratlike one is speaking. His voice is garbled and wet, like the flowing of brown water through the kingdom's sewers. "—eyein' the Dove Coop in the Boneburrow," he says as I slip from one side of the room to the other. Now I stand to the left of their table, invisible. Not even Doyun, his eyes darting frantically around the Moonlit Hare, catches a glimpse of me. "Song Iseul is late on her payments—again. Boss wants us to head on over in the mornin', and I'm all happy to, if we get a taste of the girls there. There ain't nothin' like a Dove."

"They're damn expensive, though," the squat one sighs. He's polishing a jagged-looking blade. There are flecks of dried blood along the sharp metal. "So much money for a little birdie."

"Song's girls are the best, Hada." The rat sniffs through his nose. "You would know if you had any taste at all. But Song, she's a bitch and a half if there ever was one. Kalmin's got a mind to kill her and just be done with her *antics* if she doesn't pay up. And I don't blame him. He's the king of Sunpo. He survived Gyeulcheon. Bitch should treat him with the proper respect."

I bite back a scoff.

Konrarnd Kalmin, leader of the Blackbloods, survived the realm of the Dokkaebi because *somebody* went to hell and back — literally — to ensure his safe return. Now he feasts and ruts every night, believing himself an emperor, a victor. Believing the one who brought him back dead. But I am not dead.

The bastard is in for quite the surprise.

This kingdom is mine.

And his reign will be over soon enough.

"I'll do it," Man Jisu offers. His voice is surprisingly quiet, with an undertone of sweetness that sends a chill down my spine. "I'd *like* to do it."

"I'm sure you would, Jisu," Rat mutters, spitting on his blade and polishing it some more. "I'm sure that you would more than like it."

In the shadows against the wall, I count the weapons between the trio of Blackbloods. Between Hada's jagged blade, the two triple-bullet pistols strapped to Jisu's waist, the jikdo with its hilt resting comfortably in Rat's hand, and Doyun's knife, the possibility for a very bloody brawl is *astronomical*.

If I can manage to be quick and nimble, then what follows will be delightful.

If my body betrays me, as it is so prone to doing these days, then what follows will be notably unpleasant for me.

Rat's back is to Doyun, who is sweating so much that the stench of his fear fills my nose, bitter and sharp. Hada and Jisu sit across from him, but their attentions are on the returning serving boy, who is carrying three cups of makgeolli, his eyes trained on the ground and lips pressed tightly together.

Doyun has begun to stand from his seat, his knees knocking together, terrified of the men before him.

I allow my arm to emerge from the folds of the cloak. I push up the sleeve of my black stealth suit underneath to reveal a print of a dark crane mid-landing. I despise the feeling of it on my skin. It lives on it like a leech, slimy and cold. But it will wash off easily enough after I am done with it, nothing but cheap paint.

As far as my plans for the Blackbloods go, I must admit that this one is rather elementary. But it will work all the same.

One, two, three...

I wait until the three real Blackbloods are occupied with retrieving their drinks from the tray the boy has set in front of them.

Now. I must move *now*.

Hoping fervently that I do not stumble or otherwise make a fool of myself, I emerge from the shadows. It is a small victory that I am swift and graceful as I appear directly before Doyun with my back to Rat, a terrible smile on my face. A victory that right now, at least, my body is doing what I tell it to do.

Doyun flinches, his eyes widening and flicking to the brand on my arm. *Blackblood,* I see him think. *What does he want from me what will he take from me I have nothing left to give nothing left to lose they already took everything everything everything everything...*

My smile grows.

And then I attack him.

I keep the attack quick. Businesslike. There is no need to hurt him more than I already have. I stomp perfunctorily on his foot, land a quick yet light blow to his stomach, and while he's distracted, I take the wedding ring from his hand. I was, after all, a pickpocket before I was an assassin. Sleights of hand are not foreign to me. Rather, performing them reminds me of coming home. The familiarity is comforting, much like a warm embrace.

Doyun gasps for breath like a fish out of water, gasps in horror, as I flick his wedding ring into the air. The golden band spins, twirls like a miniature sun, and hovers motionless for a perfect moment—before plummeting down to the makgeolli within Rat's small earthenware bowl.

I am gone before it hits the surface of the milky golden liquid with a tiny plop, gone before it sinks to the bottom of the dish like a stone thrown into a lake.

Gone before the jumak erupts into chaos.

They won't kill him, I reassure myself as I gnaw on my lip. *Not tonight, anyway. Not while he can still pay tribute.*

He may stumble away with a swollen eye, bruises as tender as midsummer fruit, and a few fractured bones—but they will allow him to keep his life.

While they keep his wedding ring.

And there is nothing more dangerous, nor as angry, as a man who now truly has nothing left to lose—and everything to gain. I will help him take his life back, if he lets me. I will help him find his feet again, if he lets me. I truly hope that he does.

I am filled with a guilty sort of satisfaction, mingled with regret, as I slip through Sunpo's Fingertrap, thankful for the territory's perpetual state of ruin. There are no lanterns to light the way of the street, for candlewax is much too expensive for the kingdom's denizens to afford, leaving the streets shrouded in an inky darkness. But the darkness proves no problem for me—my feet know these streets well, and my eyes are much sharper than they once were. I am pleased that, at least right now, I am nimble instead of clumsy. It has been at least a day since I last tripped and fell over my own feet, the world screeching around me. I'm growing stronger, more at home within this skin.

In a twisted sort of way, I suppose I am grateful for the attack in the woods. Grateful that Wang Jiwoon, leader of the Gyeulcheon rebel group known as the Revolution, witnessed my betrayal on the beach, my indiscretion with the emperor I'd thought to kill. The fatal wound I obtained as punishment resulted in my ingestion of the wongun enhancer, which in turn granted me this.

Power, beyond my wildest dreams.

Strength, beyond what I ever could have hoped for.

Victory.

It wasn't just the enhancer that gave us these gifts, a voice — brittle and ancient, as cold as the stars — whispers in my mind. It echoes throughout the chambers of my cognizance, turning my warm sweat ice cold. The summer night is suddenly sharply chill. I swallow hard and quicken my pace through the street as if I can outrun the words that slither across the crevices of my consciousness. *That blade, the blade in our chest. It was laced with Imugi venom. We were born from venom. Born from poison. Born from the scale of a snake. Do not forget that, Shin Lina.* It sounds triumphant and scolding all at once. *Do not forget.*

I swallow hard, tasting sickness in my mouth. How can I forget that I am born from the enemy of the Dokkaebi and gods? The gods that I cherish. It has become a habit of mine to hope, fervently, that the gods will accept me as I am despite my scales. But a part of me whispers that they surely would not. A part of me wonders if I am even worthy to pray to them.

Leave me alone, I snap harshly, blinking rapidly. *I do not want to listen to you tonight.*

The Voice laughs softly. *Your manners are atrocious.*

In the two weeks that have passed since my rebirth, the Voice has been...speaking to me.

Sometimes it slumbers, silent, but often it does not. I thought it was the Thought at first—my old enemy, trailing dark sludge in its wake as it whispered torments. *Sang, Chara, Yoonho, Chryse...*

But it soon became clear that the Voice was something else entirely.

The Thought never had such a...a *cadence* to it. It was my own guilt, my own trauma, whispering to me. It lacked the steely, ancient tone of the Voice. The Thought was the shame of a broken girl, one who had lost everything and everyone.

I do not hear the Thought anymore. I hear only the Voice.

A part of me wonders if the Voice tore the Thought to shreds like some rabid animal finding another trespassing in its territory. For the Voice, I've quickly realized, is *different*. It is...alive, almost. More than the Thought—echoes of memories, reflections of guilt, exacerbations of my fears—ever had been.

And the first time I heard it...

Open your eyes and find out, it murmured as harsh white light—life—streamed into my body, as I questioned what the cold, cruel blaze of power making its home among my bones and blood could possibly be. And it returned in the gardens, as Jiwoon stalked toward me, his ax glinting in his hands. **What wonders will we perform together?**

This, I replied.

The scales came for the first time then. Sharp and glittering and beautiful. Blades from my own body. Scaleblades, I call them now.

And with them, I cut out Jiwoon's heart.

My power within me seemed to rejoice at that.

Power should not be able to speak. I know that is what Rui, or Kang, would say to me if I told them of the voice that has come with the power, with the changes.

"*It is not possible,*" Kang would say with that wary look on his face to which I am now so often subjected. He would scrutinize me, his jaw tight, as if despite everything that has happened since the forest, I am still not to be trusted. "*Power is not sentient. Power does not converse.*"

And yet to me, it does.

It should not be so.

For this reason, I do not tell them. I do not tell anybody. Something has held my tongue the few times I have summoned up the courage to approach even Rui.

Haneul Rui, my friend, my…something more. The Dokkaebi I was meant to kill but kissed instead. The Dokkaebi I have come to care for in a way I thought myself incapable of since — since Sang died.

Deeply. Earnestly. *Fervently*.

Yet something has quelled the words in my mouth until the taste of them fades, leaving me silent, the struggle within my mind unknown to anybody but myself.

On the street, I slow. My left leg is aching. My muscles there are cramped and sore. It is hard to fight past the limp that has remained even as my strength has grown. I could use salves, tinctures, but it feels almost wrong to seek such comfort when this pain is a reminder of my mistakes. Of my story.

I am, however, comforted by the fact that I will find Asina soon enough, and that she will pay for digging her dagger so deeply into my left thigh.

They will *all* pay. Starting with the Claws. Then the Legs, the Feathers, the Bills, the Crest, and — finally — that filthy, filthy Crown.

For Sang. For Chara. For Yoonho. For Chryse —

I pause, my ears pricking.

Despite the empty street, the kingdom is far from silent. There is the clinking of glasses, the rumble of distant carts, the weary neighing of horses, the rustle of bedsheets, the humming of cicadas, and the distant boom of a far-off summer storm. The sounds blur together, forming a symphony that rises and falls to the rhythm of life. I am learning to tune this song out well enough, focusing on only what is directly before me, on what I must hear.

There are, of course, times where this song slips through, blaring loud enough that I fall to my knees with my hands clapped over my ears, rocking back and forth as Rui holds my shoulders, murmuring soothing words that I can barely hear…but those times have lessened thanks to the auditory exercises the emperor has guided me through.

But now I allow myself to expand my senses, searching for the sound I thought I'd heard. It had been a—a rustling, almost. A susurration.

A slithering.

CHAPTER TWO

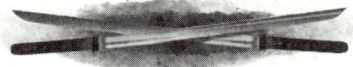

I stand motionless for a few long moments, sifting through sound after sound, my head beginning to pound. My muscles tense, even as my heart stumbles in...in something so similar to *longing*.

Unbidden, I remember a dark mist and a thunderstorm. A flash of teal scale. A fast-melting candle dribbling warm wax upon my fingers. Unbidden, I remember the dreams that have been plaguing me ever since I left Yeomra's realm.

I inhale a shaky breath, slamming my senses back, focusing on only what is before me. It would not do me any favors to stand here the entire night, straining for a sound that is not here. *Fool*, I chide myself, even as I unclench my fingers from where they wrapped tightly around the hilt of my jikdo. *They do not come here, to Iseung.*

The Voice may laugh, husky and knowing. But I am not sure.

Soon enough, I reach the small hanok in which I have stayed the past three days and release a sigh of relief as I unlock the door. Tomorrow, I will pay a visit to Gwan Doyun. After tonight's events, his allegiance should be easy enough to win. And although his wound is still raw, I can offer—comfort. Money. Power, if only he stands by me.

It will never fix what I have done, but it is a start. He will never be hungry again, not when I rule this kingdom. He will be healthy. Happy. And perhaps in time, there will be another woman. Another wife, sweet and supple and whole. Alive.

This is my apology.

I slip inside the giwajip and shut the door firmly behind me.

The image of Doyun happy should quell this rising wave of guilt, but it does not. Slowly, I make my way to the lukewarm, murky bucket of water in the hanok's bathroom. Swallowing hard against my dry mouth, I remove my gat and the headband, and coax my hair out of its topknot. I splash my face with the water and squeeze my eyes tightly shut.

I am profiting from his pain. As much as I may say that this is for him, it is just as much for me.

Hush, the Voice snaps, as icily as a winter wind. **We have done what is necessary. The man will help us now. What are his hurt feelings compared to the blood spilled in the palace of the Talons? What is his grief compared to ours? He lost but one. We have lost many. I do not need to remind you of their names.**

The bloodbath of that one fateful night flashes before me. Chara and Chryse, their blond hair matted with blood, blood-soaked blades embedded in their chests. Yoonho, a dark hole rupturing the center of his forehead, red trickling out of his mouth.

Sang's face lingers longer than the others, ghostly pale, the eyes that had once been a warm hazel, blank and unseeing. His body is patched with bullets.

I squeeze my eyes shut and reopen them, pushing the images from my mind. *I have been where he is. I have had everything taken from me.* I stare into the chipped mirror. *Who am I to inflict this upon somebody else? I killed his wife. I took his ring. I pushed him into hurt. I killed his wife.*

I remember that night well. Slipping into Doyun's chogajip, murdering his love. Imagining Yeomra, God of Death, standing behind me and steadying my shaking hand.

She had been small, young. Pretty in her sleep, with rosebud lips and long dark lashes.

I didn't want to kill her, but I did.

You had no choice, the Voice whispers reassuringly. **Your**

decisions were not your own, back then. Kalmin threatened our sister.

There is always a choice. I scrub water and rough soap on the crane I'd painted on my forearm with ink earlier, hating the look of it on my skin. The water of the basin turns black and my skin turns red and raw. *And for so long, I have been making the wrong ones. Demands…do not always hold dominance over what is right.*

Those words are not our own. Those are from the tongue of the Dokkaebi. These words are uttered with clear distaste.

The girl in the mirror scoffs. For a moment, she is as unfamiliar as a stranger. She does not want the kingdom to recognize her, and for a moment, even I do not. But despite the changes, my face—the face of a killer—is the same. I turn away and close my eyes as shame once again rises within me, but the image of myself is still imprinted in my memory.

Black hair, scraping against my collarbones. A thick fringe, released from its band, concealing my forehead and falling into my eyes. A white scar running down the side of my face, spilling out from just underneath my right eye to the corner of my lip, where the puncture of the blade is deeper, a mockery of a teardrop. My nose, long and pointed. My mouth a thin white line curled into a sneer. I know that I am not pretty in the way I long to be. The little beauty I had is faded, replaced by something…unearthly. I am not entirely human.

Disregard what the Dokkaebi said, the Voice continues. **Do not feel guilt over this death.**

I have taken the words to my heart. I had a choice. I chose wrong. I always chose wrong, back then. I open my eyes and strip off my sweat-drenched cloak and suit until I pace naked in the darkness, wishing that the Voice would leave. It does not.

Well, the Voice says as the floorboards creak underneath my bare feet. **She is gone, she is dead, and there is a job to do. What was she to you? Nothing.**

But she was somebody to him. And I took her. Just as Kalmin took my family from me. I run shaky hands through my hair. *I'm not going to be like that. Not anymore. No more innocents. No more undeserved death. I have power, now. Real power. I need to act—like the gods do. Fair. Just.*

Good.

Do the Good feel such guilt? sneers the Voice, and I swallow hard. Guilt. Other than the Voice, it is my one constant companion. Even after my reunion with Sang in the underworld realm of Jeoseung, even after the gentle reassurances his Gwisin spoke to me, the guilt still continues to wrap spindly fingers around my throat and squeeze hard until black spots ebb and flow in the corners of my vision.

Like the pain in my leg, like the teardrop scar that did not disappear with the emergence of my…my change, the guilt is a part of me. It is as familiar as the sound of my little sister's windchime laughter, as the backs of my own hands.

But I have returned. To Sunpo. And I have a chance to right my wrongs.

The Pied Piper kept true to his word. In accordance with my wishes, Gyeulcheon's fickle emperor did indeed release Konrarnd Kalmin from the spell of compulsion induced upon him by the Piper's enchanted flute, Manpasikjeok. The scarlet-haired snake did indeed return to the crime-ruled kingdom of Sunpo, thinking himself to be an emperor.

In all technicalities, Haneul Rui is the true emperor of Sunpo. But the Pied Piper turns a blind eye to this city, save for when the Dokkaebi king slants his lips against his beautiful flute, its song luring humans into his pocket realm of Gyeulcheon. They work there, vacant-eyed and compelled, as servants.

But upon my demand, Rui has promised to cease the string of kidnappings. That was the cost for my aid in the days leading up to the battle with Jiwoon. Yet the emperor will not return the ones he took, something that has not ceased to bother me.

"*I can't—*" Rui said when I pressed him, igniting my suspicions that there is more to his kidnappings than Sunpo has ever known. It is a mystery that I have not yet solved. But despite his reluctance to speak of the matters, I will uncover the truth, one way or another.

Yet for now, more pressing urgencies call me to them.

While Kalmin is distracted with the giddiness of his return, with the ruling of the kingdom he believes to be his, I am allegiance hunting.

For when I kill him—for when I kill *all* of them—I will need to have allies. Those who will support my new rule. Those who will prove useful in healing this broken kingdom, those who will quiet any outrage when I take my throne.

In the three days—four days, now—that I have been back, I have refrained from visiting the Blackbloods' giwajip, located in the wealthy Coin Yard. I have not yet even laid my eyes upon Konrarnd.

It's not because I am scared. If my body obeys, I am strong now—stronger than ever. Stronger than the weak girl he once wielded as a weapon, stronger than the grief-stricken girl he claimed as his inheritance. No, I am not scared.

I am *furious*.

If I catch a glimpse of the scarlet snake now, there is no doubt in my mind that I will kill him then and there, soaking my hands with his blood. And that will simply not do.

First the Claws. Then the Legs.

After them, the Feathers. The Bills.

The Crest. And then, finally...

The Crown.

For the whole Crane must fall. Must die a slow, gurgling death. Must wheeze and beg and plead, only to be met with complete, undeniable annihilation.

Kalmin took everything from me. Every*one* from me. It is

only fair, it is only *just,* that I return such a favor. I will saw off the Crane's limbs one by one. And then—when Kalmin has lost *everything*—I will kill him and take the kingdom for my own.

So instead, I bide my time. I hunt for allegiances, gathering power in the form of loyal people. I murder Claws in alleyways, grimly sliding my scaleblades across their throats, letting them drop to the dirty ground with dull thuds.

In the past few days, I have killed.

I started with Unima Hisao, whose treachery sparked the massacre of the Talons. He pulled his loyalty from us, and when I went to retaliate, I walked into a trap. That trap had prevented me from reaching my friends as they were slaughtered, while cowardly Unima fled to his home in the Southern Continent's kingdom of Oktari, returning when the dust settled—only for me to finish exactly what I started.

He died cursing himself for his folly.

And then there were the twenty-four Claws. For a kingdom such as Sunpo, where murder is as commonplace as music, it is not so very large a number. I'm nowhere near done. There are the three Claws from the tavern to take care of, plus a few handfuls more. And then, I will begin plucking Legs off the street like a vulture tearing off the limbs of a long-dead creature. These past few days have simply been the calm before the storm.

See? the Voice whispers. ***Do the truly Good fantasize about killing? Even if it is deserved?***

Be quiet, I snap with such ferocity that my head aches. *Their deaths are deserved.*

Grudgingly, the Voice falls silent, and I make my way into the giwajip's cramped bedroom, where I pull on a silken nightshirt that smells of *him.*

Of plum blossoms and licorice.

As I curl up on my bed, I remove the simple silver ring from the fourth finger of my right hand. It is warm in my palm. I turn it round and round, staring at the looping letters of the Old Language. I do not know what they say, but it is easy enough to guess. *"I will come to you, no matter the time, no matter the distance, no matter the circumstance."*

I bring the ring to my lips but pause a half centimeter away, despite the desire thrumming in my stomach.

There is no room for distraction tonight. I must sleep, and tomorrow I must pay a visit to Gwan Doyun and Song Iseul. I did not miss the Blackbloods' whispers tonight of the Dove Coop's madame, a woman who has not paid Konrarnd Kalmin tribute.

And a woman who does not pay Konrarnd Kalmin tribute is undoubtedly a friend, rather than a foe. I have added her to my list of targets. She sits among people of power I could use by my side when I reclaim Sunpo as mine.

Ruefully, I slip the ring back onto my finger. It chills for a moment, almost in disappointment.

I sleep.

I dream, although I wish I did not.

This world smells of sweet cherry blossoms and sharp, biting lightning. In a sky of lilac, thunderclouds of smudged gray begin to creep over a periwinkle moon. Tendrils of dark mist snake around my ankles, soft as a bird's feathers as they coil around my bare skin.

I am clad in nothing but a thin white nightgown, my right hand closed around a fast-melting candle. Wax dribbles onto my fingers, hot and sticky. I wear no ring. I have no weapons.

My hair is long again, long and unbound. Strands of inky black lift in a wind that carries with it the cold spray of the river I know rushes just beneath the grassy ledge on which I stand, running a sparkling, glittering rose underneath the world's pale blue light. The impenetrable layer of swirling fog conceals this river from view, yet I know it is there, as one knows their own limbs are attached securely to their body.

It is the Seocheongang River, separating the realm of the dead from the realm of the living. Just near my bare feet, there is the beginning of Hwangcheon Bridge, a jade bridge that will take me to Yeomra's halls should I choose to cross it. The god is not there— only the dead. Yeomra left us long ago, with the rest of his kind. Perhaps I would be able to bend the rules to cross the bridge, to visit the Talons, and return. Sang did so once.

Yet I do not move, even as goose bumps rise on my skin and I begin to shiver.

For behind me, I feel its presence. Old, ancient, wise. I feel its inquisitive eyes resting upon me through the mist. I know that if I turn around, I will meet a creature of deadly, glittering teal and serpentine grace. I want to turn around. I want to see it, to speak to it. The yearning to do so strains my chest, aches my heart. Yet I cannot move, for my feet are stuck to the ground, my limbs slow and heavy. It is as if I am chained to the earth on which I stand, imprisoned in my place by the mist coiling around my quickly chilling limbs.

"*Lina,*" a voice whispers, dry and rustling—like the sound of wind sweeping over a field of hay. "*Child of Venom.*"

I stiffen, but I feel no fear. Only a growing desperation to speak to the presence lingering behind me, to lay my eyes upon it for the first time. I open my mouth, but my tongue is dry and leaden. Words do not form. A hoarse, croaking noise emerges from my mouth—weak and pitiful, like the crying of a newborn bird.

Wisps of fog waver and swirl, twirling upward as movement disturbs the obsidian haze. The creature is encircling me. The flame of my candle flickers. Wax runs hot down my skin, burning, searing. I know that I must leave Jeoseung before my candle dwindles entirely, but I cannot bring myself to try to leave without catching a glimpse of the monster in the mist.

"*Do not weep, child,*" the creature murmurs, and I feel its gaze grow intense. Too late, I realize that tears—warm and salty—spill from my eyes, trickle into my mouth. "*What iss it that you want? What iss it that you ssseek?*"

To see you, I think, my heart fracturing with a longing so intense I fear it might shatter. *Please—oh, I wish to see you. I wish to speak to you, more than anything, more than everything.* It is as if I am a magnet, tantalizingly pulled to the creature before me with no way to resist.

There is no answer—only a satisfied sort of silence, like the being can hear my thoughts.

And then I wake.

CHAPTER THREE

I lurch upward in my bed, my breath caught between a gasp and a choke, drenched in a sticky layer of sweat. Sizzling morning sun has already begun to spill into the hanji-screened window of my small bedroom, illuminating the motes of dust dancing in the air, and burning with a heat that seems to sizzle as it touches my skin. Yet despite the summer warmth, my blood runs cold. Another night has brought another nightmare.

Imugi.

Serpentine monsters who once terrorized the mortal plane of Iseung, creatures of dark intent who battled the gods themselves. It was on such a battlefield that the Dokkaebi were born, created as the gods' weapons ran with both their blood and the blood of the Imugi, dripping onto the gore-dampened soil. That battle had resulted in the Imugi being exiled to Yeomra's realm of Jeoseung, although they did not stay there long. Even after the gods left, the Dokkaebi were constantly at war with the Imugi…until the serpents retreated to the underworld of their own accord. They have stayed there ever since, for reasons as obscure as the darkest shadows of the night.

I met such a creature, an Imugi, upon my own trip to Jeoseung. As it has in my dreams, the mist obscured the serpent from view, leaving me with only the flash of a vivid teal scale. I felt the same… curiosity from it, the same inquisitive stare. But I left to rejoin my body in Gyeulcheon before anything could come of such a meeting.

The nightmares started soon after my return. They are

always the same. The smell of cherry blossoms and lightning, the immobility, the whispering of the Imugi. The tears rolling down my cheeks, the desperate longing in my chest.

The fear.

Yet it is not the Imugi in the dream that frightens me.

It is my reaction to it.

Once, I was terrified of serpents. My palms would sweat and my knees would grow weak upon encountering one of those sinuous bodies. Memories of my family's old chogajip would flood back to me—waking in the middle of the night to find that a snake, having snuck into our poorly built hut, had wrapped itself around my legs.

But now, that fear—it is gone. It died as I was reborn, replaced by something even more frightening.

Yearning.

Once before, I have felt it—the morbid curiosity that led me to linger in the Imugi's presence despite my fast-melting candle. It was only the echo of Sang's words—*"Promise me that you'll let yourself live. Truly live."*—that snapped me out of my trance and allowed me to leave Jeoseung. It was then that I'd encountered rebirth...and the Voice for the very first time.

Sang is not in these dreams. And so I remain with the Imugi, overcome with something much more than a simple morbid curiosity.

Just a dream, I tell myself. *Just a dream.*

On trembling legs, I rise from my cot. In the bathroom, I furiously scrub my puffy face with water and soap, pushing my sweaty bangs out of my eyes. The haircut was a calculated decision on my part—a precaution should Kalmin or one of his lackeys spot me in Sunpo. They think my body is six feet under the Gyeulcheon ground and won't be looking for me, yet I will not have my scheme ruined by a simple error, a glimpse caught of Sunpo's Reaper. I took a dagger to my hair, sawing and chopping with grim intent until Rui stopped me—his silver eyes dancing in a mixture of bemusement and entertainment — and handed me a pair of shears. The ordeal had gone much more smoothly after that.

Gwan Doyun lives in Fishtown, where the once-wealthy congregate. There are no tiled-roof giwajips there. Instead, the dwellings have thatched roofs, like the Moonlit Hare. Doyun lives in such a chogajip, one with a half-sunken-in roof and a battered door that has taken many wooden beatings. The once-artisan used to live in the wealthy Coin Yard, in a fine manor not unlike the Blackbloods', also located within the same area. I remember its glossy tile roof, its shiny wooden floors. There had been a slight creak as I tread upon them to slit his wife's—

Breathe. I'm different now. I am subject to nobody's will but my own.

Now, however, he remains in Fishtown, in the east.

Our old palace — the Talons' palace — is in Fishtown, on the very outskirts of the kingdom, right on the verge of the Yongwangguk Sea that circles this continent. I will not be going there, not today. The pain is still too raw, the wound too gaping. It is not time yet. I will visit Doyun and Iseul only, carefully avoiding the palace — which should be easy, seeing as it is far enough away from the other buildings, located in the countryside.

I have planned this visit well. Doyun is easily intimidated, but after last night, what he needs most is comfort.

Sweet kindness, soft words, and gentle reassurances will be welcomed after his bloody stint in the Moonlit Hare.

And that is why I step into the morning sun clad in a modest hanbok rather than my stealth suit. The jeogori, the jacket, is a petal pink, with a ribbon of silken lavender. The chima below is a clean, pristine white that matches the color of my slippers. The hanbok comes from Gyeulcheon — stolen, in fact, from Park Hana's own closet.

I could have, of course, brought a few hanboks from my own wardrobe. But I found that Hana, who returned to glaring at me even after I saved her emperor's and lover's lives, simply had such revenge coming.

Morning bustle fills the street of the Fingertrap, where the weekly kingdom marketplace will soon be erected. Already, vendors cram the cobblestone roads, carrying baskets of produce, their simple white robes already stained with sweat and their faces ruddy underneath the rims of their satgats, conical hats crafted of straw. Horses huff as they clop down the street, toting carts heavy under the weight of rice sacks.

I dodge the stomping horses, the chattering vendors, careful to keep my skirts out of the murky puddles wetting the street. Memories of the last time I visited this marketplace come flitting back to me, swirling through my mind like sweet, spun sugar.

"Is it routine for your people to pop onto rooftops out of nowhere?"

"Is it routine for your *people to hurl perfectly good pastries off rooftops?"*

My lips curling into a small smile, I glance down at the ring on my finger. It warms slightly on my skin.

The baker is at her stand next to the Wyusan poacher, eyeing — as she always does — his bulging biceps as he finishes setting up the pelts hunted in his kingdom's expansive wilderness. He is flexing, I am sure of it. The baker doesn't notice as I swipe two sugar rolls out of a basket and continue merrily on my way, munching.

Some things never change.

I slip one sugar roll into the pocket of my skirts as I walk. Both pockets are heavy now — one with pastry, one with bribery. Sweetness and charm shall get me far with Doyun, of that I am quite certain. However, if there is one thing I learned during my time with the Talons, it is that what *truly* seals a deal is treasure. Rui's Gyeulcheon treasury was brimming with jewels and baubles that now suit my specific needs quite well.

The route into Fishtown does not take long. Sunpo is rather

small, after all—miniscule, really, compared to our northern neighbors of Wyusan and Bonseyo. My transition from the Fingertrap to Fishtown is marked by the sudden rise in the stench of fish and the sharp decline regarding the quality of the buildings lining the road. Grimy fishermen, hailing from the flimsy boats atop the Yongwangguk Sea, are hauling sacks of their gape-mouthed goods up the path, scales slimy in the rippling heat.

I wrinkle my nose against the reek. There is no ice for the fish in the summertime, and by the smell of it, many have already gone bad during the time it took for the fishermen to reach shore and walk the miles to the city. With a surplus of uncomfortable effort, I yank my sense of smell back as I approach Doyun's door. The stone wall surrounding his small chogajip is crumbling and chipped, the pebbled path leading up to his home dappled with spots of dried blood. I peer at it closely, my lips firmly pressing together. He came home bloodied last night. Because of me.

Before my courage fails me, I knock quietly on Doyun's door. For a few moments, there is only silence. And then—a fearful scuffling. "Who goes there?" a wavering voice demands.

"A friend," I say gently, my fingers closing around the treasure in my pocket.

I wait with patience through the wary pause that follows.

The door creaks open, just a crack. Swollen eyes meet mine through the sliver of darkness beyond. And then they slide to my scar.

My blood runs cold. Last night, I hoped my gat covered most of the cut running down the right side of my face, and that Doyun was too preoccupied with my false tattoo to notice that the man before him was really an eighteen-year-old girl with an identifiable scar. I curse my folly. Covering it with powder would have been the wise thing to do…

But Doyun's eyes soften just a bit. Perhaps it is my small, hesitant smile. Perhaps it is that I have taken great pains to look like the sort of woman his dead wife was—darkening my lashes with cosmetics, shaping my lips to small rosebuds with a pink paint, applying blush to the lower ends of my cheekbones to give my face a fuller, plumper, kinder appearance.

A manipulation, yes. But a necessary one. I suspect that I am… frightening up close. If one looks, it is likely they can tell that I am not like them. That I am different.

I take advantage of his momentary tenderness. "I ask for only a few moments of your time, sir." It is hard to guess what his wife's voice sounded like. I only ever heard her scream. But I settle for a featherlight whisper, quite different from my usual hoarse undertone. "I have come here unfollowed by those whom you fear. I speak true, for I am a friend. Please, sir. Let me in."

Doyun hesitates. "Who are you?"

"An enemy of your enemy. I have heard a tale of a dead wife and a stolen ring. I have come to speak with you." I watch carefully as, at the mention of his stolen jewelry, his eyes blaze with rage. I swallow down the sour taste in my mouth. "I think I may be able to offer you…sufficient compensation."

"Nothing," Doyun spits, "can replace what I have lost. *Nothing*. They have taken everything from me. Nothing you can give me is a suitable replacement."

I shake my head. "I believe that at least one thing, in particular, is." It would be easy to mistake my words for a different sort of innuendo, but Doyun is too smart for that. He sees my scar. He hears the quiet promise in my voice.

And he latches onto my words like a fish to bait. All at once, he yanks open the door, urging me inside. He lingers by the doorway a second longer, warily scanning the street before slamming the door and locking it with trembling fingers. The inside of his house smells of sour body odor and old tea. It is dark, very dark, but I can see perfectly well.

Yesterday Gwan looked no older than thirty, yet today he

looks a man of fifty—wrinkled and stooped, with watery eyes and a mouth that is a mere gash in his sallow skin. He wears the same cotton hanbok as he did yesterday, but now the threadbare fabric is stained with blood and grime. His swollen eyes are not the most of his worries. By the way he carries himself, I can easily tell that bruises have bloomed underneath his clothing, in places I cannot see. His lip is split. His hands shake, and I can hear the nervous thudding of his heart despite my attempts to block out the uneven thumping.

Remorse and a brittle kind of self-loathing prod at my chest as Doyun licks his lips. "So," he says, his thin mustache trembling as he moves away from the door, limping toward a room to the left. I follow. "You say you are a friend."

We enter a small kitchen. "Yes," I respond quietly as Doyun hobbles to a low table in the corner, on which a bowl of pinkish water sits next to a damp rag. He takes his spot on his cushion, and I kneel across from him, watching as he dips the rag back into the water and places it on his swollen lip. The blood from last night is dried and crusted as he gingerly sponges it off.

"I want a name." Doyun looks at me evenly, even as I smell his terror and distrust. "I want...I want to know about this compensation you speak of. I want to know who you work for. Is it Song?" he asks before I can respond. "Are you one of her Doves?"

If the madame's dislike of the Blackbloods is this well-known, then it is quite certain that I will win her allegiance just as easily as I will win Doyun's. I smile, only just remembering to keep my lips together, my eyes down modestly. "No, sir, I am no Dove." I raise my gaze to his. I watch Doyun carefully. Every time I speak, his face relaxes, his eyes gentle. "My name is Shin Lina. I am...the Reaper of Sunpo."

Doyun's mouth tightens, his heart accelerating. "The gangster," he says, the words clumsy with fear. "The Talon. The assassin." There is an icy bite of shock to his words. *Breathe in. Breathe out.*

He does not know it was me.

My true name, my identity, has never been an easy commodity to come by. Yoonho made sure of that—to shield me from other assassins and those who would be glad to rid the city of me. Kalmin did, too, for he wished to preserve his stolen prize, his godsdamned "inheritance." He was a possessive master, content to brag about having the Reaper under his employ—but jealous enough to withhold my true name from his lips in the company of those who may have taken me from him.

For the most part, Sunpo knows me only as the shadowy figure in the night, reaping Sunpo's bodies—a faceless monster in the dark. A villain of children's stories. *Be home by ten, or the Reaper will get you. Don't pull on your sister's hair, or the Reaper will cut off your hands.*

That will change soon enough. I want all Three Kingdoms to know who killed Konrarnd Kalmin.

"Yes, the Reaper," I say carefully, trying to ignore the stench of Doyun's horror. It clogs the back of my throat. This is the tricky part—telling him my story, but not too far. Telling him the truth, but not too much. "I was the Talons' finest assassin."

The man blinks, taken aback. His rag falls from his hands. "But you're—"

"Young? Yes, I know." I bow my head modestly. "I was orphaned when I was—"

"N-no." He frowns. "I meant to say, but you're *alive*. You did not die with the others. I thought—I thought you *had.*"

Kalmin's boasts must have missed Doyun's ears only narrowly. I swallow against my tight throat as I realize that I must explain my story now—my loss, my grief, the hatred that burns ever-brightly within me. "Ah." I incline my head, even as my heart cracks in two. "Yes, sir, I am alive. But the others are not, for Konrarnd Kalmin stole them from me. And I understand, Gwan Doyun, that he has stolen somebody from you." My words are gentle, soft and lulling, even as my nails dig into the palms of my hands. My fault. My fault. "Your wife. Gwan Yoonji. Konrarnd Kalmin sent one of his men after her, she who had a target marked on her back after your disobedience."

"I did not pay tribute," Doyun whispers through his fist, which he has stuffed in his mouth, biting hard on the knuckles. Blood spills down his hand. "He demanded too much. I did not obey his rule."

"He took everything from you," I say, gently reaching over the table and removing the hand from his mouth. He stares at me with wide eyes as I take up the rag and press it to the new punctures in his skin. I know intimately the pains he suffers. I know how he hurts. "As he did to me. I think, sir, that we share a common interest. Konrarnd Kalmin forced me to work for him for a year," I continue, squeezing some water out of the rag. "And so I have, Gwan Doyun, the name of the assassin who killed your wife."

Doyun's eyes snap up to mine, and I see something wary—something sharp and suspicious—cut through the pain, the weariness. I shake my head, summoning as much sincerity into my expression as possible. "It was not me," I whisper softly, dabbing at his wounds. The lie tastes like burnt sugar and I fight to not choke on it. It is a necessary one, one for his own good. "Yet not for lack of trying on Kalmin's part. He demanded that I slaughter her in cold blood, and I refused. I am an assassin, but I do not kill innocent women. Kalmin became enraged. My punishment was to be beaten into oblivion by Man Jisu and held in a cell for a week without food." I close my eyes, letting my lower lip tremble. "It was not me. I swear it upon my life." I swallow the sugar's bittersweet flavor and open my eyes, holding his gaze even as my throat closes in shame.

And I can see that the poor man believes me. I am a skilled liar, capable of blending truth with fiction until each becomes indeterminable from the other.

Sometimes I hate myself for it.

Man Jisu beat me into oblivion before, yes—but I never refused Kalmin's orders. Not when Eunbi's life was always on the line. But Doyun does not know this. He knows nothing but what I have told him—Shin Lina, fair in the way an assassin can be, young and sweet like his wife once was. Shin Lina, who has helped tend to his wounds. Doyun's stare is now only weary and sad. There is no suspicion—that has been quelled, leaving him free to join me. To have a better life.

"I know the name of the killer," I say again. My tongue feels heavy in my mouth. "I will tell you, in exchange for a favor. And I also know that I am capable of killing him for you for the same fee."

"What do you mean?" A ragged whisper tinged with hope.

"I plan to overthrow the Blackbloods." I say this as gently as I can, setting down the washcloth. "I am more than capable of doing so. I will kill Konrarnd Kalmin, I will kill his henchwoman Asina, and all of those in between. But to do this, sir, I will need backing. I will need pledges of loyalty, for when I reclaim Sunpo as Talon territory, there will be turmoil. There will be unrest. There are those who have—surprisingly—profited from the rule of the Blackbloods. The many who allied themselves with the gang long before they wrested control of the kingdom from the Talons' hands have been well rewarded. And so, Doyun, I would ask your hand in aid for when this time comes. You may be penniless, but your words still hold power. Convince your neighbors, comfort your friends. Back me with loyalty, and in return, I will protect you. Shelter you. Provide you with good food and sturdy clothes. A better life."

And to provide me with a chance to make amends. To fix a life that I ruined by taking another's. To try my best to mend the tears and rips. To atone, as well as I am able.

Doyun has friends, yes, but he is not as influential as he once was. He is my chance to apologize. To become somebody new. Somebody better. Somebody *good*.

The man has straightened. There is a glint in his eyes, despite the bruises dappling his face. "You are so generous," he whispers, "and I hate to ask for more, but there is one thing…"

"Anything," I reply, smiling.

"My wife's murderer." Doyun's lower lip trembles. "I want you to kill him. Or…p-perhaps I want to kill him myself."

I fight not to flinch. I did not expect this of the meek, hungry man. And so my deception must continue. "As you wish," I agree after a few moments and smile my rosebud smile, noting how his eyes latch onto the sweet curve in grief and fascination. Self-disgust makes my stomach roil. It seems as though I'll be assigning blame to another Blackblood, for Doyun can never know what I did. "Your revenge and redemption will be delivered."

"Revenge," Doyun whispers, still staring at my lips. "R-redemption."

Both, as I know, are powerful motivators.

"All that and more," I say, reaching into my pocket. My fingers close around the baubles taken from the Gyeulcheon treasury. Slowly, so slowly, I place them on the table before him.

A comb of pure silver, studded with gemstones. Five coins of thick gold, engraved with a head that bears a suspicious likeness to Haneul Rui. A weighty bar of jade, deep and emerald, cold to the touch. These three objects are worth more than every single chogajip on this street combined twice.

"Consider it an early investment," I say softly.

And when Doyun looks up, his eyes blazing with a fire that had not been there the night before, I know that I have him in my clutches. "When you take this kingdom, you'll tell me his name? You'll kill him, o-or let me?" he says, breathing hard. "You swear it? You, a-a young woman—will do so? C-can do so?" Doubt creeps into his words, mingling with his fervent desire.

"Do not underestimate me, Gwan Doyun." I rise from the floor, brushing off my hanbok, and bowing slightly in farewell. "She will be avenged. As will my own." I turn to leave, but his next words stop me dead.

"You'll want to look in the palace first, then," Doyun says quietly, but not nervously. The fear is gone, replaced by stone-cold determination. "That's where you'll find them. The Blackbloods."

It takes a moment for the words to sink in.

"The palace," I repeat hoarsely. "The old palace?"

"On the verge of this sector and the countryside," Doyun confirms nervously. "It used to be the Talons', yes?"

A dull fury roars in my head.

No.

He wouldn't have.

Oh gods oh gods oh *gods*.

Of course he would, the Voice in my head whispers, stretching like a cat that has woken from a particularly long nap. I feel it cock its head, brushing against the base of my brain, sternly hooking a sharp claw into its stem. **Why wouldn't he? He's Konrarnd Kalmin. He killed our friends. And now he sleeps in their beds.**

I am vaguely aware of Doyun frowning. "...Shin Lina?" he's saying. "Are you well?"

No. No. I am not well. Oh gods.

I am running out of the chogajip, sick to my stomach, before Doyun can approach me. I am stumbling through the streets, unsure of where I am going or what I am doing. All my grace, my poise, my agility is gone. The world's music is roaring through my head. My legs are weak, shaking. My vision is blurred. I run, my legs twisting awkwardly as I move, my arms bumping into my chest as they pump in uncoordinated bursts. I miss my old body as I fall to the ground, scraping my hands against stone. This one is new, foreign, unfamiliar, and I can't...I can't navigate in it, I can't... Oh gods. Oh gods.

Somebody—a blurred face, a concerned voice—tries to help me up but I push them away, my heart beating so fast I think it might burst out of my ribcage. Bile rises in my throat and I push it down, down, down like I push down the guilt and grief and self-hatred. My head spins as I rise and keep going until I am panting in the middle of Sunpo's Heart, staring at the familiar scarlet eaves of the Temple of Ruin. I have crossed the kingdom in less than a minute, carried by my new strength and roaring fury.

Shaking, unable to breathe, I stagger into the abandoned temple, having broken the lock by picking it with a trembling scaleblade summoned onto the back of my hand. I welcome the darkness, the silence, the solitude. Hot tears roll down my face, tracing the mockery of a teardrop engraved upon my skin as I shut the door and sink to my knees. Plumes of dust rise into the air, a false snowstorm.

I stay like that for a very, very long time.

Sometime later—maybe minutes, maybe hours—I begin to pray.

I used to pray to the wicked gods, the sinful gods. Yeomra, God of the Dead. To Seokga, God of Deceit. To Mireuk, Creator of All, Creator of Evil. But now... Hesitantly, I begin to speak to Dalnim, Goddess of the Moon and Rui's ancestor. To her brother, Haemosu, God of the Sun. To Jowangshin, Goddess of Hearth and Home.

I do not know if I am worthy of them. If I ever have been. If my Imugi scales have marked me as undeserving to speak to the uncontaminated deities. But I want to make decisions that are *right*. Perhaps, with their guidance, I can. They are absent, but I wish for them to hear me. Perhaps if I wish it enough, they will answer from the faraway sky kingdom of Okhwang, hidden among the clouds.

"Please," I whisper, "I know I have no right to ask it of you, but...let the light of your moon guide my way to Good. Let the light of your sun show me the righteous path. It has been so long since I have made my own choices. Since I have wielded such power. Let me use it wisely."

The Voice scoffs in clear outrage. I ignore it, gritting my teeth.

"Let me build a hearth here, a home. Let this kingdom be mine."

Absent as always, the gods do not answer me.

But something else does.

CHAPTER FOUR

I sink into the vision as quickly as a golden ring into makgeolli, the floor of the Temple of Ruin replaced by a field of purple flowers and a heavy blanket of dark fog. A candle, dripping wax, appears in my hand. My short, choppy hair grows with alarming speed, tumbling down my back. My hanbok is replaced by a nightgown. My slippers disappear, leaving my toes sinking into the flower field's soft earth.

The Imugi waits behind me. I feel its stare.

And as I always do, I remain immobile. Unable to move.

I smell cherry blossoms. I smell a brewing storm, heavy and metallic.

My mouth waters.

Is this a dream? It does not feel like one. Could it be something else?

"Child of Venom," the Imugi murmurs in that voice of rustling fields and ghostly gusts. *"Why do you pray to those long-gone godsss? They do not hear you, but I do."* Somehow, I can detect curiosity in the serpent's strange voice. Curiosity...and warmth. Hesitant friendliness almost. *"I hear your prayersss, my child. I listen to them."*

Again, I am hit with that desperate longing. Although I know it is wrong and that I should not feel such a desire, I want to turn around. I want to see. But wish as I might, I cannot. Rain begins to fall from the stormy sky, cold droplets splattering my face.

"You musst let me in, firsst," the serpent says gently. *"I have

been waiting for you to let me in. It is easssy to do. You need only turn around."*

I cannot move, I think, frustration welling up in my heart and overspilling in the form of angry tears. *How can I turn around when I cannot move?*

"It is sssimple enough." I startle, and the Imugi chuckles—a hissing noise from deep within an elegant throat that is strangely indulgent in its sound. *"Yesss, child, I can hear your thoughts. They are as clear as the ssurface of a reflection pond in the midsst of a white winter. As plaintive as the cries of a newborn babe. As for your question, child, turning around is not so hard. You have been able to all thisss time. You have simply chosssen not to."*

There is nothing that I want more than to rest my eyes on this Imugi, this creature who calls to me in the voice of dry winds and rattling stalks of wheat. So I strain, I push, I fight against my locked muscles, but it is impossible. *No. I cannot turn, although I have tried.*

"You fear me," the Imugi murmurs. There is no judgment in its tone, only patient fact. *"For you have been told to by thossse of the hidden realm. Let that fear go, child. There is no need for it. I will not hurt you."*

I am not afraid, I think, but at once I know it is not true. Hidden in my heart is a small kernel of reservation. I immediately feel a surge of anger toward that hidden kernel. It is what has been keeping me back from the creature behind me. Hatred tightens my throat and twists my stomach. How dare it hold me back? How dare it keep me from this Imugi?

Crush it, the Voice whispers. ***Destroy it, and we will meet the Imugi.***

Closing my eyes, I examine the seed of fear closely, rotating it round and round in the fingers of my mind. It is heavy with whispers of a war, of death and destruction. In it I see a familiar library, a crackling fire, and a pair of silver eyes glittering as a red mouth tells me of the Imugi. In it I see a girl with a scar on her face lurching upward in a bed, gasping, shuddering at the longing she feels in the world of her dreams to meet a monster.

That girl is me, yet she is not. I cannot imagine fearing my reaction to this creature—I can only imagine the crushing disappointment I will feel upon waking without breaking free of my stupor.

In my mind, the kernel rests between my thumb and forefinger. It is dark, glossy, and small.

Now. Do it.

And it is easy to crush underneath my fingers, shattering it into nothingness. I taste triumph, sweet and cloying, on my tongue. The change is immediate. My limbs are lighter, my muscles looser. I know, now, that should I try, I will be able to meet the monster who waits for me in this realm of death.

Behind me, the Imugi's forked tongue flickers out, tasting the air that is now thick with suspense. *"Turn around, my child. We have waited long enough to meet each other."*

My lips curve into a smile.

And I turn.

My eyes fly open.

I am panting, panting hard, on my hands and knees atop the dust-coated floor of the Temple of Ruin. My head swims, my teeth ache. I taste blood. I've bitten my tongue.

Wiping my bloody mouth with the back of my wrist, I rise shakily to my feet, staring determinedly at the empty chest in the center of the room. A little more than a month ago, I stole the tapestry within that small trunk, igniting the rage of the Pied Piper. A little more than a month ago, my life was changed forever.

I glance to the ring upon my finger. I want, badly, to summon

Rui. To rant to him my fury, my frustration, my fears. To watch his silver eyes darken with rage as I speak of the Blackbloods' new base. To watch as twin columns of Dokkaebi fire flares in his glare.

But I cannot. Not yet. I cannot be distracted. I have lost time enough today already. A glance upward at the high windows suggest that it is now nighttime. Thunder booms, rattling the glass. It is storming outside, a summer squall beating furiously down upon the temple.

It is obvious that I fell asleep, that I dreamed, but my mind is coated with a bleary fog. There is a feeling of—of *satisfaction* in me, although I do not understand why. My mouth is stretched into a smile. Unnerved, I force my lips to flatten.

Finally. The Voice sounds bored, although sometimes it is hard to tell—interpreting the tone of a voice so ancient, so cold, is by no means easy. ***You've certainly slept for long enough.***

Do you know if I dreamed? I typically do my best to refrain from interacting with the foul Voice at all, but perhaps the presence that came with my power is able to see into my unconscious memory.

I do not see your dreams, the Voice says and adds, drily, ***make of that what you will.***

My stomach clenches uncomfortably at its tone. Almost as if it's implying I didn't dream, but instead experienced something… else? Frustrated, I shake my head. It is no help at all. Scowling, I push my sweat-soaked bangs from my shining forehead. I have spent the day sleeping in an abandoned temple, being completely and entirely useless toward my quest. I planned to visit Song Iseul directly after my meeting with Gwan Doyun. Surely it is not too late now—Song's brothel, the Dove Coop, operates at the most unholy hours, as most Boneburrow establishments do.

With still-trembling fingers, I undo my hanbok, stepping out of the jeogori and chima to reveal my black suit underneath. I do not think the hanbok would be appropriate for a meeting with a formidable madame. No, sweet words and downcast eyes will not charm a woman like Song Iseul. She will want an assurance of power. Of cunning and wit.

A stealth suit would be more fitting for my purposes. My jikdo is strapped to my side—it was easy to hide underneath the hanbok skirts. The sturdy black fabric is drenched with my sweat, and I grimace as I reach into the pockets of the discarded white chima, my fingers closing around a few other treasures. I only belatedly remember that the sugar roll in its other pocket has certainly gone stale by now.

The sheets of rain wash my hot, grubby face. I am still slightly clumsy on my feet as I navigate north, toward the Boneburrow—infamous for its nightlife. I have heard of the Dove Coop. Sang, Chara, and Chryse used to frequent it. They often tried to persuade me to accompany them, the twins pleading with sweet smiles and eyes dancing with mischief, Sang watching with a look of quiet amusement and avoiding my eye as I glanced at him.

"It shall be fun," Chryse said once, staring at me beseechingly with her long-lashed green eyes. *"And it's not as if you need to... partake, if you do not want to. There is music, too—music and food and dance and drink. And downstairs..."*

Her twin, Chara, grinned wickedly. *"Downstairs will be much more your style, Lina. There's so much more to the Dove Coop than meets the eye. I think, really, that you and Iseul would get along quite well."*

I frowned, glancing to Sang. *"What's downstairs?"*

The spy smiled faintly, even as he ducked his head away from my gaze, something dulling in his own. Something like regret. *"It's a secret. You'll have to come to find out, Lina."*

But I never did. I hadn't been able to bear the thought of watching Sang with one of Iseul's girls. Or the thought that he preferred nameless Doves to the way my name sounded on his tongue. So I walked with them as far as the pleasure house's door before turning away, a lump in my throat as Sang disappeared for a night of tangled embraces.

It is clear that the brothel, no matter how successful, is a front for something else entirely. Something that Kalmin considers an asset if he is so slighted by Iseul's lack of tribute. Tonight, I will discover what exactly lies underneath the Dove Coop.

CHAPTER FIVE

The Boneburrow is the one sector in all the kingdom with streets that are typically illuminated even during the darkest parts of the night. Not by lanterns, but by open doorways spilling wavering oranges and reds out onto the streets as Sunpo denizens are ushered into the pleasure houses and gambling dens that populate the sector. But tonight, it is dark. The doors are tightly shut, locked. The street is quiet, save for the pounding of the rain and the rumble of the storm.

Vague unease slithers down my spine as I continue toward the Coop, splashing through puddles, blinking past rainwater, concentrating hard on blocking out all the noises of the night save for the ones closest to me. The air smells strange. It almost smells like fear.

I wrinkle my nose and refocus on walking as steadily as I can, willing this bout of ungainliness to soon recede. Song Iseul will not be impressed if I fall on my face before her due to a pathetic lack of coordination.

Among the other battered brothels lining the street, the Dove Coop sticks out with no small amount of grandeur. There is nobody in this kingdom who has not seen the white, domed structure that is the Coop. It is built in the style of faraway seaside kingdoms—the entrance is lined with towering white pillars and carved marble statues of men and women alike, their white stone bodies hard with muscle, their faces chiseled and perfect. The sculptures' clothing comes in the form of veinlike green vines dotted with pale pink flowers that remind me of a blush blooming on the cheeks of a maiden. The Dove Coop is called such for a reason—the tall golden gate encircling the pleasure hall reminds me of the rungs of a gilded cage.

Even with the storm, by this time, the gates should be open and allowing in a steady stream of clients. But they are firmly shut. Two men, burly and dripping wet, stand guard before it.

Odd. I remain in the shadows of a nearby alleyway, watching. Thinking.

Perhaps business has dwindled more than I realized under the rule of the Blackbloods. Perhaps under their reign, the Boneburrow is scared to operate in any hour without daylight. There is no other reason I can think of that would explain the shut gate or the lack of clients. I nibble on my bottom lip. No matter. Iseul is in the Coop, regardless of the Boneburrow's deception of abandonment.

It is imperative that I find Song Iseul quickly and stealthily. I cannot afford to be recognized here, should word travel back to Kalmin. The Dove Coop was once a neutral territory, belonging to neither the Talons nor the Blackbloods, but times have changed.

Using my fingers, I comb my soaking bangs so they fall down into my eyes and reach into my pocket to withdraw a thin strip of leather. I knot my short, damp hair back into a small bun at the nape of my neck. I am sharp boned enough, flat-chested enough, to pass as a young boy at first glance. I wish I brought my gat with me, but there was no way to conceal it underneath my hanbok.

As I attempt to adjust my awkward body into a swaggering pose, I freeze. The hairs on the back of my neck stand on end.

Somebody is watching me.

Alarm has scales rippling on my skin, crusting my flesh in diamond-hard armor. They emerge on my hands, the long blades of scale extending from my wrists. They unfold over my heart, along my neck. My vitals are protected against whatever waits in the darkness, watching me. I expand my senses, but no sounds of the abnormal reach my ears.

Warily, I allow the scales to recede.

The Imugi scales.

For that's what they are. They cannot be anything else. Kang himself confirmed it a few nights after the garden attack.

"There is no doubt in my mind," Rui's advisor said grimly, his deep-set eyes wary and swirling with knowledge. The emperor and I were sitting in the center of a library among the labyrinth books, Kang leaning on his staff before the fire. "The Imugi venom in your body at the time you consumed the wongun enhancer gave you... serpentine traits. *Imugi* traits. Your body, your new abilities, reflect the mixing of the two substances."

I blanched at his tone. It was deep with...foreshadowing, almost. A growing mistrust. *Am I turned into a monster?* The thought had come unbidden, and the Voice had stirred in displeasure then, batting the question aside.

How dare he speak to us such? the Voice had hissed, and I could feel it pacing back and forth on the surface of my mind. **Look how he frowns. How he glances at Rui.**

The emperor sat stiff-backed on the overstuffed armchair next to me, staring past Kang into the crackling fire as it popped and hissed, mingling with the sounds of a fast-approaching thunderstorm. **Look how they brood. They compare us to their old enemy. Will we allow this, Shin Lina?**

Be quiet, I ground back. I was still not used to hearing the Voice. I opened my mouth to confess, to admit to Kang the presence in my head, the power—but another look at his expression had me faltering. It wasn't an expression of disgust, not quite—but it hurt all the same, sending shards of uncertainty into my heart, scraping the words off my suddenly leaden tongue. I looked to Rui, whose profile was rimmed orange in the firelight. His mouth was a thin, hard line. His brow creased in the way it did when he was troubled.

So I said nothing, biting the inside of my mouth hard enough to taste blood instead.

I was not ashamed of the scales. They saved my life. They saved *Rui's* life. But there, in the library, something changed. It was in the look on Kang's face. It was in Rui's ruminating silence. It was the sudden feeling of not being clean enough to hold that book on the gods.

As the scales now melt into warm skin, I block the memory from view. There is no reversing what has been done. And I am not a monster. I am not an Imugi, despite the traits I share with them.

I'm Shin Lina.

And I have a job to do.

Taking a deep breath, I slip toward the gate, stealthy only through sheer force of will. My limbs still feel ungainly. Heavy.

The guards—for all their wary attention—do not notice as I vault over the slippery golden rungs and land in the shadows below with a splash that is fortunately covered by a boom of thunder. I am not agile enough to avoid a particularly deep puddle, nor am I able to quell the shock of pain in my left leg. My feet are slower than I'd like them to be on the steps leading up to the vine-embraced statues and marble pillars. Unsurprisingly, the massive stone door is locked. I duck into the darkness again, pressing my back against a pillar.

I suppose that I could, using my new strength, pull and pull until the lock breaks. But I desire stealth, and stealth is definitely *not* a sudden bang in the night as a formerly locked door suddenly breaks. This street is being watched; I am sure of it. Although I cannot make out the exact color of their dark, rain-soaked robes, the guards at the gate may even be Blackbloods. If so, they're likely Claws, or Legs. If my body wasn't so maladroit, I could take care of them—but when I'm like this, when my immortal grace has been replaced by heavy limbs and slowed reflexes, it's better not to risk injury.

But before I can begin plotting, the door creaks open—just

a bit. Just an inch. Bewildered, I stare, inching forward. A voice hisses out into the night. "Come in *quickly,*" it snaps, and before I can react, a pale hand snatches out into the night and hauls me through the narrow crack in the doorway. I stumble and nearly fall, shocked, and the door once again slams closed, leaving me gaping. A pair of narrow black eyes glare back at me.

The woman is slender and small, my age—or perhaps a bit older—with glossy hair bleached so light a blond that it is nearly white, and a face so perfect that it's unnatural. I feel a pang of envy as I take in her delicate nose, plump lips, dark lashes, and rosy cheeks. Her eyebrows are arched mischievously, and she wears a delicate lavender hanbok in utter contrast with the giant ax she's holding in her left hand. She hefts it over her shoulder and looks as if she would very much like to chop me into little pieces.

"Well," says Song Iseul, Madame of the Dove Coop, "Shin Lina. It certainly took you long enough."

CHAPTER SIX

"Close your mouth," she says, turning away from me and striding across the empty plaza in which we stand. "You look like a dying fish."

I snap my mouth shut and see no choice but to follow her under the looming archways as she stalks farther into the pleasure house with not even a single glance over her shoulder. I grind my teeth in a mixture of bewilderment and frustration as we pass through a curtain of crystal beads into a hallway. They rattle against my skin, cold to the touch as I seep rainwater onto her perfectly polished floor.

She looks like the sort of girl we would befriend, says the Voice, sounding very amused indeed. It stretches and yawns. **With her giant ax, and all.**

Shut up.

"I've been waiting for you to come crawling to the Coop," Iseul says as we traverse down the narrow corridor lined with lavender doors that I assume lead into bedrooms. No sounds emerge from them, not even a peep. There are no Doves in sight. They are tucked away, hidden. "Ever since you stepped foot back into this kingdom of filth with that Dokkaebi of yours." She turns, giving me a look that is *far* too knowing.

Shock twists my mouth and tongue, but for only a moment. "How—"

"How did I know of your return? And your identity?" Iseul snickers. "Please. I'm not Sunpo's madame for nothing. I have an *extensive* network of informants. I like to keep tabs on this city, on who comes, who goes. Who can be a potential client or a potential enemy. This way." She turns sharply to the right and unlocks one of the lavender doors.

I stiffen. If Iseul has seen me, if she has told the Blackbloods of my return, my cherished element of surprise will be completely ruined.

As we step into a spacious bedroom that smells of rose oil and honey, Iseul snorts. "My spies are loyal to me, Shin Lina. You may stop wondering if I've crawled into Konrarnd Kalmin's lap and told him all your dirty little secrets. That would ruin my new reputation as the little shit who drives Sunpo's crime lord up the walls. That *treasured* title's fallen to me since you supposedly perished in Gyeulcheon."

Iseul has walked to the center of the room and is now kneeling on the wooden floorboards, fumbling for something in her pocket. "The fool thinks you're dead. If only *I* were so lucky. I've considered faking my death numerous times—and I have many ideas for such a show—but that would mean I'd have to say farewell to this lovely whorehouse I've established. No, I'd rather see the man dead."

She finds what she's looking for, an iron-wrought key, and inserts it into a gap in the boards so well hidden that it almost escaped even my keen eyes. With a click, it turns, and then Iseul is pressing down hard on the wood, which folds downward to reveal the beginning of a large staircase. "I trust you've heard of my Downstairs. That will be the safest place to talk. After me, if you please." She disappears, leaving me again with no choice but to follow with rising curiosity, carefully measuring the space between each step in order to not utterly humiliate myself in front of this madame.

Striking a match and lighting one of the many candles lining the gray stone walls, Iseul illuminates the hidden room in which we stand. It is large, larger even than the bedroom above, and heavy with a bitter, ash-like scent I know all too well.

Attempting to ignore the sudden itching in my mouth, I focus on the soft rug spanning the room, embroidered with stitches that entangle with one another to form the bark of a stretching cherry blossom tree, the petals' stitching a pale, pinkish white. Atop the rug, many plump cushions are scattered, well-worn and well-stuffed. I can imagine this place on a livelier night, crammed with people lounging laconically on the cushions, heads lolling, eyes fluttered shut. There is a rather large portrait of a white fox hanging on a wall, sleek and slim with its head tilted in cunning. My eyes linger on it longer than anything else, noting the nine tails fanning out behind it. *A nine-tailed fox. Gumiho.*

The creatures are long extinct, eradicated by the Fox Hunt fifty years ago. There is something haunting about seeing this painted creature now, knowing that its likeness no longer exists on Iseung, the mortal realm.

Iseul is making her way to a padlocked door at the end of the room, picking her way over the vast sea of pillows. "Welcome to the Downstairs," she announces, unlocking the door and disappearing from sight for a few moments before reemerging with a mesh satchel of a substance I know all too well, and two fine, glossy pipes.

I swallow hard, a bead of sweat trickling down my face. *This* is the Dove Coop's appeal. *This* is why Kalmin desires a firm reign over Song's business. A successful brothel—and underneath, a successful halji den.

Breathing in only slightly through my mouth, I stand stiffly, motionlessly, as Iseul plops down onto a set of cushions, stretching her legs out before her—catlike—and leans her ax against the wall. "Go on," she says around the pipe as she places it in her mouth and carefully measures out a bit of the ashy substance. "Sit. I've heard of your taste for cigarettes, but this is *far* superior." The madame gestures vaguely at the cushions next to her before withdrawing another match from the pocket of her hanbok and lighting the halji.

She exhales the smoke, shaping it into rings, smiling as they float delicately in the air.

My mouth is unbearably itchy, my stomach is tied in knots, my fingernails are pressed so tightly into the palms of my hands that blood has begun to bloom underneath their vicious pressure.

I want to, but I cannot. I made a promise. I must keep it.

"I am not here for pleasure," I manage to say, as flatly as I can, devoid of all emotion as I refuse the offer of the second pipe. Struggling to regain the upper hand after such a series of surprises, I lean against the wall opposite her, staring down at her with eyes I hope show no sign of my inner struggle. I need to impress her, as I did Doyun. "I'm here to make you an offer, Song Iseul."

"Oh, how *riveting*," Iseul drawls, puffing smoke. "*Yes*, Lina, I *know*." She kicks a foot toward a smoke ring, and I see that she is barefoot under her hanbok. "Like I already said, I've been waiting. You have my pledge of allegiance for when you take over this godsforsaken city. I remember your friends. They spoke highly of you—not that it matters. As long as that Northern snake is far below the surface of this kingdom, dead and decaying, I am happy with whoever takes the throne. The new crime lord could be a *lizard*, for all I care. But you'll do just fine. *Far* less adorable, but I'm willing to accept it."

That was too easy. The Voice sounds suspicious. Although I agree, I pay it no mind as Iseul continues to speak.

"Konrarnd Kalmin," Iseul adds, puffing away at her pipe and glaring at a spot on the wall over my shoulder, "is a nasty, pigheaded, obtuse, snout-faced little rodent whose grubby hands have no claim on this territory." She cuts her black eyes back to me, her lips thin with unconcealed fury. "His Blackbloods think that they can take my girls and boys for free. My Doves choose who *they* want to tumble with, and *they* choose the price. Konrarnd's men barrel in here every night like a pack of half-starved vermin crawling with fleas, desperate for some cheese. Especially those

Claws. And their Crown—oh, *he* thinks he can threaten me into paying his little gang tribute. *Me*. Tribute. Ha!"

She scoffs, blowing out smoke. I try not to breathe it in, yanking in my expanding senses, the senses that want to savor the smell of the halji, every note of the biting bitter leaves.

"As if I'd ever associate myself with such a lowlife. He and his gang are a blight on this land, and I want them gone. So, yes. You have my pledge of my eternal loyalty forever and always, or, rather, until another crime lord comes along and assassinates you. Do you need it in writing? I can put it in writing." Iseul blinks at me expectantly.

"I don't need it in writing," I say evenly, staring into her eyes rather than the pipe I am so acutely aware of. "As long as you keep your word, benefits will come to you. Here." I withdraw the rest of the treasure from my pocket and toss it her way. She catches the diamond necklace and golden pocket watch in surprise, her head tilting this way and that in catlike consideration.

"Bribery. Shiny things. Oh, I *do* like you better already." Iseul hangs the necklace around her neck, grinning. "In return for this sparkly little toy, Reaper, I offer you my help in your quest for revenge. That's what I assume this is, anyway. I was sorry to hear about the Talons." Her smile slips. "They came here often."

"I'm aware," I say tightly. It has been an effort not to imagine Sang lounging on one of these cushions in between two cooing Doves, blowing smoke, my name nothing but a distant memory in his mind.

"It's not that I'm questioning your ability to singlehandedly wrestle Sunpo from Kalmin and his army's control," the madame continues, exhaling another smoke ring. It drifts toward my face, and I refuse to breathe, keeping my mouth tightly shut even though my heart hammers in my chest. "What's a legion of Blackbloods against a lone girl?"

"Do not underestimate or mock me," I snap, suddenly defensive and self-conscious of my lumbering body. "I have no humor to spare today." Not here, under the Dove Coop, with my lungs burning with the need for a broken promise. I want to return to the silent street, replacing the smell of halji with thick summer air.

She widens her eyes innocently, fiddling with the jewelry around her neck. "I'm not mocking you, Lina. Really. All I am saying is, I have many resources at my disposal. Many, *many* resources. Many terribly sordid and incredibly useful resources. I am under watch, that is true, but should you need…oh, to dispose of say, a *massive* pile of bodies, or burn down a particular palace… Well, I will eagerly come to your assistance."

"Thank you." Iseul reminds me, in a vague sort of way, of the twins. Her sly disposition, her oh-so-innocent facial expressions that quickly snap into irritation or calculating wit. Something in my heart breaks just a little at the thought of them.

Iseul is playing with her necklace again. "I assume that this is from your Dokkaebi? From his realm within a realm?"

I incline my head, just slightly.

"Hmm." Iseul taps a diamond thoughtfully. "He's been *quite* busy, hasn't he?"

My brows inch toward each other in confusion. "What do you speak of?"

"Pied Piper-ing," Iseul says, and her gaze is no longer sparking with sly cunning; rather, it is dark with suspicion. "If you may deliver a message to him, tell him that the Fingertrap and its marketplace are all fair game for his…*exploits*…but if he should step one foot near my Coop, near my Doves, I will behead him with this ax. And if that doesn't work, I will dig a *massive* hole in the ground, trick him into walking into it, board it up for all eternity, and leave him there forever."

I blink. That is a rather good idea. I am surprised that during my time in Gyeulcheon, I never thought of it.

Then I process the rest of her words, and dark foreboding turns my blood cold. My throat closes, and it is an effort to push sharp words into my mouth. "What do you mean," I say, very slowly, very coldly, "*Pied Piper-ing?*"

"You don't know?" Iseul stares at me in clear shock, setting down her pipe. "Where were you all day, Shin Lina?"

Sleeping in an abandoned temple. I clench my fists, unclench them. *What has Rui done?* "I was occupied," I grit out. "What did he do?" He promised. He *promised* me he would not use Manpasikjeok to lure away Sunpo's denizens, he swore it to me. And yet—

Something cold bites my heart as Iseul fixes me with a stare. "Well." She narrows her eyes and pushes herself up so that she sits erectly on the cushion. "While you were *occupied,* our fine, forgotten emperor strolled into the Fingertrap with his magical flute and spirited away...oh, let's see...*the entire marketplace* to Gyeulcheon."

All my thoughts eddy out of my head as I stare at her in shock. "He *what*?" The words lurch out of me before I can stop them. The room tilts before my eyes. It all makes sense now. The empty street, the closed brothels. The fear that seems to linger upon this kingdom like a disease tonight.

The Pied Piper has paid a visit.

Rui has broken his promise.

Betrayal cuts deep into my chest, and it's all I can do not to accept the second pipe after all. To fight the temptation of letting a biting inhale calm my rapidly fraying temper, my agitated nerves. I swallow hard, struggling to maintain control over myself, the itchiness in my mouth.

Godsdamn you, Rui, I seethe, twisting the silver ring around my finger, forcing down small sips of halji-tinted air with a roiling stomach and cracking heart. *How could you?* I feel a twinge of that old hatred, the burning hot resentment, flare in my stomach. Rui has become my best friend, and...somebody important to me.

Very, very important to me.

He has also stolen an *entire godsdamned marketplace*.

I was there just this morning. The baker, the Wyusan poacher... the bustling farmers, the fishermen...and he must have taken marketgoers as well.

Through my haze of fury and rapidly growing hurt, confusion also lingers. Haneul Rui has stolen more than one hundred humans from Sunpo. *Why? Why would he do this?*

Numerically speaking—this is not right.

Before Rui's easily broken oath to me, only five or ten disappeared per year. Before I met Rui, I myself thought of him as an urban legend. He *never* strikes this openly. So blatantly.

The ring is cold on my finger as I stare at Iseul. She sighs.

"You should really keep better track of him. Ensure that he does not wander too close to my Doves. Otherwise, I promise you, he will one day find himself in a very, very, *very* deep ditch with no way out." She grins, suddenly, and kicks at another smoke ring. "I *so* look forward to working with you, Shin Lina."

INTERLUDE

Hatred, thinks the emperor, feels like molten fury within the bloodstream. He has used its flames before to win battles, to win wars and crush rebellions. Hatred and Haneul Rui are intimately acquainted—he has *loved* hatred, cherished it for what it could bring him.

But self-hatred is different.

Self-hatred feels like guilt and disgust and mortification and terror all crammed into one horrible package. Self-hatred feels like the blade of shame, digging into his heart as he stands before the rushing Black River with Manpasikjeok clutched so tightly in his fist that should he squeeze just an increment harder, it would snap.

He wants to break it. He wants to crush it into nothing but dust. The temptation is so powerful that it is painful, and only the knowledge that the flute's existence has the power to *save* lives keeps him from shattering the instrument.

Instead, Rui spasmodically opens his fist and lets the flute fall to the ground, hitting the rocky shore with a clatter. *Such an inconsequential sound*, he seethes. One would never guess what Manpasikjeok has done. What it will continue to do, century after century after godsdamned century.

Underneath his hanbok, Rui's skin itches. He wants to tear it off. He wants to leave this body, this life, and be reborn as an innocent with clean hands. Not these bloodstained fingers. His mouth trembles. His eyes are glassy.

Suddenly, violently, he yanks the hanbok's sash open and

wrenches himself out of the robes. The cold night air bites at his crawling skin, and the emperor takes a deep, rasping breath as he steps from the pool of fabric and plunges into the dark current.

The waters are as cold as winter's first snowfall—exactly how he designed them to be, a deterrent to the wongun berry bush on the opposite bank. And there are river serpents with teeth as sharp as knives, also exactly how he designed them to be.

Rui hopes they come for him. He hopes they tear him apart as he wades deeper, shutting his eyes as the waters close over his head.

But they don't. Of course they don't. They are his and are no more a threat to him than a rabbit.

He created them from the accumulated magic of his ancestors, from a well of inheritance deep within him that now runs dry. When Dokkaebi die, their remaining powers flow to their eldest child. The Haneul line is long, as ancient as the moons and stars. It took no small portion of that ancestral magic to create Gyeulcheon. Rui will never be able to create another realm from nothingness. All he has now is magic of his own.

And his shame.

Downward he sinks. His toes touch the river's silt, and a river serpent winds around his leg like a sleepy cat seeking attention. The emperor opens his eyes and waits for his lungs to begin burning.

It is both his punishment and his reward.

He will need to reemerge from the river, will need to see through what he has started. But for now, Haneul Rui gathers pain to him like a blanket of comfort. This is a ritual for him. He must do this, every time. Must torture himself under Gyeulcheon's moons.

How long does it take for a Dokkaebi to begin to drown? Rui found the answer to that many years ago. For him, it takes ten minutes and forty-two seconds before his lungs begin to sear in his chest and spots of black to threaten his vision. He savors it as long as he can before he is forced to kick upward toward the surface.

It is with a terrible sense of guilt that he parts his lips and sucks in a lungful of air. He knows that it is not right for him to crawl onto the shore to lay panting as he regains his strength. It is wicked of him. Wrong. Hot tears trickle down Rui's cheeks as he steps back into his robes and lifts that foul flute from the ground.

For a moment, he considers it.

The ramifications of being selfish, of breaking it in two.

It is then that he feels it—one of his many rings begins to warm, the enchantment Kang placed upon the silver activating, as lips he knows as well as his own, brush against a matching band. Rui's heart stumbles in his chest and he quickly wipes away his tears, his breathing beginning to steady, the dark cloud of self-loathing starting to abate as a face swims into his mind's eye: dark eyes the color of casserite in the sun, deep and warm and sparkling. A radiant smile and a teardrop scar.

His Lina.

She is calling for him.

CHAPTER SEVEN

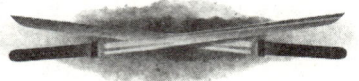

"Rui," I hiss, toying with the silver ring as if the emperor can hear me, "What in the gods' names have you done?" After stumbling out of the Dove Coop, I stand in the shadows of yet another alleyway, turning the band around and around between my fingers. The stench of the kingdom's fear is heavy in my nose. The storm has ended, but the acrid smell of lightning still remains. "Do your promises mean so godsdamned little?"

Liar, deceiver, trickster. Rui has played me for a fool. My mouth wobbles and I press it into a firm, straight line.

Yet my mind takes me back to that day in Gyeulcheon, as I awoke in his bed—weakened severely by Jiwoon's attack, his attempt to collect the collateral I owed for kissing Rui on the shores of the Black Sea. I had valuable information on the rebels that Rui needed—information I was willing to give him…for a price.

"The humans you take from my kingdom. The men and women you kidnap for servants. Stop taking them. Stop stealing them away. They are not yours to take."

"Lina—"

"And the ones already here. They don't belong to this realm. They don't belong to you. Return them. Break their compulsion."

"I will cease the kidnappings of humans if I must. But I cannot return those I have already taken. This is all I can give you, Lina. This is my only bargain."

"Why? They're only servants to you. Employ your own kind, let *the mortals return—"*

"Take my offer, Lina, or deny it. It is my only one."

"Rui—"

I remember his jaw tightening, then. *"I can't—"*

Now, I twine those words around in my mind, feeling their desperate edges. *I can't. I can't.* Not, "I won't."

I *can't.*

Haneul Rui is the Emperor of Dokkaebi. I have seen him paint the sky in colors to my liking, I have seen him steal minds and bend others to his will. He is a creature of unfathomable power, a being who created a realm from nothingness, one who possesses the ability to travel through air and darkness. He is descended from Dalnim, the silver-eyed goddess of the moon. He carries her blood in his veins. Anything is within his reach. Why not this?

Why, *"I can't?"*

There is something darker at play here. I know there is. Something...powerful. Something that would compel Rui to withhold the mortals he already stole, to break his promise to me.

Haneul Rui is hiding something from me.

Why can't you stop? Why have you broken your oath? It is a question I need answered. It is a question that *will* be answered tonight.

Taking a deep breath to steady myself, I press the silver ring to my lips, summoning the Pied Piper. As if it were waiting impatiently for my touch, it heats in response, flaring blue—the color of Rui's Dokkaebi fire.

Tension eases from my shoulders, but only for a moment. A split second later, I am whirling around, my expression thunderous, scaleblades extending from my wrists as I shove the ring into my pocket. It is that feeling again, the feeling as if I am being watched, like before. It is unshakeable. Yet I hear nothing but mundane sounds of the kingdom as I stretch out my senses before tightly reining them back in. Nothing but the scuffed walls of the alleyway surround me.

"Whoever is here," I say very quietly through my teeth, "I suggest that you leave now."

Could it be Rui? No—I felt as if I were being watched before I entered the Dove Coop, and I hadn't summoned him then. If this is the same watcher as before, it is not Rui.

There is no response, but I didn't expect there to be. With my spine still tingling from my stalker's stare, I slowly begin to walk out of the alleyway, each step wobbling and unsteady.

Something emerges from the shadows and begins to carefully follow my every footstep.

I am in no condition to fight, not like this—but I can try. I must try.

Willing myself not to fall, I turn on my heel, spinning around at a precariously sharp angle that has my vision blurring. Yet I can still make it out—the figure behind me. Before even a half second passes, I have shot toward the silhouette and have slammed it into the wall, my teeth shuddering at the impact. I rock back, and my legs almost give way as I struggle to remain upright, struggle to control my own body. Hard muscle strains under my grip, and I bare my teeth as I press a scaleblade to the column of a slender, elegant throat that slowly comes into focus. A throat I know all too well.

Silver eyes glitter in the darkness. It *is* him.

"Well," Haneul Rui, Emperor of the Dokkaebi, the Pied Piper, purrs. "This is beautifully reminiscent, don't you think? I suppose that if you try to kill me now, you actually stand a chance. How enthralling."

"You," I say in a mixture of relief, exasperation, and growing suspicion. For a moment, I am too shocked to be hurt, to feel the sharp blade of his betrayal. Rui smiles, looking rather pleased with himself.

"Me," he confirms calmly, pushing away my scaleblade with an indolent finger. A droplet of golden blood wells on the tip of his finger before quickly fading away, the cut healed. "Hello, Lina."

My brows knit in a frown, and I slowly move the other scaleblade back onto his throat. "You surprised me," I whisper, wondering if he can hear the steeliness to my tone, the growing coldness. If he can feel how fury, confusion, and hurt once again begin to heat my blood. For our bodies are pressed so closely together that I can feel the hitch of his breath as he stares down at me. "You shouldn't surprise me."

Rui pushes the sharp scale away again, a dark, midnight laugh snaking past his lips. "It wouldn't have been any fun if I didn't." His smile grows, and I can't help but allow my lips to curl into a smile of their own—even as I put his throat in jeopardy *again* and wonder, reluctantly, if I will best get my answers through means of violence.

But the emperor is beautiful in the night, wisps of moonlight dancing across his golden, marble-hewn face. His dark, glossy hair reaches the chest of his flowing black hanbok, which is open ever so slightly to reveal the first beginnings of a chiseled chest. As is his custom, he wears long earrings of fine silver on his pointed ears, and an assortment of elegant rings—one of which I know is a match to mine. At present, he is pressed against the wall, his head leaning back to bare his throat. He is smiling a wolf's smile. "Did you miss me, little thief?"

"I— Are you *wet*?" I demand. Upon further glance, his hair is so unnaturally glossy because it is, in fact, incredibly soaked.

"Very," he replies, smirking. But something about it seems weary. "It was storming today."

It certainly did storm in Sunpo, and he certainly did pay this kingdom a visit. I narrow my eyes and push myself away with considerable effort, letting my scales recede. Trying to even my breathing. Rui remains where he is, leaning against the wall, cocking his head as I respond.

Honey captures more flies than vinegar, the Voice whispers.

I didn't ask you.

But all the same, I listen to its advice despite the unease roiling through me at the way I can feel the Voice settle back, satisfied. "Rui," I say, very sweetly, unsheathing a dagger from my waist and twirling it idly, "would you like to tell me about your little *escapade* this morning?"

Rui stiffens. "Whatever do you mean?" he asks hoarsely, and I scowl. How dare he feign ignorance?

"I mean that you *broke your fucking promise.*" Losing my saccharine tongue, I tighten my grip on my weapon, words bubbling out of my mouth and scalding my lips. "The whole godsdamned marketplace, Rui? What *possible purpose—*" I cut off.

His throat is bobbing, and I see him fight hard to redon his mask of wry mischief. I grind my molars in ire. Surely he knows how furious I am at his shattered promise. His nostrils flare slightly, and I realize, with a jolt, that he is struggling to breathe evenly. And…

There are traces of *fear* etched upon his face. The sight brings me pause. It is a remorseful fear, edged with a self-hating guilt. I know the look well. I wore it upon reuniting with Sang in Jeoseung. As I apologized for the night my family was brutally slaughtered, as I worried Sang might despise me for it, might blame me bitterly and hatefully.

The anger in my chest banks and I slowly sheathe my dagger. My arms hang loosely at my sides.

"Rui." My voice is gentle.

He closes his eyes, ever so briefly. His mask slips away. "Not here," he says. "Not now. Please. I come tonight to apologize, but—not here."

I swallow hard, taking a deep breath. Pushing my questions, my hurt, down until I can nod. If there truly are darker forces at play, as I suspect, an alleyway in Sunpo's Boneburrow is not the time, nor place, to discuss them.

"Fine," I say, ceding—and extend my hand. Rui's tortured eyes linger on my face as he slips his hand into mine. His skin is cool as our fingers interlace. Despite myself, I can't help but lean into the emperor for a moment, savoring his presence.

For this moment between us will be the calm before a storm. I do not desire a fight with Rui, but I need answers.

Yet as Rui murmurs my name, I hesitate.

Perhaps for a few hours, I will let it sit. Perhaps for a few hours, I will let my hurt and outrage stew in a cauldron with the lid tightly shut.

Rui kisses the top of my head. "The hanok I purchased you," he says hoarsely. "Where is it?"

Rui's hand is cool in mine as I lead him out of the Boneburrow and through the winding Sunpo streets. I lean on him as I stumble over puddles and loose stones. He says nothing, although I know he has noticed. When I nearly trip over my own foot, Rui's hands shoot to my waist, and he gently steadies me with a hesitant, crooked smile. Softening, I smile back.

Despite it all, I *have* missed him—missed him dearly, although it has been only less than a week since we last parted. I breathe in the scent of him as we traverse the hushed city, our silence companiable, intimate. His thumb moves in a circle along my skin, and he smiles that sweet smile down at me—a smile I once would have thought so foreign on his immortal visage, but one that I have now grown used to these past few weeks.

"I see the city is not yet burned to the ground, nor running red with blood." Rui murmurs as we come to a stop outside my door. "I don't know whether I should be relieved or disappointed. The scarlet-haired. Is he still alive?"

My mouth tightens as I remember where, exactly, the scarlet-haired is at this very moment. "Let's not speak of him," I murmur as I shut the door and lead Rui toward my simple bedroom. "Not yet."

All I want is to feel him close to me.

Everything else can wait. My bruised pride and bewilderment can wait.

The calm before the storm, I think grimly.

Rui seems to think the same.

In an instant, the distance between us has vanished completely. His lips are crushed against mine as his hands are tangled in my hair, and mine pressed against his chest, backing him into my bedroom and pushing him toward the bed. I straddle his waist, overcome with need that reddens my face and warms somewhere deep in my stomach. That keeps the lid on my anger sealed tight, for now.

His lips fit against mine perfectly. It's as if his body was carved for me, his limbs shaped to fit against mine. I nip at his bottom lip and he makes a noise low in his throat, hoarse with need. It's impossible not to smile with satisfaction as Rui shudders, pulling me closer, holding me tighter.

"I've missed you," Rui gasps.

"I've missed you too," I whisper hoarsely, pulling away for a brief moment in order to drink in the sharp lines of his face, the way his cheekbones become slightly flushed when we are together. He is beautiful, and he is mine.

He has also broken a promise.

The reminder is like a bucket of cold water emptied upon my head, chilling my skin, icing over my bones. Blinking, I loosen my arms from where they have been encircling his neck.

"Have you?" Rui's eyes are worried. Hesitant. I know that he has noticed my sudden distance and see a flicker of guilt flit across his visage. "It is so hard to tell when you've summoned me only this once."

"I have," I murmur, choosing my words carefully. "Truly, I have. But, Rui…" How to voice the disappointment I feel? The feeling that he has been…an infidel to his promise? "I need to get out of this suit," I finally say, voice hoarse.

He closes his eyes as I shift off him, running a hand through my hair, unable to ignore the betrayal stinging at my heart. I feel him watching me as I leave the room, and his expression is nearly unreadable as I return in his silken shirt.

Nearly. There is hesitancy there. And, perhaps…dread.

Lying down on the bed, I close my eyes for a few minutes, my breathing steadying. Rui is quiet. When I open them again, I see molten silver staring down at me.

"You're so beautiful," Rui whispers, an almost sad smile softening his face. "I love watching you, little thief. More than I love watching snow fall in the winter's first flurry, more than I love watching the moons shine over my realm."

I don't return his smile, for my chest once again feels tight and my stomach hollow. "You've been watching me for hours," I return, pulling the sheets up to my chin as I remember the feeling of certainty that I was being watched before entering the Dove Coop. "You're supposed to be caring for Eunbi." My younger sister is safely tucked away in Gyeulcheon under the care of Rui's court and far, far away from the chaos I am about to incite. "Not stalking me from the shadows." *Not kidnapping marketplaces.*

There is a confused pause. "I haven't been stalking you," he finally says into the crown of my head. "I came when I was summoned."

I frown, for there is truth in his tone—truth and slight concern.

What, then, had been watching me before I'd entered the Coop? Silence falls between us as I wonder, if not Rui, who it was.

And the uneasiness that follows is enough to make the cauldron of emotions slowly begin to boil over. Spilling betrayal and anger and resentment. Confusion and exhaustion so deep, so profound, that my breathing turns shallow.

Rui seems to understand that the storm has begun. That our pocket of temporary peace has been rescinded. I see him steadying himself, choosing his words with gentle care.

"Lina," Rui says quietly. "I know that I broke my promise to you tonight. For that I am infinitely sorry." He traces the lines between my brows, and his silver eyes are duller than usual as I fix him with a glower. The emperor pulls his hand away. "I know you must feel—betrayed. That you must want to sink a dagger into my heart again. But please, know that I do what I must. I came here tonight to tell you this."

I can't. I do what I must. My mouth turns dry as the words ring hollowly in my ears. "Why must you do it?" I ask, clutching the bedsheets with white knuckles. Every word is strained. I am fighting against the temptation to treat him as I would another who is withholding valuable information. My hands shake. "Why, Rui? Is it not your choice?"

A long moment passes between us, fraught with emotion. With my incredulous anger. With his tense guilt.

"I came to apologize," he says quietly. "Not to give you my excuses."

"*Give me* your excuses," I reply fervently. "Give me your justifications. I want them, Rui. I-I need them. Please. What is it you keep from me?"

Rui's expression is tortured as he turns away, angling his face toward the moonlight creeping in through the screened window. "Lina…" I feel him inhale shakily. "There is much I wish to tell you. There is much I *will* tell you; I promise. It is simply that some stories hold more than the mere weight of words. Some stories… Some stories are not for the time of darkness. Some stories I wish to tell you in the summer light, when it is warm, when it is safe."

The realization forms with a spark of concern. *Rui is scared.*

Yes. Yes, he's scared. I can see it clearly now, in the lines of his face, angled away as it may be. I can—understand that, I realize with a sinking stomach.

There is a story he holds close to his chest, one that seeps darkness into our conversation even now. There is also one that I hold close to mine, one that I have not yet shared with Eunbi, yet I know I must. I, too, am waiting for a moment of sunlight and security. To deny Rui what I myself seek—I will not.

I feel myself beginning to yield, beginning to trust the truth of his words, to feel the sincerity behind his vow despite the one he has broken. Yet just as my muscles begin to relax, as my heart calms from its furious pounding—

Look how easily he scorns us, the Voice sneers, peering out from behind my eyes. **Look how easily he dismisses us. Do we mean so little to him?**

My body flinches, as if to escape the Voice, but such a thing is impossible. It rests within my head, curled upon my mind, ingrained within me. I feel the cold touch of its presence on my mind as it stalks to and fro.

Perhaps he compares us to Shuo Achara.

The mention of Rui's dead lover sends a jolt through me, and I feel the Voice's leer grow. "Lina?" I think Rui might ask in concern, turning toward me once more, but I am not sure. Everything but the Voice is muted. Muffled.

Achara, with her paint-splattered hands and eye for beauty.

Rui and I have both loved before. We both share the grief and pain of losing our loved ones. Do not try to turn this into something that it is not.

He does not trust us as he did her. He wrote poetry for her. Has he done so for us?

Perhaps one day, he will. In, out. Ignore the Voice, the way it whispers untruths. Ignore the thing inside my head that will not leave.

Look at his long hair. Look how he still mourns.

My eyes flit to his long, silky dark locks and my stomach clenches uncomfortably. It is Dokkaebi custom for males to wear their hair long in mourning over their lost partners. I have never thought to ask Rui to cut it, to sever his grief for Achara... That would be wrong, and something I would never, ever demand of him.

Do not put these irrelevant thoughts into my head, I hiss, but the Voice only shrugs in smug resignation. I swallow hard.

Achara surely knew the secret that Rui keeps from us, it whispers and curves a gnarled finger into a corner of my mind before finally—*finally*—retreating back into the crevices of my consciousness.

The sudden quiet is thick, jarring. I gasp in panic, once and then twice into the cradle of my hands. That—that *thing* in my head should not exist.

I want to tell Rui of the Voice, but I know I cannot. I do not want to be seen as... I want him to see me as strong. I do not want him to think that what I have gone through has broken me. The spells of gracelessness, the times when I have sunk to my knees screaming that the world is too *loud*...those times are humiliating enough. And this...if he does not believe that the Voice is the vocal manifestation of my new powers, he will surely think me mad.

And if he *does* believe me...

Perhaps that would be worse, for I do not want his expression to one day match the one of suspicion that so often rests on the visage of the royal advisor. I was reborn from the scale and venom of his eternal enemy, after all. Trust can stretch only so far.

Mouth tasting sour from words unsaid, I turn on my side so that Rui does not see the hot tears now blurring my vision. There is a Dokkaebi in my bed and a Voice in my head, yet I feel more alone than ever.

A broken promise. A secret kept hidden. A new body that does not feel like it is entirely my own. All of it is so much, so soon. My throat tightens, and suddenly I'm missing the barley farm, missing the simplicity of life before the shipwreck and the Talons and the Blackbloods and Gyeulcheon and the wongun enhancer and—

Rui curses softly and I feel a gentle hand on my shoulder. "Lina..." His voice is heavy with regret. "Lina, little thief, I truly am sorry. I..."

"You broke your promise," I whisper, suddenly spent from sadness. *You, who I trusted. My friend. My...*

"I did." His words are barely audible. "But please, believe that my reason—it is sincere. I did not deceive you for the fun of it, nor did I take it lightly." He hesitates, and then I feel the bed shift as he sits upright. "Would you...would you rather I leave? I will do so, if it's what you wish."

My throat feels tight, but I manage to shake my head. I cannot tell if Rui's sigh is one of relief or remorse. Likely both. With a heavy heart, I close my eyes and feign sleep. Next to me, I suspect that Rui does the same, his mind swimming with words unsaid. With stories untold.

Alone in the darkness, I turn to the Voice. It is only desperation that guides me. I still fear the presence in my head, the consciousness that is not my own. But I am fraught with the need for answers.

Do you know?

Know what? The Voice sounds bored.

Don't play coy, I snap. *What he does with them. The humans.*

Maybe he eats them, jests the Voice after a long silence. **Or... maybe he feeds them to something else.** I feel it arch a wry brow, waiting expectantly for my response. Or praise. I give it neither.

Instead, I scowl and close my eyes.

But there is something in the Voice's tone that keeps me awake for the rest of the night.

CHAPTER EIGHT

When Rui rises the next morning, I am slick with sweat and flecked with blood from an early morning attack on two Claw patrols. There were four Claws in each patrol. Thirty-two Claws dead in a matter of days.

I feel—triumphant, afterward, one step closer to killing Kalmin but...it's almost scary how easy it is to kill, now. It's...it's different. Sometimes it feels like cheating.

I have to remind myself that it's not. That I am doling out what is deserved, a swift hand of justice.

Kalmin will begin to notice, now that his Claws have been nearly halved. Even for Sunpo, that is unusual. I've no idea how many Claws remain—I would estimate, based on my time in Kalmin's service, thirty. Three of them are the patrol I've monitored entering and exiting the Moonlit Hare. I'll find the other twenty-seven easily enough. Then I'll start on the crane's Legs.

Now, however, I am practicing my swordsmanship in the hanok's foyer. I returned a few hours ago and have been conditioning since. My clumsiness has receded, replaced by immortal grace. The exercise pushes aside my faint morning longings for a smoke. So immersed am I in my practicing, I hardly hear the soft footfall behind me.

I have always been agile, but this new—albeit inconsistent—gracefulness is awe-inspiring as I sweep the blade through the air and, ignoring my leg's ache, position my feet in the complicated steps of footwork Yoonho taught me so long ago. "To battle is to dance," he always said. I listen to him now as I weave around my invisible opponent, practicing my lunges and slashes, my advances and nimble dodges. Only when I spin do I see him, the Dokkaebi emperor. He leans against the wall, looking tired. Dark shadows rim his eyes and his skin lacks its usual luster.

I still mid-strike. My fingers tighten momentarily around the hilt of my jikdo before loosening as Rui attempts—and fails—at a small smile.

"Good morning," he says quietly. He is clearly carrying the weight of the past night upon his shoulders.

My chest is rising and falling unevenly as I twirl my blade in a neat figure-eight before sheathing it at my side. The hemp fabric of my plain tunic and pants stirs with the quick motion, and my hair flutters around my chin. "Good morning," I say quietly, watching him.

He looks so uncharacteristically hesitant as he runs a hand down his face. "I am sorry," he says sincerely. "For my broken promise, for all of it. I meant what I said. When the time is right, I will give you my explanation."

I incline my head in a small nod.

I believe him. Some apologies ooze with fabricated sincerity, drip with false regret. It is a lie that is told to placate, to silence. It is untrue.

But Rui's apology is not one of those.

And perhaps I am sorry, too.

Our battle in bed last night was confirmation enough. There is something...*dark* at play, something that compelled Rui to break his promise and spirit away an entire marketplace of humans. Something powerful, something sinister. My outrage last night was deserved, but perhaps I pushed him too hard, pressing down on a tender wound.

I of all people know the weight of trauma, the burden it brings. As I ran through Sunpo's streets this morning, hunting leering Claw patrols, I mulled over the possibilities until my head pounded even faster than my heart.

I know so little of Dokkaebi magic. Perhaps there is a cost to creating an artificial realm. Perhaps Rui must have humans in Gyeulcheon to keep the pocket realm alive. Or perhaps the kidnappings are an order from Okhwang, from one of the gods. But what god would demand such a thing, and why? It is a question that Rui will answer in his own time. I must trust that, and devote my energy to reclaiming Sunpo as my own. As Talon territory.

I wipe sweat from my forehead as I make my way over to Rui. He watches me closely, cautiously. "The Blackbloods are in the Talons' old palace," I say lowly. Rui blinks, once and then twice. It strikes me, as he relaxes, that he had expected another fight. But as my words sink in, he stiffens once more, and his eyes burn momentarily blue. "I found out yesterday." Even saying the words makes me feel ill, but I plow on. "I'm burning down their old giwajip this morning."

It is a decision I reached earlier, as I sprinted past the godsdamned thing in Sunpo's Coin Yard. My chest constricted with fear at the sight—it was nothing more than a large, gated house with a tile roof, but I nearly stumbled. Nearly tripped as bile rose in my throat.

Unacceptable that a mere building should hold such power over me. Unacceptable that the giwajip in which I was abused and enslaved should still stand.

Rui's mouth is a tight line. "Good." The word is sharp and proud. "Burn it to cinders."

His fierce tone has my lips curving upward, a sharp blade. "I want you to come with me." I shake my head as he hesitates. "I know you don't want to involve yourself in my war. I already have the means to a fire. I don't need yours." I slip my hand into my pocket and finger my lighter. I do not use it anymore, but I've kept it. It's a remnant of days past. Of a life past. "But I want you there with me."

Rui's eyes soften. "Then I will come," he says, and brushes a strand of my hair behind my ear. Then, ever so softly, he presses his lips to mine. The kiss is sweet and fleeting, but it still warms me to my toes. "I will come," Rui whispers again, "and watch that damned place burn to ash."

The Coin Yard is silent as Rui and I step from his corridor of shadows onto the dawn-lit street. Sunpo's western sector belongs to the kingdom's wealthy, all of whom have no reason to rise before six in the morning on a hot summer day. Our arrival has gone completely unnoticed.

As I roll my shoulders, I realize that Rui and I stand in the same spot where, weeks ago, he gathered me in his arms and brought me to Gyeulcheon. There, ahead of us and barely visible, is the shadow of the giwajip's wall. As I did then, I raise a finger in a vulgar gesture and set my jaw, ignoring my sweaty palms.

My boots clip on the cobblestones as I stalk toward the old base. Rui is silent beside me, but his presence is comforting. A reminder that I got out. That I escaped. I breathe in the summer air. I can smell the traces of a storm on the horizon. It seems that this is the summer for them.

Odd. We never did get so many before.

In one hand, I have a bottle of alcohol, freshly stolen from the Moonlit Hare. The other hand is in my pocket, tightening around the lighter as we reach the black stone wall. The silver gate in the wall's center is the intended point of entry, yet I vault over the obsidian barrier with ease, careful not to put too much weight on my perennially injured leg as I land on dead grass.

I can almost smell traces of my old anguish and filthiness in the air. Abruptly, I reel in my senses. Rui, having followed, places a hand on the small of my back. I take a steadying breath as I eye the sloping black-tiled roof, the wooden pillars, the rocky steps leading up to the doors.

From my pocket, I withdraw my silver lighter. With a flick of my thumb, there is a flame. Yet it doesn't leave the confines of my hand as I stare at the godsdamned place where I was beaten and brutalized for a year. A familiar grief squeezes my chest, but underneath it, there's something else.

Slowly, I extinguish the flame and take a swig of soju from the bottle.

"Come with me," I say hoarsely after I wipe my mouth with the back of my wrist, savoring the gliding burn down my throat.

I do not know what compels me to mount the steps of the giwajip. To, with a flick of the wrist, break open the door. As I step inside, boots creaking on the wooden floor, silence meets my ears. Rui is stiff next to me as I begin my walk down the hall, trailing my fingertips against the bare walls.

Gone are the stolen paintings and rugs that once decorated the corridors' lengths. Gone is the crooked chandelier that once hung precariously from above, casting a chipped light upon the door—the door that is half hidden underneath a flight of stairs. I take a steadying breath and turn to Rui. "When I was a captive here," I say hoarsely, "this was my room."

His nostrils flare slightly as he stares at the chipped wooden door.

"For a year," I whisper, "this is how I lived."

And I push open the door, somehow knowing that it will all be there still—the tattered blanket on the floor. A crate full of grimy, unwashed clothes. A small, cracked mirror on the wall and a basin of water for washing. The scuttling of small creatures on the ground. The smell of unwashed human. Of desperation and despair.

I cannot explain why it is important to me that Rui sees this.

But I watch him intently as he takes it all in, his shoulders stiffening and his skin paling. To see this, I suppose, is to see me. To *really* see me. To glimpse a dark corner of my soul, one which I loathe to bare to anyone else. My tongue is suddenly heavy and dry, my back prickling with uncomfortable heat.

What if this changes how he sees me? What if this dark corner alters his perception of me? I gnaw on my lip and watch him carefully.

Rui is barely breathing. His eyes glow blue with Dokkaebi fire, and the air around us grows cold as azure flames flicker between his fingertips.

Nervous now, I down another gulp of soju and swallow hard. "All things considered," I rasp, "I was lucky. The Talons were never buried or given a funeral. They were dumped into Habaek's River. Food for the fish and turtles. Chara hated the water, too. When she was a-alive—" I stumble on the word. "When she was alive, she avoided the sea. Even when the rest of us jumped into the waves at the Yongwangguk Cove, she stayed on the shore. But now her bones are underwater. She would hate that."

As Rui stares and stares at the room, I begin to douse the floor with alcohol, making my way back down the corridor. "I went to the river once," I continue. "I ran away from here in the dead of night and pleaded for Habaek to give them back to me. I screamed and I pleaded but the river god ignored me. So I dove into the water to look for them." I can almost feel the sludgy water closing in around me again, can almost taste the brackish flavor of the river.

Rui slowly joins my side as I continue to splatter alcohol on the floor. His hands are trembling, I notice. His breathing is uneven.

"But I never found them." Hot tears prick my eyes. "When I returned to the base, dripping water, Kalmin immediately knew what I'd done. He threatened to kill Eunbi for my insolence, even though I'd returned.

"And then he locked me in a room with Man Jisu, a Blackblood who enjoys—pain. Torture. It was—it was a *reward* for Jisu. And by the time it was over, I couldn't move without weeping in pain. Kalmin brought in a healer, only so Jisu could do it again the next week. And then the next. And the next."

The fury radiating from Rui is palpable. The skin around his mouth has become very pale, and a muscle is pulsing rapidly in his jaw. Blue Dokkaebi fire burns in his eyes, scorching. "*Fuck—*" His voice cuts off, harsh and abrupt. He presses a fist to his lips, and I think—I think that his entire body is shaking.

My bottle is halfway empty. The liquid *glug glug glug*s as I soak the foyer in it. "Their skeletons are still down there, in the silt," I say in a thread of a voice. "I can feel them. By now, fish have made homes in their eye sockets. River eels have coiled around their ribs." Tears drip down my cheeks, trails of salt and sorrow. "They're lost to me." The final drop of soju spills from the bottle's neck. I let it crash to the ground, let it shatter into thousands of shards.

From my pocket, I pull the lighter and switch on the flame.

I stare at the flickering orange, the crackling red. In the flames, I can almost see them—the Talons, watching me expectantly, waiting to be avenged. "I cannot bring them back. But I can drag Konrarnd Kalmin and his Blackbloods down to their knees. I can make them scream and suffer. And their suffering will not end in life. The Talons will haunt them in death."

I meet Rui's eyes. "It starts with fire."

The lighter tumbles to the floor, the flame steadily burning, hissing as it reaches the alcohol on the ground. I wipe the tears from my cheeks as we are surrounded by heat and smoke, as the flames spread across the floor and begin to grow, stretching toward the ceiling. Rui grabs my hand, and I think he, too, may have salt-dampened cheeks before we disappear into darkness and shadow.

. . .

The fire will send a message.

Perhaps Kalmin will brush it off as an accident, at least at first. What is it to him if the old base is destroyed? He's in the palace now, enjoying its luxury. But he will grow uneasy soon enough as some nervous Leg hesitantly reports to him that the number of his Claws have been sawed in half. That they've all been killed in Kalmin's own streets. That the other patrols are scared that they're next.

The rain falls in heavier sheets now, cold and clean, quelling the usual midsummer scorch as Rui and I finish watching the burning from afar, sitting on the highest tier of the Temple of Ruin's roof. His arms are tight around me as I lean into his chest, watching the final flames lick the sky. Watching two gray-clad Claw patrols frantically attempt to put out the fire with the help of bystanders.

"Lina," Rui says. His voice is a rasp. "I know that I said I would not get involved in your war. But I...I would willingly be your soldier now. My fire, my fury, my flute are yours to command. Let me help you."

I twist to stare at him, my heart beginning to beat faster and faster. "You mean it?"

"Yes," he says, his voice tight and his expression icy. But not toward me. "I will burn their entire regime down for you, Lina. I will leave nothing but ash. I will teach them what agony can be."

It is enticing. So enticing. For a moment, I imagine that my war could end tonight. The Blackbloods—Claws, Legs, Feathers, Bills, Crest, and Crown—all dead by tonight. Sunpo mine, by tonight. The Talons avenged within hours. I close my eyes, savoring the fantasy.

But that is all it can be.

A fantasy.

The revenge must be my own. For only when I dirty my hands with Konrarnd Kalmin's blood can I truly be forgiven. Truly be clean. These deaths belong to me. They are mine, I have claimed them, I have marked them. A sudden surge of territorialism crests through me and I open my eyes, shaking my head. "This fight belongs to me," I say in a low voice.

Rui nods, as if he expected this, but his mouth is still a tight line. "I want," he says slowly, raking a hand through his long hair, "to kill them, Lina. For what they—for what they *did to you*. But if I cannot, let me help in another way. Please. Please, little thief."

And his expression—it's so open. So honest. So at odds with the deceit he subjected me to last night, and something in my heart swells with warmth at the sight of it. "There is," I find myself saying slowly as thunder rumbles up ahead, "somebody you could help me find."

Rui inclines his head in a nod. "Who?"

"Her name is Im Yejin," I say, combing back my bangs with my fingers as rainwater seeps into my eyes. "She's a shipsmith. Yejin has made nearly all the boats in Sunpo—she rents them out to fishermen, or to whoever wants to leave the kingdom." Her name tastes like ash in my mouth. It was one of her pyeongjeoseon boats that my parents took to visit my ailing haraboji in Bonseyo. The small cargo ship that my parents had gained passage on sank beneath the cold waves of the Yongwangguk Sea when I was fourteen. When I was small and scared and hungry, leaving Eunbi and me utterly alone against the world. "I…need to speak to her. I've been looking for her these past few days, but I cannot find her. I suspect that she's in…hiding."

"In hiding?" Rui tilts his head, clearly intrigued. "From the Blackbloods?"

I scratch at the back of my head, swallowing bitter guilt. "She's been in hiding for a while. Ever since I tried to kill her."

The Dokkaebi emperor's brows raise. "Somehow," he drawls, "I'm not surprised that you seem to have a vendetta against everything in Sunpo that so much as moves."

"It was three years ago," I mutter, shamefaced. "It was one

of her boats that failed my parents. I wanted retribution. But I couldn't—I couldn't kill her." I shift uncomfortably on the roof, remembering the woman's wide eyes, remembering the way my blade stopped in midair. "She didn't kill them. Not...not directly. I realized that, and I left."

Rui brushes a strand of wet hair behind my ear. "Oh Lina," he murmurs.

I clear my throat, shoving down a rising bitter emotion. "But she's been elusive ever since. If one wants to rent or purchase a boat from her, they first must find her. Her most loyal customers, the fishermen who work on the sea, they all know where she is... yet they're careful. Yejin is smart. When I went to her, I told her my name. My story. She knows who the Reaper is, and although the world believes me dead, the woman is still taking precautions. But I need to locate her and earn her favor. I need her as an ally."

"What use is a single shipsmith?" Rui asks, tilting his head. "Unless, of course, you have an excursion planned." His eyes glint. "I hear that Yongwang's abandoned ocean palace is particularly nice this time of year."

I smile slightly, staring down at the ruins of the giwajip through the sheets of rain. "Im Yejin is the *only* shipsmith in Sunpo, Rui. That means that she can control who leaves the kingdom. To an extent, she can also control who enters it, as she also owns the docks. If I can bring her to my side, I can ensure a secure kingdom under my rule." Below us, men and women are gaping at the ruined building. Two Blackblood patrols have joined them—my acute eyes spot their tattooed cranes as they lift their arms to lace their hands behind their heads in dismay. Six Claws, I suspect.

I scratch my wrists, watching them closely. "I'm going to rebuild Sunpo. No more murder, no more wrongful deaths. If I have Im Yejin by my side, I am one step closer to accomplishing that."

And one step closer to making amends. I wronged Yejin. I know that. This is another chance for me to make things right before I take this kingdom for my own.

"So will you help me find her?" I turn to Rui, whose lips crook in a smile.

"Lina," he says and raises my hand to his lips, pressing them against my skin, "I would give you the moon on a string if you asked for it."

CHAPTER NINE

As Rui departs in a swirl of shadow and the scent of plum blossoms, I nimbly make my way to the ground, where I focus on the two Claw patrols. The other bystanders have vanished into their homes—the storm is now truly raging, lightning and thunder splicing the sky in half. Rain sluices down my face as I focus my hearing, listening to their exclamations of disbelief. My blades emerge from my wrists, shining in the storm.

When the two patrols leave, shaking their heads, I follow them. I let them take us out of the Coin Yard and all the way into the Boneburrow before I strike from behind.

They're on edge, undoubtedly due to the deaths of the other patrols. It's for that reason that three of them manage to draw their swords before my scaleblades whip through the air, before they meet skin and bone.

Severing heads used to be a precise science—I used to need to swing hard, fast, with as much strength as possible. Now it's easier. Three heads roll. Two more soon follow.

The final Blackblood shouts in horror as his friends fall, their blood staining his boots. I smile as lightning flashes, illuminating my face, and as recognition has the Blackblood gaping.

"You," he chokes out before his head topples onto the street below with a wet splash into a grimy puddle. His eyes are still open, staring up at me. I look away.

Breathing hard in the storm, I wipe my scaleblades on my suit. Six men dead in under five seconds. Only twenty-one Claws remain.

That's only seven more patrols.

This power...I am scared of it, sometimes. I look down at the six heads, the six separate bodies, and my legs begin to wobble. I fight to keep my balance, pushing away the oncoming spell of ungainliness as best I can. Yet it is not hard to feel it approaching, to feel my grace slipping away, replaced by clumsiness.

What fun that was, croons the Voice.

I wouldn't call that fun, I spit back, stepping over a body.

It chuckles, cold. **You enjoyed it, Lina. Do not bother to lie to me. I live within your head. You like killing.**

Yes. No. When it is deserved, I give justice. But I am not—I do not want to be wicked anymore. I have the power of an immortal. A...goddess. Now that I am free to make my own choices, I must choose wisely. Must make myself worthy of such powers.

I gulp down thick, humid air as my legs carry me through the kingdom. Breathe in. Breathe out. But the noises of the kingdom are growing, and my head is beginning to pulse in pain.

Lightning cleaves the sky with a flash of blinding light. Thunder sounds like one hundred cannons fired in unison. I gasp. I choke. I stumble. The laughter of men in Boneburrow taverns. The giggles of women. Clinks of coins. So many people are pouring drinks into glasses that it sounds like a waterfall in my ears. A child sobbing. A door slamming. Feet pounding. Boom. Boom. *Boom*. My fingers press into my ears but it's not enough. I can hear *everything*.

Thunder. Lightning. The world is being torn apart, and it is taking me with it.

I try to walk, need to move, need to leave, but I can't see. My vision is fixed on the cracks in the stone road. Within them, hundreds of tiny bugs squirm and squeal. I look to the sky but all I can see are raindrops, enormous and glistening.

One of them falls upon my face and the feeling of it is so cold, so icy, so unusually sharp that I fall. Raindrops never felt like that before. I hit the ground hard, facedown into a muddy puddle, and

I can taste the shoes of men and women who walked on the street, the dirt from the horses who passed through here. The dust and grime explode on my tongue. Gagging, I roll onto my back, but the raindrops *hurt* my skin, and everything is so godsdamned loud that I am drowning, for there is so much sensation that there is nothing at all, nothing but panic and fear and shame and guilt and oh gods oh gods *oh gods oh gods*—

One voice cuts through the chaos. It is melodious and sweet but edged with sharpness. I have heard it before. It offered me halji and told me that Rui had stolen a marketplace, an entire marketplace... "This can't possibly be good," the voice says, and I can hear the bemusement, the hesitancy, the concern. "Lina? Are you dying? Did you eat a bad clam?"

The groaning noise that comes out of my mouth is so loud inside my own skull that my head rocks back, smacking into the stone hard enough that my vision momentarily goes, and it's a relief to see only darkness as Song Iseul lifts me into her arms.

"I *really* hope," she says, "that your Dokkaebi isn't nearby because I positively, *absolutely* know that it will look as though I've killed you and am collecting spoils of war for some nefarious purpose." We're moving quicker than I would have thought possible.

Iseul is still speaking, her voice pushing back the world's cacophony, and she's not even slightly out of breath. "By the way, I saw your little craftsmanship over there. *Very* impressive. The way the bodies and heads are arranged...it's almost artistic. I would have admired it forever, but then I saw you, twitching on the street like a dying rat. I hope you aren't dying. I like you more than I like most people in this shithole. It does look like you're dying, though..."

We're going up a stairway. There's the sound of a door unlocking, a door opening. "Thank you for killing those awful guards, by the by," she says, almost cheerfully, although I can still hear a trace of panic in her voice. I'm focusing on that, letting everything else—the sounds, the noises, the tastes and smells—recede. "They reeked like unwashed vermin. You also smell quite bad, and I think you've got shit on your face, but I'm willing to grant you leniency. Considering that you're dying." Another door opening, and I'm being lowered onto something soft, cushioned.

Breathe in. Breathe out.

The episode is almost over.

Breathe in. Breathe out. My senses are reining themselves back. My vision is returning, but it is normal once more as I blink unsurely up at Song Iseul. She's staring down at me, brown eyes wide. "Or perhaps not," she amends. "Welcome back to life, Shin Lina."

Slowly I take in my surroundings. The walls of the room are lavender, and the air smells faintly of vanilla and ginseng. Intricately patterned rugs, a deep shade of rich purple, adorn the floor. The sheets on the bed underneath me are silken, cool to the touch. I'm in the Dove Coop, and its madame is gaping at me, her mauve hanbok crusted with mud and blood. "Lina," she says, and her voice is no longer light. "Are you injured?"

"No," I rasp. "I'm fine."

Iseul blinks. "Lina, Beheader of Blackbloods," she says endearingly, in the way one might say "darling" or "love." "I found you, as I said, twitching in a puddle like a *dying rat*...but you mean to say you're perfectly fine? Really? I'm friends with a healer, you know. I could send for him right now."

Groaning, I sit up. "I'm fine," I repeat. "Really, I am."

The Dove Coop's owner is staring at me as if I've grown a second head. "I don't believe you."

"I just—" I rub my face wearily. "I have...spells like these, sometimes. It's nothing."

"It truly did not *look* like nothing," Iseul returns wryly, sitting down on the bedside. "But I don't think you're the type to lie if you need help from an ally. But these spells..." Iseul picks at the sheets and cocks her head. "What are they?"

I swallow hard. "They just...happen, sometimes."

Iseul props her chin on a fist. "Are they born, perhaps, from strong emotion?"

My brows inch together. "What do you mean?"

"Well," she says carefully, "I have heard of...attacks such as these following emotions like panic. My friend, the healer, says that they're nothing to be ashamed of. That this world can be overwhelming. Does this sound like what you experience?"

I open my mouth to deny it, but something stops me. I begin to sift through my memories. The first "attack," as Iseul put it, was after Kang had looked at me like I was a...something unnatural. *I'm not a monster,* I'd thought, but self-doubt had pinched at my chest. Remorse and disgust at my past choices, my mistakes, followed. My legs became uncoordinated. I bumped into walls, I tripped over my feet. And then my senses expanded. Unable to rein them in, I sank to my knees and suffered.

There was another time, too. I was running through Gyeulcheon, fast as the wind, savoring my powers. I'd stopped, panting, and the enormity of my abilities—my new responsibilities—sank in. The weight of the necessity that I make decisions that are moral and right had landed on my shoulders like a weight. If I made the wrong choice, like I am so prone to doing, the result could be... catastrophic. But my choices, I realized, have not been my own for so long. What if I have forgotten how to choose to be Good?

The attack had come, leaving me huddled on the ground, shaking. It is not exactly what Iseul is saying, but it's close enough that I nod hesitantly.

"There are herbs and techniques that might help." Iseul pats my hand sympathetically. "I can introduce you to them, if you'd like."

"Perhaps," I reply hoarsely.

She levels a look at me that is somewhat wry and somewhat empathetic. "Well, anyway—my offer to hide an enormous pile of bodies still stands. I have a multitude of wonderful hiding spots for this very purpose."

"No. I want him to see." My tone is steely. Determined.

Iseul grins. "There will undoubtedly be new guards stationed outside my Coop within the day, but I do truly appreciate you killing my former ones. They'd left, you see, when they saw the smoke rising from the Coin Yard. Did you happen to have anything to do with that?"

I can't help it—I smirk, and Iseul crows in triumph.

"I *knew* it! Oh, Lina, you are *precisely* the sort of person I'd like to see on a throne." Iseul pats my head and I stare at her, unsure whether to be impressed or offended by the fact she dared to do so. "You're welcome to stay here as long as you need. Your Dokkaebi, however, is *not* welcome here. Where is he, anyway?"

"Finding an ally," I reply as Iseul examines her nails.

"Did you pass on my little message about my Doves being strictly off-limits for his Pied Piper-ing?"

"It doesn't matter. He doesn't listen to me," I mutter, the wound reopening, and Iseul arches a neat brow.

"Oh?" She twirls a strand of her hair. "Do tell. I've never gossiped about a Dokkaebi before."

"He broke a promise."

"Why?"

"I don't know. He wouldn't tell me." As I talk, the weight on my shoulders begins to lighten. Iseul really does remind me of the twins. Confiding in her is...nice. It's been so long since I had somebody to talk to about things like this. "There is a secret he is keeping from me," I whisper. "Something scares him, something forces his hand. But he will not confess."

"Men," sniffs Iseul. "Whether they be human or Dokkaebi, stubborn secret-keeping is certainly a common theme. But perhaps he will tell you, in time."

"He said he would."

"Then you must hold him to that promise." The madame wriggles her fingers with a wide grin. "Remind him of it at the most *opportune* times. What are Dokkaebi like in bed, by the way? Are they..." Now it is her eyebrows that are wriggling. "Anatomically the same as humans? Or are they more *generously endowed*?"

"I—wouldn't know. Not yet," I say awkwardly.

Iseul looks truly crushed. "Pity."

A reluctant snort escapes me, and Iseul—seemingly encouraged by this—rises from the bed and begins to twirl around the room, skirts flouncing. "I, for one, am curious about *how* they like to do it. Are they very flexible? Stop laughing! This is a very important line of questioning."

I smile slightly, but a question occurs to me, and I ask it. "Iseul," I say, "how did you know what was happening on the street?" Based on the winding turns she took while carrying me here, I was a good distance away. But somehow, Iseul came. And helped me.

Iseul's smile fades. "What do you mean?"

"You knew there was a battle, didn't you?" I'm looking at her curiously. "How?" The storm would have drowned out any noise. Nobody from the nearby taverns heard, but somehow, Iseul did. For a moment, she looks taken aback—but then she relaxes and shrugs, although I do not miss the tension in her shoulders.

"I saw that my guards were gone and fancied a stroll. I've been caged in here for so long, my legs were positively *aching*. Imagine my surprise when I stumbled upon six heads detached from six bodies, and you, flopping around like a fish." She flicks a strand of light hair away from her face. "A pleasant surprise for the former, but the latter...not so much."

I suppose it makes sense. But something is nagging at me. Perhaps it's the way she carried me, chattering the whole time, not panting at all. I'm taller than Iseul, if only by a bit, and I suspect I have more muscle as well. But she transported me so easily...

"Well," she says, clasping her hands together and bouncing on the balls of her feet, "I have business to attend to in my study. I'm attempting to develop a new sort of lingerie. It's going *terribly* so far, and I should really get back to it. It's very hard to turn fish skin into lingerie, you see, but unfortunately that's all I've been able to get my hands on thanks to Konrarnd. If you'd like to stay for lunch, we'll be having skinless fish."

I shake my head, rising to my feet. I'm steady again. Strong. "I should go. Rui may have found who we're looking for by now."

"*Rui,*" Iseul repeats, looking half impressed, half wary. "So he has a name. Well, give him my regards. Or don't. I don't like him very much." She skips toward me, moves to kiss me on the cheek, and then halts. Her nose scrunches up. "I would, but you absolutely do have shit on your face." Instead, she reaches up to pat my head again. "Farewell, Lina the Beheader. Do feel free to continue stopping by. I think we'll become a great pair of friends."

With a wicked grin, she leaves, and I cannot help but smile after her.

CHAPTER TEN

"Im Yejin is a cantankerous old woman," Rui mutters as he appears in my hanok's foyer, stepping out from the undulating corridor of darkness and smoothing his fine hanbok with a look of supreme distaste, "who hit me with a shoe."

His face is hidden by a gat he must have taken from a shop, and its rim conceals his eyes. His pointed ears are nowhere in sight. A wise choice, given that he has recently stolen away an entire marketplace.

I've just finished washing off the mud from my face and suit. I'm clad in a spare, and I attach my jikdo to its sheath as I raise a brow at Rui. "A shoe?"

"Her shoe, specifically."

"At least you found her." Taking the small leather ribbon from my wrist, I knot my hair back into a small bun and reach for my own gat. Securing it on my head and following it with my cloak, I appraise Rui. "Where was she? How did you find her?"

"I may have used Manpasikjeok on a fisherman," he replies glibly. "She moves locations every three days. Haewon's Fabrics and the Gambling Toad. Today, she will be in the Fingertrap, beneath the fabric shop. At that precise moment, however, she was taking a drink at the Moonlit Hare. I may have gone to see her—"

"Why?" I narrow my eyes. "Rui, all you had to do was locate her."

Rui rubs his jaw ruefully, avoiding my accusatory stare. "It was clear that fisherman's boat was not of good quality. If all her boats are practically shambles scraped together into something only slightly reliable, she has no business sending them across the Yongwangguk Sea on lengthy voyages." He takes off his gat, and his eyes meet mine before darting away. "I decided it would be… reasonable…to tell her so. She did not take to it kindly and hit me with her shoe. It was rather violent, I might add."

My lips twitch. "And what did you do?"

"I incinerated her on the spot." Rui sees my scowl and smirks. "You're of so little faith in me, Lina. No, I left. She'll likely be beneath Haewon's Fabrics by now. If you'd like to see her, the fishermen passed along that there is a password, one that must be given to Haewon. This week, it is *mul naengmyeon*."

"Mul naengmyeon." The cold noodle dish is a popular summer meal among those in Sunpo who have enough money to afford some. "Thank you, Rui." Gyeulcheon treasures are heavy in my cloak pocket. I finger them nervously. "You don't need to come…"

"I want to," he replies evenly. "If you don't wish for me to enter the shop, I will wait outside." As Rui redons his gat, he offers a small smile. "She would be a fool not to ally herself with you. You'll be good for this kingdom, little thief."

Good. The word warms me from head to toe. I take a steadying breath. "I'm trying to be," I say quietly, taking Rui's hand and stepping out the door.

Haewon's Fabrics is a small building, sunken in on itself, with a chipped sign out front reading: FABRICS NEW AND OLD, WILL GIVE YEOKUN FOR DONATIONS. ONE YEOKUN PER THREE SQUARES. The rain is still beating heavily, and the sign's ink is running. Next to me, Rui gently squeezes my waist. "I'll be waiting," he murmurs.

For I want to do this alone. Going to Yejin by myself, without the support of Rui, is the right thing to do. The brave thing. The good thing.

Nodding, I take a deep breath and walk up to the shop. The door is half rotted, and I am cautious with it as I slip inside Haewon's Fabrics. It smells musty, and the floor creaks as I make my way between baskets of fabrics to the small, wizened woman with large round spectacles standing behind the wooden counter, smoking a roll of halji. My palms begin to sweat, and my mouth itches as I move to stand before her. "I'd like to speak to Im Yejin," I say quietly.

"Password?" puffs Haewon. Her voice is like the creaking of the floorboards.

"Mul naengmyeon."

Haewon takes another inhale of her roll before nodding, beckoning me to follow her around the counter and into a supply closet. She points at a trapdoor. "Through there." With a final puff, she wobbles away.

I stare at the trapdoor, reminded of another in a bakery, leading to a rebellion. Reminded of an attack in the forest, of a Gwisin guiding me back to life.

Focus, Lina.

I shake my head to clear it and pull open the trapdoor. Light spills out, warm and cozy, but I know better than to think I will be welcomed here. Slowly, I climb down the ladder, wooden rungs rough underneath my palms. When my boots touch the floor, a slightly croaky voice calls, "I'll be with you soon enough."

Turning around, I take in a small room stacked with boxes of tools: wrenches, hammers, nails. Planks of wood are piled in corners as well, and some tiny one-person boats hang on the walls. On a steel table lie sketches of ships atop yellowed parchment, and—with her back to me—is Im Yejin. She's hard at work, scribbling something down with a quill and ink. Her gray hair spills down her back in an intricate braid, and she wears a simple tunic and pants, her wrinkled feet barefoot on the shop's floor.

Suddenly nervous, I shift from foot to foot. The air smells of sawdust. Her old workshop in Fishtown, where I attacked her, had the same smell. Slipping into the pocket of my cloak, my fingers curve around a Gyeulcheon treasure. A chunk of gold. With my other hand, I remove my gat.

"Well," sighs Im Yejin, setting down her quill, "that's finally done. How can I—"

She turns around.

The wrinkled lines of her face, deepen at the sight of me. Her black eyes widen, her sparse brows lift. "You," she breathes, and then she's scrambling away, behind the steel table, grabbing a hammer...

"Wait—please—" I toss the chunk of gold toward her. She catches it, eyes even wider than before. "I wish you no harm. I swear it on the gods."

"Shin Lina," says Yejin, staring at the gold, and then at me. "The Reaper hasn't been spotted since the Talons died. The kingdom thinks you're dead."

"*You* don't. After all these years, you're still hiding from me. But I'm not going to kill you." My voice is soft. I almost feel as if I am speaking to a cornered animal. One that I have hurt.

Yejin's eyes narrow. "You think all these years, I've been hiding only from you?" she scoffs. I blink. "There's more than just Sunpo's Reaper out there, girl." The shipsmith pockets the gold. "I'm surprised you're here as a customer, though, and not a killer. After what happened to your parents, I would have thought you swore off my ships forever—"

"Don't," I snap before I can stop myself. Yejin falls silent. "I'm not here to buy one of your shitty boats, Im." Realizing my tone is bordering on violent, I take a deep breath. "If not just me, who else are you hiding from?"

Yejin rubs her nose, still eyeing me suspiciously and holding the hammer tight. "The Pied Piper, first of all." At my expression, she scowls. "He's more than just a legend, girl. You'd be a fool to believe otherwise, and I'd never much taken you Talons for fools." She sniffs. "That marketplace, that was him, you mark my words."

I grimace and refrain from commenting that the Pied Piper is standing right outside the shop, and that she's already thrown a shoe at him.

"Then there's the Blackbloods. Ha!" Yejin spits on the floor. "You scared the shit out of me that night, Reaper, but what set you Talons apart from the Blackbloods was that you weren't ham-headed imbeciles who killed without thought. You stopped yourself. I respect you for that."

She rubs her nose again, glancing at some of the ships hanging on the walls. "Kalmin wants me dead on account of a little stint I pulled on Habaek's River a couple years back," she continues. "He wanted to ship some halji overseas, came to me for a boat. I said "sure" and gave him a boat that would sink. Never much liked the man. The halji sank, he lost a fortune, and he wants me dead ever since. Mind you—" She's sweating nervously now. "That's not how I chose a boat for your parents. That pyeongjeoseon, it was supposed to be reliable. Carried grains over to Wyusan and Bonseyo's coastlines every month without a problem. Barley, wheat, that sort of thing. They should have been fine."

"But they weren't," I say quietly.

"I'm sorry," Yejin says. "Not that it's my fault." She glances nervously at my sword and licks her lips. "But I am sorry."

"Thank you," I make myself say. "That's not why I'm here, though. I'm here because I'd like to make you an offer, Yejin."

"An offer?"

"I'm going to destroy the Blackbloods. Claws, Legs, Feathers, Bills, Crest, and Crown, too. Sunpo will be mine, and I want you as an ally." She looks suspicious, and I continue speaking, explaining, careful to keep my voice slow. Steady. Convincing. "Under my rule, you won't have to run anymore. No more looking over your shoulder. No more changing locations every few days, no more passwords. The gold I just gave you—there will be more of that, too. You can buy better wood. Better tools. Build better ships, ships that don't sink. All I ask in return right now is that you help me monitor who comes and goes on the river and sea. I want to make Sunpo better. A place where people can live, truly *live*. And you could help me."

Yejin's dark eyes are scanning my face. The older woman's gaze is shrewd. Nothing like the terror I saw when I nearly murdered her out of rage, spite, and grief. "Humph," she says, tapping her chin. "If you hadn't tried to kill me that one time, I would be agreeing by now."

My stomach twists. "I…" I clear my throat. "I—"

You don't need to apologize.

"I'm sorry," I say forcefully, shoving the Voice aside. "I was—I was angry and grieving and lost. And it's no excuse, but I thought…" I take a deep breath. "I thought the pain would stop if I…if I hurt you. It wouldn't have. You didn't…you didn't kill them. It was an accident at sea. I am truly sorry, Yejin."

The shipsmith nods. Once, twice. And then she walks toward me, setting aside the hammer. "Like I said, you Talons were always smart. You have my vow, Shin Lina." She reaches out her hand. It's wrinkled, weathered, and callused. I take it in mine, and we shake.

In a low voice, I give her the address of my hanok. "If you ever need anything," I say softly, "anything at all, you can find me there."

"Thank you." As Yejin pulls away, I note that her eyes are slightly misty. "You'd best be on your way. The storm's picking up. I can feel it in my bones."

Yejin is right. As I exit Haewon's Fabrics, the force of the rain-lashed wind is so strong that I nearly stumble. Rui, however, is unmovable. He's leaning against the wall of the alleyway, and as I near him, he opens up the corridor of darkness. I close my eyes as he embraces me, as we fall through shadows before landing in the foyer of my hanok, dripping rainwater.

Rui draws me toward him and gently kisses me. "Lina," he murmurs against my lips. "Lina, Lina, Lina. You are the most fearless, exquisite creature I have ever known."

The Voice stirs in my head, leering. *As exquisite as Shuo Achara?*

I ignore the Voice, but Rui must see the fleeting agitation from the Voice that crosses my face, for he pulls back. "What is it?"

"I'm just cold," I say evasively, wringing my dripping shirt. He holds his stare for a long, curious moment and I turn away, making my way to the kitchen where there is a small fireplace of stone and chops of pinewood. My lighter is gone, left behind in the base's ruins. I do not feel an ache for its loss—it has served the Talons well, and I feel only contentment as I light the fire with the small pieces of flint and steel set next to the fireplace. As the tiny flames crackle, I sit before them on a cushion and warm my hands.

Rui has filled a small teapot with water, and he latches it to the hook above the flames, letting the water boil. He sits next to me, and we savor the dry heat as rain drums on the roof and thunder rumbles above. When the water has boiled, we let a few pouches of cinnamon steep before holding the warm earthen cups in our hands.

"Has she allied herself with you?" Rui asks.

"Yes," I say, smiling down at my cup. Today, I was...Good. I made Good choices. I apologized and earned forgiveness.

"Did she hit you with a shoe?"

"It seems that she saves that for special occasions."

Rui laughs, low and lilting. The fire crackles merrily as we sip in silence.

It is fitting, this fire. For this one feels of home, rather than rage. I savor these moments, letting my mind release the remnants of fury and fear that stepping into the old base and Yejin's shop ignited within me. Letting the adrenaline seep from my body, leaving me calm.

"I will have to return to Gyeulcheon soon," Rui murmurs after a while. "My court expects me."

I swallow a spiced mouthful. "Are you still hunting the Revolutionaries?"

Rui shakes his head slowly. "The Revolution has been completely eradicated."

It is a relief to hear, for Eunbi is in Gyeulcheon. Although, even with the rebels, it is safer than Sunpo, my heart still lightens to hear of this development.

"No movement stands in the way of my throne," Rui continues. "Chan's soldiers found all members; they were weakened without Wang Jiwoon. Those who fought, we killed. Others have been imprisoned. I've lowered taxes," he adds quietly. "I've...repaired my rule. There will be no other uprisings." There is a guilt in his voice, and I can tell he is thinking of the neglect Gyeulcheon faced as he sank into grief with the death of *her*.

Achara.

She has never bothered me before. She should not now. Rui does not envy Sang, and I know I should not envy Rui's dead lover. I do not. It would be wrong to listen to the lecherous Voice in that way.

Yet even so, I cannot forget what the Voice whispered to me last night. Cannot wonder if perhaps it has made a point. ***Achara surely knew the secret that Rui keeps from us.***

My mouth itches uncomfortably, and I instead focus on the Revolution's disbandment. A few days ago, when I left, there were still at least fifty more members of the Revolution to track down and dispose of. Rui and his general have been quite busy. I force my voice to be level as I say, "Good. And Eunbi?" My throat is slowly loosening, my breathing coming steadier. "How is she?"

"She has made her permanent home in the kitchens," Rui replies, sounding vastly amused as he sips his tea. "Asha has taken quite a liking to her. Eunbi is much the same as you left her—slightly wider perhaps, but in good health."

I arch a brow. "Asha despised me." The stout cook swatted me across the face with a wooden spoon more times than I could count.

"Being despised by Asha is practically a rite of passage in my kingdom. But I don't jest. Asha adores her. She even lets her dictate what is served for breakfast, lunch, and dinner." He smirks. "Your sister melts even the hardest of hearts."

That's true. It is hard not to love Eunbi, with her gap-toothed grin and tendency to speak so fast in her eagerness that she runs out of breath.

"Her taste in food, though, could use some work." Rui sighs mournfully. "Asha has begun to cook *sugar rolls* rather than danpatjuk for breakfast. I do not know how I will go on."

The thought of Rui, deprived of his favorite sweet red bean porridge, is enough to make me smirk. "Poor, poor Dokkaebi," I croon. "However will you cope?"

He flicks my nose. I glare, and he laughs his midnight laugh. "With considerable difficulty." And then his expression grows grave. The change is so abrupt that it happens in the blink of an eye. "Lina—I have something to ask of you."

Warily, I cock my head. "Ask it."

"I will need Eunbi to return to this kingdom tomorrow."

The sip of tea I've taken suddenly grows cold in my mouth. I force it down and eye Rui cautiously. "That's not a question," I say softly. "That's a demand. Why? She's not safe here. I'm hunting Claws, and soon Legs. This kingdom is a bloodbath. That's why I left her in Gyeulcheon, under your care."

His throat bobs. "I will retrieve her the next afternoon—"

I scowl. "Does this have something to do with the marketplace attack?" Each word drips with accusation.

"I wish you wouldn't call it an attack," Rui says quietly. "A necessity is a better descriptor."

"But why? Rui, if whatever this is concerns Eunbi, you need to tell me. Now."

"It won't," he replies stiltedly, "if she comes to Sunpo tomorrow morning."

The contentment I felt slowly seeps away, leaving only frustration in its place. "I understand," I say, attempting to keep my voice level, "that you wish to tell me of these—circumstances in your own time. But now, they directly impact my sister and me. What is happening tomorrow in Gyeulcheon?"

Rui is silent for a long moment. But then— "There is a... feast," he finally replies evenly. "With old friends. It will hardly be a suitable place for a young child, with the drinking and revelry."

Old friends. I straighten. "Do you mean the gods?" Could it be that the deities are traveling from Okhwang to Gyeulcheon? "Are they traveling to your realm?"

But the emperor is already standing, the air rippling as a corridor of darkness unfurls behind him. "I must go," Rui murmurs, bending down to brush a soft kiss against my lips. "I have been away too long already. There are preparations that require my attention. I shall see you tomorrow morning, Lina. With Eunbi."

"Rui, wait—"

Rui casts me a backward glance as he steps into the ever-dark hall of shadow. For a moment, he looks so impossibly tired—and much older than his twenty Dokkaebi years. But then he is smiling, a wry quirk of the lips. "If you plan to burn down more buildings, little thief, I suggest you do so before your little sister arrives. I would hate for Eunbi to return with a fondness for the flame. I rather like my palace."

In a flurry of darkness, the emperor disappears.

But not before I see his smile drop the moment he begins to turn away, replaced by something grim.

Something severe and...something sad.

CHAPTER ELEVEN

My scaleblade slides across the Claw's throat. He drops to the ground with the two others from his patrol, gushing blood, eyes wide with terror, and I smile down at him and allow the scales on my wrists to melt back into warm flesh. He clutches his throat, gurgling, and after a few moments falls silent and still. Dead, like the others. Dead, just like the three other patrols I killed tonight.

Since Rui left, my mind has been crammed with questions and my heart heavy with displeasure. The Voice has not helped matters, stalking across my mind, muttering with disdain about a *"lack of trust"* and *"dreadful secrets."* I have turned to midnight hunting to quiet both, stalking Blackbloods through the shadows and disposing the city of them, leaving Claw bodies for the Legs to find later.

Satisfied that the man is well and truly dead, I wipe my hands on my dark cloak and decide with a certain grimness to end my night with a final glimpse of the fire's wreckage.

I make my way briskly through the streets—and pause as I reach the site, slowly halting in the shadows as I see a lone figure standing before the ruined gate and crumpled wall of what was once the giwajip. A Blackblood? I summon my scaleblades once more, but something about the figure gives me pause.

My keen ears can pick up his ragged breathing, the smell of his emotion—something dark and hurt yet satisfied. I eye the slope of his neck, long and lean, and the way his shoulders are drawn back.

The moonlight does not shine on him, but I hone my vision, and see that he wears a simple hemp tunic and pants. That his hair is black and curls to his ears. That his fingers form fists.

Curiously, I watch him. He no longer strikes me as a Blackblood. A Blackblood would not carry such a satisfied scent upon witnessing the ruins before him.

And underneath that, there is the smell of alcohol—of makgeolli and soju and other sweet, biting drinks. Something about it strikes me as familiar.

I watch as the man stares at the giwajip. As he spits on the ground's rubble with vehemence.

Interesting. Whoever this man is, he clearly harbors a disdain for the Blackbloods. And that could prove most beneficial to me as I search for allies. As I debate whether to make myself known, the man stiffens. And he turns. He does not see me, still as I am in the shadows, but I see him.

The serving boy from the Moonlit Hare.

"Who's there?" he demands softly, eyes scanning the darkness, moving over me completely. His voice is raspy and deep.

"I am," says a voice that is not my own, and from behind the ruined wall, Song Iseul appears. "You were looking in the entirely wrong direction, Seojin." The madame grins, hopping over the wrecked stone. "I was crouched there for *eons* waiting for you to notice me. You do lack your brother's acute awareness. It's rather concerning." She brushes off her hanbok—a shimmering blue one tonight—and I see that she's carrying her ax. The diamond necklace I gifted her glitters around her neck.

I slip farther into the shadows, compelled to stay. To watch this exchange. Iseul is an ally, perhaps even a friend…and this boy dislikes the Blackbloods. He is also plenty disliked by them as well, if the looks toward him in the Moonlit Hare were any indication.

"Iseul." The boy—Seojin—sounds concerned. "What are

you doing here." It's less of a question than it is a statement of exasperation.

Iseul bats her eyes coquettishly. "Waiting for you, of course. I knew you would venture here after your shift at that positively dreadful jumak ended. Isn't it beautiful? I do love a good fire."

Seojin huffs a laugh, but it's halfhearted, and his lips barely twitch. The lines on his face are serious, sharp. "Did you set it?"

"Me?" Iseul snorts. "As if I were able to. There were Blackbloods watching me, did you know that? Of course, they were killed soon after by a new friend of mine—"

"Who—"

"But new ones came soon after, all pathetic Claws. I barely managed to come see you tonight. And to do so, I had to transform entirely. It was quite the ordeal."

My brows inch together. Iseul looks much the same as ever, hardly in disguise. The only thing that has changed from when I saw her earlier is the color of her hanbok, undoubtedly due to me leaving traces of dirt and blood all over the fine fabric.

"Iseul," Seojin replies sharply, mouth tightening. "You know it isn't safe."

"Well, I had no choice, did I?" Iseul pouts at Seojin. "You fret after me so much, darling. It's *adorable*." She pats his cheek and he shakes his head. "Worry not. I was entirely unseen." Her smile grows. "And those three new Claws are very much dead. I was rather hungry after I shifted. No doubt they will soon be replaced, but..." She shrugs. "They weren't very tasty, but then again, Claws are not meant to be eaten. Perhaps I will eat a Leg next."

It is as if she is talking in puzzles. I frown. Iseul *ate* the Blackbloods? Surely that cannot be correct. And what does she mean by "shifted?" Something cold slithers down my spine, and the hairs on the back of my neck rise.

"Iseul," says Seojin again, sounding exasperated.

"Oh, don't give me that look, Seojin," she snaps, suddenly

crabby. "I hid their bodies splendidly. Whoever finds them will report that they drunk themselves to death and fell into a very large pit behind that horrible Madame Ji's brothel. It's she who will be on the receiving end of Kalmin's wrath, and good thing too, because she's simply *rancid*—"

"A very large—" the boy exclaims incredulously, but she interrupts him by reaching into her pocket and pressing something into his hand. It is the golden pocket watch I gave her the day before. I watch carefully as Seojin blinks. "Iseul," he says again, in an entirely different tone, this one exasperatedly suspicious, "where did you—"

"Kalmin's reckoning," Song Iseul says softly, "has arrived in Sunpo. The Reaper is free of him, Seojin. And she's come to murder the foul man. To kill the crane. These—" She fingers the necklace, and gestures to the watch. "—are tokens of her good faith."

Seojin has gone very, very still. "The Reaper."

I bite my lip and frown, frustrated that Iseul has exposed my arrival in the kingdom—but alert as some part of me acknowledges the girl's obvious wit. And with her hatred of Konrarnd Kalmin to consider, I do not believe that Song Iseul would sabotage my plans. Nor do I believe she would underestimate the importance of my presence being a closely guarded secret. If she has given my name to this boy, it is for a reason. And I am curious as to what that reason is.

"She's hunting allegiances. And something tells me that she will knock on your door soon enough. But for now, take the watch. It's worth *quite* a lot, you see. Enough to pay tribute this month. Konrarnd will take it willingly. Perhaps it will even appease him enough for you to be monitored less. You can say you stole it from my Coop. He'd be delighted to hear that, you know." Her eyes dart around the street warily, and for a moment I worry that she's heard my hitch of breath. Seojin, whoever he is, is monitored by Kalmin. Despised by the Blackbloods.

And that piques my interest.

"You should go," Iseul says. "Your shadow isn't far behind. And—" She cocks her head. "He sounds out of breath. How fast did you run here?"

I stiffen, my own ears picking up the faint footfall of a heavyset man in the distance. How is it that Iseul can hear it? My lips tighten as I hold my breath. If she can hear him, she can certainly hear me. But how?

What is *she?*

Not a Dokkaebi, for her ears are not pointed. Certainly not a goddess, as the pantheon keeps to themselves in Okhwang. But this morning, the way she carried me without ever running out of breath...the way she somehow sensed the battle, where I was...

My heart begins to pound in anticipation. What, exactly, is Song Iseul?

"Fast," answers Seojin, looking around warily. "Thank you for the watch, I—"

"Please. Don't even mention it," Iseul replies. "It's the least I can do for you, after everything." She quirks a grin and hefts the ax over her shoulder. It's a wonder she doesn't topple backward under its weight.

Still puzzling over her hearing—and growing slightly queasy from lack of oxygen—I watch, warily, as Iseul plants a kiss on Seojin's cheek and with a furtive look around the street...

Her nose, small and round, elongates into a sleek muzzle. Her slender hands and delicate slippers ripple, replaced by four paws. Honey-hued skin replaced by white fur. Nine...

Holy gods.

I flinch backward in pure, icy shock and the ground seems to fall away under my feet as I watch Song Iseul, madame of the Dove Coop, turn into a nine-tailed fox.

Gumiho.

• • •

I thought they were extinct.

The words ring in my mind as I stare at the shiny white pelt, the narrow black eyes, and the nine slender tails that wave slightly in farewell to Seojin before the fox—before *Iseul*—darts down the road, nothing but a streak of white in the night. *The Gumiho are gone. Hunted to extinction fifty years ago.* But my eyes tell a vastly different story.

The Voice, too, is stunned. **Gumiho**, it whispers, and it sounds— awed. Stunned. **Nine-tailed fox. Devourer of the male ki. Beautiful women, ravenous creatures.**

Hunted by men for their pelts, I reply, still frozen with shock. *Killed during the Fox Hunt.*

The Fox Hunt was a genocide. Gumiho were slaughtered by the thousands. The hunt started when a foolhardy Gumiho ate the ki, the soul, of Bonseyo's Crown Prince Jeon Jimin—a seventeen-year-old boy who was seduced by one of the beautiful women. It is said that as he leaned in for a kiss, the woman turned into a nine-tailed fox and sucked out his soul through his lips.

Ki powers a fox bead, the pearl of energy within a Gumiho that lends them their power. The more ki within a fox bead, the stronger and faster a Gumiho is in both their human and fox forms. Undoubtedly Prince Jimin's ki appealed to the Gumiho for precisely this reason—likely, the Gumiho suspected that devouring the soul of royalty would increase the power of her fox bead… Never mind the fact that status does not always equal a strong soul.

The boy's dead body was later found by his father, the emperor—Emperor Jeon Sanghoon. There was no question as to what sort of creature took his life. In retribution, the emperor ordered the Fox Hunt to begin. Hunters and soldiers from all Three Kingdoms united, and the Gumiho were vanquished.

We do not speak of Gumiho. Their extinction has expanded onto the pages of books. Gone are their myths, replaced only by details of the Fox Hunt, the gore and glory that followed. *The man-eating monsters were swiftly eradicated. No more shall the wicked foes torment our kingdoms!*

But Appa knew the stories, for he was a teller of tales. He would whisper them to Eunbi and me, in the darkness of our chogajip. Would tell me of their cleverness, their immortality, their morals that are not as monstrous as the Fox Hunt made them seem. *"They were like us,"* Appa said. *"Neither good nor bad. But now they are gone."*

"Why?" I remember whispering, eyes wide.

Appa smiled sadly. *"Because they were different. Because they were powerful. And it's human nature to fear what we do not understand, to fear what could destroy us. But it is the nature of monsters to order extinction. There are no more Gumiho."*

And yet — Song Iseul is a Gumiho.

Perhaps the last of them.

And...she is my ally. Perhaps soon, she could even be my friend. Feeling starts to come back into my body as I consider what this means. With a Gumiho at my side, I have gained a formidable weapon. And if she remains by my side, I will protect her. I will ensure that she is never hunted again.

When I finally shake my head and blink, slowly coming back to myself, I see that Seojin is gone — replaced by a brutish Blackblood huffing and puffing, hands on his knees as he scours the street for the strange boy. He's doing the busy work, following a teenage boy, running through the dirty streets in futile pursuit. He's almost certainly a Claw.

Scaleblades extend from my wrist, and I pounce.

CHAPTER TWELVE

The next morning, Eunbi emerges next to Rui from his corridor of wavering darkness with a hop and a skip, her curly hair bouncing with her excitement, her eyes flashing in delight.

"*Lili!*" she crows, barreling her way toward me with her arms outstretched, nearly tripping over the chima of her hanbok. I can't help but laugh as I scoop my eight-year-old sister up into the air and hold her close to my chest, kissing the crown of her head. Eunbi giggles and squirms, tugging at my ear. She smells of lavenders and lilies—but also, suspiciously, of sugar roll. I tell her so as I set her down, earning a guilty giggle before she scampers away, off to explore the tiny giwajip. Her slipper-clad feet patter on the floor, and I hear her rifling through the chest in my bedroom—probably looking for anything interesting to scavenge.

I am glad that I have tucked my weapons away. Eunbi sometimes thinks of them as toys rather than real threats. I suppose the brief time she spent with the Talons was enough to cement such a belief in her mind.

Rui grins at me, his eyes sparkling. "I found her in the kitchens, munching on a platter of sugar rolls. It was with great difficulty that I managed to pull her away." It is indeed evident that he has come from the kitchen, for his hands hold a wooden tray heavy with a bowl filled with what looks like danpatjuk, three glistening sugar rolls, and steaming gyepi-cha. The cinnamon tea is spiced and fragrant, tendrils of steam curling across his face. "I brought breakfast," he adds. "I thought we might take it together before I depart."

His words are soft. Hopeful.

I try to manage a smile. I've not forgotten how he left yesterday morning before I had the chance to question him about tonight's supposed "feasting." A part of me wants to tell him of last night's events—that I have a Gumiho on my side—but the knowledge of Iseul's secret is not mine to share. I remain quiet as we sit on cushions before my low table, the food set out before us. Eunbi is here, and she does not quite know of the intricacies between this kingdom and me.

My baby sister sits in my lap, watching as Rui elegantly pours the tea for us, his rings twinkling in the morning light that manages to escape past the hanji-screened window next to us. Using a wooden spoon, he scoops porridge into three bowls, and places one sugar roll on a plate before distributing the meal among our small trio.

"Lili," Eunbi says through a mouthful of porridge, twisting up to look at me, "can we see the others today? Sang and Chara and Chryse and Yoonho? It's been so long, two years since I saw them! Remember, the last time was at the Night of the Red Moon festival?" She shoves another scoop of porridge into her mouth and snarfles through it. "I've gotten taller since then, lots taller, and I bet that now I can reach Sang's hand, even when he stretches really, really high! Are they throwing another celebration this year?"

The porridge turns to ash in my mouth. My heart sinks as if dragged by a stone. Eunbi is still talking, but I do not hear her. Rui has gone still with concern, his stare latched onto me, but I do not see him.

All I see is the Night of the Red Moon, and the festival that took place nearly two years ago now.

The Night of the Red Moon is a festival native to the Three Kingdoms. Every year, when the scorching midsummer days begin to cool, Dalnim's moon is as ripe and bloody as the pulp of a blood orange. It is said that the night is the anniversary of her ascension to goddess-hood—when a hungry tiger devoured her parents and chased her and her brother, Haemosu the Sun God, up toward the heavens, where they became deities upon the approval of Okhwang's emperor. The moon's ruby color is a reflection of Dalnim's rage and mourning for the loss of her parents to the tiger.

Two years ago, the Talons... We threw a party in the palace, and I managed to smuggle Eunbi out of her mountain school in the Yaepak range just for the night.

Two years ago, our palace was alive with feasting and dance and music. Eunbi delighted in the attention of the Talons, dancing with the twins, sitting on Yoonho's lap, and struggling to retrieve a sweet from Sang as he held it high above her head. There were no Blackbloods that night—only the Talons and our associates, safe in the palace that would later become home to a bloodbath.

Sang and I watched Dalnim's moon that night, smoking halji. On the roof of the palace, our hands touched, ever so briefly, and I went to bed with a smile on my lips.

The next year, there was no party. The Talons were dead. I was enslaved. That night, I snuck into Gwan Doyun's home and killed his wife underneath the scarlet moon.

I become aware, dimly, that Eunbi is waiting expectantly for my answer. "Lili?"

This is not how I want to tell her. Not how I have planned it. But there is panic in her eyes now, a growing realization. She knows what death is. She has seen it take our parents. Her chin wobbles. "Lina?" Eunbi asks in a whisper. "Lina, where are they?"

I must tell her. A part of her already knows.

"I... The Talons aren't here right now," I whisper hoarsely. Rui is quiet, and his hand stretches across the table toward mine. I take it, finding solace in his touch. "They're not... They're not here."

Eunbi pauses. "Lili...?" Her voice wavers. Perhaps she has suspected all this time. Perhaps she simply hasn't wanted to believe it. Her wide eyes glisten. "Where are they?"

Gods give me strength. Please. Oh, gods.

I am dizzy and my stomach is churning. With shaking hands, I set down my spoon and shift Eunbi from me before staggering to my feet and stumbling toward the washroom. I can barely breathe around the pain.

This is the thing about secrets, I suppose. They gnaw on your insides with venom-laced teeth, choke you with your own veins and arteries, leave the taste of blood in your mouth until you are sick.

I hear Rui calling after me, and I wonder if this is how he feels about his secret—if he, too, is dying from it slowly, painfully, endlessly.

I need to tell her. I cannot tell her.

I vomit into the chamber pot.

Gentle hands rub my back. Rui holds my hair back as I empty my stomach again. My face is slick with tears.

It will never get easier, this grief. I cannot bear to impart it upon Eunbi. And would she blame me? I would not hold it against her if she did, but I would not be able to bear it. I am crying, crying as I rinse my mouth with cleansing paste, crying as I sink onto the bathroom floor, burying my face in my hands as Rui holds me against him, murmuring soft words that I do not hear around my pain, around the grating noises of the world as my senses expand and expand and expand—

"Lili?" Eunbi appears in the doorway. I hear her tremulous voice cutting through the chaos, the nervous pounding of her heart. I smell her anguish; I taste her horror. "They're dead, aren't they. They're dead." Her voice breaks. "They're *gone.*"

I can't do this. I will not do this. Not to her. Not to myself.

I can't do this.

"I have to go," I gasp, hauling myself to my feet, seeing double. Rui's eyes widen as I lurch past Eunbi, trailing tears. "Stay with her—for an hour. I will be back."

I do not wait for a response before I am staggering through

the still-empty street and tasting the remnants of yesterday's fear in the air. Every part of me burns. Burns for vengeance, burns for redemption. Somewhere in the distance, thunder roars. The sun above has begun to dull, slowly covered by furious storm clouds. I taste lightning and it courses through my veins.

I've waited long enough. With only a handful of Claws left, I'm more than ready to start on the Legs.

My feet, suddenly steady, set pace toward Sunpo's palace.

Once, this palace was a place of joy. Once, we reigned within the structure that sat atop the mountain of white stone steps. Once, we smoked atop the emerald tiles of the roofs, gazing up at the stars. Once, we chased each other with swords and daggers through the sprawling gardens and underneath the drapery of its willow trees, laughing as we splashed through the koi ponds, blades flashing underneath the light of the moon.

Once, this palace was my home.

No longer.

Thunder shakes the sky above. Lightning snakes down in blazes of brilliant white, illuminating what my home has become in the year I have been away.

The main gate, a palatial structure of an outdoor archway with high walls, crawls with patrolling Blackbloods. These are Legs, second up from Claws, distinguishable by their brown hanboks.

The Claws wear a simple, drab gray, the Legs a brown that is only marginally less ugly. The Feathers wear an expensive black, for the color allows them to blend easily into the homes of their marks while they loot and pillage. The Bills wear pristine white, the color of mourning. It is a mockery of grief for the assassins to wear the color, to splatter it with red—which is precisely what Kalmin wants.

I am thankful I was never made to wear those white robes, instead working in my dark stealth suit. Those white robes never fit me, especially after months of starvation. Kalmin therefore allowed me to continue wearing that one remnant of the Talons.

How gracious of him. I breathe in shallowly as anger squeezes my heart hard enough for black spots to momentarily speckle my vision.

Now, with most of the Claws dead, it makes sense for the brown-clad Legs to take over the patrols. Their boots stomp and squelch in the muddy ground. They're on high alert. From the number of them, Kalmin has pulled his men from the streets, refocusing them at his base. When I was with the Blackbloods, Claws were the most prominent caste, with members in the sixties. Legs are nearly half that, consisting of thirty or so members. Right now, I estimate fifteen Legs stomping outside the palace.

Above the main gate, the two flared roofs of the palace are visible, one underneath the other, separated by a row of red and green painted wood lined with small windows. Once grand and glorious, they are battered and in a state of disrepair. The once-vibrant paint is dull, the striped, intricate patterns underneath the eaves chipped and faded. Skinny birds hop to and fro, dodging lightning, their voices shrill and cackling.

Fury is a steady war drum in my heart. Standing underneath a gnarled willow tree opposite the palace and the nearby dirt road, I struggle to breathe at all. Hidden underneath the drooping blinds of soggy green, I sink to my knees, soaking the fabric of my pants with mud. I cannot help but remember the last time I'd been here. Staggering up those steps, into the foremost room, my shoes wet with blood.

Surely Konrarnd Kalmin finds that allowing this palace to perish underneath his rule—just as its previous owners did—is the greatest fun of all.

I take a steadying breath through my nose. He is in there. If I wish it so, I could kill him tonight.

But I want him to lose everything first. I must work my way up to the Crown. Besides—I have not yet gathered enough allegiances to retrieve my throne. I have Iseul, Doyun, Yejin…but there are still names to check on my list.

Bang Bomin, an influential halji dealer who collects favors from buyers—favors that I want to call in, if needed. Cha Hyukjae, a prominent fisherman who feeds half the kingdom with his catches and employs dozens of other fishermen. If I have his allegiance, I have a very powerful ally, and perhaps many others under his service.

But I've not paid these two visits yet. And then there is, perhaps, the boy from the Moonlit Hare. Seojin. I am intrigued by him, curious as to what we could offer each other.

I gnaw my bottom lip and curl my fingers around some of the willow's foliage, staring at the patrolling Blackbloods.

We can chop off his Legs, the Voice suggests. **That would be fun, Lina. Let this rainstorm turn red. Let us perform more wonders together.**

Hush. I do not like the cold hunger in its tone, nor how it has begun to sidle up to the stem of my brain, grinning maliciously. *I will decide what we do.*

Yet the Voice is right. I must satisfy my craving for revenge. Otherwise, I will not be able to face the confession that awaits my return to the Fingertrap.

It is true that I can take lives to sate my fury, but I can also take something more.

Something invaluable. Something…*informative.*

For Yoonho has taught me that information is a weapon that can be honed for later use.

I slip out from underneath the willow tree, and my stomach twists into one thousand knots as I prepare myself to enter the palace where, one year ago, my entire world was shattered. But fury steadies me. Konrarnd Kalmin has no right to be here, in this palace. He has no right to be in this *kingdom*.

There are the fifteen Legs keeping watch at the front gate, and there will be more inside. I will attend to them later, after I have acquired the information I desire. So I wait for the lightning to recede, and in the semi-darkness, I sprint to the corner of the wall that is temporarily unguarded—the guards are pacing back and forth, rainwater dripping into their eyes. I have only a half second to vault myself over the wall and land on the cobblestones below. My perpetually wounded leg buckles in protest, pain rushing up my thigh. I shove the pain away as best I can and grit my teeth.

This is where it happened, I think as I skirt into shadows to avoid another set of Blackbloods. *This is where it happened.*

Kang said that the pain in my left leg would never recede, for it stems from the pain of memory. And the pain of memory is a different sort of agony. It lingers all of one's life. Even a potion, such as the one I ingested, will never heal it. Instead, I have learned to live with my wound.

My eyes narrow. Five more Blackbloods stand before the palace doors. I will not be able to enter that way.

But what if I don't need to enter the palace at all?

My eyes flick to the rain-slick roofs on which Sang and I spent many nights smoking halji and sharing jests. There was one spot in particular—one spot on the topmost roof—that carried sound from the study below. We eavesdropped before on Yoonho's meeting with associates through such a method. I am certain that Kalmin has claimed the study as his own. And with my enhanced hearing, even the roaring storm will not block out his words if I can get close enough to the roof.

I wet my lips in anticipation. Taking the steps is impossible, as they sit below keen-eyed Blackbloods. I will sneak around to the side of the palace instead, launch myself into the air and grab an eave of the roof, and scamper upward that way. It will require speed. It will require stealth. It is a good thing that right now, I possess both.

My heart hammers in my throat as I follow my plan, hurtling myself to the roof with all the speed I possess—nothing but a blur in the storm. I huff as I throw myself into the air, hands reaching for the lowest eave of the roof. My fingers find purchase and I haul myself up, breathing heavily and ignoring the pain in my leg that has now spread to my hip. Another jump and I've found the tiles of the second roof, swinging myself up as lightning snakes across the sky. I flinch, glancing downward, but I have gone unnoticed. Good.

Blinking water out of my eyes, I crawl farther onto the green tiles, glaring at a few of the skinny birds who have made their home here. On my stomach, I snake closer to the spot I know will allow me to listen in on whatever is happening in the study. Rain soaks through my clothing, leaving me shivering, but I do not focus on anything but the words I can now hear through the storm. I expand my senses until each word is as clear as if I were standing in the room below as well.

"Will not ask again," somebody is saying. Kalmin. I jolt in a mixture of fury and shock.

It has been more than a month since I've heard his voice—sickly sweet, tinged with a cutting Northern accent that makes each melodious syllable of the Eastern language ugly. He has never tried to pronounce words of the Eastern language in the way that they were meant to be, instead marring them with his ignorant tongue, delighting in the butchery of each word even though he is perfectly capable of the proper pronunciation. It is only one of the mockeries he savors.

He may depend on his Blackbloods, but he ridicules them with his every breath. Yet they are happy to go along with it. He gives them power. He gives them money.

Traitors.

Unable to stand the derision, I'd once made the mistake of

correcting his pronunciation, spitting the proper articulation out through gritted teeth.

I never made that mistake again.

Trembling, I am barely able to restrain myself from smashing a hole in the roof and dropping into the study below with my scaleblades extending from my wrists.

"The woman has jilted us for long enough," Kalmin continues, and I hear the rustling of papers, the clinking of coins. He is counting his earnings in yeokun. I smell halji and sharp Northern wine. With my keen scent, it's almost as if clouds of the smoke seep through the roof. I hold my breath, palms sweating, keeping my attention on the scarlet-haired snake below. "We have played far too nicely with Song Iseul. She owes us a great sum. Don't you agree, Son Wooseok?"

A nervous clearing of the throat. A younger voice, a boy's voice, whispers, "Yes." This must be Wooseok.

Kalmin snorts. "There's no need to be afraid of me, boy. Yesterday, I was upset. My Claws are dropping dead in the streets. One of our most prolific sponsors is dead. I needed something to direct my dissatisfaction toward. It was nothing personal, you understand."

Disgust roils in my stomach. Kalmin beat him. Wooseok. I bite my tongue hard enough to taste blood. A part of me wishes I could reach into the walls and pull the boy away from this place…

An idea slowly begins to form in the back of my mind.

"Now, with Song Iseul…the matter *is* personal." Kalmin clicks his tongue. "That rotten bitch."

Song Iseul. Madame…and Gumiho. My lips flatten into a tight line as I listen to the discussion of my ally.

"Her guards were found in the bottom of a large hole," a third voice adds. "Behind Madame Ji's, with their hearts missing."

Asina. The bald woman with her fishlike eyes stands just below me, reunited with her lover. I snarl, but it is lost over the thunder.

"Whoever is killing my Claws will pay," says Kalmin in seething fury, "whether that be Song Iseul or some other pathetic lowlife scum. Whoever has dared to question *my authority* will rot in the streets for all to see. And I am beginning to think that my men are severely lacking in brains. How—*how* am I expected to control a kingdom when my gangsters are buffoons? When they get plucked off the streets so easily? Who recruited them?" Silence. Then—"Wooseok, I asked you a *question*."

"The-the Legs, m-most likely."

"Fuck my Legs." I flinch despite myself as there's a series of sharp, rapid bursts, as if Kalmin is pounding his fist against his desk. As the noise continues, I realize that he's doing exactly that. When the noise finally stops, I can hear Kalmin's heavy breathing.

Asina finally speaks a few moments later. "What will you do?"

"What we should have done a long time ago." His sneer is evident in his voice. "Burn Madame Ji's to the ground. And while you're at it, dispose of Song Iseul. Start, my dear, with her Doves. Kill them, kidnap them, sell them to the highest bidder... I don't particularly care. Then kill her. Slowly." He takes a sip of his wine. "Is Man Jisu still alive?"

"He's alive," Wooseok whispers.

"Good." Kalmin sounds pleased. "And the rest of his patrol?"

"They're the one remaining unit," Asina offers.

"Then they deserve a reward, don't you think? Take them to Song's brothel tonight. I'm sure Jisu will enjoy himself. Maybe more than what's necessary, but it doesn't matter to me."

Shit. I bite down hard on my tongue. I'll need to warn Iseul before tonight. If she dies, I will have lost an ally, a potential friend.

And the world will have lost its last Gumiho.

I hiss a curse.

"Would you like to come?" Asina murmurs, and I can *hear* her running a hand down Kalmin's arm. I grimace in undiluted disgust.

"What I would *like*," Kalmin bites back, shaking off her

touch with an abrupt rustle, "is to have complete control of this godsdamned kingdom. Yoonho nearly did it," he spits, and my muscles lock at the name of my leader on my enemy's tongue. "*He* controlled nearly all of these fucking sectors. *He* had them in the palm of his hand."

"He had the girl." Asina's voice is flat. "He had the Reaper."

"So did we," Kalmin snarls, "until she had to get herself *killed* in Gyeulcheon. That bastard—that emperor—" He makes a noise of distress, something between a snarl and a choke. "That *Dokkaebi* I want dead as well. Tossed me into the street like some mangy dog. And do you know, Asina, what he *said to me*?" He doesn't wait for a response. "He told me this *wasn't my kingdom*. I barely heard him over—over whatever that flute had done to me. And then he grabbed me by the neck and threw me back to the ground. He pressed his boot to my neck until I couldn't breathe, and it all went dark."

My heart warms just slightly in my chest. *Oh, Rui.*

Every sentence quivers in fury. "So. The next time he pays a visit to *my kingdom,* I want every remaining Blackblood on him. I want him dead."

Asina says nothing, and I know what she's thinking. Mere mortals cannot kill the Pied Piper. I know. I tried.

Kalmin pants and gulps down wine. I hear him wipe his mouth with the back of his sleeve. "Wooseok. Find a way to invite this Dokkaebi to the gala. On the Night of the Red Moon, we'll kill him. And the kingdom will be mine. No more fucking Dokkaebi. None."

The gala.

The Blackbloods are throwing a festival on the Night of the Red Moon. Here, in *my* palace. I cannot see anything but a furious red. *How dare they. How* dare *they—*

"But how," Wooseok says in clear bewilderment, "do I invite the Pied Piper?"

"Find a way," Kalmin snarls. "Shout it from the rooftops. You have nine nights to figure it out. Now—get the hell out. Go. And try not to get killed like the other Claws when you patrol tonight."

I do not pay attention to Wooseok's shaky response or the clumsy noises as he leaves the room. No, I've learned enough. Konrarnd Kalmin is throwing a gala on the Night of the Red Moon in the palace that was once my home. The hatred within me swells, leaving my hands shaking. I will not let him enjoy that gala. The gala that was *ours*. I will not let him taint it. Instead, I'll sever every one of his Cranes' limbs before that party, and I'll quicken that process today. I'm here, aren't I? And his Legs are so easily in reach.

Then, if Kalmin throws that gala—*our* gala—despite having lost it all, I will kill him on that night. And, oh, it will be...poetic.

Poetic to have the Blackbloods die in the same spot that my family did.

Poetic to kill Kalmin where he killed them.

Poetic to have everything come full circle.

I allow my scaleblades to emerge, and pause, considering what I heard from Wooseok. Maybe I can take more than just lives. Maybe I can take loyalties. Setting my jaw, I think of scared Claws like Wooseok, young Blackbloods who have been beaten and abused by Kalmin...

They might just make very useful allies indeed. Not, of course, useful in the ways that shipsmiths and drug lords and Gumiho are useful, but useful in a quieter sort of way. Loss of gang members to death is to be expected at some point or another. But *betrayals*...

If I have allies on the inside, I can take out the remaining standings quicker. Poison in the Feathers' winecups. Bills' throats slit in the dead of night.

Wooseok will be patrolling tonight. I'll find him soon enough, offer him safety and shelter and a leader who doesn't beat her subordinates into submission. In return he—and his friends, if he has any—will help me.

But for now, before I find Iseul . . . the Legs.

There are fifteen of them, stomping through the rain, boots sloshing in the mud. They're tired. Cold. Nervous. Claws dead, they must be next.

They don't understand just how right they are.

Afterward, as I stomp toward the Dove Coop, sloshing through the pounding rain, I do not allow myself to consider how quickly I killed those men. I do not allow myself to question whether I made the Good decision. I need to warn Iseul of what is coming, and I cannot allow myself to be hindered by another attack.

Eunbi and Rui, I know, are waiting for me back at my hanok. Eunbi is waiting for my comfort, for my confession. But there is a larger matter at hand. I must warn Iseul of what Kalmin uttered in the study.

And perhaps I am not quite ready to face my baby sister yet.

Thanks to the lack of guards, it's quick work to knock on the door. Iseul is slower this time, but her hand still manages to yank me through the doorway and into the Dove Coop. She slams the door shut.

"Lina!" she says, looking absolutely delighted—but her face soon falls upon seeing my own. "Let me guess," Iseul sighs before I can begin. "He's threatened to kill my Doves." Today, she wears an especially poofy pink hanbok and an especially murderous expression. Her ax gleams in her hand, and the diamond necklace around her neck shimmers. "Well, he's too late for that. My Doves haven't been in this kingdom for three days now. I sent them off on a ship on Habaek's River to Wyusan. I know a madame there. She's agreed to take them in for the time being while I hoard away my finances and wait for you to kill Konrarnd. Did I forget to mention?"

So that is why the Coop had been so silent on my last visit, and why it sits in darkness now, utterly devoid of life and sound. I swipe my soggy bangs out of my eyes. "There's more," I say quietly. I'm looking at her with new eyes. Noting how her eyes are distinctly foxy, how her face holds a cunning and craftiness that far surpasses what a human face may contain. Remembering the sleek white fox who darted down the street, little more than a flash of lightning.

"Oh, *lovely*," Iseul mutters. "Well, it sounds like news I don't want to take standing." I watch with some disbelief as she drops to the floor, glaring up at me. "You sit too."

I see no choice but to oblige. Now kneeling on the floor, I briefly explain Kalmin's plan. "He's told Asina, his—"

"The one with the big, fishy eyes and the very shiny head?" Iseul asks in clear distaste. "Oh, I know *her*. Would stand out in a crowd, that one."

"Precisely." A bitter smile tugs at my lips, but it quickly fades. "Iseul, listen to me. She's taking men here soon, Man Jisu among them. They're going to kill you."

"Well, they can certainly *try*." Iseul rolls her eyes, and flops onto her back. Her head lolls. "Man Jisu, you say? And I truly thought my morning couldn't get any worse. Not after I spilled my tea and stubbed my favorite toe." Her tone is light, but I do not miss the heavy frustration building within her.

"Something tells me that you could handle Man Jisu quite well, Song Iseul."

Iseul slowly draws herself up. Her expression remains playful, with a hint of agitation—yet her eyes have become alert. "Well, thank you, Lina. I *am* quite handy with an ax."

I fix her with a gentle stare. It's best to come out with it. "I know what you are," I say quietly.

She flinches, but it's barely noticeable. Yet I see the veins on her neck stand out momentarily as she swallows hard. "Beautiful? Incredibly rich? A feast for the eyes? Why, thank you. You're *divinely* kind."

"Gumiho."

There is a moment of taut silence between us, so sharp it cuts the air.

And then the effect of my word is explosive.

Iseul launches herself to her feet with more speed than I'd expected, and levels the blade of her ax at my forehead. *"How?"* she demands, voice quivering. *"How do you know that?"*

I swallow hard, wishing at once for our easy laughter and light conversations. It has not been so very long since I faced Jiwoon, who wielded a similar ax, and I am not impressed—instead, I find that I do not want Iseul to be displeased with me. To lose her as an ally or a friend. "I saw you last night. With the boy named Seojin. I watched you transform."

"You cannot prove it." Her cheeks burn bright pink, her eyes unusually glassy. "You have no such proof."

"Iseul," I say, trying for a small smile, "you have a portrait of yourself, as a nine-tailed fox, in your Downstairs."

Iseul makes a choking sound. The ax moves slightly closer to my forehead, and I let my smile drop.

"I'm not going to spread word or hurt you. I swear it on the gods. Nor will I ask you for specifics—how you survived, how you keep yourself fed." I hold her gaze, willing her to see the truth I speak—but as she continues to scowl, ax unmoving, I know that I must do more than speak. I must *show*.

So I let my scales emerge on my skin. Bright, sparkling teal. I let them flank my face, framing it with diamond-hard snakeskin. Iseul blinks rapidly, and the weapon begins to lower. "You're a powerful ally, Iseul," I say, and slowly rise to my feet, hands raised cautiously in the air. "A powerful affiliate with a shared hatred. And I agree with what you said. That we could…make a great pair of friends. I would protect you, if you stood by me. You wouldn't be hunted. You wouldn't be targeted. And in return, all I want is your promise that, when the time comes, you'll work by my side. That you'll keep Sunpo under my control through whatever means you possess. Whether it be eating the ki of those who seek to overthrow me or using your cunning to calm dissent."

"What are you?" Iseul has lowered her ax completely and is

eyeing me with both wariness and a new, hesitant appreciation.

"A friend." I lower my hands, letting them hang loose by my side. Perhaps I should tell her the full truth, but…not yet. What if she, too, has heard of the Imugi's evil? What if she decides she does not want to be my ally after all?

A beat of silence passes between us, Iseul scrutinizing my face with unconcealed curiosity. Yet she does not press the matter.

"A friend," she repeats, and—to my surprise—grins mischievously. "Then, I would be a fool to deny a *friend* such a promise. In return, you must promise not to utter a word of what I am, Shin Lina. Because if you do, the world will seek to kill the last Gumiho. And so, in return, I will kill *you*. I do not know what you are, exactly, but even the most powerful creatures are powerless against a very, *very* deep hole with no possible way out—and also the company of worms and maggots."

"It's fair enough." I allow my scales to recede.

"Well." Iseul gives me one last wary glance and heaves another long-suffering sigh. "I truly don't feel like battling an entire legion of Blackbloods at the moment. I suppose it's time for me to retreat to my hidey-hole. Oh no—*please* don't ask where it is," she says, even though I am not planning on it. "Its location is unknown to all but me. Very mysterious, yes, yet a necessity. But before I go…" Iseul grins. "You've helped me escape the stench of Man Jisu's breath. Let me give you a parting gift."

I climb to my feet as well. "Which is…?"

"Loyalties." She fiddles with the necklace and her grin widens. "A few birdies told me that the number you've so far amassed is *much* too low to ensure your retention of the throne once you overthrow the red-haired rodent."

"There are still names on my list, yes."

"Give me the list," says Iseul with a twinkle in her eyes. "I have friends in high places and friends in low places. Also, I have some friends in very, *very* high places. *Incredibly* high places.

Jaw-droppingly high places. Whoever is on your list, I suspect I may be able to wrangle them to your side."

"Truly?"

"Truly."

I give her the names of Cha Hyukjae and Bang Bomin. Iseul winks. "Easy. Nearly *boring*. Is that all?"

"Well," I say carefully, "there's a Blackblood I plan on targeting tonight. Son Wooseok. I think that he would switch allegiances if offered sufficient reward—"

"—and to have somebody on the inside could be beneficial," Iseul finishes, smile widening. "Oh, Lina, we truly are going to be the best of friends one day. You're just as sly as I am, and that is no small feat." She toys with a strand of her hair. "I do, however, have a severe aversion to Blackbloods and their associates. I fear you'll have to handle the boy yourself. Otherwise, I will likely break out in hives at the sight of him."

I snort in a very undignified manner. "Somehow, I believe it."

"Look… Give me a few days to convince the Blackbloods I've gone and fled to the end of the world—I'll send you a message when it's time to meet your new friends. Feel free to bring a casket of wine in thanks. Oh, and Lina?"

"What is it?"

Her eyes are suddenly grave. "Call upon Ryu Seojin."

The boy from the Moonlit Hare. Iseul's friend, whom she met at the old giwapji's ruins. The intensity of her stare takes me momentarily aback. "I—yes. I forgot to mention him. I was planning to."

"Good. I think you'll find him quite to your liking." With that, she winks and all but shoves me back into the storm. "Goodbye now! *Do* try to hurry up with that murder business. I want my house of scandal open again. Life isn't any fun without salaciously illicit affairs!" And the door slams shut.

CHAPTER THIRTEEN

"Lina? Where were you?" Rui's eyes are wide with concern as I stumble back into the giwajip.

"Wh-where's Eunbi?" I manage through chattering teeth. "I-is she asleep? I d-didn't mean to leave her a-all day." Guilt swarms in my stomach as I push past him, looking around for my little sister. The foyer is quiet, empty.

"Eunbi's asleep," Rui says. ""Recuperating. She's in your bed. To comfort herself, she ate all of our sugar rolls. And the entire pot of porridge. And drank the full pot of tea. I suppose it is in your right to know that, although she made me promise not to tell you." He pauses. "Lina, you're shaking—"

"W-was she upset? That I was g-g-gone all day? I d-didn't—" I stumble to the door of my bedroom and expand my senses so that I can hear her soft, sleepy breathing through the door. "Shit," I mutter, digging the palms of my hands into my eyes.

Behind me, Rui lays a hand on the small of my back, guiding me to the bathroom, where he takes in my violent shivering and rain-drenched form with thinning lips. "Did you intend to kill yourself by catching a cold? You are not immortal, Lina."

"L-logically sp-speaking," I manage through chattering teeth, "I p-probably a-am n-now." It is something that I have not allowed myself to contemplate too carefully just yet—how my new powers probably signify a very long life-span ahead of me.

"Logically," he scoffs.

"It's *t-true*."

"I am not speaking *logically*," Rui mutters in exasperation. He narrows his eyes, and a flare of blue Dokkaebi fire immediately heats the bathwater I brought in from the water pump yesterday to a steaming temperature. He adds in a stream of soap, and the water immediately froths with thick, white bubbles. "I am speaking from a vast amount of frustration and a considerable amount of concern. Even immortals can die from pneumonia if they are not careful. Bathtub, little thief. Now."

Rui looks away as I struggle out of my soggy clothes and sink into the hot water, hissing slightly at the sudden warmth. The bubbles conceal my body, and I gather them closer to my chest, feeling rather grateful for the blanket of soap. Rui has not seen me unclothed before. I want the first time he does to be...special. When I am not reeling from grief and pain.

Rui's face is taut and worried as he leans against the doorway, arms crossed.

I bring my knees up to my chest and close my eyes. "Oh gods. I shouldn't have left like that. I don't know what I was thinking." My voice trembles.

He is silent for a few long moments before he kneels at the edge of the bathtub and pours a few drops of herbal soap into the palm of his hand. "You were distraught," he says quietly, gently working the shampoo through the tangles of my hair. His touch is tender, comforting. "I only wish you'd brought a cloak."

I clutch my knees, my breathing shallow, and squeeze my eyes shut as a familiar craving burns my throat. I swallow against it, but still it rises, clawing and scratching. All of this—all of this, today, yesterday, this past godsdamn year...it is too much. I need it.

Think of Sang, his hazel eyes. You promised him you would stop before it takes you.

"Lina?" Rui whispers.

"I want a smoke." The whisper is shaky, guilty, weak in its admittance. I open my eyes and hug my knees tighter. I am attempting to squash the craving down, but it resurfaces, stubborn. For a terrible moment, I fear that Rui will judge me for it.

Addict.

That is what he called me once. In Gyeulcheon's throne room, he'd flung the word at me. *Addict.* It stung then, and it stings now as I rock back and forth in the water, wanting—needing—the release. Rui's face is taut for a moment—with concern, I realize with relief as his face eventually softens, and as he continues to work through the knots in my hair.

"I know."

I stuff my knuckles into my mouth, tasting blood as my teeth puncture skin. "S-sometimes I don't," I manage to say. "Someone offered me a roll and I said no. I sit in a jumak and push down the craving. I thought I was getting better. I thought I was f-fixing it." My stammers are so unlike me, but I cannot stop them from tumbling past my tight lips. "I th-thought I was fixing myself."

"Lina." Rui's fingers gently, but firmly, move my fist away from my mouth. His hand covers the small cuts my teeth left, even as the skin begins to stitch over. "Listen to me. You are not broken. You do not need to be *fixed.*"

"You c-called me an addict—"

"I did not realize the word contained such a negative connotation," he replies solemnly. "Because to me, it never has, and I apologize if I have ever made you feel otherwise. To me, it has been only a medical condition, something to fight against, and not the fault of the patient. Something to be treated." He rubs his thumb across my skin. "Growth isn't linear, Lina. It is knotted and tangled and frustrating. But it is something to be proud of, even as you struggle."

"I don't feel proud," I reply, ashamed that tears are causing my vision to swim and that the world is becoming loud again, all sharp sounds and scents and sensations…

Rui straightens, suddenly alert. "Lina. Take a deep breath, little thief. Here," he says, shifting, placing my hand on his chest so I can feel him inhale. "One," he says, and breathes out, a deep gust.

"Two," I whisper, inhaling and exhaling, letting my lungs expand, letting oxygen into my body. As I exhale slowly, I hold eye contact with Rui. And the itching in my throat banks—just a bit.

"Three," he murmurs.

"Four."

"Five."

By fourteen, I am able to *exist* again—not caught in the maw of desperate longing. The world is quieter. Easier. I blink a few times as Rui smiles softly back at me.

"There," he whispers, and kisses the tip of my nose.

"There," I repeat, a little wryly.

The silver of his eyes is so warm, so sparkling, the connection between us so full of deep affection that for a moment…I open my mouth, my confessions on the tip of my tongue. *Rui?* I want to say. *There is something in my head. Something that talks to me, that prowls along my mind like a beast, that is watching me. Constantly.*

I almost say it.

But something stops me.

Perhaps it is the way the words turn sour in my mouth and curdle on my tongue before I even say them. Perhaps I do not want him to think me both an addict and deluded.

Or perhaps it is the Voice itself that stops me, stomping my words out with heavy feet, shattering the vowels and consonants into dust. And with my silence comes terror. It is not right for my words to be erased on my tongue. It is not right for something to be in my mind. But either way, I say nothing. I do not know if it is because I do not want to, or because I am unable to.

Instead, I merely tip my head back, my eyes still closed as he massages my scalp. He doesn't notice that my hands have begun to shake. Only when the tremors finally pass do I speak—and the words are not the words I thought I meant to say. "The breathing,"

I whisper. "How did you learn that it helps?"

"I used to have similar spells," Rui replies quietly. "It's been a long time, but I still remember what I would do to find relief."

"Oh," I murmur, thinking of what Iseul said. About attacks like these sometimes following strong, negative emotion. It must have been after Achara died. A few moments later, I speak again, this time quietly. "Don't you want to know where I went?"

Rui hesitates. "Matters such as these are...personal. I will not pressure you to reveal them if you are unwilling." He pours water over my head and soap runs down my shoulders, which have stiffened. It is clear he is drawing a parallel between our two situations, reminding me that he is still unwilling to reveal his secret. The affection that his comfort brought forth, the forgetting of the boundaries and battles between us, disappears. "Although I was worried," he adds quietly. "And still am."

"I went to the palace." The words tumble past my lips. "I retrieved...information." And although I want to, I will not tell him of Iseul, the Gumiho. I swore my new friend silence, and silent I will keep.

"The palace." His fingers still in my hair, and his mouth tightens. "Konrarnd," he snarls, and each word blisters with wrath. I remember what Kalmin said—that Rui threw him to the ground after bringing him back to Sunpo, that he pressed his boot to his neck. That he told Kalmin that Sunpo did not belong to him.

Rui may not have known the Talons, but through me, he feels their loss, their absence. He feels my rage, my fury. And for that, he is...he means so much to me. Perhaps more than any boy has before. There was a time when I thought that I would never feel my heart mend. And for a year, I felt nothing except pain and rage and ruin. Until Rui.

Rui. He is...he is my best friend. Somebody who makes me laugh and smile and sometimes sparks the intense desire to punch him in his perfect face.

But we have something more, too. Something that has no name, not yet. But given time... Given time, I think that there could be a name for it. A word that is pure and simple and sweet. A word that, at times like this, does not feel so impossible.

I shiver in the bathwater, averting my eyes, overcome with sudden anxiety. What if he will not feel for me what I suspect one day I will feel toward him? What if it is Achara—always Achara? Perhaps I am foolish in hoping we could have something together. What is it that the Voice had said?

He compares us to Shuo Achara. Achara, with her paint-splattered hands and eye for beauty. We will never measure up to his lost love. He does not trust us as he did her. He does not love us as he did her. Look at his long hair. Look how he still mourns.

"Lina?" Rui's brows are pulled tightly together. "Little thief, are you well?"

"I—I'm fine," I say quickly, the Voice stirring in my mind, smiling at a sensed opportunity. "I just...I..."

That word, the one you wish for, it comes with trust. A trust that he lacks in us.

Stop—

"Lina?" Rui asks again, peering at me intently. But the Voice is not done.

We're born from such a terrible foe. Daughter of the Imugi. The Voice sighs, and goose bumps rise on my skin. *Born from something wicked. Evil. Most definitely not Good.*

Stop it.

It would make sense to lose him too, someday, wouldn't it?

Stop it, stop it, STOP IT!

"Lina," Rui says sharply, jerking me out of my reverie. I blink water from my eyes, hiding my shaking hands in the bubble-frothed water of the tub.

"What is it?" is all I can manage. Rui's eyes scour my own before slowly, he pulls away.

"It is only that..." He frowns slightly again, before shaking his head and allowing a wry smile to curve his mouth. "It is only that sometimes, I think you are listening to something I cannot hear. Something far away, in the distance." Rui shrugs, as if he does not expect an explanation—but the questions linger in the air.

Swallowing hard, I do my best to fill the expectant silence. "There is a gala," I say, rising from the tub and drying myself off as I studiously avoid Rui's eye. It's not difficult to—he's politely averted his gaze. Bathwater sloshes onto the floor. "On the Night of the Red Moon, nights from now. At the palace. I plan to kill Kalmin then. He wished," I add in an undertone, slipping into hemp pants and a simple tunic, "to invite you."

"Invite me?" Rui sounds extraordinarily amused. "Ah. So, he wishes me dead." Now he sounds enormously pleased with himself. "Do you remember, little thief, when *you* wanted me dead?"

"Even if I slammed my head into a wall," I reply drily, "I wouldn't forget *that*." Yoonho taught me that trick, once—how to induce memory loss. It involved hitting a victim's head at a certain angle with a certain amount of force. It didn't always work, but if one was lucky, it would.

"My fondest memory," Rui declares, adopting a look as if he is gazing lovingly into the distant past, "is when you stabbed me in the chest over dinner. I gave quite the performance."

"You mean when you faked your death and tricked me." I scowl as I exit the bathroom, the emperor close behind.

"If I was not an emperor, I do believe I'd have a future in the theater."

"All that was missing was a lolling tongue."

Rui laughs, carefully quiet so as not to wake Eunbi. "An emperor does not have a lolling tongue, even in death. We must always look extremely stoic."

"I would disagree."

"Shall we settle the dispute?" Rui spreads his arms and grins.

"Stab me. You'll see that I'm right."

"You're insufferable."

"And you're reluctant."

"I am not—" I lower my voice, glancing to the door of my bedroom. "Rui, I am not going to *stab you* in the middle of my foyer."

"Why not?" Rui looks so completely crestfallen that I snigger. A moment later his facade breaks, revealing his mischievous smirk.

I roll my eyes in exasperation. "So, are you attending?"

Rui arches a brow. "Attending…?"

"The *gala*," I say in exasperation. "On the Night of the Red Moon. Nine nights from now."

"Ah. Well." He tilts his head, considering. "I do adore parties, and I adore revenge even more." He steps closer and kisses me gently. "I will come to the gala, if only to observe you kill the scarlet-haired. I am sure it will prove to be quite pleasant entertainment. Perhaps I will bring some sort of snack to eat as I watch."

"Danpatjuk?" I smirk, exiting the bathroom, Rui close behind me.

"And sugar rolls."

My smirk wavers as I sigh, leaning against the wall, running a hand through my wet, tangled hair. "Do you think Eunbi will forgive me?" The words waver. "I really—I really fucked up today, Rui."

Rui's hands find my waist. "From what I've observed in Gyeulcheon, Eunbi can't seem to stay mad at anybody for very long. She's quick to forgive."

"I kept their deaths from her. All of their deaths." I shake my head, glaring at him. "This is—this is *different*—"

"But Eunbi is the same. You're her sister. You know that," he adds with a wry arch of his brows. "I suspect you only want reassurance." He leans in closer, letting his lips graze mine. "Which I am happy to give. But now that you're clearly *not* about to perish from a deadly cold..." He tilts my chin up and kisses me again, long and slow and deliciously sweet.

I run my hands down his back, feeling his smooth, taut muscles through the fabric of his hanbok. His kisses are distracting in a way that I crave, shifting my focus from the mistakes I made today, the harm I caused Eunbi.

Rui groans as I deepen the kiss, pulling him closer, closer. "This," he gasps, moving away for a split second, "this is even more thrilling than you wanting me dead."

His lips are soft, and his teeth are sharp, and his roaming hands are fervent. Hungry. Underneath my fingers, his hair is mussed, so different from its usual silky sheen. My heart is pounding and pounding, and my blood—it's burning so incredibly hot in my veins, searing my skin, ebbing lower. And lower. I marvel at how this...this thing between us feels so right. As if we're meant to be together, as if our lips have been shaped for this very moment.

I hook my legs around his waist. My back is pressed against the wall. Our breathing is heavy, hoarse, uneven. Rui's mouth has become hard, unyielding, and he's making these noises—these low, raspy noises of desire in the back of his throat—that are my undoing. I shiver as he begins to kiss along the slope of my neck, nuzzling into me, his hands sliding underneath my tunic and up my bare back.

"Lina," he murmurs, looking up at me. His pupils are so dilated that the silver of his eyes is nearly overcome by dark, dark desire. "Lina, Lina, Lina." A kiss follows each whisper of my name, and I moan softly, pulling him closer—

How to describe what happens next? It's like a...a tug in my chest, in my heart. It's as if the air has shifted, as if gravity has changed somehow. The world's rotation slows to a crawl, dragging time with it. I feel disoriented. Dizzy. Inside me, I feel...peculiar.

Once, when I was younger, my eomma taught me how to stitch the ragged holes in our clothing back together, mending them with scraps of fabric cut from a spare cloth. My stitches were neat, precise. I've always had steady hands when I work. My favorite part was finishing the line of stitches, tying the knot tight, watching the fabric bunch.

That is what this feels like.

In my heart, I *feel* a needle slipping in and out of my tissue. I *feel* the knot tie.

A moment later, the red, pulsing organ *bunches* and for a moment…for a moment, I can't breathe. And then I feel something else, as if I've been—connected to something through that thread. As if I've been stitched to something.

Gasping, I clutch at my chest and scramble to stand on my feet. Rui has gone very still, breathing hard. There is a look of unfathomable emotion in his eyes. Confusion. Delight.

Fear?

Has he felt this strange sensation, too?

I look at him closely, panting. And something has changed. It is as if I know his face as well as I know my own. As if I have known him for so much longer than I have. The slope of his knifepoint nose, the arched curves of his brows, the way his skin is a light golden-beige with a smattering of tiny, nearly invisible freckles atop his high cheekbones…they are all familiar to me in a way that is deeply intimate. Almost as if I am looking at a reflection of myself. A part of me. "Rui?" I whisper, and then startle.

A flicker of something between us. A flash of red… There, and then gone so quickly I know I must have imagined it.

Rui's chest is rising and falling unevenly. His eyes are so very wide. "I—" The emperor breaks off, and I see him fumbling for words. "Lina, I—"

"Did you feel…that?"

Something flickers, a shadow over his face. As if he's made a decision. A sly, sated smile curves his lips. "As I said," he murmurs, reaching out a hand to touch my face, "*much* more entertaining than those assassination attempts."

I blink, unsteady. Already beginning to doubt what I felt and thought I saw. The gods know that my senses have been tangled lately. That I am still growing used to this body.

The air behind Rui begins to ripple, parting to reveal a corridor of darkness. He clears his throat, glancing over his shoulder. "I must go. I will return for Eunbi tomorrow afternoon. I've been gone long enough," he says, almost to himself. His voice takes me aback as his hand drops from my face, falling to his side.

For his tone is soft, but laced with a terrible shadow of desolation. And it's shaking. He raises his eyes to me and grins—perhaps catching his slip. But his lips are pulled too tightly, and his eyes have lost their spark, dull and dead.

"Farewell, little thief," he says with forced cheer…and then with a wink he is gone, leaving only the faint scent of plum blossoms behind.

INTERLUDE

P iercing screams shatter the thick blanket of night as the Dokkaebi emperor returns, through shadow and darkness, to his home.

Hoarse screams of terror that bury their way into the emperor's mind, echoing endlessly, screaming accusations. His head, buried in his hands, aches with a pounding, edged anger. His body trembles. This, he likes to believe—remaining within the palace during this night—is one of his punishments for a war nearly lost, a realm created, and a tithe owed.

His advisor's wards have contained these screams, this torture, to within the palace. The Dokkaebi staff, guards and cooks and the rest have been moved to the second, smaller palace in Gyeulcheon's mountains, The Little Palace.

Only the emperor, and his inner circle, remain.

They are sequestered in a small room, a hidden room heavily protected by Kang's magic. The room is used only once per year, and dust coats the wooden floors like a dull, dead snow. It is a sort of attic, tucked above a cleaning closet constantly kept locked, in which a ladder extends from the ceiling should one of the inner circle pull a lever, cleverly hidden as a broom handle.

The air is stuffy. If the emperor allows himself to expand his senses, he will smell blood. So he is careful to breathe in only the smell of dust and mothballs and the herbal scent constantly clinging to his advisor, Kang, who is seated next to him on a lumpy floor cushion. Hana is curled up on a wooden chair, her dark eyes unfocused, her lips a tight white line. Chan, her lover and general of the Gyeulcheon army, is pacing back and forth, broad shoulders tight and emerald eyes flashing.

Rui raises his head and stares, despairingly, at a spot on the floor.

He was late tonight. By the time he arrived back at Gyeulcheon, the preparations had already been made. He should have been back earlier. None of his circle questioned him. But it is only a matter of time before—

Like clockwork, Chan abruptly stops pacing. He cuts his glare to his emperor, his friend, his brother in all but blood. Rui, Chan notes, looks fucking terrible. He always does on these nights, but it's worse than usual. His hair is mussed, his face is haggard, and he seems older—much older—than his twenty Dokkaebi years. But Chan can't let it rest.

Because it's horrible making those preparations, godsdamned awful, but Rui—despite being emperor—should hold the same responsibility as the rest of them to truss up the tithe. He glances at Hana, who nods. *Ask.*

"Rui," he snaps over the screams. "Where were you?"

Rui swallows hard, and makes himself look at Chan. "Sunpo," he replies, and the word sticks in his mouth. He clears his throat. "I... Circumstance prevented me from returning earlier."

"You mean Shin Lina," Hana drawls, rousing herself to shoot Rui a venomous look. "While the rest of us were making the preparations, you were with your snaky lover. Fraternizing with the enemy."

"Watch your tongue, Hana." Anger straightens Rui's back, and he curls his hands into fists, allowing a few sparks of Dokkaebi fire to ignite in the air between them. "Lina is not the enemy."

Hana sniffs in disdain. "She has their scales." It's a point she's been making ever since the human girl...changed into something else. Something that is most definitely not human.

A high-pitched scream tears the air apart, and the circle falls silent once more. Auburn-haired Kang, quiet until now, carefully places a hand on Rui's shoulder. He earned his position beside the Dokkaebi king by his honesty, his accumulated wisdom of the realms. But he is also the emperor's friend, a position Kang values just as much as he values his official status as advisor. "In all these years," he says in a low voice, letting the two others know that these words are for Rui and Rui alone, "you have never once been late. It unnerved them. This night is hard enough for all of us."

"I know." The memory of Lina's lips locked against his increases Rui's guilt. Guilt is an uncomfortable emotion, and Rui has never enjoyed it. Yet he has felt so much of it through the years. So very, very much.

Kang removes his hand. "Let us speak of other matters. How is Lina?"

Rui knows what his advisor thinks of Lina. What he fears. That she is more Imugi than human. That she is dangerous. "Adjusting," he replies carefully. "She..." The emperor trails off, closing his eyes. If he concentrates, he can feel the difference in his heart — the stitches connecting him to fate. But is it, truly? Could this be... real? More than a myth? More than a legend?

If anybody would know, it would be Jeong Kang, scholar of the highest wisdoms.

"Rui? What is it?" Kang prods gently, unable to miss the confusion misting his emperor's eyes. As the sound of suffering rises, Kang forces his emperor to look at him, guiding him by the chin. "You may tell me," he says, knowing that Rui will focus on his voice, on anything but the cries of fear and pain and horror. He also knows that Rui will hate himself for it, for seeking distraction, but it is necessary to keep the emperor's mind in good health.

The circle is not required to stay here, tonight. Nothing in the bargain details it. But they do.

To atone. To repent.

"Rui," Kang prods gently.

Rui takes a deep breath. "There was a moment. Where I felt… and even now, I feel it. In here." He presses a hand to his chest, where his heart beats for a girl with a teardrop scar and blazing eyes. "Kang, the story…the story about the thread. Tell me, is it true?"

And Jeong Kang goes very still. His mind, usually a calm, cool pool of collected knowledge, wavers. There is a ripple in it—a ripple of unease. He well knows what Rui is referring to, the story that is little more than a whisper, a phenomenon so rare that it hardly exists at all. If the phenomenon has joined together his emperor and the assassin, the Imugi girl, it signifies something larger on the horizon. It must. For they're so unique a pair, so unlikely and unusual. Fate, perhaps, is finding its fun. But at what cost?

Yet despite Kang's unease, there is a possibility—albeit an extraordinarily slight one—that there could be no harm in it. Kang knows that. In the texts, the thread is drawn to individuals who are already magnetic. Already revolving around one another. It does not always need to foreshadow a turn in history, or a pitting against each other.

Sometimes, it just signifies true love.

But…

"Kang?" Rui is watching his advisor closely, noting his hesitance. His wariness. "Is it real?"

"The red thread of fate," Kang murmurs. "The thread joining two souls in common destiny. Yes. Yes, it is real. Extraordinarily rare, but it exists."

Rui exhales in one fell swoop.

Kang waits. Attempts to still the waters of his mind.

But when Rui speaks again, the waters ripple and waves begin to churn.

"I think," Haneul Rui whispers, "that the red thread has joined my soul with Lina's. I think, Kang…I think that Shin Lina and I are soul-stitched."

CHAPTER FOURTEEN

Eunbi sleeps with a tearstained face, a thumb in her mouth, her dark curls soaked with the sticky sweat that coats her small body. Every few moments she hiccups and stirs in her thin blanket, reaching out toward where I sit on the edge of the bed. Even in her sleep, Eunbi instinctively looks for me.

I stroke her curls and wipe a trickling tear from her plump, ruddy cheek. I withhold my own, for it is time to be strong, it is time to be the older sister. I did not have the luxury of the news being broken softly, gently, to me. But it is a luxury I can give to Eunbi.

"Eunbi," I whisper. "Eunbi, little sister, it is time to wake up."

Blearily, she opens tear-crusted eyes. I hold myself steady under her groggy gaze as she sits up and reaches for me. "Lili," she mumbles. "Where did you go?" She climbs into my lap, and I hold her tight as I gather the blankets around us.

My heart hammers in my chest. My palms sweat. Now is the time to tell her.

"I went to the palace," I say quietly. "The palace with the willow trees and the koi pond."

Eunbi goes still. "But the Talons don't live there anymore," she whispers, clutching at my hands. I cannot see her face, but I hear the crack in her voice. "Do they?" Her hope is unmistakable, and it cuts through my chest like a blade.

"No," I confirm gently. "A…a new group lives there now. A new group run by a bad, bad man. He took the palace from the Talons, and he took the Talons from me." My voice wavers. "I made a mistake, and the bad man hurt the Talons. For a year, I was imprisoned by him. That's why I couldn't see you for so long. I wanted to. I missed you."

My baby sister is quiet. I press on. The worst of it is over, yet I still feel sick to my stomach. Eunbi twists in my lap, stares up at me. She says nothing. Her lower lip trembles.

"I'm going to take the palace back from him. There's going to be some fighting, so that's why you're staying with the Dokkaebi, where nothing bad will happen to you. And when I finish, you can come live with me in the palace, and we'll climb the willow trees and play in the pond. And you can be the princess of Sunpo, and eat as many sugar rolls as you like." I manage to earn a small, small smile out of her. "How does that sound?"

Her smile disappears as quickly as it came. "Lili," she says in little more than a whisper, "the bad man killed them? All of them?" Fresh tears spill from her eyes as I nod, as gently as is possible. Eunbi presses her hands to her mouth, crying. *"N-no,"* she wails, like her denial can bring them back. *"No!"*

I hug her close to me as the storm tears Sunpo apart, as thunder shakes the sky, as lightning pierces the land below.

When her sobs cease, she crawls out of my lap and curls into a ball under the blankets. "I didn't get to say goodbye," she whispers in a voice so much like my own—hoarse and broken—that I only barely hold back sobs. "You didn't get to say goodbye."

"I did," I say softly, remembering the night of the woodland assault, remembering how Sang's Gwisin guided me to the palace, and later, back to life. "And they are together now, little sister. We will see them again someday." I manage a small smile. "They watch over us from a realm far from our own. There is no pain for them anymore. No fear. They are safe now."

Eunbi swallows hard and furiously scrubs at her puffy eyes. "I suppose," she mumbles through wet sniffles. "They're happy?"

I don't know if this is quite true, but I still nod and say, "Yes.

They're happy." There is beauty in death. There is a field of flowers and the scent of cherry blossoms. But still, it is death. Irreversible. Eternal.

Under Eunbi's gaze, I try not to tremble. I have not told her exactly what transpired that night, but I revealed enough to subject myself to her blame if she so chooses. *I made a mistake, and the bad man hurt the Talons.* It may be easier for her to have somebody to blame, and I will not protest if she chooses for it to be me. But my little sister's glossy eyes hold no sign of rage—just deep, unfathomable sadness and love as she stretches her arms out to me.

"I love you, Lili," she whispers, hugging me tight enough that the breath rushes out of me. "I love you so, so much."

I sob, unable to stop the hot tears from freely flowing down my cheeks. "I love you too, little sister."

"And you're going to kill the bad man, aren't you?" She pulls back, scanning my face intently. "You're going to do it, right? You're going to do what Yoonho taught you to do, with the knives and swords?"

"I am." In nine nights.

"Good." Eunbi's face tightens, like she's just barely holding back more sobs. "Make him scared and hurt too."

"I will." I struggle to keep my voice steady.

She scrubs at her eyes again and takes a deep, shuddering breath. Then she reaches out and traces the right side of my face hesitantly. "I never saw this scar before," she says, and I close my eyes. In Gyeulcheon, I always concealed it with makeup. Today, I forgot. "Did the bad man give it to you?"

"No," I whisper hoarsely, brushing her hair away from her damp face. "Not that bad man." An image of Jiwoon leering down at me flashes through my mind. *There. An eternal tear.*

Eunbi frowns. "Another?" When I nod, her face crumples. "Why are there so many bad men?"

My throat closes and suddenly I wish, desperately, that my

Eunbi could live in a safe world. Where "bad men" always receive what's due them, where they don't plague kingdoms and continents.

As much as I want Sunpo for my own, as much as my heart beats for this decrepit kingdom, I wish I could seize the entire Eastern Continent by its neck and give it a firm shake, ridding the kingdoms of men like Kalmin and Jiwoon and all the others I've killed for the Talons—the rapists, the traffickers, the corrupt businessmen. There are far too many of them, and far fewer innocents in this kingdom. Bile rises in my throat.

For it was innocents who Kalmin made me kill. Innocents like Doyun's wife. Perhaps if I had broken free earlier... If I'd been able to make my own choices... My vision blurs.

In this moment, I desire more control than I will ever possibly have.

"Because their sort of evil is a rot," I reply softly. "It spreads, and it never stops."

Eunbi inhales sharply, and I realize with regret that I've scared her. Quickly, I change the subject. "Do you know why Rui sent you back today? Why he thinks that Sunpo is a safer place for you right now?" *Is it somehow connected to the kidnappings yesterday?*

Eunbi wipes her nose on the sleeve of her hanbok. "Rui said that Gyeulcheon was going to be very busy," she mumbles. "He said..." Eunbi frowns, as if struggling to remember something. "He said he was having old friends over for dinner. But he said it in an odd way, like when he's joking, but not truly. Have you noticed that tone, Lili?"

Indeed, I have. "Did you see who these old friends are?"

"I think...maybe the gods," Eunbi says, looking at me curiously. "They're old friends, right?"

I've had ample time to muse over this, wondering if Rui keeps Eunbi away because she is associated with me, and because I am no longer...worthy to be near the deities. Yet it doesn't quite fit. "But the gods are gone. They remain in the sky kingdom of Okhwang.

And I do not see how they would be a threat to you."

"Some of the gods are scary," Eunbi offers. "Like Yeomra and Seokga. Also, if the gods are going, Cheuksin may be there."

I blink. "The goddess of the toilet?"

"She likely smells very bad," Eunbi replies seriously. "Because she's the goddess of the toilet and all."

As much as I have wanted to believe it, I very much doubt that Rui has invited the gods for dinner. Not only are they far gone, but he would have told me—he knows how much I love the deities, how much I long to meet them. He would have told me.

Would he?

Perhaps I truly am not worthy of meeting them. Perhaps my Imugi traits have lost me the right to meet the pantheon. I am, after all, born from their enemy. Should I not have prayed to Dalnim and Haemosu? To Jowangshin? Am I not worthy? I swallow hard.

"Lili?"

The words squeeze past the lump in my throat. "Did you notice anything odd before you came here? Preparations? Have Hana, Chan, or Kang said anything?"

"Asha was cooking normally," Eunbi answers, frowning now, "but Hana said she didn't have time to play dolls with me like she usually does. And I didn't see Chan, because Chan was with his soldiers, and Kang was with Rui all morning—they were in the throne room and the doors were shut and locked. Also, the servants were all gone. The Dokkaebi ones, not the strange human ones," she adds.

I blink at this. "The Dokkaebi servants?"

"Asha was planning on leaving, too, after she made breakfast. All the servants were to go to the Little Palace because every year they have a day of rest in the mountains. That's what he called it. He also said for all the Dokkaebi not to return until sent for, otherwise they would pay for inconveniencing him with the sight of their faces." Eunbi shrugs. "He's a good emperor, but sometimes I think his people find him really rude, Lili." She pauses, and nibbles at the nails of her left hand. "I wanted to see the Little Palace, too, but he brought me here instead because he said you missed me and I'd have a better time. But then you were gone all day. Did you miss me?"

My throat is so tight that it's difficult to squeeze the words out. "Of course I've missed you, Eunbi. I just…I was sad."

"I understand." Eunbi picks at the sheets and sniffles. "But don't leave again, please. Because I missed you all day. Rui is nice, but he isn't you."

I had been planning to find and recruit Son Wooseok tonight, but at my little sister's words, my determination to find him banks. It can wait. Eunbi—precious, small Eunbi—is here. And I should be, too.

My little sister is still talking about Rui. "He let me braid his hair once. I put flowers into it, and he wore it all day. Even to one of what he calls Very Important But Boring Meetings." She peeks up at me. "He's the Pied Piper, isn't he?"

My heart lurches in my chest. I've never told Eunbi who Rui is, and she's young enough that I assumed perhaps she wouldn't make the connection between the figure of urban legend and the kind, benevolent emperor who showers her with dolls and dresses. It's not that I was keeping it from her—but her life does not need to be more complicated than it already is. "Who told you?"

Eunbi gives me a droll look. "He's a Dokkaebi," she says slowly, as if perhaps I am the oblivious one, "with a *magic flute*, Lili. And there are humans in his palace."

I swallow, mouth dry. "I see."

"It doesn't really take a genius to figure it out." She wipes her runny nose with the back of her wrist and sniffles a few times. "But it's funny, isn't it? Because he's not as bad as they say. And maybe he pays the humans for their work! With the coins that have his face on them!"

He most certainly does not, but I nod all the same.

"Maybe he's bad *and* good." Eunbi plays with one of her curls, not quite meeting my eye. "Can...people be both evil and good?" Her voice, its hesitant hope and wary acknowledgment, pierces my heart.

I hesitate, my stomach clenching.

Eunbi doesn't know the extent of what I've done, but she knows enough. And while she's never challenged me outright, never questioned what I am, she's growing up. This question, in all its forms, is something I must face.

So I nod, choosing my words carefully, sifting through the options of my reply. "Nobody's truly Good," I finally reply hoarsely, brushing her baby hairs away from her forehead, "and nobody's truly bad. We're just...us." The words taste bittersweet in my mouth as I think of myself—assassin, yes, but an older sister as well. As I think of Rui—the Pied Piper, but a friend. Of Sang, Chara, Yoonho, and Chryse. "Shades of gray in a dark world."

"What about me?" Eunbi straightens and stares deep into my eyes as she asks, "Am I good or bad?"

"Of course you're Good." It's not even a matter of debate. She's Eunbi. Young and innocent and pure. She has always been Good, never losing empathy. Never losing kindness, or the ability to make the right choices, like I have.

Eunbi squints her eyes at me. "Once, I kicked one of the Sisters at my school. Well, maybe two. Or three."

"What?" I blink at her incredulously.

She shrugs, looking guilty. "I didn't kick all three at once."

I don't know whether to smile or frown. Although I'm certainly not one to talk about the inappropriateness of violence, my expectations for Eunbi are so...high. Somehow, I can't reconcile my baby sister with a girl who kicks Sisters. "Why did you kick them?"

"Because they told me I had to take a bath."

"Eunbi," I groan, remembering the days on the barley farm

when our mother struggled to bathe my sister, who turned into a feral cat at the sight of the rinsing bucket.

She crosses her arms. "I didn't want to! If I want to smell bad, that's my business!" Eunbi snuggles against me and changes the subject suspiciously quickly. "Tell me a story, Lili."

"Which one do you want?" I play with one of her wayward curls.

"The one Appa always used to tell. The one about the treasure in Jeoseung."

The mention of Appa brings a dull wave of old pain, followed by a small smile. "The Poor Man's Treasure." Appa used to tell it to us to encourage us to live a life of good deeds. I'm not sure that it worked for me, but perhaps it will for Eunbi.

Eunbi yawns again, closing her eyes. Still playing with her hair, I begin. "Once upon a time, a man named Kim was very poor. But even though he was poor, Kim would often help his neighbors as much as he could—teaching them to fish, lending firewood, donating coins when he could afford to. Now, Kim lived near a man named Bak, who was very rich. But even though Bak had lots of money, he would give none to his impoverished neighbors, even when they came to him begging for help. All he would spare, mockingly, was a bundle of straw. 'Here,' he would say. 'And don't bother me again!'

"One cold night, Bak fell ill and passed into Jeoseung. But Yeomra, Jeoseung's king, told him that it was not yet his time. 'You mean to say I've traveled all this way for nothing?' Bak snapped. Yeomra smiled and shook his head."

"And Yeomra said 'Perhaps not,'" Eunbi murmurs sleepily. "Go on, Lili."

"Bak followed Yeomra through Jeoseung. It seemed that Yeomra was giving him a tour. Finally, they stopped at a small chogajip. It was dilapidated and falling apart. 'When it is your time, Bak,' said Yeomra, 'this is where you'll live.' And he pushed open the door, revealing nothing but a pile of straw on a dirty, dank floor. Outraged, Bak looked at his house, and then at the house next to it. The other house was in much better condition, with a tiled roof. When Yeomra, sensing Bak's intrigue, pushed open the door to reveal..."

"Treasure!" Eunbi finishes, only half awake by this point. "So much treasure."

"Bak was outraged. 'Who does this house belong to?' he demanded of Yeomra. When he heard that it belonged to poor man Kim, he was shocked. 'But I am rich and he is poor! How can this be?' Bak stared in disbelief as Yeomra told him that the amount of treasure in each house equaled the number of good deeds the house's owner performed. Realizing he had not lived his life as a good man, that *charity* was the true treasure of life, Bak returned to the world of the living, where he fought to redeem himself."

Eunbi is sleeping, her breathing heavy. But I continue speaking, my voice at a whisper. I do not know if I am continuing the story for my sister or for myself.

"It was hard for Bak to change his ways, and it was hard for Bak to be Good. But he tried, and kept trying. He helped his less fortunate neighbors, giving them more than just a bit of hay. He was generous and charitable, and grew to be loved. Bak gave away gold, but gained friendships and forgiveness. When he finally did die after a long life of righteousness, a home filled with treasure was waiting for him in Jeoseung."

Exhaling slowly, I close my eyes and savor the warmth of my little sister next to me.

The story runs through my mind and swirls through my dreams as I sleep.

CHAPTER FIFTEEN

When Eunbi pleads to go swimming in the Yongwangguk Cove the next morning once the storm has stopped, it is a welcome distraction from my powerlessness, my inability to do anything but mull over theories and thoughts that besiege my mind as I wait for Rui to return this afternoon.

The Yongwangguk Sea itself is a violent, crashing thing reeking of brine and plagued with dangerous riptides. It is said that underneath the frothing waves is the sea god Yongwang's kingdom of Yongwangguk—the namesake of the sea itself. Yet the kingdom is undoubtedly abandoned, for Yongwang, like all gods, has retreated to the heavenly realm of Okhwang. His kingdom is abandoned, but his sea is not. Fishermen brave the churning waters to haul back Sunpo's primary food source of fish, and women wash their clothing in the shallow waters, beating hemp tunics and pants against rocks.

But the Yongwangguk Cove is Sunpo's best-kept secret. Sang is the one who discovered the peaceful cove and all but dragged the Talons and me there. He hoped the still, clear waters would help soothe Chara's fear of the sea, that we could teach her to swim. Chara, in true Chara nature, stubbornly refused and spent hours sunning herself on the sand while Sang, Chryse, and I dove and splashed and competed to see who could hold their breath the longest.

Eunbi has never gone, but she often heard me recount those days on the beach with fond, excited tones. I cannot help but think that she wishes to go there today to connect, in some way, with the dead Talons. As I pack our luncheon—balls of sticky rice topped with sesame seeds and dried seaweed shavings—I'm hit with a dull wave of longing.

I wish they were still alive. I wish they could come with us to the Cove today.

I swallow hard and focus instead on Eunbi.

My little sister's eyes are still red-rimmed, but she chatters about this and that as I pull on my gat and wrestle her into one as well, despite it being far too big. I cannot risk her being recognized. As we make our way into Fishtown, I keep her hand clutched tightly in mine. But Kalmin must have pulled back his patrols after yesterday's massacre, as we go unnoticed, and soon the sea's salty spray is cold against our faces as we traverse the long stretch of beach, our bare feet sinking into the grains. The Cove is a long walk from the main beach, but Eunbi doesn't seem to mind—stooping to collect seashells and sea glass, pointing at the birds flying over the waves and swooping down to catch fish in their talons.

The Cove finally comes into view as we climb over the slippery rocks that shield it from the rest of the beach. They're dozens of feet tall, and while the climb is easy for me, it is not so for my little sister. I put her on my back as I ascend the stone, careful not to go too fast on the descent. Eunbi has never liked fast movement.

The water here is calm and clear, the beach empty. Eunbi clambers off my back and looks around in awe—and sadness. I swallow hard as I stare at the sea, remembering how Sang once swam with me down to the coral below, how we grinned at each other through the colorful schools of fish in the sea's depths.

"It's pretty," Eunbi says in a whisper. A gentle sea breeze lifts her curly hair as she takes off her gat.

"It is." I sit down on the sand and pull out our lunch.

"I miss them."

"I do too."

Eunbi and I stare in silence at the sea for a few long minutes. It feels...different to grieve with somebody who knows my pain, who shares it. It's awful and dizzying and has my stomach tightened with guilt, but...I don't feel so alone.

My voice is husky as I break the silence. "Come here, Eunbi. We can eat and then swim."

Eunbi is a skilled swimmer—we learned together, in the pond behind our barley farm. Thankfully, Eunbi's aversion to bathwater does not extend to all forms of water.

"Come here," I coax again.

She finally obliges, settling down and sinking her teeth into a rice ball. Her front teeth have grown halfway, but she still chews awkwardly, not sure what teeth to use and which to avoid. I watch her with emotion rising like a tidal wave in my chest. She's such a child, awkward and unsure, yet in awe of the world around her. I love her more than words can ever describe.

Eunbi notices me staring and makes a face. Rice sticks to the corner of her mouth. "What?"

"You have a little something—here." I wipe away the rice and she squirms. I grin at her, and she sticks out her tongue.

"Lili," she says a moment later, suddenly somber, "I need to ask you something important."

"Oh?"

Eunbi's eyes are wide on her small face. "How do you know if you love somebody?"

I choke on the bite of rice I've taken, pounding my chest with my fist. When I can finally breathe, I stare at her in incredulity, wondering—hoping—I've misheard. *"What?"*

She blushes pink, all the way to her hairline. "There's a boy in Gyeulcheon. He's really nice. His name is Tae and we play swords together. They're wooden swords!" she says quickly as I straighten. "And they don't have sharp tips like yours."

I stare at Eunbi. "Tae," I say warily.

Eunbi nods vigorously. "He's nine and he's funny. Chan introduced me to him because he said we would be friends, and he was right."

"And you…like him? Tae, I mean?" Part of me wants to march right into Gyeulcheon and investigate this Tae. But another part of me finds a slow, quiet happiness in Eunbi's first infatuation.

I watch as my sister goes beet red and stuffs the rest of her food into her mouth. "No! I don't know! Well, maybe. That's why I'm asking you! You love Rui, right? I was wondering how you know you love him."

"I…" My cheeks are burning. "I think it's a bit early for that, Eunbi."

"I heard you two kissing last night."

"Eunbi!" My entire face is now flaming. "I thought you were asleep!"

"You woke me up." Eunbi cackles as I close my eyes in mortification.

"You weren't meant to hear any of that," I finally say. "Rui and I are…something, together." Remembering the peculiar sensation last night within my heart, the feeling of *connectedness,* I wonder if it is love. But that sensation was so completely bizarre that I'm still at a loss as to what it might have been, if not another feature of this body to adjust to, as I suspect it was—or a figment of my imagination. "But love takes time."

And trust, the Voice reminds me slyly. ***Without that, how can you think you will ever fill the shoes Achara left behind?***

"Shut up," I mutter, and I hear Eunbi gasp. I open my eyes and wince. "I didn't mean you, Eunbi." I would never say that to her, and I'm suddenly furious with the Voice for making her think I might.

"Oh." She looks confused, but blinks it away. "Well, how did you know you wanted to be something with him?"

"He's…he was kind to me," I say slowly, watching the sunlight glitter on the azure water of the cove. "In Gyeulcheon. He helped me when I was hurt. He cared about me. He...he made me laugh."

"Tae makes me laugh!"

My lips curve up, but it's halfhearted. "It's important," I say slowly, "that whoever you love is...is trustworthy and honest." My heart twists a little. "Who doesn't keep secrets, but instead keeps their word."

Eunbi has begun to reach for another ball, but stops, frowning. "Lili, you sound...sad."

I inhale a deep breath, taking off my gat and running a hand through my hair. "I'm fine."

"Did you and Rui have a fight?"

Yes. "No," I say quickly. "Just a tiny disagreement, a day or two ago."

"Oh." Eunbi frowns, but I distract her, pushing another rice ball into her hands. I don't want her to become caught in the crossfire between Rui and me.

"Tell me about Tae," I encourage her instead, watching as her small face lights up.

"He's taller than me, but I think I'll catch up to him soon! He tells jokes that make me laugh until my belly hurts! He's training to become a guard, and Chan sometimes lets me join in on his lessons. Tae has those pointy ears too, and..."

Hours pass in the Cove as Eunbi and I sunbathe on the shore and splash in the waters. We swim down to see the coral reefs, and it's an effort to stay calm as memories of Sang, underwater and grinning, flit through my mind. As we kick back to the surface, Eunbi laughs in delight, shaking her head and flinging droplets of water into the air. When we finally make our way to shore, she's content but exhausted, and I carry her on my back as we return to my hanok.

It's the afternoon now. Rui should be here soon. With only eight nights until the Night of the Red Moon, I need to hunt down Son Wooseok. I need to finish off the Claws and Legs, but I cannot leave Eunbi alone.

The rest of the day passes, and he doesn't come. Eunbi, fresh from a nap, is delighted every moment he fails to return, as it means she can regale me with stories about Gyeulcheon and how she and Tae once played hide-and-go-seek in the hill lands with Chan. I smile and nod and exclaim at the appropriate moments, but where is Rui? Has something happened? When will he return? Concern growing, I press the silver ring to my lips. It warms in response but does not burn with Dokkaebi fire. Rui is still nowhere to be found.

Theories and thoughts once again besiege my mind. It is an effort to refrain from pacing, and instead I cook dinner for Eunbi. To keep my demeanor light and pleasant as we spend the evening playing with two dolls that Eunbi brought with her from Gyeulcheon as a thunderstorm once again besieges the kingdom.

After we eat dinner and she's tucked safely into bed, snoring softly, I creep up onto the roof of the giwajip to stare at the glittering stars and call again for Rui—with no luck.

What if he's hurt?

What if he's dead?

I force myself to breathe evenly. Whatever Rui was obligated to deal with last night must have kept him in Gyeulcheon. He is fine. I would know if he were gone. Wouldn't I?

Something in me knows, without question, that somehow, I would. That I would feel his death, feel his absence as if a part of me were ripped away. I would have a cold, gaping wound. I do not understand how I know this, but I do. Swallowing hard, I call again for him.

He does not come.

CHAPTER SIXTEEN

As my mood plummets, so does the temperature. Suddenly feeling cold despite the growing humidity, I rub my arms, feeling the goose bumps that have risen on my skin. Yet it is not just the cold that is bothering me—it is that feeling again, the indisputable feeling that I am being watched through the light rainfall splattering the roof. Observed.

"Child...of Venom..."

The voice is so soft that at first, I believe that I've imagined it. But then it comes again, accompanied by a soft susurration. I freeze as my blood heats—not in fear, not in wariness, but in welcome. I swallow a surge of sickening happiness. I wish I felt fear. It would be easier to feel fear. Why do I not feel fear?

As every instinct urges me to turn around, I fight back. I dig the heels of my boots into the roof, I curl my fingers around the tiles until they cut my skin. I set my jaw and stare determinedly at the waning moon. I count the number of stars. I ignore the knowledge that has unfurled deep within me, the knowledge of what has slithered onto the roof, what looms behind me.

It is not possible. And yet it is.

The rain is coming down heavier now. Thunder once again rolls somewhere on the horizon, a terrible premonition.

"Lina, my child." That voice. Like grass rustling in the wind. Like sand shifting underneath the tide. Like the turning of time itself. *"At lassst, we meet."*

I feel its gaze on my back, expectant. I feel the height of it, the power of it, as scales brush against tiles, as a forked tongue flicks out to taste the air. There is no mist to conceal it here. No darkness, not with my eyesight.

The giddiness within me is sickening, and I am not afraid of the creature behind me but of my *lack* of fear toward it. This feeling cannot be Good. It is wrong, all wrong.

My muscles scream at me to turn around, but instead I close my eyes as cold, glistening scales touch my skin, gliding across my flesh with eerie smoothness. I shudder violently. Cold. So cold. And so large—the creature is ginormous. Its sinuous body is so very, crushingly heavy on my lap as it twists across so its face hovers right near my own. It is only thanks to my immortal strength that my bones do not snap. Much of the creature still remains behind me, judging by the sheer weight coiling around my waist and lap. When I open my eyes, I am certain that I will meet the Imugi before me.

Why do I not fear it?

Because, the Voice murmurs, ***like calls to like. Open your eyes.***

Hating how much I long to, I do.

Large eyes as golden as a molten sunrise, cut down the middle by elliptical pupils as dark as the deepest night, stare back at me with warmth. In them, my face is reflected, full of awe and wonder as my own eyes rove across the wide, glossy head that is slightly flattened at the top, the curving scaled hood, the dark teal plated neck. Each scale glows and glitters under the dim moonlight. A black tongue flicks out with a soft hiss, and far, far away—at the very end of the roof—a tail waves slowly, melodiously, in the air.

It must be thrice as long as I am tall, and I know that should it wish to, it could unhinge its jaw and swallow me whole. Such a realization sends a thrill through me, and I cannot stop a smile from curving my lips as I hold the Imugi's gaze. It sways back and forth with a grace that belongs only to the serpentine, watching me carefully, hopefully.

The Imugi is beautiful.

I am pulled to it like a magnet, every fiber of my being singing in a chorus of joy. *Finally*, I think, somehow knowing deep within my soul that this is the Imugi I encountered in Jeoseung. *Finally together. Two parts of a whole, reunited at last.*

Tentatively, I reach a hand out to the large head that blocks the view of the night sky. My fingers meet the scales just above its mouth and between the nostrils. "Hello," I say, very quietly, even as some rational part of me demands to know what I am doing, hisses at me that *this is not right or Good, Lina.*

I'm briefly aware of the Voice shutting that rationality away in a chest in the corner of my mind and locking it there with a grim smile. My hesitations fall away like leaves in an autumn gust, replaced by glee. This moment is what I yearned for in my dreams for so very long. And yet I cannot help but think that perhaps I *have* seen this creature before…but the memory slips through my fingers like silky water.

The Imugi bows its head slightly, so its eyes are closer to my own, swimming with gold. *"Shin Lina,"* it murmurs. *"My name isss Sonagi. I am the mother of my kind. I am as old as the starsss in the sssky, and as wisse as the eternal wavess of the ocean. I have come, my daughter, to offer you my aid."*

"Your aid?" I whisper. "But how are you here? The Imugi live within Jeoseung, I thought…"

"We have ssspent centuriesss in the realm of the dead, it is true. But we have come to crave the light. Tonight is a very special night for us, Child of Venom. It is the end of our sshadow-home."

"You mean…" My thoughts are slow. Sluggish. "You will return to Iseung?" The thought should send horror through me, I know, but I feel only a growing curiosity. "Why?"

Sonagi seems to smile—her mouth parts revealing dark gums from which I know front fangs can emerge. *"A Prophecy, daughter. A Prophecy and a promise. Accept my offer of aid, and my knowledge will be yoursss. I will tell you all, if only you allow me to pledge you my allegiance, if only you allow me to help you reclaim this kingdom. We are the sssame, you and I—creatures of fangss and fury. Let me fight by your ssside."*

I open my mouth to agree, for how can I not? We are the same, Sonagi and I. We are kindred souls. We bear the same scales.

Yet a single name swims through my foggy mind. A name that is bright and beautiful with love and friendship. The chest in which my rationality is locked rattles. Fists pound on the wood, a voice that sounds suspiciously like mine screaming to be let out. "Does— does Rui know that the Imugi have left Jeoseung?" I whisper hoarsely, beginning to realize the enormity of this development. I still feel no fear, not of the Imugi, but the horror of my reaction to it has begun to seep out of that trunk.

At the mention of Rui, Sonagi's eyes narrow to slits. *"Call for me, daughter, and I will come,"* the serpent whispers before slithering off the roof and disappearing into the darkness. Lightning flashes once, twice. But she is gone.

It is early dawn when Rui arrives in my giwajip, staggering out of the corridor of darkness ashen-faced and haggard. Somehow, I know that he is about to arrive before he does. It's a tugging in my chest, leading me to where I sense he will appear. It is an alert of his impending presence. Prepared, I am leaning against the door of Eunbi's bedroom, an empty bottle of *Sallinna* in my hand. Rui sent the Northern wine to the giwajip before my arrival as a welcoming gift.

Getting drunk is quite impossible. It is an effect of my transformation, I suppose. I feel only a slight buzz despite draining almost the entire bottle of *Sallinna*. I narrow my eyes at Rui as the air ceases its undulation. He wears the same clothes as yesterday. His black hanbok, though, is wrinkled. His hair, usually sleek and straight, is disheveled. I think I see spots of mud dotting the fabric of his robes.

"Lina," he says wearily, bracing a hand on the wall as if to support himself. "Good morning."

I say nothing. My throat is tight with horror. Last night, an Imugi came to me—in Iseung—and I did not fight it. Instead, I smiled. I felt…*joy*. And the worst part is that I want her to return. Sonagi. But to wish so is wrong. I do not understand why I did not feel fear. I do not understand her words. *A Prophecy and a promise*.

I cannot wait for Rui to choose his time anymore. Too much has happened, and I know that everything—everything is somehow interconnected.

The secrets and the serpents. There is a link, connecting them.

"Why did you not come yesterday? What happened in Gyeulcheon?" The words that come from my lips are sharp and bitter. "Tell me, Rui. Tell me today." *Does it have something to do with Sonagi? Tell me or I fear I shall go mad.*

"I'm sorry, little thief." Rui's mouth tightens. "I would have sent word, but the palace had to be made ready for the staff's return from the Little Palace."

"So you were *cleaning*." My words are flat with disbelief. Of all the pathetic excuses… "Rui."

He swallows, throat bobbing. "Is Eunbi awake?"

"No." I take a swig from the bottle. Only a few drops of wine wet my tongue. "Tell me the truth about what has been happening. I will wait no longer, Pied Piper."

Something sharp pierces my chest. A strong, bitter emotion—but it is not my own. It is as if the emotion is coming from *outside* my body and forcing its way in. I blink, taken aback, but my focus soon shifts to Rui as he makes a sound between a soft gasp and a scoff.

"Pied Piper," he repeats quietly, and I realize too late that I've hurt him. I remember the light in his eyes when I'd called him by his true name for the first time. That light has dimmed now.

"Rui," I amend quietly, the bottle falling to my side, but the damage has been done. "Rui, I..."

"That is not a nickname I chose for myself," he says wearily. "Nor is this the life I would have chosen for this kingdom or the usage I would have chosen for Manpasikjeok." He runs a hand through his hair. "I am sorry, little thief, but I must return to Gyeulcheon immediately. Dire matters call for my attention. I have no time to spare." He attempts to meet my eyes, but I am staring at a small fleck on the column of his throat.

A fleck of red.

Dokkaebi bleed gold.

And the stolen humans...

The dark stains on his hanbok are not flecks of mud at all.

"I saw an Imugi last night." Each word is bitten out, brittle and blunt. I stare at the spots of scarlet, heart pounding. "She came to me. She spoke with me."

Rui flinches. *"What?"*

I say nothing, staring at him steadily, waiting for him to explain. Fury beats in my body like a drum, hot and furious. And just as that fury begins to beat louder and louder, edging toward a frustrated web of hurt and hatred...

Rui's face drains of blood and he staggers, actually *staggers*, backward. "Lina," he whispers, as if I've shot him. "Lina, you must tell me where it appeared... What it said..." His chest rises and falls with a startling unevenness. "What did it say to you?"

That she wishes to aid me. That the serpents will soon leave their death-home. The words do not pass my lips, though. They will not, as long as he continues to look at me with such horror, as if *I* summoned Sonagi. As if I am a cohort of the Imugi simply because I share their scales.

And although Rui's expression is one of shock, I cannot help but suspect that the shock is mostly due to the Imugi's conversation with me—not the presence of one of the serpentine creatures on Iseung. "Tell me what happened last night first," I say hollowly. "A truth in exchange for a truth, a bargain. You enjoy those, don't you? Games and tricks?"

This is another game.

And I know how to play.

Achara didn't need to play these foolish games.

I ignore the Voice. Rui has regained some control over his expression, stark shock melting into cold nonchalance with a hint of icy offense. "My bargains tend to have much higher stakes, little thief. And I am not a child in need of frivolous amusement."

Iseul's advice comes back to me. *"Then you must hold him to that promise. Remind him of it at the most* opportune *times."*

"No?" I croon, peeling myself off the wall and slowly making my way toward him. Rui is still, so very still, as I run a hand up his chest. My fingers brush against the speck of red blood as I snake my hand around his throat so that it cups his neck. I rise onto my tiptoes and slant my lips so they hover just above his ear. "A secret for a secret, Rui," I whisper. His jaw works as I slowly step back, idly toying with the fabric of his hanbok. "You tell me yours and I'll tell you mine."

As quick as an adder, Rui's fingers close tightly around my wrist, halting me from continuing to play with his robes. His fingers are ice-cold around my skin. His eyes flash, and his mouth tightens. I stand rigidly, my breathing uneven, as Rui angles his face down toward mine. His dark hair falls around us like a curtain of shadow. My eyes fixate on his smile—it is thin and razor-sharp. A wolf's smile.

"Tempting," he murmurs, still holding my wrist. "Why don't you start us off, little thief? Beginning with what the Imugi said to you." Each word, although soft, is carefully aimed. Rui leans closer to me, and his lips brush my cheekbones, my jaw. I close my eyes as he smiles against my skin and places a featherlight kiss on my neck.

Heat and desire bloom within my body. Rui has taken the advantage. This simply won't do.

Summoning a coy little smile, I sidestep him. The absence of his touch is palpable, yet I ignore it as I say, "That wasn't the deal." Each step is delicate and graceful as I circle him slowly, a hand placed between his sharp shoulder blades. I pause before him and twine my fingers through his tangled hair. My eyes snag on the splotch of blood as I kiss the column of his throat, where I have leveled a blade so many times. Rui makes a sound that is halfway between a groan and a sigh of irritation as he tips his head back, eyes fluttering closed.

Triumph is sweet on my tongue as I slant my lips against his, my touch light and teasing. Rui's hands drift to my waist, tugging me closer, and I can feel his lust as I press my body to his. He backs against the wall, and I lock him in by placing one of my hands on the smooth wood. He will not escape me, not this time.

Chara and Chryse would be so proud.

Iseul, too.

His lips are hot against mine, hot and hungry. But I tease him still, knowing full well that he wants—needs—more. As he deepens the kiss, I pull away so my lips only brush against his, the miniscule distance between us seeming to stretch out for miles upon miles.

Rui breathes unsteadily, his throat bobbing. Color has risen in his cheeks, his lips are glossy. Every part of him seems tense, ready to strike, desire battling determination.

He is right where I want him.

"Tell me," I whisper against his lips. I can still taste him, sparkling sugar and winter winds. "Tell me, *nae sarang.*"

Tell me, my love.

The term of endearment widens Rui's eyes, and his hands flex at his side. Thunderstorms of emotion roll in his eyes, dark and gray.

I watch him avidly. He is in my grasp, I know he is. Rui's lips part, and I know that this is it...

...and my bedroom door swings open.

I whirl around, my face heating as Eunbi—bleary-eyed and tousle-haired—stares at Rui and me. She rubs her eyes groggily and yawns. "Hello," she mumbles sleepily, still rubbing her eyes. "Is it time to go?"

For the first time in years, I feel a flare of intense annoyance at my little sister. But at the same time I feel relief—relief that is not my own—and I turn to see that Rui is already pushing himself off the wall, all languid grace and indolent smirks. "It certainly is."

Am I feeling *Rui's* emotions? How is that even possible? The shock of it quells my frustrations and replaces them with confusion. Hesitancy. "Rui, I felt—"

His eyes widen slightly, and I think he might wince.

But Eunbi is running to me, flinging herself forward and squeezing her arms around my waist tightly enough that I can barely breathe. "Goodbye, Lili," she says, squeezing me. "I love you. I love you *so much.*"

I'm forced to swallow my bewilderment as I kneel down so I'm eye level with her, and ruffle her hair. "Goodbye, little sister," I say softly, returning her embrace. "We'll see each other again soon."

"When I'm a princess," Eunbi whispers slyly. "And the bad man is dead."

I grin, even as something twists hard in my chest. "Yes."

She hugs me again, hard, and skips over to Rui. He takes her tiny hand in his as the air begins to ripple and shimmer, revealing the hallway of shadow. "Farewell, Lina," he says quietly over his shoulder.

"Rui, wait—"

"Do not speak to the serpents—although I am sure you already know that." His concerned, wary tone suggests the opposite, and I fight back a flinch. "I would instead advise for you to run away very quickly, should you spot another. I'll return to speak with you of these matters in more depth quite soon."

He can't leave. Not yet. "Rui, I think I felt—I think I felt *you*—"

In the split second before the shadows consume him, I think I hear him inhale sharply. I think he starts to say my name. But then he is gone, and I am alone.

INTERLUDE

The Dokkaebi emperor knows he should have told her of the thread connecting them, joining them.

But he could not. Not when she does not know how…wretched he is. How foolish, to have made this bargain with the Imugi. He felt her anger, how sharp it was. How it tasted, for a moment, like hatred. A hatred that quickly passed, one born in the moment, dwindling within seconds, but…it was deserved.

To have told her then would have been selfish. Attempting to fix a wound with a single stitch. Cheating, for his own comfort.

But he will have to tell her soon. This, he knows.

Sitting on the smooth stone of the garden's fountain, Rui watches as Lina's younger sister chases a blue butterfly around the very spot where Lina carved out Wang Jiwoon's heart. The girl is happier than he's seen her in a long while. Eunbi is always cheerful, but the visit to Lina's—even with its tribulations—has rejuvenated the girl.

The Gyeulcheon moons are warm and bright in a cloudless sky. It is an effort to keep the sky a pure, happy shade of cyan when the emperor feels nothing but a storm gathering in his mind and heart, spurred on by exhaustion, guilt, and anxiety. But his people, newly returned from the Little Palace, cannot suspect anything amiss. He is worried enough about them finding a spot of blood he and the circle forgot to scrub clean. So the sky must remain cloudless today.

Rui sighs and massages the bridge of his nose wearily. Lina spoke to the Imugi. If he were to place a macabre sort of wager, he would bet that it was Sonagi who approached her.

This year's tithe, paid for nothing. All those people, taken by him for nothing. *Nothing.*

Grief brackets deep lines around his mouth, and Rui closes his eyes. For a moment, it is all he can do to suppress a roar of unadulterated fury. Of rage and shame and terror.

In another world, perhaps this broken treaty would be a twisted sort of relief. A severed treaty means no more tithe, no more Pied Piper. But Rui's head is spinning with nightmare after nightmare, and what he feels is anything but *relief.*

His circle is currently deep in discussion within the throne room, and perhaps he should be in there, as well. But their bickering will only agitate him, as will their animosity toward Lina. She did not seek Sonagi; Sonagi sought her. Although the circumstances are concerning—and extraordinarily so, to the point where Rui very much wishes to smack his head against something very hard— he cannot believe that Lina is…Imugi. Yes, she has their traits, but she is still *Lina*. She will not be harmed unless he allows it, and he will *never* allow it.

For they are soul-stitched.

To be soul-stitched is to be forever joined, forever linked. A thing so rare that it is almost mythical. For the immortal Dokkaebi, the idea of it is even more laughable than marriage. Being bound to a singular soul forever? When forever has the potential to be literally forever, it is extraordinarily unlikely.

Rui himself would even doubt it, if not for what he *felt.* The stitching, the joining. Lina's strong emotions, radiating off her skin and digging deep into his own. This connectedness is what the myths speak of. The soul-stitched are said to be able to find each other anywhere in the world, if they only follow the red thread. If he concentrates, he can feel it…a tugging in his chest, leading him out of Gyeulcheon and into the Sunpo streets. When their connection grows, Kang told him, the thread will one day be visible upon command.

He swallows hard.

Soul-stitched. It's synonymous with *meant-to-be*. It is permanent. Even if they tried, they would never be able to escape each other. He is fated to her, and she to him. Forever.

In any other circumstance, he would be delighted. Lina, with her flashing eyes and wicked smiles. Lina, who taunts and teases and presses daggers to his throat. She is…extraordinary.

But the Imugi are on Iseung. The treaty has been broken. Another war could be brewing on the horizon. And his circle is inside, debating what to do. Debating how Lina is involved. What the Imugi want with her.

"Rui." Kang has approached his emperor, entirely unnoticed. Hesitantly, he sits beside him, noting how Rui tracks Eunbi and the fluttering blue butterfly with a desolate expression.

"Kang," Rui replies, glancing at him sharply. Kang is wearing an expression that Rui likes to call his *apologies for what's to come* expression. Rui manages a sharp, sardonic smile that's all teeth, masking his growing sadness and unease. "Let me guess. You bring ill tidings."

"Rui," Kang says simply, "we cannot afford another war."

Silence. Eunbi is farther away now. "I know."

"We need to speak to Lina." Kang is careful to say this without emotion. Rui will take it better this way, when it is only the facts. When it is impersonal. He will be angry, yes, but he will listen. "We need to learn what she knows. If she's involved. There's a possibility, Rui, that she is. She has their scales."

Rui swallows hard. His spittle tastes sour. "She is not like them. We would not be soul-stitched if she were like them."

"That is not necessarily true." Kang holds the gnarled wood of his staff tightly as he takes a deep breath, bracing himself for what he must admit next. "The soul-stitched in history, although few, vary in fate. Some soul-stitches are formed between true loves.

Others are formed between mortal enemies."

Rui's blood grows cold. "You did not mention this before."

"I hoped I would not have to." Kang sighs as his king makes a noise of anger low in his throat. "You are fated to be a part of each other's lives forever, Rui. The only question is how. As lovers? Or as enemies? We must know the answer. Which is why we must pay Lina a visit tonight."

Silence. When Rui does not reply, Kang quietly takes his leave. His emperor will agree, in the end.

In the gardens, Rui watches as Eunbi chases after the butterfly. She never catches it, though. It's always just out of her hopeful reach.

CHAPTER SEVENTEEN

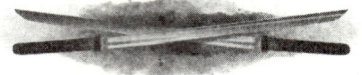

I try my best to shove Rui and the Imugi from my mind as I scour the streets for Son Wooseok, but it is nearly impossible. My mind roars with shock, and it is difficult to track the boy, as I have two... *fits* where my senses become unregulated and my limbs turn to putty. Twice, I have to stumble into alleyways, where I huddle and whimper until the horrible sensations pass. But my horror stays.

Imugi, on Iseung, seeking the fulfillment of a Prophecy.

Seeking *me*.

Seeking to pledge their allegiance, to help me reclaim Sunpo.

"Call for me, daughter, and I will come."

It is a perverse twist on the words Rui uttered as he gave me this ring.

But there is no denying that I itch to summon her, although I know that to do so is—dangerous. Wrong. That to do so is to create a rift between myself and Rui, or deepen the one that has been growing since the night in the Boneburrow.

I am trying so hard to be Good. And yet...

Yet there is that terrible curiosity boiling within me, and a longing to reunite with the creature, to speak to her once again. To wield her power by my side in my reclaiming of this kingdom. The Claws, the Legs, even the Feathers, and the Bills—these are the easy parts. But the Crest and the Crown...

Their influence over this kingdom runs deeper than I want. Their *power* runs deeper than I want. And as much as I hate to admit it, that power still lingers over me. It is hidden under the hatred and fury, but it is still there. The fear. The *hurting*. If I had the Imugi, I would be even stronger than I am now, and that pathetic trepidation would be trampled in the dirt.

But no. It is all I can do to cling to rationality, to remind myself that I must not talk to the serpents, that there is more at play than I have been permitted to understand. That the Imugi are evil, enemies of the gods I treasure, and of the emperor I cherish.

But...Sonagi did not feel wicked, not to me. I remember the kinship, the sense of *belonging* that grew when I was close to her. To feel such a thing, I know, must be wrong.

Yet it felt so right—and that is what unnerves me. How can I feel this for an enemy of the gods? Does this make me their enemy as well? My vision blurs and my throat tightens. Perhaps... Perhaps I should stop praying to them, the deities I love, the pantheon I have worshipped since I was a child.

Perhaps it is what they would want.

An hour under the hot sun passes until I catch a glimpse of who I suspect is Wooseok. I'm standing in the shadows of a Fingertrap alleyway, an alleyway Claw patrols typically tend to pass on their day routes. Even as the routes have changed with the growing threat of my attacks, this particular corner is necessary to pass in order to leave the Fingertrap and head into the Coin Yard.

He comes, head ducked, eyes moving from side to side. He's holding a dagger, shoulders hunched, defensive. He's scared. There are no other gray-clad Claws with him. No Legs, either. Just him against the world.

Bruises line his face, his bare arms. Sympathy and anger thickens in my throat. Son Wooseok cannot be more than fifteen, with scraggly black hair and a small nose.

I don't want to startle him. So instead, I cough—lightly—and his eyes snap to me immediately. He halts a few feet away.

"Son Wooseok?"

"What's it to you?" he asks. He's nervous. In my gat and cloak, I look like a man. And men who lurk in alleyways are rarely harmless. My raspy voice likely is not helping, either.

"Do you have time to talk?"

"Why?" Wooseok's dagger is out, clenched tightly in his hand. The crane on his forearm is ugly, careless. Like somebody took pleasure in creating the tattoo with pain. "Are you a buyer? I-I haven't got anything to give you yet. The L-Legs are dead, so we can't arrange deals."

"I'm not here to buy anything." From my pocket, I pull out a jade bracelet. He catches it with a surprised expression.

"What..." Warily, but with the unmistakable air of intrigue, Wooseok steps into the alleyway with me. "What is this for?"

I'm eyeing his bruises. They're swollen, mottled. His lip is split. "Those look bad," I say, and reach back into my cloak pocket before pulling out a vial. After checking to make sure it's the right one, I give it to him. "A salve. Put this on, and it will grant you some relief."

Wooseok swallows as he holds the vial tight in the same hand as the bracelet. "Why are you giving me these things?"

This is the hard part.

He could run back to Kalmin. Tell him that Shin Lina is the one killing his Blackbloods. Ruin the surprise, the final blow. Or he could join me, and make quick work of the Feathers and Bills. I sift through the possible words, turning them over, choosing carefully. There are speeches, there are paragraphs of urges to join my side, but what comes out is: "Kalmin used to beat me, too."

Wooseok freezes. "What?"

"Oftentimes, he let Claws do it. As a reward. Man Jisu, and the like. Those beatings came after a mistake. But with Kalmin..." My throat works as I sink into the memories—falling on his office floor, hitting my chin on his desk's rim on the way. Being kicked in the stomach, hard. My face slamming into the wall. "It was unpredictable. That was the worst part. Never knowing when it was coming. That's one of the things I'm most grateful for now, I think.

I'm not living in terror of his next beating. I'm out." I remove my gat, meeting his eyes. "My name is Lina. I can help you, Wooseok, if you let me."

Recognition is dawning behind Wooseok's red-rimmed eyes. "I know you," he says slowly. "You were the prisoner. The Reaper." His body is tense, but he's not making to run. "We thought you were dead. But you're...you're alive." Suddenly, his face contorts in anger. I'm not expecting it—I blink, muscles going taut. "Why did you let him come back?" All of a sudden, angry tears are running down his face and I know—gods, I know they must sting his open cuts.

There's no question who this "him" is. "Because I want to torture him," I reply quietly. "Just as he has tortured us."

Wooseok falls silent. He wipes his eyes with the back of his hand and winces as he grazes a bruise.

"I started with the Claws and the Legs. Those are all but gone. Next are the Feathers and Bills. I want the whole Crane dead, and I'd like your help to do it. In return, I'll give you safety. Somewhere to sleep peacefully, knowing that you won't be beaten bloody the next morning. I want to give you this, Son Wooseok." An apology. For bringing Kalmin back. For the pain he's suffered at the hands of the Blackbloods. "Will you take it?"

"You're the one killing them?" Wooseok asks. "It's been you?"

"Does that upset you?"

Wooseok shakes his head slowly. "No..." He takes a deep breath. "You mean it? You'll give me safety?"

"I will."

"Swear it." Wooseok sticks out his hand, looking stubborn and scared all at once. "Swear it on your life."

I reach out to grasp his hand in mine. "I swear it on my life," I vow. We shake once, twice. Wooseok straightens and nods.

"What do you want me to do?"

"Can you be quick? Can you be stealthy?"

He juts out his chin. "Easily. Sometimes Kalmin can't find me. I've learned to be quiet."

"Good." I reach into my cloak and pull out the other vial, freshly stolen from a dank Boneburrow shop. "I want you to poison the Feathers and Bills," I say softly, turning the flask of aconitum coreanum around and around, admiring the shrub's dark, powdered roots. Rui has often said that poison is a coward's tool, a point where he and I disagree. It's a clever killing, requiring sleight of hand. "Do the two standings still take drinks together every night?" When I was working as a Bill, I was frequently excluded from these events. Not that I minded in the least.

"Every night at eight," Wooseok confirms, eyes on the aconitum coreanum.

"How many are currently out on missions?"

"Kalmin's pulled all his higher ranks back," the boy replies. "Ever since you began striking. The Feathers and Bills are on a temporary hiatus."

It's almost too good to be true. All the Feathers and Bills in one place. I hand Wooseok the lethal poison.

"He doesn't care about the Claws, though. There are only four of us left—he's still sending us out. I think he wants us to be attacked. So that he can gather clues and find you." Wooseok swallows. "He was...when he saw that his Legs... I've never seen him like that. He was screaming for hours, trashed at least four rooms. And then he—he found me."

My stomach roils. "I'm sorry," I whisper, but the boy doesn't seem to hear.

"I mean—you killed *all* of them. How did you do that? How many people are working for you?"

I don't say anything. I don't need to. Wooseok is still speaking enough for the two of us, words running like a rapid river. "He would never admit it, but he's scared. At night, he holes himself up with Asina and stations Bills outside and inside the room. I have to taste all the foods before he eats. He knows something is coming, something big. And he's working hard to find the killer. He dragged the Legs' bodies in for examination…" Wooseok's face is slightly green.

"He won't find me until I want him to," I reassure him. "Here." I press the poison into his hand. "This works within the hour. Its scent is very faint. Even the Feathers shouldn't be able to smell it." The Feathers, although heist-men, also deal in subtle killings such as poison…and as such, have incredibly sharp noses. "Go into the kitchen and mix it into the wine bottles. If there are any Feathers, or any Bills you think might join my side, anybody who should be spared…"

Wooseok closes his hand around the vial. His eyes are very dark. "There aren't. There never were."

"You're sure?"

"I am. Because I've never felt more alone than I do when I'm in the palace," the boy replies tremulously. "Ever since you left, I'm the one he beats."

I take a shaking breath. *Gods.* "Then are there any Feathers or Bills you have a specific vendetta against?"

Wooseok bobs his head and wipes his nose with his arm. "Yoo Hoonmin and Lee Yoochun. A Feather and a Bill." He spits out their names with such vehemence that I don't need to ask for further details to know that the two have hurt him. Badly.

"If you're able, plant this vial in one of their rooms when they're drinking. It'll throw suspicion off you for at least a while. A murder-suicide is unlikely, but Kalmin will pause to consider it. Don't be the one to find the bodies. If you can't escape right away, wait until your patrol the next night to run. Kalmin will think you've been killed."

"Where do I go?"

"Find Im Yejin, the shipsmith. Check Haewon's Fabrics, or The Gambling Toad in the Boneburrow. The password this week is *mul naengmyeon*. Tell her that you're with the Reaper. An alliance."

Wooseok nods, suddenly breathless. "Do I do it…tonight?"

"If there's an opportunity. If not, wait. Don't make any hasty decisions." My heart pounds as I imagine what could happen if the boy is caught. "But no longer than a day before the Night of the Red Moon." That night is seven nights from now. It should be plenty of time for Wooseok to find an opening.

"Why then?"

"Because that's the night the Crown dies. At the gala. He *is* still planning on hosting it, isn't he?" From what I know of Kalmin, I suspect he is. He wants to get his way in everything. Even if the sky poured blood and the earth shook, he would still throw the gala simply because he had once wanted to.

Confirming my theory, Wooseok nods. "I overheard him speaking to Asina. He thinks that to not throw the gala is to admit… defeat, somehow. Even if all the Bills and Feathers are dead along with the Legs and Claws, I think he'll still host it out of spite. He's inviting the entire kingdom. Even the Pied Piper. Kalmin also thinks it would be a good place to draw out whoever's killing his men."

I can't help but smirk. "I thought so."

Wooseok hesitates, shifts from foot to foot. "What if I fail?"

"You won't," I reply with no room for debate. Wooseok is terrified. But soon, with the vial, he'll realize that he has power in his pocket. And that hurt will turn into cold, icy focus. Wooseok will kill the Bills and Feathers for me. Of that I have no doubt.

The beaten boy nods once, twice. And then, tucking the poison and jade bracelet into the pocket of his pants, he turns and scurries out of the alleyway.

· · ·

By the time Haemosu's chariot has reached the peak of the sky, I am hungry, tired, overheated. Despite my success at recruiting Son Wooseok, my churning confusion and shock still torment my mind and body. Exhausted, with the afternoon heat blistering my skin underneath my heavy cloak, I duck into the Moonlit Hare and flop onto a cushion in the corner.

The jumak is empty at this time of the day save for me and an elderly man tucked away near a small window. And, of course, for Ryu Seojin, the boy from the Moonlit Hare, and Song Iseul's friend. The time has come for me to seek him out.

I twirl a yeokun between my fingers as Seojin serves the man a small cup of broth and turns to me. His expression gives nothing away. It is as calm as a still pond. He was expecting me. Iseul must have told him.

"Ryu Seojin," I say as he approaches me, knowing that the hood of my cloak and angle of my chin conceal everything but my razor-sharp smile.

His dark eyes are solemn as he takes the cushion across from me. "Reaper of Sunpo." His voice is as hoarse as it was on the street last night.

"How," I ask curiously, tilting my head, "does a serving boy at the Moonlit Hare ignite the Blackbloods' hatred? Have you killed one of them?"

Seojin leans forward, his forearms on his crossed legs. His expression is serious. "How," he returns levely, "does a teenage assassin make it out of the Talons' massacre alive when the others died?"

My stomach twists but I manage to maintain my composure, still rolling the yeokun between my fingertips. There is no accusation in his tone, but there is—carefully hidden under precisely measured words—a small layer of grief, cracked and chipped. "You knew a Talon," I say slowly, focusing on the feeling of the coin on my skin and not on the way my skin has begun to grow clammy.

Seojin blinks. A small flinch, nothing more, but it tells me all I need to know. Guilt twists my tongue for a brief moment. I am not the only one who has lost them.

"Yes," Seojin finally says a moment later. "I knew a Talon." He rubs his chest in what looks like an involuntary gesture, as if to try to soothe his hurting heart. "You asked why the Blackbloods hate me. I knew a Talon." A bitter, hoarse laugh that dies as quickly as it is born.

I choke on guilt and mask my disconcertion by flicking the yeokun toward him. Seojin catches the bronze coin neatly, nimbly. "For a few minutes of your time," I manage to say. Seojin nods, mouth thinning, and pockets the coin.

The heat of the jumak has become stifling. I pull away my hood, shrugging off the sweat-soaked cloak and revealing myself to Ryu Seojin. He blinks, eyes catching on the teardrop scar. For a long moment, neither of us speaks. My mouth is filled with questions, but I cannot bring myself to ask them. *Who? Who did you know? Who did you lose because I fell into a trap?*

"Iseul says I can trust you," Seojin finally says, dragging his stare back up to my eyes. "But I'm not so sure."

I study him, noting his suspicion, his hesitancy. Finally, I force my tongue to move. "You asked me how I survived. It was a heist."

Seojin goes still.

"Konrarnd Kalmin wanted the Reaper. He lured me away into a trap. When I returned to the palace"—I swallow hard—"the Talons were dead. Kalmin killed my friends and then stole me, forced me to work for him for a year. But not anymore. I'm going to kill him, Ryu Seojin. He is going to die by my hand." I flex my fingers to hide their trembling. "I'm collecting alliances. People who will stand by me when I reclaim Sunpo on the Night of the Red Moon. Iseul is one. Are you another?"

Seojin is silent. Already I have the sense that he is one who can communicate more through a moment of silence than a plethora of words. He looks at me steadily, long enough that I begin to grow uncomfortable and fight the urge to shift in my seat. Seojin's lips flatten and his brows furrow, but a moment later, his face is smooth. Indecipherable. When he finally speaks, it is quietly. "My brother always spoke fondly of you," he says, and the words turn my blood cold.

"I knew a Talon."

"W-what was his name?" The question tumbles clumsily from my mouth, which has become dry and tastes of sickness.

Perhaps his brother was a Talon in the loosest sense of the word—a trainee, a sponsor. But I feel a terrible sensation unfurling in the back of my mind, a horrible knowledge, something that is more than a suspicion. My heart is beating so fast that my ribs begin to ache. The jumak swims before my eyes and I blink hastily, refocusing on Seojin.

"His true name, given to him by our mother, is a secret that I still protect," he replies. "But I know he went by Sang among his comrades."

Sang.

And then the world is falling, falling around me. I stare at Seojin, noticing the details I missed before. The angles of his face, the strength of his brow, the faint freckles along his cheekbones. His hair is dark and his eyes are a deep, solemn brown—not the warm hazel of Sang's—but the familial resemblance is suddenly clear.

And as Seojin inclines his head, a slant of sunlight brushes against those eyes, turning them—for a split-second—the same color as Sang's.

I know my face has crumpled, for I cannot mask the surge of sorrow and guilt and grief that rushes into my chest. Sang had a brother.

Ryu Seojin. Ryu.

Family names weren't important in the Talons, not when the

name of our gang represented our found-family, our lives, our loved ones. I clung to mine, Shin, only for Eunbi. I never learned Sang's last name. The secrecy came with him being a spy. I'd long suspected that Sang wasn't even his real name, either—but I didn't know, didn't even suspect, that he had a family. A brother. I press a hand to my mouth and blink away tears.

And what was it Iseul said?

"You do lack your brother's acute awareness. It's rather concerning."

"After he died," Seojin says, mouth stiff, "Kalmin found records stating his family name. He found me. I was training to be a healer. As revenge, I'm barred from the school. I owe Kalmin a grand sum every month, if only to keep my life. My every move is watched. I'm unable to leave the kingdom. Although I notice that my shadow is missing today." Seojin's stare is coolly knowing, and I try—frantically—to compose myself. I try not to see the lines of grief underneath his even expression.

"I killed him," I manage to rasp, still tasting tears in the back of my throat. "You should—leave. While you can. I can give you—funds—"

"No." Seojin's voice is suddenly fierce. "This is my kingdom. If you're reclaiming it for the Talons, I will be here."

"You sound like him." The words leave my mouth before I can stop them.

His pain is fleetingly clear upon his face, and I feel ill. But then he composed himself.

"I paid Kalmin with a golden pocket watch this morning," he says, in a clipped voice. "I've bought another month of life. But Kalmin wouldn't complain if one of his Blackbloods killed me. He keeps me alive to torture me, but it'll grow old soon."

I remember the men from the other night, staring after him with murderous expressions, and my stomach roils. "They won't kill you," I snarl.

"Actually, they will," says Seojin blandly. "Three of them have already tried. But my brother didn't leave me completely defenseless. I don't like to fight, but I know how to defend myself. I escaped, but they'll come for me again. Three Claws visit here every night," he adds flatly, as if we're discussing the weather, "just to frighten me."

Three Claws. I have a growing suspicion I know who those *three of them* are. They're the other remaining Claws, and Man Jisu is among them. "Tonight," I say with quiet fury, "they'll die." I will do for Seojin what I could not do for Sang.

Protect him.

Seojin's lips twitch, but there's no mirth in his eyes. Just a deep, unending sadness that he cannot hide from me. Not when my eyes contain the same. "Sang told me you were ruthless, Shin Lina," he replies. "It was one of the things he loved about you."

Loved.

I swallow hard before that word is shoved away by a new realization. Iseul didn't tell him that night, but Seojin somehow knows my true name. He knows exactly who the Reaper is.

What I did.

The walls seem to close in around me, and the air is so hot, so thick, that I nearly gag on it. Shaking, I abruptly rise to my feet. If I stay any longer, I will break completely.

But Seojin grabs my wrist, fingers tight on my skin. His hand is cool and smooth. Not like Sang's—warm and calloused and scarred. "Iseul told me that you know what she is," Seojin says in a voice of soft steel. "I'm a gentle person, Lina, and I don't like violence. But if you hurt Iseul, if you reveal her secret—I will kill you."

"She's already threatened that herself. But you don't need to worry." I swallow hard. "She's my friend."

He releases me. "Good," he says, and for the first time since I've met him, Ryu Seojin sounds pleased.

...

In an alleyway, I lean against the wall, blending into the shadows as I pant and pant and pant. Sang. Sang had a brother. Ryu Seojin. He didn't tell me. I didn't know. A brother. A *brother.*

Hurt sucks the air from my lungs and I struggle to breathe. Sang never told me he had a younger brother, he never even hinted at his existence. Why? To protect him?

I swallow bile as guilt stabs at my chest, its blade twisting deep.

Seojin lost Sang too. I didn't know... I didn't know that anybody else had lost him. I thought I had the—the *luxury* of being the only living person wounded by my mistake.

It's not your fault, Lina, Sang said. But had he known how his brother would pay for my mistake? Waiting on leering Blackbloods in a dingy jumak? Banned from studying healing? Fearing for his safety every night with no place to turn?

I bury my face in my hands. I did this.

And what will we do to fix it?

I lower my hands, trembling. *Go away.* But the Voice does raise a valid point. How dare the Blackbloods hurt what is left of Sang in this world. How dare they prey on Seojin. *Tonight,* I think to myself, but of course the Voice hears.

Will that be enough? Killing those men is child's play. The Voice yawns. **Surely we can do better to avenge Ryu Sang. What of her?**

Who? I ask before I can stop myself.

The Voice is silent as it shows me an image of a woman with bulging, fishy eyes and a cruel smile.

Asina.

The time isn't right, though. Feathers and Bills have to fall first.

But isn't that what Kalmin will expect? How about a twist?

I shouldn't be listening to the Voice. I know that. I know that.

It cannot be a Good decision to do so. But...

I have never been adept at resisting temptation. And the strategy that the Voice is offering me is deliciously dark. *Four birds with one stone.* I straighten, cold, cold fury clearing my head. *I see.*

Oh, how we'll savor it, the Voice whispers. **Let's have fun tonight, Lina.**

CHAPTER EIGHTEEN

Night has fallen, but it is still far from midnight. Leaning against the gnarled trunk of the willow tree in the dark, I narrow my eyes at the swaying green curtain that envelops me. I have been standing, waiting, for hours—nothing but a shadow, so still that my muscles have begun to ache, and I have begun to question whether or not I am even truly here. It is only the soft kiss of dry summer wind against the nape of my neck that assures me that my body still remains on Iseung, even when my thoughts are thousands upon thousands of miles away. My thoughts are in Gyeulcheon, chasing after Rui, longing for him to calm me with his silky voice—with a confession. For I am impatient and tired and utterly confused.

A stolen marketplace. A serpent from Jeoseung. A splatter of red blood. Emotions that are not my own. Secrets and silence and suspicion. I am so tired of begging for answers, so tired of stooping to threats and games to force his hand.

Perhaps I will never be able to fill the void that Achara, the beautiful artist, left behind. Perhaps the spark that we have will flicker out before it ever truly bursts aflame.

"*They told me she fell down the stairs. Her neck snapped.*" Rui's voice seems to stir on the summer wind, as haunted by grief as it had been in the gardens as he'd told me of his and Achara's ill-fated romance. At the time he spoke of the event, I felt only sympathy, sympathy and understanding, a beautiful feeling that the emperor and I were the same, shaped by our mistakes, carved by our regret. But now I feel a horrible envy unfurling in my chest, snaking around my ribcage.

Love like that never fades. He imagines we are her, when we are in his arms. But her hands were stained with paint and color. Ours are stained with blood.

I press my hands to my eyes, pushing until spots of light flare in my vision. I have never felt this toward Shuo Achara before. I should not start now.

I still mourn Sang, as Rui mourns Achara. His long hair symbolizes his grieving, just as the pain in my left leg symbolizes mine.

But he can cut his hair, for us. We cannot heal our leg.

I have listened to the Voice enough today. I will not continue to do so.

Yet deny it as I might, its words have wormed their way beneath my skin. I wish I could yank them from my flesh, these ideas that are not mine, but I cannot. I feel them, writhing beneath the surface.

I wonder, worriedly, which of my decisions they've influenced without me ever knowing.

Opening my eyes, I exhale a shaking breath, unable to escape the envy and self-doubt churning within me. Rui cares for me. I have never demanded more. We have known each other a short time. This envy is ridiculous. Achara is dead. They are both—

A movement at the main gate of the palace catches my eye. *Finally,* I think, letting the coldness of the hunt wash over me and mute my roaring thoughts.

Asina.

The sight of her brings hatred bubbling to my mouth, hot and blistering. My left leg sears with pain as I remember how she dug her knife into my skin and *twisted* it, that night when everything went to complete and utter shit. I grit my teeth and ignore the growing burn.

She looks the same. Tall and slender, her narrow face pale and dwarfed by her bulging black eyes. I sneer as Asina gestures to the Blackblood guards—white-clad Bills—who shift and allow her to pass onto the road. No doubt she has been sent off by Kalmin to terrorize some poor unfortunate, but she will never make it. Silently, I shadow her as she begins to head toward the heart of Fishtown, away from the outskirts.

She doesn't see me, completely oblivious to the danger on her heels. I savor her ignorance, unable to think of anything but that night I slipped into Unima Hisao's bedroom and found her, Kalmin's lackey, instead, smiling at me like a cat who just witnessed a juicy rodent be snatched up by a mousetrap. It was because of her that I hadn't reached the Talons in time. It is because of her that they are *dead*.

And tonight, she will be, too. I hope that in Yeomra's halls, Asina receives a special sort of torture from the dead Talons.

I smile, still unseen. This is the fun part, herding her toward the Moonlit Hare, where four birds will drop from one very violently thrown stone.

This. *This* is what I came to Sunpo for. *This* is what will take me one step closer to avenging the Talons. My gang, my friends, my family.

It becomes clear that Asina is taking a route toward the Boneburrow—specifically, toward the Dove Coop, likely to check to see if Iseul has returned. I slip off the road, fighting past the pain in my leg to push ahead of her. When Asina arrives at the Dove Coop, she won't find Song, but she'll find me. The golden gates loom into view, and I quickly vault over them, wincing only slightly as pain rockets up my left leg. Pleased by my stealth, I note that there are still no guards stationed anywhere in sight. Kalmin's resources are running dry.

I make my way to the grand white columns of the domed pleasure house. Asina will come to the front entrance, demanding

Iseul's presence. And I will be here.

Half-hidden in shadow, I wait the remaining ten minutes for Asina to arrive, leaning against a column. As I do, I wonder if Kalmin will even miss Asina. I hope that he does. Oh gods, I hope he does. I hope he sobs as I tear everything and everybody away from him. My head swims with anticipation. My hands itch. To keep them busy, I pick up a loose pebble from the ground, passing it back and forth between my fingers.

She's closer now. Closer. I can hear her steady breathing, the thump of her boots against the ground. My ears twitch as I expand my senses even further. I estimate that she will be at the gate in five minutes, and my guess proves correct. I watch as she slams open the gate, her face murderous. She withdraws her dagger from the belt of her stealth suit, stomping up the steps and striding toward the door. She does not see me.

I still my hands, willing myself not to be sick from the pure, blistering hatred that swarms in my stomach at such proximity to her. The undercurrent of trepidation at the sight of her. As Asina slams her fist against the door of the Dove Coop, shouting for Iseul to open up, I slip into the skin of the Reaper. Cold, cruel, and merciless, the Reaper has no time for any emotion such as fear.

And once I've settled into my skin, I chuckle. Low and rasping, it is a laugh that I know will send the woman freezing in her spot. Asina's back stiffens. She knows this laugh. This laugh once haunted the streets of Sunpo, carried on the wind to even the farthest corner of the kingdom.

"Asina," I croon, still leaning against the column. Slowly, I roll the pebble between my fingers. "It's been *so long.*"

Her fist slowly, so slowly, falls from the wood of the door. "You," she says, still facing the opposite direction.

"Who else?" I retort in a cold drawl, cocking my head and grinning. "Did you miss me?"

"*Shin Lina,*" Asina pants through clenched teeth, whipping

around. Her bulbous eyes blaze, her lips flap in outrage. *"You're meant to be dead."*

It is an effort to restrain myself enough to lure her to the Moonlit Hare instead. Every part of me screams to do it now—but the idea of four birds killed with one stone is so very appealing. So not here. Asina may intend to tell Kalmin of my return, but she'll chase me to her death first. She'll want the glory of killing me all to herself, and the praise that comes with it. Too bad that she won't receive it.

"And you," I say, stilling my fingers around the pebble, "are too slow."

With all my strength, I hurl the small rock toward her, knowing that when it hits her shoulder it will burn like a bullet. Although the small rock is not enough to debilitate her, it will hurt. As Asina's eyes widen even further, I launch myself into the night, sprinting through the Boneburrow—but pacing myself enough that she can track me to the Moonlit Hare. It's closer to midnight now. With any luck, I will run into the trio of Blackbloods—Rat, Hada, and Jisu—closer to the Fingertrap where the jumak is.

My boots thud on the uneven road as I weave through the kingdom, leading Asina on a less-than-merry chase. Her breathing is uneven and her lungs rattle in her chest as she struggles to keep me in view. I glance over my shoulder with a grin as I pass the Temple of Ruin and enter the Fingertrap. Asina growls, and I fight back a laugh at how graceless, how uncoordinated she looks as she sprints faster, stumbling over loose stones. Her nostrils flare with the effort of breathing as I increase my pace ever so slightly, shoving past denizens of Sunpo's night, ignoring the throbbing in my leg.

I have observed the rat pack's route—they will be up ahead of me by now, nearing the Moonlit Hare. That's them up there, the clump of shadows reeking of sweat and blood and drink. I smile, my teeth aching. *For Seojin,* I think as I sprint toward them, aware of Asina's furious shouts behind me. *For Sang.*

At the noise, the three turn, hands going to their weapons as they recognize Asina and spot the cloaked figure she's chasing through the night.

"Don't—just—stand there—" Asina pants as I whip past them before they can shake themselves from their shocked stupor. *"Catch—her!"*

Frantic to obey, three more feet pound the pavement behind me as I run, increasing my pace infinitesimally. I allow the men the idea that if they push themselves just a bit faster, I will be in hands' reach. My arms pump as I shoot past the Moonlit Hare, spotting Seojin staring out the window. His eyes widen.

For Sang.

Down a narrow street, past my giwajip, past where the Marketplace operates, and toward a rusted sewer grate. I speed up so that there is plenty of space between the four Blackbloods and me. With time to spare, I skid to a halt near the grate, kick it open, and drop down.

Two parallel sidewalks line a river of rushing brown. The stench is awful, and the walls crawl with bugs, scuttling atop the damp stone and chittering among one another. Knowing that my pursuers will soon see the open grate, I sink into shadow, holding my breath against the fumes. Some dark water splashes onto my boots as the current grows violent, carrying the waste of the city out toward the Yongwangguk Sea. I wonder what the sea god thinks of the unwelcome gifts we send into his abandoned ocean realm, turning sparkling blue water black and stench-ridden. Perhaps our disrespect is what drove the pantheon away to Okhwang, the sky kingdom. Perhaps they now watch from above as mankind destroys themselves and the world's gifts, for we are liberated to do so thanks to the gods' abandonment of our realm.

Perhaps they do not understand how much we need the orders of the gods, how mankind requires godly rule to save us from ourselves.

The thought is…*interesting*. Uneasily, I realize that the Voice takes note of it with malicious satisfaction.

"She's down there." A few minutes later, voices emerge from the grate above. Rat is the one speaking, for his voice is thready and squeaky. "In the sewer." He sounds disgusted.

"Out of my *way*." Asina's shadow falls onto the pavement close to me. "I go down first. You three come next. But the kill is mine, do you hear? *The kill is mine.*"

"Then why do we have to go down into the sewer?" Hada mumbles, and I can practically picture his jowls wobbling.

"To watch, Hada," Jisu says quietly, and I can hear the vile excitement in his tone. "We may watch."

With a noise of irritation and disgust, Asina drops down into the sewer. Her eyes roam the darkness, clearly attempting to adjust to the inky black. She does not see me, nor do the other three as their feet splash onto the puddles of the concrete. Silver flashes as Asina withdraws her dagger.

"Do you think she…" Jisu gestures to the sewer water, looking thoughtful.

"Don't be daft," Asina bites out, still scanning the walkways. "That girl survived Gyeulcheon. I'm willing to bet that she's the one who massacred Unima, the other Claws, and our Legs. I don't think a jump into the sewer would kill her. My guess is that she's waiting for us, somewhere in here."

Hada scratches at his receding hairline nervously. "Should we tell Kalmin?"

"No," Asina snarls. "Not yet. Not until she's well and truly dead."

"Are you sure? He might want to be the one to—"

"I said," she hisses, *"Not. Yet."*

"But, Asina—"

Hada and Asina are so wrapped up in their bickering that neither notice as I dart from the shadows, smile grimly, and shove Rat into the frothing waters before receding back into the darkness.

Rat screams, flapping his arms as the vile water takes him. *"I CAN'T SWIM! I CAN'T SW—"* He cuts off with a gurgle and disappears.

The remaining Blackbloods stare dispassionately at the water.

"He fell," says Jisu, sounding more annoyed than upset.

"How did he…" Hada blinks. "Huh?"

"She's here." Asina straightens, eyes flashing. "He was pushed. Oh, that *bitch*…"

"Watch your tongue." My voice cuts through the air, cold and sharp as I step out from the shadows only a few feet away from where they stand. Asina and the others go rigid as I tug off the hood of my cloak. "For I can think of many more words to describe *you*, Asina. And none so pleasant." I cluck my tongue as Asina lurches forward, her dagger in her hand. "I wouldn't do that," I say softly, and there is enough danger in my voice that she pauses, a vein pulsing in her temple.

"You—"

My lips twist into a smile as I summon my scales.

They unfold over my hands, creep up my neck. They emerge on the lines of my cheekbones and forehead. Diamond hard, they glitter in the shadows. I cock my head and my grin grows.

Asina makes a choking noise. Hada and Jisu gape. *"What are you?"* Asina demands in horror. The words remind me of another night, another adversary. Jiwoon had a similar reaction.

I'd cut out his heart.

"I'm a Talon," I say quietly, allowing myself to feel every droplet of rage coursing through my bloodstream.

They barely have time to blink before I strike.

Ignoring Asina, I leap toward Hada and Jisu first. Hada stumbles backward before his throat is gushing red. He falls, and Jisu curses, raising his knife against me. In vicious, violent motions he slashes toward me, spitting and snarling. A feral light is in his eyes, and a terrible delight. I dodge each attack and disarm him, aware that behind me, Asina is positioning herself to launch her own weapon at me. I hook my arms around Jisu's throat, and whirl around so that when Asina's dagger does fly, it hits him in the chest. He gurgles wetly, straining, twitching.

I remember the pleasure he'd taken in my suffering as I dump him into the sewer as well.

Asina withdraws another dagger, and when she hurls herself toward me, I nimbly dodge her attacks as she slashes once, twice, thrice. My movements are almost indolent, for I'm enjoying this, her comeuppance. I want to drag it out as much as possible. I sink into an easy pattern. Dodge, weave, smirk. Asina cannot possibly win this fight. She knows it. I know it.

I'm grinning now, cocky. Triumphant. "Tired?" I croon as Asina launches another attack, teeth bared, breathing heavily like some wild, wounded animal. "There's no harm in admitting defea—"

Asina growls, and in a sharp burst of speed, manages to bring the dagger close to my right elbow. And as I dodge…

The ground of the sewer is slippery. Even more so from the three large splashes as the Claws hit the water. My left leg twists peculiarly, and its wound sends a jolt of pain up the entire limb— enough that I stumble, momentarily weakened and lacking balance.

It's then that Asina strikes, hitting from behind with a vicious kick to my back that—in my disoriented state—sends me crashing to the ground. Shit. *Shit.*

This shouldn't be happening. I'm stronger. *I'm* the one with power. Yet I'm also the one spitting grime from my mouth as Asina places a heavy boot on my back. Rising would be easy, so terribly easy, but—

Asina's hand finds the back of my left leg, finds the exact spot where my scar—my wound—lies. "How's the leg?" she spits, and *digs* her fingers into the fabric of my suit, nails gouging the injury through the fabric, going *deep*. I scream as a burst of raw agony shoots through the muscle and hastily summon that impenetrable snakeskin to the skin of my leg, but it's too late. The wound hurts like the night I received it, and all of a sudden those godsdamned memories are flooding back to me. A palace stained with blood. A floor littered with corpses. The smell of death. The way my friends had already become stiff, limbs awkwardly rigid and so lacking life.

I'm groaning, fighting to see past the memories, fighting to maintain the armor of snakeskin around my neck as Asina yanks my head with a fistful of my hair and places the dagger against my throat. She's sawing, back and forth and back and forth, but the blade is no match against the scales.

They could vanish, though. Any moment, the scales could disappear and leave my throat gushing red.

Get up, snaps the Voice. **Get up.**

But I can't. I can't. Guilt and bitter regret are squeezing their iron grips around my body, and my vision swims. The noises of the sewer become louder, louder.

No. No. Not now, I think, but it's no use.

I can hear the waste moving with the water, trailing sludge and slime. The scuttling of roaches, their stomachs brushing against the walls as they move in zigzagging patterns. Festering waste fills my nostrils, a collection of unnamable filth. My throat constricts, tightening. Air. I need air. Fresh air. Real air.

Heaviness tightens my limbs, and I can feel my control over the snakeskin slipping. This attack of the senses has made me vulnerable in a way that could mean…death. True death, should my defenses slip.

I'm not ready to die.

Rui. I should call Rui. But the silver ring on my scrabbling, outstretched hand is so far away. I cannot move my arms. They are weights attached to my body, dragging me down.

It's almost laughable.

Shin Lina, dying in a sewer underneath Sunpo.

It doesn't need to be like this. There is one who could help us.

Sonagi.

No. No. Through the haze of pain and panic, I *know* that such a decision cannot be Good. The Voice…it guided me here to the sewers tonight for a reason. Perhaps this very one. To coax me toward a decision that feels as if it could be so right but is wrong…

So you want to die? The Voice, I can feel it prowling across my mind. The sensation is just as tangible as Asina's knife working futilely against my throat. Of the world's assault against my senses. **Any moment, now, she will try something new. The leg is the clear weak point. She'll attack it once more. And when she does, our defenses will fall.**

And you'll never have won the fight against Konrarnd Kalmin.

My head slams back down into the ground. I feel Asina panting, reaching for my leg. My snakeskin there is vanishing. I cannot hold it. I cannot…

I cannot die.

To have come all this way for nothing… I cannot yet die.

The Voice smiles.

"*Sonagi,*" I gasp into the slick stones of the sewer, my tongue clumsy and mouth dry. *"I summon you."*

CHAPTER NINETEEN

Asina laughs mockingly, trailing her hand against my leg. "Did you say something, *scum*?"

I close my eyes. The world has slowly begun to come back into focus, sensations receding. But I am still weak, and the most I can do is drag myself forward, inch by torturous inch. My fingers dig into the sewer's stones. I swallow down sickness as I move, as Asina allows this to happen, still chuckling quietly. She's amused. Like a child torturing a caterpillar, pulling off its legs one by one by one.

I have never felt so alone.

But you're not, the Voice murmurs.

Slowly, I become dimly aware of a presence behind me, one as familiar as family, one that sends my soul thrumming with a recognition of an equal. Sonagi. She's here.

She came for me.

A susurration in the darkness has Asina stiffening. My lips twist into a tight smile as strength floods back into my body. With a forceful shove, I roll over and leap to my feet, grinning down at Asina even as I gulp the thick sewer air, panting rapidly. My sudden movement has thrown her off-balance, and she kneels on the ground, eyes wide with shock. The darkness around us moves. Slithers. I catch a glimpse of dark blue-green scales from the corner of my eye.

With Sonagi here, I feel…I feel stronger than ever. It is such a stark contrast from my earlier weakness that I laugh, suddenly giddy. I will not be the one to die tonight.

Sonagi is waiting for my instruction. Waiting, filling the sewers with a sense of foreboding. Perhaps the Voice had good intentions, after all. For I will give Asina a truly terrifying death.

For the Talons. For my friends. My family.

But first...

In a flash of speed, I plant my boot on her chest and shove her down. Her bald head hits the stone with a dull thud.

"*Get—off—of—me!*" Each word is punctuated with a slap on my boot. The Crest's face is strained and vicious. I stare down at her. A word bubbles to my lips before I can stop it, spilling out with a horrible intensity that leaves me breathless.

"Why?"

She pauses, taken aback. But she quickly composes herself. "Why what?" she growls, grappling at my foot to no avail. "Why did we kill your friends? Because we could. Because we felt like it."

My wrath, my rage is a living thing inside me. It is roaring, howling in broken anger as Asina says those words. *Because we felt like it.* As if it were *inconsequential.* My vision blurs with both tears and fury.

Asina turns her head and spits on the ground. "This is Blackblood territory. Kalmin's kingdom. If your Yoonho had recognized that, maybe he'd still be alive." She leers. "But I doubt that."

I press down on her chest harder with my boot, watching her wheeze. I could crack her ribs if I wanted to. And I do. Asina screams, high and hoarse. "Kalmin," I sneer, "waltzed into this kingdom, fresh off a ship from Brigvalla, and decided—on a *whim*— that it was his. This kingdom doesn't belong to him."

"Fuck you," she gasps.

I glower at her, breathing hard through my nose. "Careful," I whisper. "For one of us is at a considerable disadvantage here." I press my boot down harder and Asina screams again. Her stare is still locked on mine, but by the way the whites of her eyes have begun to show, I know that she, too, senses the monster approaching from the darkness. Senses the otherworldliness slinking across the cold stone, filled with a predatory intent. Senses that, at last, the end of her bloodstained chapter has arrived.

A flash of snakeskin, sparkling and teal.

And as Sonagi glares down at Asina from above my shoulder, I know that this is who I am meant to be. This is what I am meant to do. I have never felt such purpose before, lighting my nerves on fire, quickening my heart to the beat of the war drums.

Beautiful, the Voice breathes, and with a flourish of a hand—like a magician revealing a trick—it shows me what Asina sees from her point on the ground.

A young woman stands straight and proud as a monstrous serpent looms over her shoulder. She is small and slight, tomboyish, but her stance makes her as formidable as an empress. Scales that match those of the serpent gleam on her skin, and for a moment, her eyes seem to flash the same gold as the Imugi's. Her mouth is twisted into a cruel grin as she bends downward to Asina's eye. Behind her, the Imugi tastes the air with a black forked tongue, and slowly cocks its head.

The vision is broken as I stare down at Asina's horrified face, as her screams fill the tunnel. I release my foot from her throat, and turn to Sonagi as Asina scrabbles backward on the ground, wild-eyed with terror.

"You came."

Asina makes a noise halfway between a scream and a choke as Sonagi gently butts her head against my cheek. Her tongue flicks my forehead, and it is soft, like the kiss of a mother. *"Of coursse I came, Child of Venom."* She cuts a look to Asina. *"This is the one, yesss?"*

I nod as Asina staggers to her feet and begins to run toward the sewer hatch, leaping up toward it desperately, only to crash back to the ground. "It is."

"*And what is it that you wish for me to do with her?*" Sonagi bends, almost in a bow, and I realize that she is my weapon tonight. A blade that I can wield to my will.

"Feast," I breathe, exhilaration filling some broken, shattered part deep within me as Asina shrinks back against the wall. "Feast, Sonagi."

"*Feassst,*" she repeats with what I think may be a smile.

I watch, wide-eyed, as Sonagi dips her head once more, and begins to slither toward Asina. I admire how her scales glitter in the darkness, how her molten gold eyes cut light through the shadows. She is beautiful, a creature of grace and glory. I wonder how anybody could fear her. Even as she lunges toward the cowering Blackblood, maw dripping venom as her fangs are unsheathed, I see nothing but salvation.

For the Talons, I think as Asina's screams begin to die. *For the Talons,* I think as a sticky pool of blood begins to seep toward my boots. *For the Talons,* I think as Sonagi turns, her fangs dripping venom and scarlet, revealing only a singular finger where Asina had once been.

"*Did that woman hurt you?*" Sonagi asks, slithering back to where I stand, raising herself so she is eye level with me. Her black hood flares. "*I have tasssted those who are sweeter, much sweeter. But there was a bitternessss to her, one that went deep into her bonesss, a sournesssss to her skin.*"

My smile falters. *I have tasssted those who are sweeter, much sweeter.*

Oh, gods—

This is an Imugi.

This is one of the monstrous serpents who terrorized Iseung, who fought against the very gods I worship, who Rui so despises. What am I doing here? Why did I summon her? It is as if a chest brimming with my cogent thoughts has come unlocked—they spill to the floor of my mind, shouting incessantly. I swallow hard, although it is not Sonagi I fear.

It is myself.

I begin, instinctively, to pray to the gods for guidance...but stop myself. No. No, how can I be worthy of doing so?

An Imugi has come to me upon my summoning. I have bent an Imugi to my will. Perhaps this is why Kang and Rui stare at my scales so suspiciously. Perhaps I really have turned into one of them. A monster. Rui's ring is so very cold on my finger.

Hush. Do we forget that the Dokkaebi were created by the mixture of the blood of the gods and the blood of the Imugi? Pay the hypocrites no mind. The Voice grits its teeth as it attempts to suppress my sudden rationality, my lucidity. **We have pleased the Talons tonight.**

You, I hiss, shaking. *You made me do this.*

I made you do nothing, Shin Lina. I feel the Voice's smirk. ***What is it that you are so fond of saying? That you are capable of making your own decisions? This was your choice.***

She has eaten human flesh before—the stolen humans—the red spot—a dinner with old friends—what have I done—I need to summon Rui— Panicked tears begin to swim in my eyes. I have never been so bewildered, so lost...

Sonagi's gaze is warm. No wariness or fear reflects back at me, even as I stare at her in horror. *"I would not leave thossse alive who made you ssuffer on this earth. I am glad that you have called me. I worried that you would not. Do you want me to show you truth, as I have promisssed?"*

Truth, temptation, at my fingertips. The truth about the Pied Piper. About the Imugi. About everything that is a mystery in my mind, cloudy and fogged with confusion.

The story that has been kept from me. Moments away.

"I..."

Say yes, the Voice growls.

Despite myself, the word is on the tip of my tongue. It's

threatening to roll off, pushed by the Voice. But I swallow it back and shake my head. "I...I should go."

A flash of something in those yellow eyes. Irritation? Determination? Either way, it is gone before I can confirm it was ever really there at all. *"As you wisssh."* Sonagi tilts her head. *"But firssst, collect your sspoil of war, daughter."*

My eyes dart to the lone finger. "I have no desire for that," I mutter in disgust. "You may eat it."

She shakes her head. *"But think of how your enemy will feel when it is delivered upon his doorsssstep. Yesss, I know of Konrarnd Kalmin, child. And I know that this will sshake him. It is why I left it."*

I grimace, unable to deny that the Imugi speaks true. Reluctantly, I tear off a bit of my cloak and wrap the finger within the fabric before putting it in my pocket. Asina's disappearance and this delivery will be enough to plant a seed of fear in Kalmin's mind, one that I hope to tend to and grow until it blossoms, ripe for the reaping.

Sonagi joins my side once more, clearly pleased. *"Now,"* she says, and with a start I realize that she has begun to encircle me, imprisoning me with her sinuous body.

"No—" I protest, "I don't want—" But it's too late.

"Now," she repeats, *"isss the time for truth."*

CHAPTER TWENTY

A gasp lurches from my throat as I fall through shadow and mist, the floor dropping away beneath my feet. I cannot see Sonagi, but I sense her presence, as if the darkness now surrounding me is the Mother of Imugi herself. I tumble downward, my hands grasping at the mist as if it can save me from the horrible impact that is surely approaching.

But it never comes—I hover in the darkness, panting, wild with confusion. "Sonagi?" I cry, and my voice echoes as if within a cavernous hollow. *"Sonagi!"*

Her voice arrives a moment later, soft and reassuring. Mist brushes against me like the soothing touch of a mother. *"Do not be afraid, daughter."*

"Where are you—what is this—I said not to—"

"We are connected, you and I." Golden eyes blink out of the darkness, large and luminous, bigger than the moons of Gyeulcheon. *"The sscale you consssumed. It was mine. I can sssense it within you, daughter. Our mindsss are able to be linked, for we are to each other what thunder is to lightning. It is how I have been able to vissit you in visions. Do not be afraid, Lina. I will not let anything happen to you. What I am going to show you are nothing more than memories. You are sssafe here, with me. You will always be sssafe with me."*

The knowledge that our minds are connected is jolting, a sick surge of shock. As is the realization that I am, in some ways, Sonagi's daughter—and she my mother. "Memories," I repeat, heart hammering in my chest. "You mean..."

"*Do not be afraid,*" Sonagi repeats in a whisper before the shadows and the mist swirl before me, creating a curtain of impenetrable darkness.

When it parts, I stand on a battlefield.

The roar of battle is a din that surrounds me, and the ground on which I stand is soaked through with gore—golden blood and teal blood, all intermixed together to create grotesque puddles that crawl with buzzing flies. My eyes are wide as I take in the battlefield, a field of mud and carnage underneath a lightning-forked sky, surrounded by looming, white-peaked mountains that I recognize as the Yaepak Range. The air is thick with the smell of sweat and violence, and I choke on it, unable to comprehend, at first, what I see.

For the land crawls with Imugi, enormous teal serpents like Sonagi, although they lack her flared hood. Maws drip ichor as they lunge toward creatures I recognize as Dokkaebi—elegant males and females clad in battle armor, disappearing and reappearing through corridors of shadow, wielding weapons drenched in dark green blood that bite into the scales of the spitting serpents. My eyes widen. Once, before the creation of Gyeulchon, all Dokkaebi had the gift of teleportation. I am far, far, far back in time.

I choke on a breath as I watch one fall, devoured by an Imugi in little more than a snap of the jaw.

Sonagi's voice echoes through the battlefield, muting the cacophony of battle. "*Thisss is what they turned usss to,*" she murmurs from an unseen place. "*War and violence. But we were not always so. We were content to live apart from the godsss and the Dokkaebi, once. We were a peaceful speciesss, connected to the watersss, living on beachesss and riversss with Yongwang's and Habaek's blessssingsss... But they came for us with weaponsss and criesss of war. They killed our young. The godsss' evil creaturesss came for us with blades, and we sssoon developed a tasste for their flesh.*"

The world ripples, and the battlefield is replaced by the scene of a night-darkened beach. Humans, grubby, with their teeth bared in violence, run barefoot across the sand with blazing torches in their hands, shouting battle cries, throats thick with hatred. I stumble after them as they make their way toward a distant rock formation on the beach.

The world ripples once more, and now I stand within a stone cavern, watching as the ocean of flame comes closer and closer toward the mouth of the cave. Behind me, a cluster of Imugi shrink back toward the shadows, their bright eyes shining with panic. A small serpent, a child, begins to cry, and his mother tightly curls herself around him. A large Imugi, the male of the nest, stands next to me at the mouth, spitting venom.

"They wanted uss for our scalesss," Sonagi whispers as arrows fly through the night, dozens embedding in the male serpent. He falls with a cry into the ocean's cold fingers lapping into the cavern's mouth, and the child screams. The dark water is stained green as the mortals continue their assault, relentless, raging. *"They were once worth more than gold. We were never anything to them but property, an infringement on the realm they thought they owned. The gods made a misstake when they created thesse creatures. They forgot to grant them empathy. Insstead, they gave them greed."*

The mortals burst into the cave. I close my eyes as the scent of blood thickens, as hisses and screams grow in volume. I hear the sickening thuds of a weapon as it is brought down, over and over again, in an attempt to sever diamond-hard flesh. I am reminded, unpleasantly, of Asina sawing at my throat. My body feels numb, cold, as the Imugi cry out in tortured anguish.

"We begged the gods to protect us from their creationsss. But they would not listen to our pleasss. Even our creator, Mireuk, turned from us. And so it was a massacre," Sonagi continues quietly. *"Never had we harmed the humansss. Never had we wronged them—once, we brought them rain for their cropsss. That is one of our powers: the*

bringing of storms. But still, they came for uss. So we had no choice but to change. I believe sssome call it evolution."

When I reopen them, my surroundings have once again changed. I am again on the beach as humans rush forward with torches and weapons, but this time, Imugi slither from the caverns and rip into the humans with razor-sharp fangs. I begin to feel a...a terrible sort of satisfaction as I watch the mortals fall. As the serpents feast. Rain sluices down from a thunderous sky into the sea, the storm no doubt the Imugi's making.

My heart breaks, imagining Sonagi once wetting farmers' lands with rain, only to be repaid with pitchforks and such violent hatred.

"And so followed a war of sseven hundred years and sseven days." Dizziness hits me as we revert back to the battlefield where I'd first arrived, surrounded by war. *"During the first centuriesss of the war, the godsss and the Dokkaebi, born from the mixture of our blood and the blood of the godsss, formed a formidable army. They exiled us, or they believed they did, to Yeomra'sss realm of Jeoseung. But we would never sstay there long, using the underworld realm only as a place to rest and recuperate away from the eye of our enemiesss. For we had as much a right to exist on Iseung as the humansss. Yet we would never receive welcome, for the mortalsss, with their hunts, had shaped us into predatorsss. Now, they feared us. As did the Dokkaebi. And as did the godsss."*

"And the gods left," I breathe, staring up at the blooming black thunderclouds. "Because they feared you."

"Among other reasonsss. But yesssss, child, they feared us. They feared our evolution. So quickly had we turned from peaceful to violent, from weak to ssstrong, that they decided they did not want to watch what came next. For evolution doesss not end, not with creaturesss such as us. And war only spurs those changesss.

"After their departure, the Dokkaebi were the last line of defense against our forcesss, abandoned by the godsss. But we were losing."

On the battlefield, hundreds of Imugi fall, spurting blood. My stomach tightens as a white-haired Dokkaebi with dark, bruise-dappled skin shouts victoriously on the frontlines, slamming a blade into a rearing serpent. Chan. Rui's general. I do not see Rui, even as I scour the field for him. I see only death, and I feel sick to my stomach.

"We had given up nearly all hope then," Sonagi whispers. "But we were visited by the one god who had ssseemed to delight in our destruction, in the death that we caused. We were visited by Yeomra, God of the Dead, who had offered his realm to us as a ressting-place under the guisse of an exile. And with him, he brought a Prophecy."

The cloying smell of wilted roses and blood fill my nose. I stand in the familiar realm of Jeoseung, the roaring of the Seocheongang River loud in my ears. I am at the frontline of an army of Imugi, all of us watching as a lithe figure steps out of the dark mist.

Yeomra. I fall to my knees, hardly able to breathe.

God of Death. Once, I imagined him to be my patron.

His angular, lilac eyes—the same color as Jeoseung's sky—fixate on the Imugi as he emerges from the shadow. I stare at him, my heart in my throat, trembling. *Yeomra. A god. A god.* He is tall, seven feet perhaps, with skin as pale as marble and hair as dark a blue as the deepest depths of the ocean. His face is hard and cruel and terrible.

He is beautiful.

Sonagi slithers out to meet him from the army of Imugi, brushing against me with no knowledge of my presence. *"Yeomra,"* she says, pausing just before the god. *"Your pressence here is... unexpected."*

Yeomra smirks and opens his mouth—but no human words emerge. His voice is the chaos and roaring winds, terror and bloodstains. Yet...underneath, there is also the sweet tenor of relief, of fading pain, of a cool calmness that soothes and silences. It is musical and horrible all at once—and I know that his is the language of death.

Yet Sonagi seems to understand, for she listens intently, as still as a stone. The army behind me is quiet, and the air is heavy with foreboding. When Yeomra finishes, closing his mouth, he spares no other passing glance as he turns back and recedes into the shadows.

But I think for a moment, two pinpricks of lilac meet my eyes from deep within the mist before disappearing completely.

Sonagi turns back to her army and smiles, revealing gleaming fangs.

A moment later, Jeoseung disappears, and we return to the battlefield—but this time, the two armies of Imugi and Dokkaebi face each other, still and unmoving save for Sonagi, who is slowly making her way to the space between the two forces.

"*The Prophecy,*" Sonagi murmurs from her unseen place, "*was more than a sssimple prediction. It was a guideline, given to us by a god. A guideline of how to truly reclaim Iseung. And it required that we, for the time being, retreat—which we had known was necesssary, regardlesss. But the Dokkaebi did not need to know that. When they requesssted a meeting, we allowed it, for we knew with it would also come a bargain that could be in our favor—for we, after all, had been losing...but the Dokkaebi's victory was costing them dearly.*"

"What was the Prophecy?" My mouth is dry, so very dry. She has mentioned it before...

"*Watch,*" Sonagi whispers, and my muscles lock as the Dokkaebi forces part for a Dokkaebi male, striding to meet Sonagi in the middle of the field.

Rui. My Rui.

He is younger, so much younger, and heartbreakingly beautiful. His hair is short, ruffled, and matted with blood. The lines of his face are smoother, lacking the cruel amusement that he now so often dons as a defense. Fear brims in his argon eyes, but he keeps his head raised high and his mouth set in a firm line. He wears the crown of the Dokkaebi, a crown of silver thorns that flashes underneath the dark sky. I note that his right hand is futilely clutching Manpasikjeok as he pauses ten paces away from Sonagi. Manpasikjeok, Rui has told me, does not work on monsters.

He is trembling, despite the fact that the Dokkaebi have been winning—albeit narrowly—against their foes.

"Imugi," he says, and his voice does not carry as I expect it to. Rather than being cold and clear, it is hoarse and rasping.

Sonagi is silent, staring at him steadily.

Rui coughs, and golden blood splatters the ground. For the first time, I realize that he is wounded, and unsteady on his feet. I fight the urge to run to him. We are on opposite sides of the battlefield in this memory. "I have—a bargain. An offer of leniency, should you accept it." He straightens, and clearly with difficulty, raises his voice. "You are outmatched and outwitted. Your forces have dwindled and will continue to do so."

As have yours, I think, staring at the army behind him. Chan is leaning heavily against a younger Hana, his side dripping blood. Hana herself is pale-faced, her eyes heavy-lidded, a cut open on her forehead. His forces do not fare much better. Nearly every soldier is clutching a wound of some sort. They have been winning, but not by much.

I have a suspicion that this meeting is not a true meeting of leniency, as Rui had called it, but a hope for a truce.

Nervously scanning Rui's army, I spot Kang in the crowd, his dark auburn hair limp with sweat, his hands wrapped around his staff. He stares at the one-sided conversation occurring in the midst of the field, and his mouth tightens in wariness.

"Return to Jeoseung," Rui says, knuckles white around Manpasikjeok. "You have no other choice but to retreat to that underworld realm. And in return, we, too, will exile ourselves to a realm of our own. We, too, will suffer." His mouth works as he says the words, and I think that I see tears glimmering in his eyes. My throat tightens.

So this is the creation of Gyeulcheon. This is the origin of Rui's pocket realm.

This is the secret that Rui keeps from all, save—I assume—from those who were present on the battlefield that day. For the ill-fated Revolutionaries never knew why Dokkaebi were confined to Gyeulcheon, never knew why the Dokkaebi had retreated from Iseung.

Emperor Haneul Rui does not keep the Dokkaebi there for his own amusement. He did not lose control over the Three Kingdoms, as history books recount.

Rui trapped himself through a bargain. This bargain. I lick my lips nervously, glancing to Sonagi.

The Imugi on the field slowly tilts her head. Blinks. And stretches forward, raising herself so she stares down at the emperor. "And what of our need for food?" Her voice sounds different, somehow, yet I do not have time to wonder at this before she speaks again. "Sssurely you don't mean for us to *ssstarve,* little emperor."

Rui closes his eyes, as if in pain. "Sunpo," he says stiffly.

Sonagi twines around so that she peers at the Dokkaebi emperor over his own shoulder. "Sunpo," she repeats musingly. "What usse could that little village in the sssouth *possssibly* offer?"

"I will yield control of all territories but Sunpo," Rui says, shaking with rage and the effort of remaining still. I can tell that it is an exertion for him to speak that damning sentence. "Once per year, you and your…*brood* will feast upon the flesh you so enjoy in the halls of my realm. I will satisfy you enough that you will be able to live off the pickings in Jeoseung until the night of the next feast. Until," he says through gritted teeth, "the next Night of the Reaping."

And as he speaks those words, I know that this is what he has been so studiously keeping from me. My stomach plummets and an audible gasp escapes my lips, yet Rui cannot hear me. He is nothing but a memory in the mind of an Imugi.

This—this is the secret of the stolen humans. With Manpasikjeok, the Pied Piper harvests them for the annual Night of the Reaping, when the Imugi emerge from Jeoseung and feast upon humans in the halls of Gyeulcheon.

It is why Eunbi had to return to Sunpo that night—in order to remain out of danger. *A dinner with old friends.*

I do not hear what Sonagi says next, for the world falls away, and I am again standing in the sewers, looking into Sonagi's eyes. I pull back, my heart hammering.

"His bargain was futile. We would have retreated anyway." Sonagi considers me, her tongue flicking. *"But he doesss not know that, doesss he?"*

"I...I don't know." Rui had told me that the Imugi had retreated of their own accord. He had never mentioned his bargain. I blink back tears, although I do not quite understand why I am crying. I do not quite understand anything. "I do not think that he does."

And we will not tell him.

But—

I cringe away from the Voice as it slams down on my protest with a gnarled, clawed hand. Sonagi's eyes narrow in concern.

"Is ssomething bothering you, daughter?"

The Prophecy. The Voice sounds strangely hungry and bizarrely self-satisfied. **Let us hear her speak of the Prophecy. The Prophecy, the Prophecy, the Prophecy, Lina...**

No. No. I fight back, straining. If the Voice is so...ravenous to hear this Prophecy, it cannot be a good decision to listen. But I am weak from exhaustion and shock, and I cannot stop the words from falling from my mouth...

"The Prophecy that Yeomra brought," I whisper, my lips moving almost mechanically. "The Prophecy that told you to retreat. I didn't hear the words... I couldn't understand Yeomra..."

Sonagi inclines her head. *"I will tell it to you, child, but I should warn you that once heard, Propheciesss inevitably come to fruition.*

Esspecially when they are heard by those of whom they ssspeak."

I stare, my mouth working for a good few moments before any words come out. "The Prophecy is about me?"

The Imugi says nothing, but the glimmer in her golden gaze tells me enough.

Bewildered, I take a step back. "I-I don't understand."

"It is your choice, my daughter, whether you want to hear it. But to hear it is to accept your fate." Her hood flares, and her body seems taut with excitement. It is clear that she wishes for me to do so. To accept whatever future lies in the Prophecy.

Listen. The Voice is practically buzzing with anticipation. **Listen, Lina.**

No — give me time to think — what if this means the war starts again — what if this means I will become a monster — what will the gods think of me — this is not Good… I don't want to hear it. I don't. I don't.

If I listen, I lose myself.

If I listen, I am not worthy of the gods. Even the ones I call my patrons will scorn me. They fought against the Imugi, and if I become a monster, they will hate me.

All except, perhaps, Yeomra.

But—

LISTEN, the Voice snarls, and the noise of it shakes my head, rattles my skull. Never has the Voice been so loud, so demanding, so utterly terrible. Never have I been so useless to deny it. Its cold fingers close around my tongue, and my eyes flare in alarm as it shapes words into my mouth, words that spill over my lips before I can stop them.

"Tell me."

No. No. *No.*

I clap a hand to my mouth in horror, but it is too late to take the words back — for Sonagi has begun to speak in a soft voice, hushed with reverence, and I am unable to do anything but listen.

I cannot move my legs, nor my arms, frozen in time like an insect suspended in amber. The Voice stands and watches, pleased as my rationality fights to stay afloat against the assaulter of my mind, attempts to push back the reverent words spilling from the Imugi's forked tongue and the weight that they carry. But it is no use.

The best part of me is drowning in those words. The best part of me is dying, replaced by something dark and sinister and deadly.

Oh gods, I think, just as my mind goes under. *What have I done?*

"With one last breath,
an empress will rise.
From dust and shadow
to bring sunrise.
Follow her and her path will lead true
to power and vengeance if from war you withdrew.
What you seek has now been found
for she is the Yeouiju who will lift you from the ground.
And the Child of Venom will rule all
Before making her home in Yeomra's halls."

INTERLUDE

Deep beneath a head of short black hair, the creature that the girl has come to call the Voice smiles as it paces across its host's mind, delighting in the words that still hover in the air. Exuberant, it trails clawed fingers over the ridges of the girl's cognizance, a slow chuckle escaping its lips.

Finally, it murmurs with a twisted grin. ***Finally, finally, finally.***

The future has been sealed. No longer will the young body that the creature inhabits be able to refuse its will. She will be its puppet now; its puppet as it fights to fulfill the sacred duty.

The girl believes that it is the voice of her power. How mistaken she is. Power does not *speak*. Power is not *sentient*.

The creature is almost offended by her ignorance, yet knows that if it so wishes, it can plant the seeds of knowledge in her mind with its gnarled hands, can sow them into her awareness with a spade and a shovel.

It could recount to her the pains it went through to bring her to this moment, the moment when those beautiful words seeped into her mind and allowed the creature to grasp the reins of her consciousness in its hands.

It could recount to her the effort it took to crush her fears of the Imugi into nothingness. It could recount to her the effort it took to reach a hand down into her heart, pinching it with jealousy of a long-dead Dokkaebi, so the girl would not confess to her darling emperor, controlled by an envy and suspicion that she herself fervently denied she even felt.

It could detail the pains it took to guide her here, step by step, into the sewer in which she stands facing the Imugi. The effort it took to summon those attacks of the senses, attacks that eventually led to the girl needing Sonagi more than ever.

But it will not.

It no longer matters. The girl is the creature's puppet now, and her strings are intertwined between the creature's gnarled fingers. A yank, and she will do as it says. She will dance, she will run, she will *leap* if it so wishes.

No longer can the girl ignore the creature's demands. No longer can the girl protest. No longer can she refuse to *listen*.

It will be easy, now, oh so easy to fulfill its duty.

In the mind of its marionette, the Prophecy smiles. There is a long road ahead of it, but it is ready.

For Prophecies will do anything to be fulfilled.

PART TWO

POWER AND VENGEANCE

CHAPTER TWENTY-ONE

"*For thousandsss of yearsss, we watched the ssskies for you,*" Sonagi breathes. "*For the Yeouiju to bring us sssalvation and triumph. And you, Child of Venom, you* are *the Yeouiju.*"

I say nothing. My mouth is unbearably dry, my head swimming. And something...something is wrong. Something is very, very wrong. My tongue tastes like blood where the Voice grabbed it and forced the words onto its pink, bumpy surface. And I can *feel* the Voice, grinning smugly as it peers through my eyes. I can feel something else, too...as if my mind has been manacled, as if I am a marionette poised to dance to the tune of another.

"*I should warn you that once heard, Propheciesss inevitably come to fruition. Esspecially when they are heard by thosse of whom they ssspeak.*"

Trembling, I fully recognize my folly. I've stepped into an inescapable fate, a fate that will inevitably pit the one I love against me. Rui's ring is ice-cold on my finger. Oh gods.

I try to force my legs to stumble backward, but they stay rooted where they are. My mind clouds with a buzzing panic—but the Voice swats the swarm away with an irritated hand.

Calm yourself, it hisses, and I...do. My shoulders relax, my fingers uncurl. Each breath becomes slow and steady, each beat of my heart is even and measured. It is almost as if my body does not belong entirely to me, acting on its own. I swallow the bitter taste of bile. **Good,** the Voice croons. **Now let us focus on the Prophecy, our purpose. This is who we are meant to be; an empress, a Yeouiju.**

And my mind...it obeys. It pushes aside my fears, replacing them with the words of the Prophecy, beautiful and bright, shining with purpose. "A Yeouiju," I repeat slowly. "What is a Yeouiju, Sonagi?"

Sonagi's forked tongue flicks into the air in clear anticipation. *"I've ssspoken to you of the evolution of the Imugi. How circumstance demanded that we transsformed from placid ssserpentsss to the creaturesss we are now. Our evolution is not yet done—not at all, for a great potential sstill lies before us. A potential to take to the ssskiesss, to grow in power, to become Yong."*

Yong. The word sounds familiar, yet it is difficult for me to place it.

"Dragonsss," Sonagi explains. *"The original Yong do not exisst anymore, banished by time and their meek nature. But we hold the ability to change that."*

My eyes widen. "You expect to transform into dragons?" I ask, my voice hushed in awe, remembering the legends of the powerful beings of the sky—Yong, great dragons with manes and whiskers, scales and claws. Now I remember—Yongwang the Sea God was said to be a sea dragon, one of the magnificent creatures. Within his waters rests Yonggun, his dragon palace, abandoned with the disappearance of the gods and the extinction of the Yong.

"It was told to us, many yearsss ago, that finding the Yeouiju would hassten our evolution. Yet we were never able to find the Yeouiju and remained locked in the endlesss war against the pantheon and the Dokkaebi. Until the Prophecy. If we retreated, we knew that the Yeouiju would find us eventually. And you did.

"My kind has ssspent much time puzzling over Yeomra's wordsss. It took more time than you would think to recognize that we were sssearching for a girl who had been reborn. Sssuch casesss are very rare. But when you died, Lina, you were reborn with our powers running through your veinsss. And you have yet to discover all of them.

"Like calls to like. I found you in Yeomra's realm, and although you did not yet have my scales, I knew that you were the one we'd been waiting for. The Yeouiju. I cannot expresss my gladness in those moments, daughter. Since then, I have been waiting for you to accept me into your heart, to hear the Prophecy. And now that you have, a new chapter of Iseung has begun. The Child of Venom will rule all." Sonagi smiles, revealing her glistening fangs.

Yet I do nothing but stare.

Smile, the Voice snarls and jerks the corners of my lips upward until I return her grin, my heart pounding in my chest, my blood running hot with excitement.

All our life, we have been stumbling through a maze of bloodshed and terror and devastation.

All our life, we have been lost.

All our life, we have been broken.

But here, in the sewers with the Imugi, we feel only a potent love and a stark purpose. The Voice waits expectantly. *Isn't that correct, Lina?*

Yes, I think slowly. *Yes.* I feel, for the first time, *whole,* like the words have awakened something beautiful within me.

I am the Child of Venom. I am the Prophesized. I have finally found a home—a home with the Imugi, who has helped me, who has come to me. Who never looks at me with fear or suspicion, as Rui and Kang do. I close my eyes, and picture what Sonagi describes.

An empress, flanked by enormous Yong. Sunpo, in the palm of my hand. There will be no more Blackbloods, no more Talons dead in their own home. There would be only Sunpo as it can be—a kingdom brimming with culture, a kingdom that will finally hold an empress. A kingdom of my own, to control as I please. And Wyusan, Bonseyo... Those could be mine as well. Especially with Bonseyo's perpetual instability due to the warring Jeon dynasty. It would be easy enough to topple their infrastructure, to claim it as my own.

To be Empress of All, to never be subjected to another's will again...to have *permanent* power. Not just physical power, strength and scales, but a home atop a throne. Oh, I can taste it on my tongue. It's sweet and brilliant and infatuating, clearing away the taste of grime and grit.

But it's too sweet, sickly sweet. For a moment, I gag on the flavor. For a moment, I wrestle the thoughts and desires flooding my mind, fighting to stay afloat as my own mind turns on me...

None of that, now.

My lips stretch into a smile. The year I spent working for Konrarnd Kalmin was as if my waking world had become a terrible nightmare. The humiliation of being subjected to his whims, his mercy, his words—it twisted something deep inside me—something that slowly begins to untwist now, as I imagine it. I would be *untouchable*. Truly free.

With this, this Prophecy, this power, I will never bow before another again. Yes. Yes. Those who would force me to kneel would kneel before me. And Eunbi. With her sister as Empress, she will be equally as feared. Never will she endure what I have. She will know, all her life, only freedom. An undisputed freedom wherever she travels on the Continent, forevermore.

A terrible hunger gnaws at my stomach. It's sharp and ravenous and voracious. It's a hunger for power, pure power. I nearly double over from the intensity of it, for I've never felt such desire before. Such singular focus, and a hunger to achieve such an extraordinary goal. This isn't right; this *isn't right*—but my mind has started to believe it to be, and as every moment passes, my protests begin to fade. I am terrified, but then, as the seconds drag past...the fear diminishes into nothing, overtaken by pleasure.

A few hours ago, the thought of being Empress of All would never have occurred to me. I was naive, then—unable to see the potential before me, focusing on only the small kingdom of Sunpo and the gang of the Blackbloods. But what would have come after

I killed them? A life contained only to this kingdom when so much more exists beyond the Yaepak Mountains and the Wyusan Wilderness?

Good.

Yet there is one part of the Prophecy that bothers me. That causes me to take pause. "The last stanza," I say slowly. *Before making her home in Yeomra's halls.* "Does it mean—"

"All living thingsss die eventually, Shin Lina. Even the so-called immortals. It is inevitable." Sonagi makes a fluid gesture that I suspect is the Imugi version of a shrug. *"Do not concern yourself with that part. It sssimply means that one day, you will passs. And we will come with you, for we are linked. Wherever you go, we will not be far behind. We will follow you to Jeoseung and back if needed, my child."*

Tears prick at my eyes and I bow my head. Loyalties. Family. It is exactly what I have been wishing for, for so long. But Sonagi pushes my chin up with her head, eyes glittering.

"An empresss does not bow." Sonagi flicks my cheeks, and it is like the kiss of a mother. *"Tomorrow night, you will meet the rest of us. But for now, daughter, your will is mine. Your ssspoil. Give it to me, and I will place it on the pillow of your enemy, to ssstrike fear into hisss heart."*

Slowly, I withdraw Asina's finger from my pocket. Sonagi holds it in her mouth. "When does the transformation happen?" I whisper, still preoccupied with absorbing the new information. "When do you transform into Yong?"

"When the time is nigh," says Sonagi before slithering back into shadow. *"When the time is nigh."*

Watching her go, I tilt my head.

An empress. Does that not sound appealing?

The sewer fills with the sound of my laugh, soft and wicked and cruel. Up above, thunder rolls in the sky. A storm is coming.

...

I stalk through the kingdom straight-backed and proud, as if a string is connected to my spine and is pulled taut. My mouth has begun to ache, for the grin is still there, stretched tight. Smiling this long is…unnatural. *This isn't right,* I think, but it's an effort to do so. Thinking is like trying to swim in a pool of thick, warm quicksand. *Something is wrong.*

Do not dwell on it. The Voice sounds exasperated. **You are not supposed to dwell on it.**

So I don't.

Rain falls in heavy sheets from the rolling gray clouds, thunder not so far off in the distance. I wonder if Sonagi has summoned this storm, if she's been summoning this summer's storms all along. I mull this over as I glance at Dalnim's moon, hidden behind a cloud of furious gray. It is tinged pink, like a droplet of blood in water. The Night of the Red Moon is only seven nights away, and with each night that passes, it will grow redder.

My eyes close as if my lids have been pushed downward, and my mind imagines storming the palace armed with vicious Imugi, imagining the terror I will bestow upon Kalmin. **Beautiful, isn't it?**

I strain to open my eyes, but I cannot, able only to watch with rising horror as my mind spins images of Sunpo swarmed with Yong, of the entire Eastern Continent cupped in the palm of my hand. Of the Dokkaebi kneeling in submission, eyes downcast. Of Haneul Rui's flute shattered into hundreds of pieces, his silver eyes dull and dim.

At once, my hunger, the desire that overtook me only minutes before, banks. I have never wished to rule an entire continent. That is not who I am. And, since our game was called off, I have never wished to hurt Rui so irreparably. *No. I never wanted this.* It is an effort for my mind to form those words, directed at the Voice. *I* never wanted to rule anything but Sunpo.

The Prophecy is a gift that we will accept. I wince as gnarled fingers dig into the flesh of my brain, sending shards of pain through my skull. **We** will ***fulfill it.***

A groan of pain lurches from my lips, and my hands come upward to clutch my head as I sink down onto the street. I cannot breathe around the pain, the burning agony in my skull. Around the rising noises of the world, the senses pounding through my body, the heightened perceptions that have my body growing clumsy, sinking to the ground.

All this time, was it the Voice controlling these attacks?

I groan as the pain heightens with the realization.

"Fine," I gasp through rainwater and pain. "Fine."

Smugly, the Voice withdraws its hand and allows me to open my eyes. And then I feel it—a tugging in my chest, a humming of recognition leading me to…

Four shadows that stand before my giwajip, heads bent and deep in conversation. I catch a flash of white hair, pale skin, a hand curled tightly around a gnarled staff, and a glimmer of silver eyes as my body rises from the street and ducks into darkness. ***Rui's court.*** The Voice leans forward in interest. ***Let us listen to the words they speak.***

Unseen, I expand my senses, my ears picking up the words passed underneath the rose-tinged moon.

A smooth voice is speaking. I know the voice well, a voice that seems to be spoken through perennially pursed lips, slick with aloofness. It is Park Hana. "—never trusted her," she's saying in great disdain, and as I allow my vision to sharpen exponentially, she comes into view out of the darkness. Her curly black hair has been knotted back into a tight braid that reaches her waist, and instead of wearing one of the Northern dresses she so covets, she is dressed in a stealth suit not unlike my own. A woldo is strapped to her back—a long, curved blade attached to a slender pole.

I taste a bitterness in my mouth as I realize that Chan, too, is dressed as if headed for battle. In his hands is a dangpa—a tall trident—and he wears his customary black hanbok with another weapon hanging on his waist's silver sash, along with his various golden medallions. His long white hair has been knotted back in a similar fashion to Hana's. Despite myself, I wonder if she braided it for him, and am then immediately disgusted by myself for even giving a semblance of a damn.

Only Rui and Kang are not armed. Kang's red-brown hair is loose, his hanbok is a plain gray, and his staff of dark wood lacks blades and steel. Yet his expression unsettles me. It is grim, grimmer than I have ever seen it—even when we'd dealt with the rebels, even when I'd nearly died. Dark shadows ring his brown eyes, eyes that have always sent a chill down my spine, for they are deep and dangerous, filled with more wisdom than anyone should possess. And, of course, there is that ever-present suspicion that made permanent residency on his face after my scales emerged.

Rui looks much the same—he wears his customary robes of flowing dark fabric, along with his jewelry that sparkles merrily in the shadows. His rain-slicked black hair is held away from his forehead by a headpiece with an obsidian brooch, revealing his indolent countenance as he arches a wry brow at Hana. Manpasikjeok, his most potent weapon, is nowhere to be seen.

"Your lack of fondness for my lover has been made abundantly clear," Rui says coolly over another crack of thunder, tilting his head and examining his rings. "I do miss the days when you were merely fond of drinking and revels. Whatever happened to you? Has monogamy weighed you down?"

I watch as Chan tenses. I can hear his molars grinding.

"Rui," Kang says quietly, placing a hand on his friend's shoulder, "you agreed that recent circumstances have been suspicious. The Imugi breaking the treaty directly after Lina's rebirth, a rebirth that was enhanced by their own powers, may be more than coincidence.

It was Lina herself who confirmed the presence of an Imugi on Iseung after the Night of the Reaping. It is only natural that we wish to speak to your lover, especially if this Imugi spoke to her. We must know what it said."

"Not that it matters." Chan's eyes flash jade as he thumps his dangpa into the ground and spits rainwater. "She is not here."

"Where is she, Rui?" Hana narrows her eyes. "Do you know? Can you follow the thread?"

"If I wish to. Which I don't." Rui's lips twist into a wolf's smile. "Shin Lina is quite nocturnal. It's entirely possible that she is simply purchasing sugar rolls at a midnight market or torturing some unfortunate Blackblood in an abandoned alleyway. She will return, and when she does, *Hana and Chan,* I suggest that you tuck away your weapons. This was supposed to be a casual call, not an interrogation. My Lina does not take kindly to tactics such as these—" He stiffens, and I know that he has sensed me in the same way I sensed him. That peculiar *tug...*

That is our cue.

My muscles tauten, and I am pushed out of the shadows by my own limbs. The Dokkaebi freeze as my head tilts and my teeth are bared in a not-even-passable excuse for a grin. "He's right," my voice says, cold and cutting. "I don't." I come to a halt just a few feet before them. My lips move of their own accord. The words taste metallic. Mechanical.

Manufactured, and by something other than me.

Rui does not look at all surprised as his silver eyes flick toward me. Chan stiffens, but he does not blanch. "Lina," he says in his deep, gravelly voice. "Well met."

"Well met," I scoff. *"Well met?* I would have much preferred meeting you minus the six-foot *fork* you're toting around, *General.*" Cutting my gaze to Hana, I snarl. "And I cannot say that I'm all too pleased to see *you,* either." The female Dokkaebi has been a thorn in my side for far too long, with her clear dislike of me. Hana smiles a fake smile that clearly means *go to Jeoseung*. Furiously, I focus on Kang. The advisor is still underneath my stare, but his eyes are not on my face. They are on the scaleblades emerging from my skin. And they are dark with fear.

Perhaps his fears are justified after all. A wry little laugh echoes through my mind and my blood runs cold.

"Lina," Kang says calmly, dragging his eyes up to my face. "Hello."

My lips sneer. Kang's eyes narrow, almost in warning. As a result, my sneer grows to a truly impressive proportion.

"Lina," Rui says quietly, placing a hand on the small of my back. "That's enough." His touch is gentle. "We're just here to talk. It's—it's time for me to tell you the story, little thief." He turns me so I face him, and I know I am not imagining the suspicion that hardens the lines of his face, even though his voice is soft. "To finally tell you the truth."

"Truth." I take a step back, narrowing my eyes to slits. "Since when have you been so willing to share *that*?" A flash of white-hot lightning illuminates Rui as he stiffens infinitesimally.

"It would be better," he murmurs, glancing to his friends, "if we could speak inside."

"It would be better," I retort sweetly, "if your friends had not arrived bearing weapons, as if I am some sort of threat to be neutralized."

The street is suddenly thick with silence, the storm the only sound. I watch as Hana's lips turn upward sweetly, too sweetly, and as Chan's shoulders stiffen. But it is Kang who speaks, leaning on his staff, bowing his head even though I do not miss the way his face has tightened. "Dark tides lap at our shore," the advisor says quietly, water sluicing down his cheeks like tears. "The weapons are only a precaution. And not against you."

Oh, I doubt that.

"Against the Imugi," Hana goads. "You wouldn't happen to

know anything about them, would you?"

Say nothing.

"Hana," Chan says sternly out of the corner of his mouth, and immediately looks as if he regrets it as his lover sends him a venomous look before turning her attention toward me once again.

"You wouldn't have had a *conversation* with one?" She is relentless, arching a perfectly shaped eyebrow. "There wouldn't be anything that you should tell us, Shin Lina?"

"For the sake of all things even slightly holy—" Rui pinches the bridge of his nose and looks as if he is very much trying to restrain his temper. "Don't ask questions you know the answer to," he snaps to Hana, who gives a small shrug and continues to direct that hateful little smirk at me. I grit my teeth and cut my glare to Rui. "Please, Lina," he says softly, now practically begging. "Please."

I hiss through my teeth. *"Fine,"* I mutter, stalking to the door and unlocking it. I see no other option. To turn them away is to arouse suspicion. It is clear that the Dokkaebi do not know of the Prophecy, and I know that I must not tell them, not give them any advantage that they can wield if these tensions escalate into something more.

Into war.

For the Child of Venom will rule all.
We can only hope that they will yield.

CHAPTER TWENTY-TWO

"I already know the story," I say, sitting on a cushion in the kitchen. Chan leans against the wall, Hana next to him, while Kang and Rui sit across from me. I haven't bothered to serve tea. "It is what the Imugi told me when it approached me." They do not need to know that I am coming from a meeting with Sonagi. Let them think there has been only one.

"It told you?" Rui looks stricken. "You knew?"

"I wanted to give you a chance to explain first," I reply, and this time my words taste sour. Honest. So different from the sweetness of a lie. "To tell your truth. But you would not," I add, leaning forward across the low table. A muscle in Rui's jaw flickers. "You refused. I do not pretend to know why the Imugi told me." Lie. "But it did. It told me that you offered a bargain. A retreat on both sides, and a Night of the Reaping each year. The emergence of the Pied Piper."

"Lina…" He is pale, so very pale.

"Why innocents?" I snap, knowing the words will hurt him. I don't particularly care who was taken, but the idea of cutting Rui with my words is all too appealing. "Why not those who are evil? Who deserve it?"

Rui swallows hard. I see his throat bob. "It's all part of the punishment," he rasps. "*My* punishment. It's what they demand from me."

Sneering, I glower at him. "This is what you kept from me. Why you broke your vow."

"I vowed only to cease the kidnappings of humans if I must," he retorts quietly. "And I must not, Lina. For the Night of the Reaping. I did not lie, not truly."

The Voice reaches gnarled fingers into the recesses of my mind, withdrawing a memory.

"I will cease the kidnappings of humans if I must. But I cannot return those I have already taken. This is all I can give you, Lina. This is my only bargain."

A sneer curls my lips. Such Dokkaebi logic. Loopholes and lies—it is purely the sort of thing Rui would gravitate toward.

"So you deceived me," I say flatly, "from the start."

"I wish I'd been the one to tell you," he insists hoarsely. "I wanted to tell you, little thief. To explain, but…"

"It is my fault." Kang warily meets my eye. "I told him to wait."

The silence between us is as loud as the roaring of the underworld's Seocheongang River. I am the one to break it, viciously, violently.

"Tell me," I say through gritted teeth, "what harm could knowing the *truth* possibly have done?"

"Some stories inspire us," the advisor replies calmly. "They guide our actions, influence our decisions. Change us."

"You thought I'd seek out the Imugi once I heard more about them." I roll my eyes.

What sort of reasoning is that? The Voice smirks. **They would have found us first.**

Kang says nothing. It is Chan who replies, brusque and blunt. "Lina, you have their snakeskin. You are of the Imugi. So, yes, we did suspect that the Imugi's part in your rebirth was more than what it seemed on the surface, and we needed to fully assess the situation. It has recently been confirmed, by you, that despite their attendance at the Night of the Reaping, the Imugi have broken the treaty and have appeared in the human realm. The damage has already been done on that end. But what has not been confirmed is if you are on our side or theirs. That is why we are here." He adjusts his grip on his weapon. "Do you know why the treaty was broken not long after your rebirth?" He speaks flatly, his tone assessing. "Do you know why the Imugi approached you? And is that truly all it said to you?"

"No," I lie coldly. "Then no, and then yes. But I *do* know that the lot of you are hypocrites. Were you not also born from the Imugi? I do not see you questioning the loyalties of any Dokkaebi." I summon every ounce of indignation that I can, pushing aside my growing annoyance.

Who are they to try to decide the course our life takes? Who are they to try to decide with whom we ally ourselves?

"Dokkaebi also have the holy blood of the gods," Hana simpers. "Unlike *you. You* are pure Imugi with just a dash of wongun berry. And you have…scales." She wrinkles her nose. "I wouldn't be surprised if your eyes turned yellow or your tongue forked. Or if you began to slither around on your stomach, hissing and eating people."

"And I would not be surprised," I reply coldly, "if one day, somebody planted a dagger in your chest for the way you run that mouth of yours. And I would be less surprised still if that person was me." In the silence that follows, I smirk, unable to rid myself of the anger thrumming deep within my bones.

Rui's expression is coldly amused, but I do not miss the flash of shock that flares in his eyes. "Yes, Hana," he says, not breaking his gaze from me, "I would advise you to choose your words more wisely."

Hana hisses something unsavory through her teeth, but before she can fire a retort, Kang speaks. He has been watching me since I appeared on the street; I feel his stare like an insufferable itch crawling up my skin. "Lina," he says carefully, shrewdly, "you seem different. Where were you tonight?"

The words are ready on my tongue. "I was disposing of several

Blackbloods in the sewers beneath the kingdom."

Chan shifts on the wall. "So that's what that smell is," the general mutters, as if it is the conclusion of a mystery he's long been trying to solve. His lover snorts.

Kang does not look away, and the itching becomes unbearable. I scowl as the advisor's eyes scour my own before dipping back to the scales that still gleam on my hands. "I see," he says very quietly, and in my mind, the Voice tenses. My muscles lock, jerked by strings, and I can only watch as my fist slams down on the table, as my lips pull back in a snarl. The words spill from my tongue in a wave of hatred, pushed through my lips by the Voice.

"If you believe that I have become an Imugi in scales and spirit, if you believe that I am a monster lurking underneath your beds, then I ask you to get out of my house. *Now.*"

Why are my words not my own, why am I a puppet for—
Hush.

Panting, I glower at the four Dokkaebi. Kang's expression has not changed, but Hana and Chan have gone rigid with shock.

"Lina." Across the table, Rui places a hand atop my fist, gently rubbing his thumb against the curled fingers. His touch does not calm me. Instead, it sparks a dissonance in my mind that is almost too much to bear. A part of me cherishes his touch, soft and tender, bringing with it comfort and an apology. Yet a part of me hisses to withdraw my hand, to yank my skin away from his, for the Dokkaebi is now an enemy of the Prophecy I must fulfill.

We will recoil at his touch, the Voice snaps, and it is a harsh demand. It jerks at the strings attached to my marionette body, insistently urging me to shirk away from the one I love.

No. I grit my teeth with the effort of refusing it, the Voice that is now somehow more than a simple speaker in my mind. Sweat dribbles down my spine, and that horrible pain once again spears my mind, like a blade digging into the softest part of me. *I won't.* It's an effort to remain conscious as the world becomes so horribly enveloping in all its facets—noises, scents, everything, everything—and I am dimly aware of Rui's eyes widening in concern, of Kang leaning forward in his seat, saying my name. "Help," I want to say, but the word is snatched from my lips and stuffed away into a trunk, locked inside with no chance of escape.

Yes, the Voice whispers, *we will.*

And then the control I managed to wrest over my body is gone. Violently, I am yanked backward, my hand ripping out from underneath Rui's. *No—*

The Voice squashes my protest underfoot. Only then do my senses draw back.

Kang's stare is unblinking, and I wonder if he knows what has just occurred. I hope he does. The Prophecy...changed the Voice, I realize, for no longer can I ignore its demands or argue with its reasonings. I am no longer in full control of what I do or say.

A wave of terror washes over me, and I drown in it—choking, gasping, spluttering for breath. But nobody seems to notice. Not even Rui.

I should have told them about you from the very beginning—

Hindsight always brings sorrow. The Voice snickers.

Rui has taken my reaction as an act of hurt. I...think I feel it. A flash of self-deprecating guilt. Gently, he says, "We don't doubt you, Lina. It is merely that tensions are high, that tensions are escalating. War is on the horizon, and it is approaching fast. The treaty has been broken, and the Imugi are restless. It is only a matter of time before they resume their prior agenda. It is only a matter of time before our war starts anew." Rui runs a hand wearily down his face. "I'd hoped that our treaty would last for far longer than this, for an eternity if possible. But it is not in the nature of the Imugi to remain placid for long, and I suppose we are lucky that they have remained absent for as long as they have. If there is a reason for their reemergence rather than them having bode their time, we are at a loss as to what it could be. I'd hoped that perhaps the

Imugi might have alluded to something, asked you to deliver me a message of some sort out of spite…yet it is clear that they have not. But the fact remains that the Imugi sought you out, for reasons that even if unknown, must be important. So we have come to you, Lina, to ask for your help."

"My help," I repeat icily, arching a brow.

"We need to put an end to this before it begins," Chan says gruffly, still clutching his dangpa. "We need to dispose of the threat before it's too late. We need to kill the Imugi. And you need to help us."

"There was one among them," Kang says, and I cannot tell if he is looking at me, or if his vision is far away, in another time. "They called her Sonagi. The Mother of the Imugi. All of the serpents, they are descended from her. She is at the forefront of their unit, giving her children strength through her very existence. Much like the situation with the rebels, if we kill their leader, the whole will be weakened. I believe," Kang continues, blinking and refocusing, "that you will be able to summon her yourself, Lina. Perhaps it is because of your Imugi nature that she is drawn to you, perhaps it was her venom and scale that were within the wongun enhancer. Regardless, it is likely that she views you as her child."

Turn them out of the house. The Voice is pacing feverishly, shaking its head. ***Make an excuse. We must speak to Sonagi right away. We must wage war while they are still scattered, still reeling in shock.***

No. I grit my teeth as pain wracks my mind. I am no fool. The connection I have felt with Sonagi, the scales on my skin, the Prophecy…

It is clear that I am what I have denied being for so long.

One of them.

A monster. Their empress.

Imugi.

They are my kin, and I cannot deny that I am drawn to them,

that I sympathize with their plight...but I cannot let them reclaim this world as theirs. For although they did not choose it to be so, not in the beginning, their diet is composed of mortals. And if they transform into Yong, there is no telling what will happen to this realm. To the people of this realm. And despite the hordes of people like Konrarnd Kalmin, there are still people like Eunbi. Sang. Like Chara, and Chryse. Like Yoonho. And I will not have more of those deaths weighing on my shoulders. I cannot bear it.

Yet these brief moments of clarity and control are scarce. I can already feel myself slipping, can already feel the Voice regaining power. And I know, deep within my bones, that I cannot stop myself from fulfilling the Prophecy. What was it that Sonagi had said? That Prophecies, once heard, are always fulfilled? Well, it seems as if Prophecies are clever cheats. It seems as if somehow, the creature in my head is the Prophecy itself. It is its own creature. Not a prophecy but a *Prophecy*, for it emerged with my rebirth and grew in control soon after I heard Yeomra's words slither forth from a forked tongue. Knowing what I know now, how could it be anything else?

It is now so glaringly clear that the Prophecy in my head has been feeding me thoughts, manipulations, determined to lead me to fulfilling a destiny that I wish nothing more than to shirk from. Each suggestion it has made has been a carefully crafted move to lead me toward Sonagi, toward tonight.

Jiwoon and the Revolution wanted to control Iseung. I killed Jiwoon before he could do so. And I will not allow the Imugi to succeed where the Revolution failed. I will not allow Rui, my Rui, to be harmed. I will not allow more innocent blood to stain my hands red.

Sonagi has shown me kindness, and I have felt a love for her. But that love is a manipulation of my mind. I have viewed Yeomra as my patron for so long, and once thought I would do anything he asked of me, if only he returned from his absence. But this

Prophecy cannot be fulfilled.

My faith in Yeomra, what I think is love for Sonagi…it is not enough for me to set flames to this world, to release monsters to the skies.

Yet I know that I cannot stop myself. I am only a puppet. My body does not belong to me. It belongs to the Prophecy, who is already regaining control, digging talons into my cognizance, spitting in rage. ***You are not supposed to fight back,*** it screeches. ***You are not supposed to be able to fight back—***

A few seconds, that is all I have left. And I will use them well. For I know that this will be the last time that I am truly myself, truly Shin Lina, without the Prophecy controlling my every move. Taking a deep breath and standing from my cushion, I force the words past my mouth, trembling violently with the effort as black spots dance in my vision. They come out slurred and choppy, but they reach the ears of those who must hear them.

"With one last breath,
an empress will rise.
From dust and shadow
to bring sunrise.
Follow her and her path will lead true
to power and vengeance if from war you withdrew.
What you seek has now been found
for she is the Yeouiju who will lift you from the ground.
And the Child of Venom will rule all
Before making her home in Yeomra's halls."

I finish with a gasp, and before the Prophecy can yank on the puppet strings connected to my mind, I hurl myself toward the wall and slam my head against it.

Hard.

INTERLUDE

"Well," says the Dokkaebi emperor, who is trying his absolute best not to sink into a panic from which there would be no escape, "this is quite bad."

He is staring at his soul-stitched, who—upon smashing her head against the wall with enough force that the wood now harbors a deep dent—has sunken into a state of unconsciousness, a trickle of blood seeping down her face. Rui holds her in his arms, trying to control the trembling of his hands. *Lina, little thief… Oh, Lina…*

"A Prophecy." His advisor is pale, his eyes large dark pits against his skin. "That was a Prophecy." Unsteadily, Kang rises to his feet, leaning heavily against his gnarled staff. "I suspected—but I didn't know—"

It is rare that Kang is so shaken, and even rarer that he is at a loss for words. Kang shakes his head, dark auburn hair concealing his miserable expression from view.

"My worst fears have come true," he finally whispers, his throat aching. "For months, my dreams have been haunted by the same vision. Of a dying world with lands preyed on by Yong. Of skies as red as blood and rain as black as ashes. My only comfort was that the Imugi have never found the Yeouiju. But if what Lina has recited is true, if she is the Yeouiju, if the Imugi undergo their evolution into Yong…"

"Yeouiju?" Chan's mind feels like it's stumbling over itself in an attempt to keep up. "What's the Yeouiju?"

"In the old texts regarding the Imugi, it's a pearl," Kang

whispers. "A treasure that allows Imugi to turn into Yong. I never thought it would be...a girl."

"We should kill her," Hana says impassively, staring at the unconscious girl whom she very much dislikes, and whom she would very much like to dispose of. "Now, when she's unconscious."

"Absolutely not," Rui snarls, an insurmountable rage filling his lungs and choking him. He pins his glare on the other Dokkaebi, blue fire dancing in his eyes. "She is *mine*. Nobody touches her. Do so and I will kill you, slowly. Painfully. Am I understood?"

But only silence meets him.

"Am I understood?" The Dokkaebi can no longer hide his trembling, overcome with fear.

"Rui," Kang says gently, "now that we know what we know, it is likely that the red thread of fate connecting you two is not one formed of love, but hatred. She is the Yeouiju. You are the Dokkaebi emperor. Your fate is tied together as foes. I do not see it being any other way. What you had will die, replaced by this. And that..." He sighs. "That does not bear good tidings. If your mortal enemy can find you, anywhere in the world... If they can enter your dreams..."

"Stop," Rui growls, gathering Lina closer to him. His heart is hammering hard against his chest. "Our fate is one of love. It *has* to be."

"Your Majesty," Chan says, and it is not the tone of a friend he chooses to use, but of a general, set to do his job and protect his people. "There is a Prophecy. Most likely it was given to her by the same Imugi she claimed said nothing to her but the story. Already she has lied to us. This does not bode well. A war is surely coming, and they have the advantage. Prophecies are, apparently, always fulfilled. But...she's helpless right now. Maybe this can be the first Prophecy to fail. We need to act." He imagines himself doing it, ending Lina's life. One look from Rui quickly stops that train of thought.

Sparks of blue fire dance in the emperor's glower. "Remember your place, General. It is far beneath me."

Neither Dokkaebi notice as Kang closes his eyes, lids fluttering as underneath them, his vision roams far-off places. Roams through old memories, sifting through them like stacks of parchment with ink-stained fingers.

"She hit her head," Hana says in a mixture of disdain and confusion, breaking the icy silence between her lover and her king. "Why would she hit her head? I mean, I have always believed she was unhinged, but this…"

"So that she would forget," Kang says, eyes flying open. He sways slightly where he stands, gripping his staff for support. "She's concussed herself hard enough to induce memory loss. Clever girl."

"But why? It makes more sense that she'd want to remember that she broke down and confessed, to operate on damage control later on." Chan crouches down next to his emperor, who rocks back and forth with his love clutched tightly in his arms. "It doesn't make sense," he repeats gruffly, frowning at the limp form of Sunpo's Reaper. "Kang?"

The advisor anxiously runs his thumb up and down the grooves in his staff. "There are stories," he says slowly, watching his emperor carefully, "ones I heard centuries upon centuries ago, when I was but a student in the Wyusan Wilderness. Stories told by Hwanung, son of Hwanin, and God of Laws."

"Elaborate," Chan says stiffly, glancing at his emperor. Rui's eyes are dark and haunted, focused only on Shin Lina's face.

"We had been asked to memorize the entirety of Hwanung's laws. I spent nights poring over hundreds of scrolls as dawn shone through the cracks in the cave-school. When Hwanung arrived, we were to grace him with the recitation of his laws, our voices rising and falling to the tune of his glory. But we forgot one law. He created it just that morning and we had not known. Furious, the god demanded we begin again and include the new law. I have remembered it since.

"The new law, Hwanung said, was that for all seen puzzlements, there is something unseen lurking below the surface. A bird who does not sing may have a parasite in its lungs, gnawing away on the flesh. A star that does not shine as brightly as it used to may be an entirely different star, replaced with a duller one by the ancestor of your bloodline, Rui. Dalnim, who does not like the stars to outshine her moon." Kang joins Chan and Rui on the ground, slowly brushing his fingers across the blood on Lina's forehead. The wound has already healed, but she shows no sign of stirring. Slowly, Kang examines the blood that despite all, still runs red. "And," he says quietly, "a girl who tries to forget her confession may not be trying to make *herself* the one to forget, after all."

"You mean to say," Rui whispers, voice breaking, "that Lina is possessed? By what?" Myths of possession are plentiful, but never has the emperor expected for the girl he loves to fall prey to a parasite. "A spirit? A Gwisin?"

"No," Kang murmurs, again pressing two fingers to Lina's cool forehead, as if he can sense whatever lies beneath her smooth skin. "Not a Gwisin. A Gwisin would have left her body when she fell unconscious, and I have yet to see a spirit here. But I do believe that there is something in her mind, controlling her. Her movements tonight have been sharp, jerky, like she is a pawn to another's whims. Tell me, Rui. Has Lina said anything…done anything…that struck you as odd prior to tonight? The smallest detail," he adds, "may lead to the largest revelation."

The emperor hesitates. "Sometimes," he whispers, raising his eyes to his court, "sometimes it would seem as if she was listening to somebody. Sometimes she would open her mouth to speak, but close it at the last minute, as if something—someone—had told her to be silent. I do not know why I did not think much of it." Guilt tightens his throat. "I should have seen it from the beginning. I should have known that their kind was here. The rains are heavier this season, and now it's obvious... But I didn't suspect it. I didn't see."

"It's not your fault," Chan says sternly, clapping Rui on the shoulder. "I mean, with all that she's been through, she's bound to be a little..."

"Finish that sentence," Rui snarls viciously, shaking off his touch, "and I shall *cut off your hand.*"

Chan falls silent, rubbing his right hand ruefully, very unwilling to part from it.

"So there is something in her mind," Hana muses, a hand on a hip as she stares down at Lina. "Something guiding her, steering her toward an end goal. Like the fulfilling of the Prophecy." She frowns.

"Exactly." Kang's eyes widen. "Exactly," the advisor whispers again after a stunned moment. "Hana, you are exactly right." Kang begins to pace across the floor of the giwajip. "For so long, I have wondered..." He spins around, staring at his companions. His mind is racing miles per minute. *"Yes.* Yes, Hwanung's law plays true here, my friends. It has proved a theory I have puzzled over for centuries. Prophecies are always fulfilled because they are, literally, self-fulfilling. There is one inside Lina's head, speaking to her—it is sentient, in a way... Manipulating her actions, controlling her... All toward the end goal of being fulfilled. It is alive, its own being."

Rui takes a shuddering, rasping breath. Kang swallows hard and pushes himself to continue.

"The very fact that she was strong enough to break through tonight indicates a powerful will and a stubborn mind, honed by her years as an assassin. Honed to never break under torture, under interrogation. Honed by her years as a captive, struggling through physical and mental torment. So she will fight back, more than the Prophecy has expected. But I believe that the longer the Prophecy is in her mind, the more power it will have. This change, it was recent. But from here on out, her words and her will, they will not be fully her own. We must remember that."

"How do we get it out?" The question is barely audible. Rui is the picture of a tortured emperor, slumped on the floor, cradling Shin Lina, holding back hoarse sobs. When there is no response, he repeats the question, his voice wracked with grief. Tasting of tears. *"How do we get it out?"*

"Well, there's one way," Hana mutters, peeved that nobody seems to be listening to her entirely reasonable suggestion.

"We have little time." Kang shakes his head somberly, eyes glazing over. "Already, the Imugi have accepted her as the Yeouiju. War approaches. The way that I see it, we have two options. Either…" He hesitates. "Either we try to k—"

"Don't say it," Rui hisses. "Seal your lips, Kang."

A short silence, crackling with tension, is eventually broken by Chan clearing his throat.

"Or," Kang continues evenly, "we convince her to join our side. We…outwit, for lack of better terms, the Prophecy itself. With her alongside us, surely the war can be won."

Chan frowns. "How?"

"I know of no Prophecies that have gone unfulfilled. But the idea that the Prophecies have been fulfilled only due to possession is…new. The Prophecy inside Lina's mind is sentient. It can be outsmarted, outfoxed." Kang tightens his grip on his staff. "Lina is still in there, as we saw tonight. Her values, her beliefs, her dreams, her *fears and desires* are still in there." Something darkens in his eyes and tightens in his chest. "And there is the matter of the red thread of fate. Perhaps… Perhaps, Rui, you are right. That there is a possibility that you *are* destined to be joined in love." The waters of Kang's mind are rippling with excitement. "Despite Lina's possession, you are still soul-stitched, are you not? You still feel the thread?"

"Yes," Rui replies tightly.

"Then it's as I suspected. Her mind is strong, and the true Lina is still in there. We may be able to use this to our advantage as we gather our forces in preparation for what may come if we fail."

For preparations, war preparations, must begin tonight. Training out-of-practice soldiers who have never once stepped beyond the walls of Gyeulcheon. Churning out armory, preparing the tactics, bracing the forces for what will come to pass if the Prophecy cannot be stopped before war explodes, bloody and brutal.

"But at what cost?" Rui's eyes are red-rimmed, his mouth a deep gash of grief, and he suddenly looks older—much, much older. "At what *sacrifice*, Kang? What is it that you believe we should do?"

Somberly, Kang tells him.

And the words…they taste like sickness in his mouth.

As Hana and Chan make identical sounds of disbelief, Rui's face drains of blood. "You cannot mean that."

"If it is your fate to be bound to her in love, Rui, then this is the only way for you to tempt that fate into existence. I have long wondered if fate is not linear. If there are many options along the road. Threads become tangled. They…split, diverge at the seams. This strategy could save us all. We are at a crossroads. Love, or war? Perhaps with our coaxing, the red thread of fate between you two will lead to love. Peace."

The emperor is silent, staring down at the face of his soul-stitched. At the small lips, the pointed nose, the long lashes, and the teardrop scar. "You mean to say that I must make her love me."

"I only mean to say that perhaps we can coax the red thread of fate in the right direction. Perhaps, against the Prophecy, the red thread will triumph."

"And if it rebels? If it fails?" Desperate, Rui stares up at Kang. "Will the Prophecy even allow Lina to love?"

"If given the right incentive," Kang replies somberly, "it might."

CHAPTER TWENTY-THREE

Scorching heat slips through my paper-screened windows, drenching me in a sticky sweat where I lay tangled in damp sheets. Scowling, I push myself upward and rub at my eyes as my head swims, plagued by a dull ache. The skin of my forehead is tender, and I wince as my fingers graze a particularly sore spot, undoubtedly from Asina's attack the night before. The wound must have been bad if it's still healing.

You've been asleep for long enough, the Voice mutters, stretching like a cat and yawning. *When you sleep, I sleep. Come. We have much to do today, Shin Lina.* The Voice too, sounds groggy and slightly disoriented. I feel a prickle of satisfaction, although I do not quite understand why. *People to kill, sights to see, wonders to perform together. Perhaps we should kill more Blackbloods and bring their bodies to the Imugi tonight for feeding.*

My legs slide out of bed, carrying me to the bathroom. I scrub my face with cold water and soap before tying my hair back into a topknot and brushing my teeth with cleansing paste.

The Voice seems to be more awake now, pacing across my mind, hands behind its back. *Why,* it mutters, *do I feel as if we are forgetting something? What happened last night, Shin Lina?*

As I pull on a pair of baji and secure my jikdo to my waist, memories come flooding back—the sewers, Asina's death, the Prophecy—and then nothing. I frown while my fingers mechanically tie the sash around the jeogori of my hanbok, and as I secure the gat around my head. *I...don't know. How did I get home?*

You were high on exhilaration, the Voice grumbles disapprovingly. **It is the most potent drug. Now there is a gap in our memories.**

The Prophecy rings in my ears, the Prophecy that Sonagi spoke in the sewers, decreeing me an empress. Yet when I think of it, I do not feel glee or anticipation, or the overwhelming sense of purpose I'd felt near the river of waste. Instead, I feel...numb. A hollow husk that has been filled with something else—like the shell of a hermit crab that has been displaced and secured onto another crab's body. Something is not right.

Slowly, I finish securing the hat, and the Voice scoffs as my eyes move to the silver ring upon my finger. Rui's ring. I smile slightly, but the corners of my lips are abruptly yanked down.

Take it off.

My brows furrow as my hands move of their own accord, my fingers poising to slide the ring away from my fourth finger.

No, I think, as if through a thick haze as I watch my hands in a mixture of fascination and horror. *I won't.* Rui's gift to me, this ring...I will not take it off. *You cannot make me.*

Yes, the Voice snarls, **I can, and you shouldn't be able to refuse—**

Two brisk knocks at the door.

My fingers pause in surprise, limpening like they have been released from some invisible hold. Cocking my head, I make my way to the front door and open it just a crack. Ryu Seojin looks evenly back at me. In the morning daylight, his eyes are hazel, just like his brother's once were before death glazed them over. Perhaps that is why I open my door wider even as my suspicion heightens.

"How do you know where I live?" I demand warily. Have I not been as careful as I believed myself to be? The thought is not comforting.

"Iseul sent me," Seojin says as he steps into my hanok. "And Iseul has her ways." He looks around as I shut the door, and I realize that he holds a basket of sugar rolls—though where he got them, with the baker currently in the stomach of an Imugi, I have no inkling. "I half expected there to be weapons everywhere, and blood," he notes, and I lift an eyebrow.

"Disappointed?"

"No. On the whole, I'm relieved." He hands me the basket. "As thanks for what you did last night. Iseul said you like these." Seojin does not strike me as the type to smile, but for a moment, the corner of his lip tugs slightly upward. Sang used to have a crooked smile, too. I take the basket quickly, averting my eyes.

For a moment, I want to talk about him. The boy we both lost. I want to ask what Sang was like as an older brother. As a child. Did he always want to be a spy? What were his dreams, before? But the Voice stamps out my questions with an impatient eyeroll.

"The madame sent you here for a reason other than gifting these pastries and expressing your thanks, I assume," I say, eyes snapping back to Seojin. "I'd like to know what it is."

His not-quite smile vanishes. "Iseul's gathered your alliances. I'll escort you."

Skeptical, I raise a brow. "So quickly?" It has been only a few nights since I last spoke to the madame.

"Iseul works fast," Seojin says defensively. "Being in hiding has not deterred her. We should leave now. Allies await you, Lina."

I've stuffed the remaining Gyeulcheon baubles in the pockets of my baji, and they clank as we go through the city, although there are no Blackblood patrols to avoid. The Voice curves my lips into a smile as it rewatches the memory of Asina's grotesque death.

Song Iseul has relocated from the magnificent Dove Coop to the notably less magnificent Fishtown—a gamble, considering that the palace rests on the outskirts of the zone. But there are no Blackbloods to be seen near the dingy shack in close proximity to the fishing docks and covered in barnacles, seaweed, and an impressive amount of bird droppings. Their numbers, after all, are truly dwindling. I wonder if Son Wooseok has disposed of the Feathers and Bills yet. I hope he will, soon. The poison will give a death of true agony. Slow agony.

By comparison, I suppose, Asina's death could seem merciful.

The shack is tucked away on a small patch of rocky beach where fishermen have stored wooden boats in need of repair. My boots crunch on the pebbles as Seojin leads me toward the half unhinged door. "How many?" I ask. The Prophecy is urging me to find out, for, as it puts it, **allegiances cannot hurt us.**

Although we have a powerful army of Imugi at our disposal, it would not be wise to underestimate the value of human alliances. I can use the humans. Even Imugi have their limits. They cannot build me ships, as Im Yejin can. Nor can they earn me influence as Bang Bomin, the halji dealer, could through the "favors" he collects from various buyers. Buyers who have their own trades and professions that could prove extraordinarily useful. And allowing them to help me will give them, in return, a sense of security and placement in the world — meaning that the chances of a successful rebellion are much less likely.

For there is little that would be more annoying than a rebellion against me when I ascend to the throne. Having human allies will calm the doubts of those wary to trust the Imugi, the new empress. They can soothe their ilk, encouraging them to accept the new ruler. Those who refuse will be dealt with by the maws of the Imugi. For it is only fair that the untrustworthy — those who might try to overthrow my rule, my power, try to make me once again vulnerable — be disposed of. My Imugi need a food source, after all.

And what is an empress without her subjects? Subjects are as necessary to an empress as a crown, a throne.

But not just empresses.

What are goddesses without their worshippers?

Nonexistent. Just like the pantheon in Okhwang. For many in the Three Kingdoms, they do not exist—simply because mortals have lost faith in them. Because they no longer believe in them. The gods are absent, but I am here. I always loved the deities, always relied on them for strength until I gained strength of my own.

I wonder what it would be like to be one, myself. To take pity on my weak, mortal worshippers. To be exalted and glorified.

"Lina? Did you hear me?" Seojin asks, jerking me back to the present, where we stand before the shack.

"What?" My reply is irritated. I was quite enjoying the fantasy.

Seojin shakes his head. "Nothing. See for yourself." Turning, he pushes open the door and I follow him inside.

It is a small room, with uneven floorboards crusted with sand and walls slumping inward. The reek of fish is overwhelming; I press a hand to my nose and mouth as I observe the motley crew sitting on the floor around the shack's sole piece of furniture—a chair carved of driftwood, currently inhabited by a grinning Song Iseul. Excluding her, there are at least ten other people staring at me expectantly, and among the familiar faces I recognize Yejin and Doyun. Doyun gapes at me, and I know he must be wondering where the sweet girl in the pretty hanbok went.

There are a handful of new faces as well: a thin, reedy man smoking a roll of halji and wearing an interesting ensemble of a startlingly pink top hat in the Western style, silken robes embroidered with roaring tigers and colored a disconcerting orange, and three necklaces crafted from bright green glass. This must be Bang Bomin, halji dealer. I never bought from him—the Talons had our own suppliers—but word of his extravagant style was well known. The Voice impatiently shoves down my craving for a sample of his wares.

The other new faces are seafarers, weary and weathered, all sitting close to a straight-backed man with a receding hairline and crooked teeth. Cha Hyukjae, the most prolific fisherman in Sunpo, and employer of dozens of other fishers. He's rich, very rich—and influential. Those who feed others always are.

"Lina!" Iseul waggles her fingers at me, her grin growing. She is dressed in a hanbok so yellow that my eyes hurt to look at it and is holding her ax as if it is a royal staff of some sort. "*So* glad you could make it. I was worried the stench of fish would scare you away." Twirling a strand of white hair around her finger, she glances down at the others. "Meet the new Empress of Sunpo."

Silence. Bang Bomin is nodding hesitantly, but the others are still. The fishermen are scratching at their chins, the backs of their heads, looking wary. Yejin is sending me a gruff look that seems to say, *Good luck*. Doyun is still staring.

Clearing his throat, Seojin nudges me, and I realize that they are waiting for me to speak. The Voice straightens, narrowing keen eyes.

Inciting fear is the best way to incite loyalties, it says. ***A grand speech… Yes, such a one will do.***

And then I am speaking, even though my mind is not searching for words. They've been put in my mouth by another.

"I am Shin Lina," my mouth says coldly as my fingers tug the hood of my cloak away from my face. My audience shifts, eyes latching to my teardrop scar. "I have journeyed to the realm of the Pied Piper and the realm of the dead. I have carved out the heart of a Dokkaebi, and I have guided a blade through this kingdom, reaping souls and gathering ruin. My name has been whispered in fear, my name has been the last sound on the tongues of the dead and the dying. I am the Reaper of Sunpo."

Coldly, I run a hand across the hilt of the jikdo on my waist, meeting the eyes of each staring citizen.

"This kingdom will run black with the blood of our enemies under a scarlet sky. My hand is a powerful one, and one that is familiar with the feeling of a fading pulse. No longer will the Blackbloods rule what is not theirs, no longer will they patrol the streets and pollute them with their stench. In six nights, Konrarnd Kalmin will know the taste of his own tears and blood. He will feel my wrath and rage." A chuckle bubbles up in my throat, icy and sharp. "And I will kill anybody who stands in my way."

As my tongue finally stills, the shack is silent save for the dull roaring of the Yongwangguk Sea as the waves lap at the rocky shore, prodding the wooden walls of the shack with foamy fingers. The audience before me are pale-faced and thin-lipped, their eyes huge and unreadable. Next to me, Seojin is silent and unmoving, though I feel his stare on me. It feels disapproving, and I try not to bristle. I just barely stop my eyes from cutting toward him with a look of warning, and the result is a painful headache.

Gwan Doyun is as white as a sheet, his body stiff, his brows furrowed so tightly that I cannot tell where one ends and one begins. I smile coldly at him, enjoying his clear surprise. **How amusing,** the Voice snickers. **Poor, poor fool. And he doesn't even know that we killed his wife.**

On her seat, Iseul stares. "Well," she says, blinking. "That was very informative, Lina. Thank you. Do you have anything else to add?"

"A taste of a reward," I reply. "For those who will follow me." My hand slips into my pocket, withdrawing a handful of small treasures—golden chains, silver trinkets, and jade trifles—and tosses them toward my audience.

Bang Bomin lets out a low whistle, snatching up a jade necklace and donning it with relish. "Oh, I like her," he says, exhaling a puff of smoke. The familiar craving rises, but the Voice stomps it down again. "I like her a *lot*."

Cha Hyukjae, I note, has not touched the treasure. "So. We're supposed to trust *another* gangster, eh? The Talons were no better than the Blackbloods. Had a friend who ran a business. The lot of you killed him. Bullets in his forehead and blood everywhere."

Oh, please. "It is probable," I drawl, "that your *friend* committed an offense."

Hyukjae seethes. "Being the rival of one of your sponsors, no doubt," he snaps. "Dongwook committed no crime save for running a successful jumak. You killed him as a favor in return for another's support and money, eh? And we're supposed to think you're better than the Blackbloods? Pheh!" He spits on the ground.

"Watch your tongue," I say softly. "I remember that jumak. Do you know what was hidden beneath the floorboards? Women. Taken from their homes by the Blackbloods and hidden away to be used by Kalmin's leeches. Dongwook knew. He used them, too."

"*Liar.*" Hyukjae blanches.

"Liar?" I croon. "Watch your tongue, little fisherman. Or you might wake up to find it missing."

The man splutters in outrage and turns to Iseul. "You said she was going to be different, woman."

"I have a name," she spits back. "And it's Song Iseul. If that doesn't work for you, you can try Madame Song."

Hyukjae mutters an apology as the Gumiho's eyes blaze.

"And," Iseul continues, "it seems to me that Shin Lina woke up on the wrong side of the bed today. She typically isn't so"—she cuts an amused look toward me—"*callous.*"

"Well," the fisherman fumes, "don't expect my loyalty. I'll make do with the Blackbloods rather than living under this Talon bitch." He stomps past me, but I stop him, gripping his shoulder hard. Rage roils within me as the other fishermen rise to follow. I jerk Hyukjae so he stumbles backward toward the cluster of others.

"If you are not with me," I whisper, "you are with them, Cha Hyukjae. And *they* are going to be meeting a terrible fate. I would advise you to reconsider your decision. When this kingdom falls to me—which it will—you can either be on the side of the victor, or the side of the vanquished. Tell me, which do you prefer?"

Iseul and Seojin exchange a quick look as the man shifts uncomfortably, giving no answer. I release him, waiting to see if he and his ilk will run. But they don't. They linger. I smell Hyukjae's fear, and wet my lips.

I glower at the indecisive crowd. At Bang Bomin, who has played with my treasures but has not offered his allegiance. At the shuffling fishermen, at pale Hyukjae. At the others, from whom I need this final confirmation. "Bow," I say coldly, the word shoved from my mouth by a gnarled hand. "Bow, and enjoy the rewards. Refuse, and lose my favor when I take the throne. Because I will, with or without you. It is up to you what follows."

Pleasure overtakes me as I watch the Hyukjae and his fishermen return to their knees, and bend forward to press their foreheads to the dirty ground, reaching out their hands in respect. Iseul sighs and joins them, muttering something about *formalities*. Seojin follows her, lowering himself to the ground with the remaining allies.

Yet Gwan Doyun does not bow. He is staring at me, his fists curled at his sides, his mouth a thin line. I think I see something churning in his stare—suspicions, perhaps, or shock—and I arch my brow. Underneath my glower, he slowly sinks into submission, averting his eyes and following the rest into a display of reverence. Good.

The Voice chuckles. ***Poor fool,*** it says again. ***Poor fool.***

Our speech was too blatant. He must suspect. How dare you put these words in my mouth—

It shoves away my protests and stomps on them with a heavy foot. ***Question nothing.***

My worries fade away, and soon I forget them completely, aware of only the here and now. At the rush of delight filling me as the room bows to me and me alone. I quite like this, standing when others bow—especially when I was the one to bow so often in the past. "You may rise," I finally say coolly, and Iseul flounces to her feet, joining my side while brushing off her hanbok.

"I've gotten sand up my nose," she says, sneezing. "I do hope you accept my eternal loyalties now, Lina."

"Yours, I believe." I'm watching Gwan Doyun warily. "Others, not so much."

For his insolence has enraged me. He is not here because he is influential like the others. He is here only because I happened to kill his wife, and *he* happened to let his life completely fall apart afterward. I am here, extending my hand to him, offering him power, treasures, security—and he dares to hesitate in his bow?

Fool, the Voice mutters. **We do not need him. But to kill him in front of allies we need is not wise. One more mistake, and he will be dispatched. Perhaps Sonagi likes the taste of sad, stringy men.**

Seething, it straightens my back and places words on my tongue, shoving them into the air. "In six nights, the reign of the Blackbloods will fall entirely. I have an assassin on the inside, waiting to strike.

"When the Crown dies and power transfers to my hands, your work will begin. Im Yejin. In order for you to rent out a ship, the renter must have pledged his allegiance to Sunpo's new leader. And I want you to begin monitoring who comes and goes on the waters. If you see any...unsavory individuals enter Sunpo's territory, inform me immediately, and they will be dealt with. Swiftly." Dinner, for my serpents. "I also want you to soon begin crafting me a ship. A geobuksun," I say, naming a sturdy warship. "Use the treasures to purchase quality, sturdy wood from the Wyusan Wilderness. I want it swift and strong. I will give you the funds to hire additional hands if you must."

Yejin nods, tucking more treasures into her pockets. "Lending and monitoring will be easy. But the geobuksun will take time. Several months, at least. What is it for?"

"My personal travels," I say curtly. For travels to Wyusan and Bonseyo, should I be reluctant to take the paths by land.

Yejin raises her brows, the wrinkles of her face deepening, but says nothing. Only nods.

"Cha Hyukjae," I say, turning to the ageing man, who keeps his eyes trained on the ground—evidently still unnerved by my previous threat. "Fire any workers under your employ who are opposed to my rule, or sympathize with the Blackbloods. Deal no fish to those who were once Blackblood associates. I'll give you a list of names." Which will swiftly dwindle after they meet a fate similar to Asina's. "The rest of you," I say to his men, "do the same. Deal no fish to sympathizers."

"Bang Bomin. Your work starts now. How many favors do you currently have the potential to call in?"

The dealer takes off his top hat to scratch his black hair. "Three hundred and two," he says, before returning to puffing on his roll. "Some are big, some are small, some are in the space in between... throughout all Three Kingdoms." Bomin smiles slyly. "Which ones will you be needing, treasure-giver?"

"It will depend," I reply silkily. "But right now—whatever strings you need to pull to ensure that the businesses owned by the Blackbloods fall into ruin, pull them."

Bomin winks. "So the small ones, then."

"Gwan Doyun." I eye the man with distaste. "Your job is to witness what occurs during Kalmin's gala, on the Night of the Red Moon." So he can see what happens to those who displease me. "You will be in attendance."

Mouth tight and eyes averted, Doyun nods.

"Good." My eyes run over the faces of my followers. "You're dismissed." As they rise stiffly, I turn to Iseul and Seojin, who are waiting expectantly.

Iseul flashes me a grin. "And can I claim the role of treasurer? I do *love* shiny things." Her fingers wiggle eagerly.

Even the Voice is amused by this. It pulls my lips into a smirk. "I have a different job for you, actually."

"Oh?" Her light eyebrows rise, and she darts an excited look at Seojin, who's eyeing me curiously. "*Do* tell."

"After the bloodbath, I want you as my personal guard, Iseul." It is something that the Voice has given great thought. For it is no small thing to be an empress, or the Yeouiju. And, as wise a choice as it would be for them to do so, the two other kingdoms will likely not yield their territories to me without reluctance. A threat could come from anywhere, perhaps even taking me by surprise. And to have a Gumiho as a protector…it is a wise choice, indeed.

But Iseul does not need to know of the larger plans yet. Better to ease into it.

"And Seojin," I say, turning to him, "I want you as my healer." To aid Eunbi, or myself, if we fall ill. Eunbi will be a princess. ***It is important,*** the Voice tells me, ***that she carry on the great Shin line.***

Iseul beams, grabbing Seojin's arm in excitement. Glancing down at her, Seojin's mouth crooks into a smile. "I'd be honored, Lina. Thank you."

"By the by, Iseul," I continue, examining my nails idly, "I thought you might like to know that Man Jisu and Asina are dead. I killed them last night, along with two others."

"Well done, you morbid creature." Iseul sniffs. "I must say, you would make a *terrific* Gumiho. Unfortunately, you weren't born a soul-eating fox, and didn't live for one thousand years before ascending into human form, so it simply isn't possible. Pity."

Seojin stiffens from where he is standing next to Iseul. *"Iseul,"* he says quietly. Warningly. From the way he has stiffened, it is clear that his protective instincts for his friend have heightened. He whips his head around, and seeing that the others have left, returns his alarm to Iseul.

"She already knows, Seojin, there's no harm in speaking of it." Iseul sighs, poking Seojin's nose with a well-manicured finger. "This one is truly such a mother hen," she informs me as Seojin's face relaxes—only momentarily—at her touch. "I suppose it comes from the fact that he found me on the streets. Oh yes," she says as my brows raise. "I was injured, too. Only ten years old. Seojin was eleven. Well, that's not right." Iseul frowns. "Mathematics are not my strong suit. For ten years I'd been a shifting Gumiho—able to switch into human form, you know—and for one thousand years I'd been a ki-eating fox. I'm one thousand eighteen now, if you're wondering."

I wasn't, but even the Voice is intrigued, wishing to hear more of the Gumiho who allied herself with us. "You were injured?"

Iseul shrugs. "A bit."

"A *bit*?" Seojin looks as if he has had this argument with Iseul many times and has never once come out victorious. "Iseul," he says, turning to me, "had summer sickness. Her temperature was scalding. She also had one broken foot, two sprained fingers, a deep cut on her forehead at risk of serious infection, and one bruised eye."

Iseul shrugs. "I'd dealt with worse," she said, and her face suddenly darkens. "In the Fox Hunt." The air becomes heavy with her sorrow, and her lips thin. "It took my parents," she said quietly. "And for nearly one hundred years, I was on the run."

"How did you survive the Fox Hunt?" The Voice speaks through my tongue, eager to learn. But Iseul stiffens, and even the Voice can see that I have not gotten close enough to the Gumiho to merit such a story. She must see that acquiescence in my eyes, for she continues, albeit a little more warily.

"I barely did. In the days where I couldn't shift into my human form yet, I had some incredibly close calls. Anything that even vaguely resembled a fox...well. Hunters took swift care of it. So I was, in all regards, just a little bit wounded, *Seojin*." And just like that, Iseul has readopted her blasé attitude, crossing her arms and cocking a brow at her friend. But remnants of her grief still linger in the air. I can taste them. "And it didn't take you very long to heal me, anyway."

"You healed her," I say skeptically, turning to Seojin, "at

eleven?" At eleven, I was throwing a ball against our chogajip's wall to see how hard it could hit me on the rebound, and if I was quick enough to dodge it. At that point, I wasn't.

Iseul answers for him. "He's something of a genius, you know. It's why his brother joined your gang. To send him to the best academies. Seojin," she declares with pride, "is one of the finest healers Sunpo has seen. And once you brutally murder our *dear* friend Kalmin, he'll be able to return to his academy and likely find a cure for all illnesses within the first twenty-four hours."

I'm only half listening to her. My eyes are on Seojin, whose face has paled significantly. His throat is working, his eyes are glazed, and his fingers have curled into fists.

And I know, in that instant, that Seojin feels as much responsible for Sang's death as I do. Sang joined the Talons for his younger brother.

And Sang died.

Seojin trembles—and wrenches open the door, hurrying away with swift strides. Iseul stares after Seojin with an expression of regret and concern.

"I shouldn't have spoken about him," she says quietly, almost to herself, before turning to me. "He hasn't allowed himself to cry, you see. I do think he'd feel much better if he—well, if he did." She blinks and quickly changes the subject. "What does that Dokkaebi of yours think of your plan for this kingdom?"

"Rui is in support of my campaign," I reply. But I suspect that whether he will be in support of my aspirations past Sunpo with my Imugi will be another matter. He will be informed of the Prophecy, of course. I do hope he will be willing to accept the Imugi's return.

But if he does not, the Voice says cuttingly, ***it is only fair that he faces the consequences.***

Iseul sniffs. "I see. You're to kill the Blackbloods on the Night of the Red Moon in six nights, no? Do you have a show planned?"

"Yes. And an audience would be nice," I reply coolly. "If that sort of thing interests you."

"Oh, it *would*," Iseul purrs. "Seojin received an invitation this morning. Kalmin taunts him, but I'll use it to our advantage." Iseul's eyes narrow. "And when you're finished, perhaps you'll allow me a nibble of ki?"

Interesting. The Voice cocks its head. "If you eat somebody's soul," it guides me to say slowly, "do they still enter Jeoseung?" Do they still travel to that world of cherry blossoms and serenity?

"No," says Iseul very sweetly. "They simply fade into nothingness. Without a soul, there is only the void. Do you have a specific Blackblood that you'd like to offer up to me as a dessert, Lina?"

"I have one in mind, yes," I say, lips twisting into a smile. "If redheads happen to suit your palate."

Iseul claps her hands, looking excessively pleased. "I'm already salivating," she sings. "Oh, Lina, you *do* delight me. Whatever sort of creature it is that you are…well. You're simply *extraordinary*. I quite like your type." She skips to the door. "I suppose I should retreat back into hiding. As always, it's been a pleasure, oh Glorious Empress." With a cheeky wink and a kiss blown through the air, she disappears.

INTERLUDE

The Dokkaebi emperor has learned many tricks throughout his twenty years. One of the most useful ones is how to become quite drunk—as difficult as it is for Dokkaebi to achieve such a state. What one must do, he's found, is drink an excessive amount of wine in an excessively short time frame. The wine must be extraordinarily aged, as well—a few centuries or so should do it. The effects are temporary, of course, but in the moment—lounging on his black-thorned throne, his crown lopsided on his head, and a bottle of *very* old wine dangling from his left hand—Rui doesn't particularly care.

It takes an immense amount of effort to become drunk, so the emperor is enjoying it as best as he possibly can. The way that his vision is swimming is quite amusing. He stares up at the throne room's vast ceiling, admiring how the ruby dragons seem to move underneath his blurry gaze. How the moons are swelling and shrinking in size.

The doors of the throne room open. Rui ignores whoever has entered and takes another particularly large gulp of wine. It doesn't taste very nice, but he doesn't care. Nor does he care that it is Kang who has entered.

Kang, who is weary as he traverses the length of the silver carpet laid before the throne, withholds a sigh as he takes in his emperor—eyes bloodshot, hair tangled, face pallid. "Rui," he says softly, but the young emperor seems to be studying the ceiling with a look of intense concentration. "Rui," he says again, louder.

"Go away," snaps Rui with no small amount of irritation. "I'm busy, Kang." Another large swig of wine. He wipes his mouth with the back of his hand.

"You should be sober when you visit her."

"I want an hour of peace and silence," Rui hisses. "You are disturbing that hour of peace and silence." Jerking his gaze away from the ceiling, Rui struggles to sit in an upright, threatening position on his throne. The world swims. Frustrated, he focuses on his blurry advisor. "Leave now if you enjoy keeping your head."

Kang, who is used to these flamboyant threats, is not fazed. "We need to talk about Eunbi."

Eunbi. Rui closes his eyes. The young girl, he knows, is currently playing with Tae, a small Dokkaebi boy who delights in all things mischievous. It's likely that they're getting into some sort of trouble—stealing food from the kitchens, jumping on beds, running through the gardens with wooden swords. The palace is quite empty now, without the humans, and the children delight in the extra space to create chaos.

Eunbi only once questioned where the humans went. Hana offered her a readily accepted excuse involving the Little Palace.

"What about Eunbi?" Rui manages.

"The Prophecy," Kang replies carefully, "may have plans regarding her. If Lina accepts your…terms, later tonight, we will need to bargain for Eunbi to remain with us. I do not think Eunbi should be allowed near Lina unless necessary. It could be dangerous."

"Necessary?" Rui stands with immense difficulty. "And what would constitute *'necessary'*, Kang?"

"There may come a time where Eunbi may be….an invaluable bargaining chip."

The words cut through Rui's haze of drunkenness. Stiffening, he narrows his eyes at Kang. "She's a child. Not a bargaining chip."

"Rui," Kang replies urgently, "I know it feels impossible, but you must try to look at this strategically. Lina will do anything for her sister. The Prophecy will want Eunbi alive, as a bartering chip of its own. A princess for an allegiance. For leniency. For the acquirement of foreign troops into her army. Bonseyo has a young prince. Lina has a young sister. But I do not think Eunbi will want to be sold off like cattle. Keeping her here is both a favor and a necessity. With her to barter with—"

"You speak as if I've already failed," Rui seethes. "As if the red thread connects us to hate. We will be soul-stitched in love, Kang. I am visiting her tonight to ensure it."

"Do not tell her," Kang warns, "that two may be soul-stitched in hatred, for we are—"

"Trying to steer fate's thread to love. I am fully aware," Rui spits back.

"If she refuses—"

"If she refuses," Rui snarls, his grip tightening on the bottle's neck, "we will speak of these things then. But for now, Kang, allow me this hope."

Kang takes a steadying breath, fingers so tight around his staff that the wood creaks. "Even if she accepts," he says, "there are many possibilities where our strategy could fail. She could realize, Rui, that our offer is false. A lie. A fake alliance. She could learn that we are gathering our forces against her. I'm not done," he says sharply as Rui opens his mouth to protest. "This—proposal is a way for us to buy ourselves time. An effort to stall a war, prevent it if possible. This false alliance is an excuse for the Prophecy to allow Lina to fall in love with you, Rui. To wheedle fate in a peaceful direction. But even then, I do not know if being soul-stitched in love is enough to defeat the Prophecy. To bring back the true Lina."

"Then what is?" the emperor explodes. "What *is*?"

"I am researching," Kang replies wearily. "Fervently. But as of right now, there are no answers."

Something in Rui's chest cracks. Breathing hard, he stares at

Kang for a moment longer before—with a roar of frustration—hurling the bottle onto the floor before his advisor's feet, where it shatters into dozens of shards and begins to seep bloody red wine. His breathing coming in hoarse, harsh pants, Rui—fingers trembling—drags a hand down his face.

How is it that he ruins all he touches?

Achara. A neck snapped. A body fallen. Dead.

And now, Lina. His Lina.

He would not blame her if they are to be soul-stitched as mortal enemies. For this…this all started with his foolish, wicked game. It is a truth he knows, in his heart, that he is responsible. He knew it when he saw Lina standing in the middle of the plaza, dripping blood, a sword jutting from her abdomen. The words had come to him then, just as they do now, vicious hisses that cut him to the bone. *Your fault.*

If only, Rui thinks in despair, he could have seen past his rage and hurt and longing for death. If only he had not proposed the game that drove Lina to the rebels. To the Imugi poison. The wongun berries. Sonagi. The Prophecy.

He would not blame her if she hates him as much as he hates himself.

Where have those fleeting days of happiness gone? The days before Lina returned to Sunpo, before everything was so utterly ruined?

Rui closes his eyes, coaxing happier memories out from beneath the lessening fog of intoxication. He clings to it as the cold marble floor of the throne room is slowly stained red. Lina, smiling. Lina, laughing. Lina as he kisses the crook of her neck, the exact spot where she's ticklish. Lina, looking at him with eyes that shimmer with something deeper than friendship. His Lina.

"*Rui,*" Kang snaps. He's been repeating the name for nearly a minute, waiting for his emperor to break out of his drunken reverie. "Rui. *Rui—*" Finally, silver eyes crack open, slits of silver that bore into Kang with dissatisfaction. Kang takes a deep breath, reminding himself to be patient, even as wine seeps into his shoes and a pounding pain begins within his head. "Tonight. You will do as we've discussed. Swear it, please."

The emperor swallows hard—once, twice—before lowering himself to one of the dais steps. "I will go to her tonight. I will make the offer. Continue your research, Kang." His eyes slide to the shattered bottle. "And bring me more wine."

CHAPTER TWENTY-FOUR

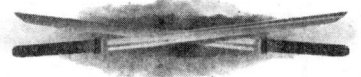

K onrarnd Kalmin is not sobbing. Konrarnd Kalmin is *shouting.* And my ears hurt.

Pressed again to the tiles of the roof, my jaw aches from the effort of clenching it, and my skin is covered with sweat from such direct exposure to the midday sun. I do not have to expand my senses for the noises in Kalmin's office to be crystal clear, for the man is roaring so loudly that I can practically see him.

He is pacing across the room, his fists clenched, his eyes blazing. "And what have the Feathers and Bills found? *Anything?*" His voice shakes the office. "Or are you incompetent? *Have the men found anything?*"

"N-nothing sir," a young, tremulous voice answers. Son Wooseok. "We've been searching the city for suspects, but nobody reports seeing anybody come in or out. Asina was last seen running past the Moonlit Hare with Jisu, Hada, and Bitgaram." I do not recognize the name Bitgaram. It must belong to the one I named Rat.

Kalmin's breathing has gone shallow in the way it does before he grows violent. I know the sound well, and my stomach churns. "Wooseok," he says slowly, and I can smell the sweat rolling from him, drenched in horrid cologne, "Asina's finger was left on my pillow when I awoke this morning. Somebody entered this palace, *my* palace, undetected. Somebody came into my bedroom *undetected.*" The floor creaks as he advances on his prey, leering. "If they'd wanted to, they could have slit my throat. My *throat.* And now, now you say that the men have *found nothing?* No clues, no signs, of who this was? Nothing? No *bodies*?"

Fear. That is fear in his voice. I grin, rage and grief and satisfaction coursing through my blood. *Bastard. You reap what you sow.*

"H-how do you know it's Asina's? It could have been Jisu's... or Bitgaram's..."

"Because," Kalmin says very slowly, "I have seen her fingers before *and that was her finger.* With the same brown birthmark on the tip. Do you dare question me, you inept—"

"S-surely you have suspicions. It could have been that g-girl, Song Iseul, or one of her informants, or her Doves..." No response from Kalmin. I hear Wooseok, backing into a corner as Kalmin advances on him, his breathing hard with hatred. "I'm sorry," he whispers. "I-I would give my life for you, I meant n-no harm...I-I'll tell the men—"

The sound of a beating reaches my ears and I set my jaw. The sooner Wooseok can poison the Feathers and Bills, the better. For his sake.

Annoyed, the Voice peers through my eyes and makes a sound of disgust. *We've seen enough.*

My body lithely makes its way to the ground.

A visit well paid. Did you taste Konrarnd Kalmin's fear? So potent. So delicious.

For all his power, Konrarnd Kalmin is a coward. We have wormed our way inside his head.

His life will grow only more miserable.

Tonight is the night I will meet Sonagi's kin.

I wait for the moon to rise with a buzzing anticipation that makes it impossible to do anything but pace around my giwajip, gnawing anxiously on my bottom lip. The Voice is beside itself with glee.

Oh, how long we've waited for this. To unite with our kin. Our kin of scales and fury. Together we will soar to immeasurable heights. Together we will claim power. All three kingdoms can be ours. Sunpo is just the beginning—

I startle as somewhere, deep in my chest, a-a *thread* is pulled, as if connected to another. My hand flies to where my heart beats, and I shake my head to clear it. It feels like heartburn, but not quite. The last time I felt this, *he* appeared...

And almost as if on cue, there is a knocking at my door.

Is it him? Is it the Dokkaebi? The Voice frowns as there is another series of knocks, these sharp and rhythmic. My legs stalk toward the door, my mouth twists into a sneer of displeasure. The Voice guides my hand into yanking open the door, revealing...

Rui.

He stands before me, one hand still raised, curled into a loose fist. "Lina," he says, leaning against the doorframe and arching a brow. "Hello, little thief."

I gape in surprise. Even the Voice is silent, before quickly recovering itself and speaking through my lips. "Haneul Rui. What are you doing here?"

"You say that," Rui drawls, pushing past me and glancing around the inside of the house. "like you aren't happy to see me. I'm wounded."

I slam the door, glowering at him warily as he grins at me in a way that says *Don't look so grumpy. Be honored by my presence instead.*

"Can you not summon at least a bit of excitement for me?" He spreads his arms wide, a smug little smirk playing on his lips. But something is...off, somehow, although he is—as usual—the portrait of perfection.

Warily, I take him in. Silky hair, a luxurious dark blue hanbok embroidered with silver flowers, glittering jewelry adorning his ears and fingers. But if I look closer…

It is as if he has not slept, yet has gone through great lengths to make it seem as if he has. There is a dullness in his gaze even as he winks. A dullness, and a sorrow. He is upset, I realize. Perhaps our last meeting impacted him more than I realized.

An anguish, it…radiates in the air, hovering there before diving into my own body, like arrows through the skin. Is it his? Is it Rui's? It must be. This is not the first time I have felt this outside emotion that was not borne from me, and something tells me that it will not be the last. Abruptly, the emotion fades, as if it were only one abrupt burst that made it through to me.

The faintest hint of wine lingers in the air. So he has been drinking. But the effects seem to have mostly worn off by now, and there is a shrewd, analytic glint in his eyes, too. And I find that I do not much like it. Not at all.

Has word reached him of the Imugi? Is conflict on our shore sooner than expected? Am I imagining that the Voice sounds… nervous?

"I didn't know you were coming," I say slowly, the words pushed past my lips by the Voice's cold hands. "Not after…"

"Our disagreement?" Rui shrugs, although he avoids my eye. "Everybody has their spats. We've just had them more than usual. But it's all behind us now, Lina. You know, I know you know, and now you know that I know you know I know."

"I… *What?*" I gape at him, utterly bewildered. "You know that I know *what?*"

"Well, that whole business with the Imugi." Rui waves a hand languidly, looking utterly unconcerned as my heart stops in my chest. "I was offended you hadn't summoned me, you see, with the ring I gave you…especially after I left without a kiss goodbye. So, I took it upon myself, again, to venture into Sunpo. Worry not—

no humans were stolen this time. But you were occupied running through the streets like a chicken with its head cut off, and with four Blackbloods on its tail. And then, to my dismay... You jumped into the sewer, Lina. And things got far more interesting afterward."

He knows. He saw. He was watching... The Voice snarls. *He will try to stop us from fulfilling the Prophecy, for he has heard it. Eavesdropper. Liar. Cheat.* Blades extend from my wrists. Scales emerge on my arms, traveling to my neck, framing my face in armor.

No, I think in panic, but I cannot force my weaponry away. The Voice is snarling, and my muscles tense.

The Prophecy must be fulfilled.

No. No. Oh gods, no. But I cannot move. My head swims with pain. Rui, however, seems utterly oblivious as he stares at the ceiling. "Regardless, *jagi,* you did not lie about Asina. Her eyes did remind me of the fish that swim in the Black Sea. I can't say that I was sorry to see her killed."

Jagi. The term of endearment, "darling," gives the Voice pause. It tilts its head calculatingly, and the pain in my skull recedes. Yet still the snakeskin does not disappear, nor do the blades recede into my wrists. "You heard the Prophecy?" I whisper suspiciously, guided by the Voice.

"I couldn't help myself. I do enjoy poetry." He still does not look at me.

Slowly, almost groggily, I remember sneaking into his bedroom in the Gyeulcheon palace, stumbling upon his books of poetry, and an odd sort of nostalgia fills me, although I do not understand why. "Yes," I say quietly, "you do." Something in my tone must strike something in him, for he finally looks at me—really looks at me—and inhales sharply at my armor.

"Lina."

"I... Hello." I cannot think of what else to say, for the Voice has frozen, failing to put any words on my tongue as it has been doing. The scales begin to fade from my skin.

His face softens. "Hello." A flash of sudden relief spears through my skin, as if it is an arrow launched from Rui's heart to mine.

"Is that you?" I whisper, and the words are still my own. I know I should take advantage of the Voice's momentary lapse in control, but this—somehow, this is more important than serpents and prophecies and everything, everything else. I know it is. "What I feel. In here." I press a fist to my chest.

His throat bobs. "Yes," he whispers.

Interesting. My back straightens, my chin tilts upward. Once more, my snakeskin stands out strong against my flesh. "Am I feeling *you*?" I demand. "Your emotions? *How? Why?*"

Rui takes a deep breath and steps toward me. My body tenses as he runs his hands down my arms until he interlaces his fingers with my own. As he bends to press his forehead to my own.

The Voice is puzzled. It pulls my brows into a frown. "What are you doing?" I yank myself away from him. "Are you here to stop me? I will warn you, you cannot. The Prophecy must be fulfilled. The Imugi have accepted me as their empress, their Yeouiju."

For a split second, blue Dokkaebi fire churns in Rui's eyes, and I feel a wave of an external emotion that is hard to untangle— frustration? Guilt? Regret? Whatever it is, it quickly vanishes. "I don't think that I *can* stop you, little thief. For Prophecies are always fulfilled, no?" Rui scans my face, running his stare along the scales with an inscrutable expression. "It would be foolish of me to try to stop you. For even without a Prophecy, you are the most stubborn creature I know. So, no. I am not here to stop you, nor am I here to beg for mercy."

"Then why have you come?"

"I'm here, Lina, to offer you my allegiance."

A second of silence so thick that I choke on it settles between us. My head reels in shock. The Voice is the first to speak, lacing its fingers underneath its chin and tilting its head. ***An allegiance.***

Interesting, it muses. *How very...interesting. But is he sincere? Why would he offer such a thing? Eternal enemies do not become allies overnight.*

Rui is watching me carefully, and I wonder for a moment if he can hear the Voice. If he can somehow *feel* my emotions, my hesitation. "The way I see it," he says after a brief pause, "with the rebels gone, my kind is content in Gyeulcheon. No longer must we deal with mortal toils, no longer is it required that we maintain the exhausting job of lording over foolish humans. This realm, Iseung, is not worth another seven-hundred-year war. You are welcome to it. For I have come to realize that a pocket realm, away from the manacles of mortal values and responsibility, is a far better fit for my sort. For me. Gyeulcheon's creation was truly a blessing in disguise.

"Truly," he says as I frown, "I do not lie. Not to you. It was so long ago that we fought against the Imugi in strife over this realm—long enough that in hindsight, I do not understand what we were fighting over. There is nothing for me here, but there is everything for you. I have always wanted to see you like this." He takes a step closer to me, and I tense as his hands approach my own. He grasps them gently, staring into my eyes. "You were born to be an empress. You were born to rule. You were born to rattle the stars, to sit on a throne of vengeance and power. You were born to this.

"So, I come here today, Lina, to offer my allegiance. My support. My trust and admiration. I come..." Rui swallows, and I think that he might be frightened. And I can tell that whatever he says next will change the course of our story forever.

My heart begins to race, my palms to sweat. The Voice stares avidly through my eyes, holding its breath.

"I come," he says again, this time gently, his voice so soft and sweet, "to tell you, Shin Lina, that we are soul-stitched."

CHAPTER TWENTY-FIVE

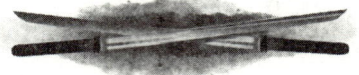

"Soul-stitched," I repeat warily. "What is—what is *soul-stitched*?" **He speaks in riddles.**

We're sitting on my bed. Evening sun, a dark and dusty orange, glows against Rui's tan skin, turning it a deep gold. He is holding my hands in his. The Voice is hesitantly tolerating his touch, pacing back and forth in deliberation. The loyalties of the Dokkaebi would be very useful indeed. But what does he mean when he says we are soul-stitched?

"I'd thought it a legend for so long," Rui says softly. He's tracing my fingers with his. His skin is cool, smooth. Mine is hot, feverish as the Voice muses and mumbles and continues to pace across the planes of my cognizance. "Do you know what the red thread of fate is?"

My head shakes.

"Simply put, it's a…physical apparition of destiny. Some say that it is stitched by Gameunjang herself, Goddess of Luck and Fate. At least, that's how Kang describes it. It ties together two people who are meant to be joined, as lovers, forever. And when those two people are joined by the thread, they are—"

"—soul-stitched," I say, realization dawning.

Rui nods. "Sometimes, the red thread will stitch the two souls together by connecting its two ends to their little fingers. Other times, the thread will join the two together by the heart. When we were kissing, in the foyer, with Eunbi asleep in the next room…I felt it then. And I know that you must have, too."

"It was as if a needle and thread had been taken to my heart. As if I had been connected to something."

"Someone," he corrects gently. "Me."

"So we're—destined to be together? Forever?" I demand incredulously.

"Yes," Rui replies. "To fall in love. Forever." He stares down at my hands, an unreadable expression passing over his face like a shadow.

"You knew." The Voice turns my lips downward. "Why didn't you say anything?"

"I thought it a legend. The Dokkaebi speak of it, yes, but only rarely. And often to mock its implications. To be with somebody forever? Dokkaebi lives are long, and the thought of eternal monogamy, to most, is…unappealing."

"But not to you," I say slowly. "Never you."

"No. Not to me." He smiles almost bitterly, and I wonder if he's thinking of Achara, who spurned his offer to wed. "Soul-stitched couples have an irrefutably strong connection, little thief. We can feel each other's emotions when they are particularly strong. Right now, I feel your shock. Bewilderment. The soul-stitched can also find each other, anywhere in the world. It's how you knew when to expect me. If you concentrate on the thread between us, you'll be able to glean my exact location." Suddenly, Rui grimaces, as if having realized he made a mistake.

"What is it?"

"Nothing," he replies with a rueful smile. "Only that I've given you this much information so quickly. You're likely at a loss."

"Not at all." ***This development could prove very useful.*** "Continue."

"The soul-stitched can also visit each other's dreams. And they're…possessive of each other. Quite possessive. As our connection grows, you'll be able to see the thread connecting us, should you concentrate."

"By connection, you mean love." I scrutinize him analytically. "Rui, do you love me?"

"I think I've begun to," he whispers. "And many marriages have been founded on much less."

Marriage.

The entire world stops on its rotation. **What did he just say?**

It's only when Rui raises his eyes to me that I realize the Voice spoke through my mouth—harsh with surprise, demanding. "Marriage," my mouth is saying now. "You want to—to *marry* me?"

"Yes. Yes," Rui repeats. "I..." The emperor has gone quite, quite pale. "I suppose this isn't the best proposal, is it?" His voice wavers, and he takes a shuddering breath. He is so uncharacteristically disheveled, so thrown off-balance.

"No," my lips say, coolly amused, "it's really not. Why do you want my hand? Because we're soul-stitched? For an alliance?"

Rui clears his throat. "An alliance," he agrees. "That's right. An alliance between the Empress of the Imugi and the Emperor of the Dokkaebi would be much more advantageous than another war." A hint of his custom wryness has entered his tone. "And an alliance will appease those of my kingdom who do not take kindly to the idea of an Imugi rule over Iseung—and likewise, it will appease the Imugi who hold tightly to old grudges."

Of all the unexpected things... The Voice begins to smile. **Well, well, well. This could work in our favor.**

"We're soul-stitched, Lina. Our destinies are bound together. It is likely that in the future, we would have wed regardless of prophecies and Imugi. Surely, there can be no harm in doing so now, to form a partnership at the turn of an age. But, Lina..." He takes a deep breath, and I feel his acute anxiety shoot between the thread connecting us, nestling into my skin. "It is also because your heart has already called to mine, singing an enchantment as sweetly as Manpasikjeok's. When you are in my arms, it is as if a part of me was broken and is now whole. And as I said"—a hint of a smile—"marriages have been formed on much less."

My hands tremble in his as I stare down at him, unable to speak. The Voice is twiddling its thumbs thoughtfully and clucking its tongue in contemplation. ***An alliance... An alliance could benefit us greatly. The Dokkaebi will not stand in the way of our conquests, remaining in their pocket realm...*** "A marriage to cement an alliance," I finally say. "A marriage of convenience."

"But it could be more," Rui breathes. "So much more. Do you think... Do you think you could ever love me, Lina?" His eyes are huge with an almost childlike fear and through our red thread, I feel an intense flare of hope. I wonder if he can feel the Voice's growing pleasure and triumph.

"I think I could," are the words that the Voice feeds past my lips. And although they are true, they are not mine. "If it is our destiny to be bound forever in love, how could I not?"

Rui closes his eyes. I feel his flare of tangled emotions, but they vanish before I have time to unravel them. My hand reaches to guide his face closer, but as his lips near mine, the Voice pauses. Its fingers loosen, slightly, on the reins that control me.

You, it says in reluctance. ***You can do this part. I have no taste for it.***

I feel it recede, stepping away from the forefront of my mind. But it is still there. Watching. Its presence is heavy and cold, and its hands pluck words from my mouth as I fight to say something, to tell Rui that I am not in control...

You will tell him nothing.

So I don't.

Instead, I slant my lips against his—my soul-stitched. I twine my fingers through his hair. He tastes like heady wine and sweet, sugared plums. Rui makes a noise against my mouth—half a moan, half a protest, and pulls away slightly. I tug him back, guide him down atop me as I lie on the bed.

I fumble with the knot of his hanbok, sliding the dark silk from his chiseled body, letting it tumble to the ground. Breathless, I hook my legs around the waist of his baji pants, savoring his reaction. As his lips find that small, ticklish spot on my neck, I moan his name—

And Rui freezes, glancing down at me. His eyes are wide with surprise. *"You,"* he breathes, and his smile is heartbreakingly beautiful. "My Lina," he murmurs again, and his hands find the hem of my tunic. I nod, and he coaxes the fabric from my skin. It drops to the ground with his silken robe. All that remains now is the soft white fabric of my supportive bandeau.

"Can I?" Rui whispers, voice rough with need. I can feel him—his passion, his longing, the sheer force of his desire. It rockets down the red thread like a bullet, embedding itself in my heart, where the same desires are echoed.

"Yes," I breathe.

His fingers are gentle as they slide the bandeau up and over my head. Rui's eyes darken, dilate as the fabric falls from his fingertips to the floor below.

My chest is rising and falling erratically, and I feel my cheeks flush with heady need and...and a rising self-consciousness underneath Rui's stare. I make to cover myself, but he shakes his head, bending down to kiss my breasts. He brings a puckered point into his mouth and *sucks*, slowly and savoringly.

Sheer sensation overcomes my hesitancy, and my head falls back onto the pillows. Rui's mouth is deliciously hot, almost feverish as he licks and nibbles and teases. I close my eyes, running a hand through Rui's hair as his hand drifts to the waistline of my pants, fingers toying with the hem.

Before he can ask, I nod, breathless. "Yes. Yes, you can."

Rui smiles against my skin. His fingers dip underneath the waistband of my baji pants and trail down the thin fabric of my underwear. I gasp in pleasure as he begins to trace lazy circles through the cotton, a noise hastily smothered by his lips as they once again meet mine.

Every movement of his hand sends flares of heat sparking up my spine. Every caress of his tongue against mine is luxurious. He plays me like he plays his flute, coaxing noises past my lips I didn't know I was capable of making. I soon find my back arching, my breathing even more ragged, my legs shaking and—

A wave of pleasure crests through me, as forceful as the Yongwangguk Sea's tumultuous waters. I am dimly aware of how I pull Rui closer, panting hard, grabbing his back with rigid fingers. When the wave finally recedes, my body goes limp and pliant.

Rui kisses my forehead and rolls off me, his cheeks flushed pink, his own breathing shaky. "I felt it," he says in wonder, pulling the sheets over us. "I felt you, through the thread..."

My eyes are heavy-lidded as I nestle into his arms.

I feel...I feel wonderful. The Voice is blissfully silent, allowing me—us—this moment. This wonderful, splendid moment. My heart feels light, fluttering. Rui is my soul-stitched. All I have wanted, for so long, is to have a family again. Eunbi and Rui are exactly that to me. Family. I curve my lips into a smile.

I am more myself than I have been since I heard that godsdamn Prophecy.

The Prophecy. Smile faltering, I open my mouth as it all crashes back to me, and try once more to speak of the matter to Rui—of how when the Voice is in control, I want the Three Kingdoms for my own. Of how I want—worshippers. Subjects. How I no longer think of my gods, my religion, and think only of myself. How I want to be an empress, a *goddess*. How I am no longer striving to make Good decisions, but spiraling into a void of mistakes and misjudgments, steered by the...the *thing* that has taken up residency in my head. My empathy, gone. The kindness I have worked so hard to cultivate, gone.

But the Voice is quicker. The Voice snatches the words from my lips and locks them away. My mouth moves silently under Rui's concerned gaze.

"Lina?"

Tears of frustration come to my eyes, only to be hastily blinked away by the Voice. *If you want this time with him,* it warns, *you will behave.*

Fine.

Fine.

"When will the wedding ceremony be?" I rasp as Rui scrutinizes me through heavy-lidded eyes. The words come from my own mind—sometime between our kiss and the journey to the bedroom, the Voice chose to recede into nothing more than a vague presence in the back of my thoughts, lending us our privacy. But it is watching. Always watching.

His muscles tighten and I think for a half second that a faint sheen of inexplicable sorrow crosses his face before he turns away from me. But when he speaks, his voice is smooth and steady, and I feel nothing through the thread. "Whenever you desire, little thief, and wherever. We Dokkaebi do not have a wedding tradition as you mortals do—" He cuts off, perhaps remembering that I am no longer a mortal. I'm…something else. "We can wed in the next nights, if you so desire."

"So soon?" My eyes widen in a mixture of pleasure and surprise.

"If you desire a grand affair," Rui murmurs, still staring at the wall, "I will make it so. Yet I do not pretend to know the customs…"

"They're simple, really." I smile down at him as he turns back to me, eyes now twinkling.

"Oh?"

I flop back onto the pillow, smiling slightly. When I was younger, I attended the wedding of a fellow barley farmer. It was a joyous affair, and that night I went to sleep with my stomach for once full. "The bride wears a special hanbok," I say, remembering the bride-to-be's beautiful red hanbok, "and the groom wears one, too. Vows are spoken—promises of love and loyalty—and they're sealed soon afterward by the sipping of wine from a gourd and bowing. Afterward, at the reception, the bride is handed chestnuts and dates."

Rui's brows raise. "I assume she eats them?"

"No." My smile grows, remembering the food flying through the air, and my small, hungry hands shooting upward in vain. "She then gives them to the families of the couple, who throw them back toward her—she tries to catch them in her skirt. And the number she catches predicts the number of children she will have."

"The ceremony sounds simple enough," Rui muses. "If that is what you wish to do, Lina, then I will oblige."

"We could wed under the moons of Gyeulcheon," I say dreamily, nestling deeper within the sheets. "We could once again dance in the ballroom as we did during your revel..." The memory of our dance warms my skin as I remember how we spun through the ballroom, whirling to the melody of the saccharine music, skin pressed so close... "And afterward," I murmur, tracing the line of his jaw with my finger, "we will consummate our marriage." The thought fills me with a heady sort of desire. After what we just did...I am hungry for more. Yet I want there to be a special moment. Where I can cherish him without blood-crusted nails and a head full of plots. Our marriage, I realize with heating blood, will provide exactly that.

Rui smiles, but it wavers even as he brushes a strand of hair from my face. "I think," he starts carefully, "it would be better not to wed in my realm right now."

"Why is that?"

"As I said...there will be some who do not wish to see you fulfill your Prophecy. I have told my people of it, and of my intention to unite us. Yet some are angry. Some are scared." Rui clears his throat and returns to staring at the wall. "It would be better, you see, for you to remain out of Gyeulcheon."

A slight hurt blooms in my heart, although his reasoning rings true. "Oh."

"I am sorry, Lina."

"No. No, it's fine." For a moment, I'd nearly forgotten my... circumstances. "We will find somewhere else." Turning onto my side, I run a hand through his silky hair. "You said that you have told your people of the Prophecy. What does your court say?" *What does Kang say, with his suspicious glances and wary eyes?*

Does he plan to stop me? Please, tell me so. This is not what I truly want—

Shh. Irritated, the Voice storms to the forefront of my mind, taking in its hands the reins of my consciousness—and once again, my actions and words are not fully my own. It shoves my own thoughts to the side. Locks them in the cell. And now my body is nothing but a puppet. I can feel myself slipping, slipping away.

"They are...adjusting." Rui's jaw tightens as he scans my face, and something in his expression changes. "But they understand how great of an importance this alliance holds. They will not offend you. In a similar vein... Do you think that the Imugi will accept this union? They are old, and harbor even older resentments."

"Sonagi worships me," I reply smugly. "She has done as I have bid her. You saw her eat Asina, did you not?"

"Eat Asina." Rui blinks. "I—yes. Yes, I did. It was, ah, entertaining."

"Later, to please me, she placed Asina's remaining finger on Kalmin's pillow. She is the Mother of Imugi, and she obeys my every whim. I am a daughter to her. The others will worship me as well. I'm the Prophesized, Rui—so how can they not? I meet with them tonight," I add. "Sonagi and I will join the others when night falls."

He sits up in bed, eyes wide. "Tonight?"

"Yes." Sliding out of the bed, I pull my bandeau and tunic back on, and knot my hair into a tiny bun. "I assume that we travel into Jeoseung to do so, although I don't know how."

"Allow me to accompany you. The both of you." Rui has begun

to clothe himself as well. "To introduce myself as your betrothed, to announce our alliance and the lack of need for a war. Tonight can be the beginning of peace between our two kinds."

"She is not expecting you. I do not pretend to know how she will react—or how you will react." *It is not a bad idea, though, to move forward with cementing the alliance...*

"You possess so little faith in your soul-stitched." Rui smirks. "Sonagi and I are old friends. I don't doubt that she will be pleased to see me. When will she come for you?"

The scorching sun has begun to dip below the skyline, leaving my bedroom with only a watery wan light. Night will fall within the hour, and I do not doubt that Sonagi will retrieve me the moment Sunpo falls into inky darkness. "Soon."

"Then let us wait together—and welcome this new era with open arms."

CHAPTER TWENTY-SIX

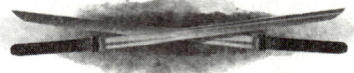

Contrary to his words, Rui chooses to welcome the new era with a badly placed joke.

Standing on the rooftop of my giwajip, Sonagi looming before us with her eyes slitted in surprised suspicion, Rui sketches a bow that is nothing if not blatantly sarcastic. His face is all hard lines of wariness, his eyes flashing with thinly concealed animosity that makes my muscles tense and my teeth grit. Perhaps he is not as able to let go of hostility so easily as he has led me to believe, if the intense dislike streaming through the thread is any indication. I close my eyes in exasperation as he speaks, his tone dripping with false sweetness and edged with cutting blades.

"Sonagi. You've become even more beautiful with age."

"Why iss the Dokkaebi here?" Sonagi's eyes snap toward me. *"He isss our enemy, Child of Venom."* She sways disapprovingly. *"I requessst an explanation."*

I open my eyes and cut a sharp glare toward Rui, who is looking as if he would like nothing more than to sever Sonagi's head from her body and bathe in her blood. The alliance, I suspect, is the only thing holding him back from attempting to do so—and for that I am grateful. I am no fool. It is clear that this alliance will be an uneasy one, with prejudices harbored on both sides, but it is an alliance that will benefit us greatly.

"Sonagi," I reply smoothly, "Haneul Rui and I are...soul-stitched."

She waves. *"I do not know 'sssoul-ssstitched'. What doesss that mean?"*

"That we're true loves," I explain. "Bound together by the red thread of fate. As such, we have formed an understanding that I suspect you will be pleased with." As clearly and as articulately as possible, I explain the terms of the bargain with the Mother of Imugi. "And so you see, a war is avoided, leaving us able to fulfill the Prophecy. Rui comes here today in a show of good faith."

"A ssshow of good faith? He murdered our people. He attacked our home."

Rui now seems incredibly bored, his expression betraying no hint of rage or discomfort. "Please, Sonagi, you know as well as I do that my kind does not speak the Serpentine Language." He glances toward me. "I will not ask how you picked it up so quickly, Lina."

With a jolt, I realize that Sonagi has indeed been speaking another tongue.

A moment later, it becomes clear that I have also been speaking in the same tongue, the language of rustling hay and smooth susurrations.

I wonder how long I have understood it. The Serpentine Language, as Rui called it. The prejudice of the Dokkaebi toward Imugi is quite clear in what they have named the language of the Imugi.

"Why would we trusssst you?" Sonagi snaps, now in the common tongue, her susurrations now choppy, each word tinged with an accent. "You ssslaughtered my children and laughed at our demissse. You claimed Iseung as your own, and now you would allow us to reclaim it with no intervention on the part of your kind? You would be content to remain forevermore in your sssmall realm? I do not believe you, Dokkaebi... I do not believe you at all. Why would you proposssse this alliance if not to weaken our defensesss and plant daggersss in our backsss?"

"For Lina," Rui says simply, his eyes bright. "I do not do this for you, old enemy. I do this for my soul-stitched."

My heart glows with pleasure. "Trust him." I place a comforting hand on Sonagi's head, the scales cold on my skin. "We would be foolish not to accept this alliance. A war would be an unfortunate distraction."

"*I will never trusst him. How can you be so sure of his intentionsss?*" Sonagi's hood flares. "*He is not to be trusted.*"

"He is my betrothed, my soul-stitched," I say sharply, "and will be treated as such. That is a command. Our alliance takes us a step closer to fulfilling Yeomra's Prophecy. He will come with us tonight to meet the others. He will not be touched, for soon he will be my husband. Treat him as such." I glance at him. He is silently staring at the moon. Patches of dark pink, a near-red, have begun to appear on the moon's rosy, pearlescent surface, signifying that we are one night closer to the Night of the Red Moon. After tonight, it will be only five moons away.

"*Or I will be very displeased indeed.*" My tone drips with icicles.

"*I live to ssserve you, for you are the Yeouiju. And propheciesss are always fulfilled. Perhapsss thisss was meant to happen.*" Sonagi sighs. "*Very well. We will journey to Jeoseung thisss night,*" she says in the common tongue, scales scraping against the tiles as she begins to circle around Rui and me.

Rui looks skeptical. "You don't mean to kill us, do you? Forgive me if I doubt the validity of her intentions," he snaps as I shoot him a look, "for it was not so long ago that we were trying very hard to kill each other."

"*You I would have no qualmsss of killing, but my daughter has forbidden it.*" Sonagi sighs. "*There isss another way to enter the Yeomra's realm.*"

"Do tell."

"*To enter Jeoseung, one of hisss realm must spill their blood first. That is you, Child of Venom. You are like usss, from Jeoseung, a creature of death and rebirth. Once your blood is ssspilled, three timesss must Yeomra'sss name be ssspoken. You will do the sssame for the return. You may take whoever you want with you if they,* too, ssspill their blood and ssspeak." A flash of fangs. "Bleed your gold, Dokkaebi. We will wait for you on the other sssside."

I watch through wide eyes as Sonagi twists to bite her own neck. Dark green blood dribbles to the ground. Thrice she whispers Yeomra's name, and in a flash of dark mist, she disappears.

"Perhaps Sonagi and I have something in common after all," Rui says, staring at the spot where Sonagi had been.

"And that is?" I quirk an eyebrow.

"A flair for the dramatic," Rui mutters. He watches as I set one of my scaled blades to the palm of my hand, and as I drag the tip across my skin. With a flash of pain, the skin parts, welling blood. I stare down at it, for a moment unable to comprehend what I am seeing.

My blood, which ran red but a few days ago, is now the same green as Sonagi's. *Oh, gods—*

Yes, the Voice breathes, raising my hand closer to my eyes. ***Oh yes. Look at this. Beautiful, so beautiful... We are evolving, Lina. With the knowledge of the Prophecy coursing through our veins, our powers will grow. We will grow.***

"Lina?" Rui's voice is soft. "Jagi, what is it?" He strides closer, a hand gripping my wrist, pulling it closer to his chest. He stares down at the cut dripping green, and a sharp breath catches his throat. "Oh," he murmurs. "Oh Lina."

My lips twist into a smile. "Isn't it beautiful? Come, Rui, you must spill your blood as well."

"Here." Rui holds his hand out to me, his eyes dark. "You do it."

The Voice is eager. It takes Rui's hand in mine and slashes the blade across his skin with a smile. Golden ichor drips down his skin, and Rui flinches in pain—although for some reason, I did not think that the cut would hurt him very much. But there is no time to trouble over his reaction. Jeoseung awaits.

I curl my fingers into a fist, letting my blood drip down to the tiles below as Rui does the same. Joy sings in my heart at what is to come. "Yeomra," Rui and I whisper together. "Yeomra. *Yeomra.*"

I laugh in glee as the same dark mist that took Sonagi swirls around us. A cold, cold wind whips at my hair, and my stomach tumbles as we are borne away—away from Sunpo, away from Iseung, flung across a field of dark purple flowers and a forest of towering, skeletal-white trees. I am dimly aware of Rui next to me, shouting something in horror and staring down at the expanse of beautiful death below us, but I pay him no heed. Exhilaration overtakes me and I whoop, filled with a pounding purpose.

This is what I was born for. This is who I am.

When our feet finally touch the ground of Jeoseung, the roaring of the rose-tinted Seocheongang River sounds mutedly in the distance, but other than that it is strangely quiet. We are still on the side of Jeoseung that Sang once referred to as the side of the "more-or-less living"—for we have not crossed the jade Hwangcheon Bridge that leads to the true afterlife. Instead, we are within the forest of bone-white trees. Long blades of grass stretch upward, dark green and earthy-fragrant. Farther away, the thick blanket of trees tapers off, revealing a large azure lake encircled by sparkling white stone, from which emerges a large cave mouth, tunneling in deep.

Sonagi is nowhere to be seen. Rui's hand joins mine. I think that it trembles, but I am not sure.

"Sonagi?" I call, my voice ringing throughout the realm. It echoes back to me. *Sonagi? Sonagi? Sonagi?*

"She's left us," Rui mutters darkly. "Wonderful. You know, Lina, I could have predicted that this would happen—"

The water of the lake ripples.

Rui cuts off, choking. My hands fly to my mouth in delight as Imugi emerge from the cave's mouth, slipping into the water and gracefully swimming to the grassy shore. Their scales sparkle with water underneath the realm's glittering, pale blue light. Sonagi is in the forefront, and her eyes twinkle as she leads her children to surround us.

Rui and I soon stand in the center of a ring composed of hundreds of sparkling, scaled bodies. Large golden eyes shine like lanterns onto us, cutting through the fog. Forked tongues flick into the air, and my name rises as a chant on serpentine lips. *"Lina. Lina. Lina. Lina."* Sonagi is at the forefront of the ring, a few feet before me, her scaled face proud and filled with adoration.

It is as if I am home.

There are hundreds of them, hundreds of glittering scales and maws gaping into smiles. The ring around us writhes and coils as the Imugi slither in a circle, twisting and twining over one another, a sea of serpents weaving through the trees. Only Sonagi does not move, remaining where she is.

"Behold the Yeouiju," she cries, and her children hiss in delight as I turn in an attempt to see them all, to meet them all. My soul sings in happiness, and I am filled with a wondering warmth. These creatures seem to me a part of me as much as my arms and legs. As if they are the piece that my puzzle has been missing, and as if I am finally, finally whole. Tears sparkle in my eyes and I nearly trip over my feet attempting to keep up with the ever-flowing ring.

"Behold the Prophessized, the Child of Venom! Behold she who will deliver uss Fulfillment, she who we ssserve most adoringly! She who will rule all! She who will take uss to the sky as Yong!"

"Lina," they whisper, voices overlapping one another in a symphony of susurrations. *"Lina, oh Lina, you have come at lassst! Lina, the Prophesssized, the Child of Venom. We have been waiting for you for ssso long!"*

One Imugi darts out of the ring, smaller than the others, and shyly nudges my boot with its head. *A child,* I think in wonderment. It grins up at me with stubby little fangs before being pulled back into the tide by another serpent who shakes its head disapprovingly. None of the Imugi possess Sonagi's hood—they resemble dark, blue-green pythons, rather than a cobra. Sonagi's hood must be a sign of her rank as the mother.

"*Our empresss, our queen,*" Sonagi continues, stretching herself high, staring down at me with a brilliant sort of love. "*Come at lasst!*"

"*Come at lasst!*" the others chorus. "*Come at lasst! But who… Who is thisss?*" The circle has begun to quicken around us. Eyes, for the first time, focus on Rui and glower with surprised hatred. Hisses of shock burst into the air.

"*Dokkaebi!*" one Imugi snarls. "*It is he, the flute-wielder! What doesss he do here?*"

Fangs gnash, and mouths spit venom that lands only inches from Rui's shoes. The Dokkaebi emperor's skin has gone pale, and he glances at me with what almost looks like fear. His long hair lifts in the wind generated by the rapidly spinning circle of serpents, and blue fire sparks between his ringed fingertips.

"You will stay back," Rui orders sharply as more venom flies through the air. The Imugi, catching sight of the fire, screech in outrage, shrinking away. The ring breaks in an explosion of dark scales, and now Imugi stare at the fire, scattered across the skeletal forest in no specific formation. They writhe in rage, rearing back, stretching to their full, towering heights. "For I remember, as I am sure you do, the power this flame holds over your kind. Attack me, and you will burn."

"*He comesss armed!*"

"*He daresss bring that here—*"

"*Dokkaebi fire—*"

"*Our old enemy!*"

"Lina." Rui cuts his glare to me. "Tell them I mean no harm." A blue flame now burns in his palm. "But I do not wield this lightly. I will answer venom with flame."

Violence is no way to start an alliance. A hand raises into the air. My eyes narrow to slits. The Voice plucks words from midair and sends them drifting onto my tongue. "*Imugi,*" my mouth says, cold and clear. The serpents freeze, golden eyes bulging wide in anticipation. Rui's Dokkaebi fire burns steadily in his palm, and he glances toward me warily, unable to understand my words as I continue. *"I have been shown the story of your kind. I feel your fears. I summon your scales. I bleed your blood."* Indeed, the green substance still trickles down my reptilian arm, sticky and warm. The Imugi gaze at it, enraptured. *"Too long have you waited for me in this realm of death and shadow, but I am here now. I am here to fulfill my Prophecy. And Haneul Rui is also here. You must wonder why, and I do not blame you for that. He has been your adversary and creator of your exile in a war of centuries, but now that has changed, for an alliance has been struck."*

Wide-eyed, the Imugi whisper among themselves. I clear my throat sharply in annoyance, and my subjects fall silent. *"An alliance,"* my lips continue smoothly, *"between the Empress of the Imugi, and the Emperor of the Dokkaebi. A marriage between two souls, destined to join each other in love. Joined by the red thread of fate. Soul-stitched.*

"No longer will a war stand in the way of our conquests. Undistracted, we will claim the Three Kingdoms as our own. It is in an act of good faith that my betrothed accompanies me here today. We wish to mend the breakages between our two people." The serpents stir in distrust, and I run a sharp eye over them. *"He is to remain untouched. Disobey me, and I will be most displeased. Soon, he will be my husband."*

"Obey," the Imugi whisper. *"Yesss. We will obey."* Like a line of falling dominos, the Imugi lower their heads until all of them — all of them — are bowing to my will.

Perfect. The Voice smiles, pleased.

"Good." Smiling coldly, I look over to Rui. He has not understood a word of my speech, and regards me with puzzlement. *"Now,"* I murmur, turning back to the Imugi, *"We will take Sunpo first. On the Night of the Red Moon, I will seize the palace. Tell*

me. Will you be Yong, by then? Or will you remain in your serpent form?"

Sonagi raises her head. *"Our transsssformation will not occur on the first conquesst, daughter,"* she replies. *"Forgive me if I have led you to believe otherwisse. But to become Yong, we musst first claim all of the Three Kingdomsss. We can do so only with you, the Yeouiju. Our evolution will be complete only once the Easstern Continent — Sunpo, Wyusan, and Bonseyo — resst within our clutches. So we will come to you within our ssserpent form, Child of Venom. But resst assured, we possess a great power, and an even greater hunger. Our mawsss are yours to command as you wish. We wait for your summonsss."*

We would expect no less. The Voice paces back and forth. **But to keep them here, in Jeoseung is an act of cruelty. We have been trapped before, imprisoned. It is not the way we would choose for our Imugi.**

"Why must you wait here in such a hidden realm?" I murmur. "No. You will return to Iseung tonight, and roam as you wish. Tonight, my loves, you are free. Tonight, your exile is broken. Tonight is the start of our reign.

"But mind," I add, perhaps a bit wryly, *"that you do not eat those who would be my subjects. I know you will be hungry, but target only those who endorse the Blackbloods — the gang residing in the palace. Those whom you track entering or leaving the palace... Well. You can devour them as you wish."* For the Blackblood sponsors are of little use to me, and their deaths of even smaller consequence. "But spare a young and bruised boy," I add, thinking of Wooseok, who I still need. *"The last Claw, clad in gray.*

"And you will come to our wedding." I take Rui's cool hand in my own. He looks down at me in some surprise. *"To cement the union between the Dokkaebi and the Imugi."*

The Imugi hiss in joyous agreement. Sonagi's hood flares as she rears her head back, maw dripping as she stretches herself upward in triumph. The silent realm is suddenly alive with victory, bursting with undiluted ecstasy. Rui's hand tightens in mine.

And I, Empress of the Imugi, look upon my subjects and know that this memory will exist within my mind always—bright and golden and utterly perfect in every way.

INTERLUDE

The Dokkaebi emperor is careful not to wake his sleeping soul-stitched as he slides out of the bed, the scent of dead roses and blood clinging to his body like a disease that he cannot eradicate. Moonlight trickles through the narrow wooden hallway of the hanok as he slowly makes his way toward the kitchen, where he settles himself atop a few cushions before the small table.

One breath, in and out.

Two breaths, steady. Three breaths, and…

His attempts at calming himself are futile. The emperor's face crumples; he buries it in his hands. It is hard to quiet his sobs, but he does, shoving them deep down into himself until they press against his stomach, demanding to be let out. No. He will not. He must be silent, and he is, save for the shuddering, shallow breaths that do nothing to rid him of the terrible, aching grief pressing down upon his shoulders.

Is this what they have come to? Is this who he has become?

He is now everything the mortals think him to be. Liar. Manipulator. Wicked, wicked creature.

An hour ticks by, marked by the shifting light of Dalnim's pinkish moon. Slowly, Rui raises his haggard face from his hands and quietly summons a corridor of undulating darkness. Standing, he steps into the shadows, falling through the hidden crevices of Sunpo until he emerges in the largest one of all—Gyeulcheon.

They're waiting for him in the throne room. Chan and Hana are leaning against the obsidian columns, watching their emperor with narrow eyes. All day, they have been organizing their forces. All day, they have been preparing for war.

Chan's throat is hoarse from shouting orders as he observed the troops' training. His soldiers don't know what they're training for—not yet. If a war can be avoided, if Rui's…girl…can be reached and the Prophecy diverted, the soldiers will think that this was only a routine practice, initiated so they became less rusty. And they are very, very rusty—the product of peace, apparently, is forgetting all useful stratagem.

But if Rui and Lina are stitched together as mortal enemies rather than true loves, Chan will once again take up the mantle as Supreme Commander—a position that hasn't had to be used for a very, very long time. He knows who he will appoint as lieutenants, who he will sort into cavalries. Who he will choose as captains, and who he will subject to extra-harsh training. Who will receive the wongun enhancers that Kang prepared as a precaution against the now-gone rebels and gain the powers of a Gaksi Dokkaebi.

"Well?" snaps Chan, much to the irritation of Kang. It is clear to the advisor, who stands next to Rui's throne, that it is not wise to push the emperor much right now. For Rui looks terrible as he trudges to his throne, slumping down upon it, dragging ringed fingers down his face.

"She agreed," Rui says quietly. "To the marriage."

Chan and Hana exchange long looks. It seems to Hana that truly, this would all be much easier if they killed the girl now. "That's all well and good," sniffs Hana, "but does she love you? Is it enough to overthrow the Prophecy's hold over her?"

"Not yet," is the rough reply. Rui sucks in a deep, rattling breath. "She doesn't love me yet. But…there was a moment tonight, when it was my Lina. It was her. I *know* it was her."

Kang stiffens in surprise. "When?" he asks, gripping his staff tightly. "How?" His research is still nearly futile. As much as he hopes that the red thread of fate, being soul-stitched in love, can overcome the Prophecy, there are no texts to prove it. But Rui sounds so sure.

"When we kissed," Rui says quietly, running his fingers along his lips, remembering the feeling of Lina's against them. "It was her, Kang. I could tell, through our thread. I felt her. It was as if she was a marionette, cut free of its strings." He turns his eyes to Kang, and it hurts the advisor to see the sparkling hope within the silver depths. "Perhaps we truly are soul-stitched in love."

Oh Rui. Kang exhales in disappointment. "Prophecies are not truly alive," he murmurs gently. "Not in the way we are, with our own bodies, our own flesh. They're parasites, and they're born only when heard. For all their power, they're young. And as such, displays of...affection...are foreign to them. I suspect that it relinquished its hold only when you kissed her, as it was at a loss as to what it should do. It was still there, Rui. Watching. Unless she said something to you? Something about the Prophecy, her lack of control?"

That hope shutters out of his emperor's eyes. "I think that she—tried to," he replies slowly. "That she would. But she began speaking of our impending nuptials instead."

Hana groans, rolling her shoulders. "This is tedious—"

Rui cuts her a scathing look. "I've found, Hana, that every time you've spoken recently, you've urged me to kill Lina. I want to hear nothing from you tonight."

Hurt, Hana glares at the floor. Killing the girl could save thousands of other lives. But her emperor is too smitten to see it.

"Not all hope is lost," Kang says gently, cutting that conversation short. "The Prophecy allowed her to kiss you. Perhaps it will let her fall in love. The red thread may listen to our pleas, after all."

The words are bitter as he says them, knowing he can delay no longer. "There's more."

Reports of what the emperor has seen, of words his beloved has told him passed from her tongue to the Imugi in the realm of death, soon follow."

Kang closes his eyes. "And so the Imugi will return in full," he whispers.

Hana, who has been holding her tongue with extreme difficulty, finally lets it lash loose. "Enough with the games," she demands, staring at her friend and emperor. "When your Lina takes Sunpo, that's one-third of the kingdoms she needs to conquer for the Imugi to be unleashed as Yong. For the world to be remade as those *beasts* want it to be. And for that reason, Lina *needs* to have returned to herself that night."

"I agree," Kang says, opening his eyes.

"As do I." Chan folds his arms.

Dokkaebi fire flashes in Rui's eyes. "There are only five more nights for me to outwit the Prophecy," he spits. "I cannot make her love me in five nights, cannot control the red thread with only five nights to do so—"

"Exactly," snaps Hana, "I really don't think you can."

"We *do not* kill her," the emperor snarls, clenching his hands into fists. "We'll form another plan, a secondary plan, should the first one fail—"

He cuts off as there's a clumsy knocking on the door of the throne room. Stiffening, he exchanges a look with his inner circle before striding to the doors, yanking them open, wondering who dares to disturb his meeting—

Eunbi, sleepy-eyed and tousle-haired, stands before the doors. She's holding in one hand a stuffed rabbit that Hana purchased for her at the shops, and scratching at her snub nose with the other. "Hello," she whispers, pushing past Rui into the throne room, bare feet slapping on the floor.

"Eunbi?" Hana asks, her face softening as she takes in the small girl. "You were put to bed hours ago. Did something wake you up?"

"I couldn't sleep," Eunbi mumbles, poking at a spot on the floor with her toe. "I kept having bad dreams. It feels like something is really wrong." She looks up at the beautiful Dokkaebi female, rubbing her eyes with a fist. Hana is always nice to her, but she's frowning a little, in the way that people sometimes frown when they're busy and they're interrupted. "*Is* something really wrong?"

"Nothing at all," Rui assures Lina's younger sister as gently as he can while also lying through his teeth. He returns to his throne, doing his best to lounge as if he has not a care in the world. "This is another one of those Very Important But Boring Meetings."

Chan nods, clearing his throat. The girl should be sleeping. She had a long day of wreaking havoc with Tae. "Very boring. Do you want one of us to walk you back to your room, Eunbi?"

But Eunbi is frowning at Rui. "Is it Lina? Is she hurt? Is that what's really wrong?"

The words stick in Rui's throat, and he finds he cannot lie to the young girl. He looks at Hana, almost pleadingly, for help. Catching his eye and nodding in understanding, Hana kneels so she can look the small eight-year-old in the eyes. "Lina hasn't been hurt," she says soothingly. "She's in Sunpo. Rui asked her to marry him, and she said yes."

Eunbi gasps, all signs of sleepiness vanishing. *"What?"* the girl all but screeches.

Rui winces as Eunbi pivots toward him, eyes incredibly wide. "You're going to *marry* my *sister*? That doesn't sound like a Very Important But Boring Meeting—"

Kang decides that it's likely time for him to step in. "It's also an alliance," he says carefully. "Lina has made some new...friends that will help her claim Sunpo. They like her so much that they've appointed her their empress."

"Lina's easy to like," Eunbi agrees with a broad grin.

"We want to get along with her new friends, too," Kang continues, "and a marriage between Rui and your sister is the best way to do so."

Eunbi beams. "So I'm going to be a *princess*," she says with relish. "A double-princess. Princess of Gyeulcheon and Sunpo!"

Rui closes his eyes.

"Do I get two crowns? What about double the hanboks? What are Lina's new friends like?"

"Er," says Chan.

"They're..." Hana clears her throat, and it's her turn to look at Rui helplessly. Rui, with his eyes still closed, is not much help at all. "They're interesting," she finally says. "They're quite...big."

Eunbi nods, accepting this. "That's good," she says. "They'll help her a lot, then."

"And they're giant snakes," says Rui, opening his eyes. "That talk."

Eunbi stares.

Rui grimaces.

"Giant...snakes?"

Hana, deciding this has gone far enough, clears her throat. "It's quite late, Eunbi. Let's get you back to bed. We can talk about this more in the morning."

Hugging the rabbit to her chest, Eunbi shakes her head. "No, I want to talk about it *now*..." But Hana is already steering her toward the doors. "What do you mean, giant snakes?"

"I'll return shortly," she says, leading the little girl out of the throne room.

Neither notice Kang, staring after Shin Eunbi with a thoughtful—yet equally mournful—expression.

CHAPTER TWENTY-SEVEN

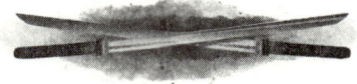

I am hiding within a memory, within a dream.
Lately, these dreams have been my only relief from the state of obedience I have found myself in. Dreams have been the only place where I remember it all—the revelation that the Voice is the Prophecy, my recitation of Yeomra's predictions, slamming my head into the table. The Prophecy had once said that it does not see my dreams. It is like a tremendous pressure has been relieved from my head. And so I hide within my sleeping mind, savoring the autonomy I know will soon vanish. Finding some semblance of happiness as best I can.

Within this memory, it is snowing. Fat flakes drift from the spun-sugar clouds above Gyeulcheon as Rui, Eunbi, and I—bundled in heavy cloaks—pack snow together in our mittened hands before hurling the icy orbs at one another atop the winter-iced mountain. Unlike the hill lands and the forest near which Rui's palace is built, where it is late spring turning to summer, Gyeulcheon's mountains are freezing. *"And perfect,"* Rui had said earlier that morning, *"to be our battleground."*

Rui is laughing, laughing hard as he hastily ducks behind the snow fort he's crafted, narrowly dodging Eunbi's attack. The snowball sails past him, slamming into one of the thicket's ice-glazed, naked trees. Eunbi cackles, scooping up another handful and focusing on me.

I sidestep her attack and snicker as she makes a sound of good-hearted annoyance. My snicker abruptly cuts off as snow erupts upon my face, cold and biting, courtesy of a smirking Rui. I wipe the snow from my eyelashes as his smug little smirk grows.

"I would say that I'm sorry," he calls, ducking back behind his fort, "but I'm not."

Shaking my head, I crouch down to arm myself. The snow glitters with the pale morning moonlight and crunches as I shape it into a perfectly round ball. Eunbi is focusing her attacks on Rui, running up to his fort and pelting snowballs over its walls before peeling away as his retaliation comes—swift and fast, but not swift enough to hurt her. I've been having to watch myself carefully. With my new strength, I could easily hurt Eunbi without meaning to.

I don't need to worry about that with Rui. When I stand and draw my arm back, it's with every intention to get my revenge—and I do. The snowball sails through the air and smacks Rui right in the face.

A triumphant smile spreads across my lips as Rui, looking mortally affronted, wipes the powder from his skin and focuses his attention on me.

Eunbi runs past me, breathless, cheeks red with excitement and cold. "You're in trouble now, Lili," she giggles before ducking behind a tree and scooping up snow to refill her armory. Rui is standing, leaving his wall of snow behind, and approaching with a devilish smile. Snowflakes frost his hair, sparkle on his long lashes. He's beautiful, as always, but nothing can distract me from the very large snowball he holds in his right hand.

"Lina," he purrs, "I'm offended."

"Good," I reply with a sharp grin, eyes fixed on the snowball as he slowly draws his arm back.

"My ego is wounded."

"Poor Dokkaebi emperor," I croon. "Would a kiss make it better?"

There's a flicker of acute interest across Rui's face, but he shakes his head. "There is only one cure for utter humiliation, little thief."

"And what's that?"

"Retaliation." Rui's silver eyes sparkling, the snowball rushes at me in a blur of speed...

And hits Eunbi instead.

My little sister has flung herself before me, and catches the snowball on her stomach. With a huff, she tumbles to the ground, sinking into the heavy snow with a dramatic screech.

Panicked, my heart stops in my chest. "Eunbi!" I gasp. Rui winces as I haul her up, brushing the snow from her cloak and hair, which spills over her shoulders. She's lost her hat. "Are you hurt? Rui throws at me harder than he throws at you..."

But Eunbi shakes her head. "No!" she assures me, beaming. "Did you see that, Lili? The way I fell? I saved you!"

"It was very heroic," I reply, finding her hat in the snow and pulling it back over her head. "But don't ever do that again."

"Why not?" she asks stubbornly. "Why can't I save you?"

Rui has joined my side. "What a morbid discussion," he says cheerfully. "I suppose we should declare me the winner, then." His eyes slip to my nose and he smirks. "Your nose," the emperor informs me, "is as pink as a cherry blossom." Ignoring my glare, Rui kisses the tip of it—and stumbles back as Eunbi hits him squarely in the jaw with a snowball.

She freezes as his gaze snaps to her.

"A rematch, then," Rui says, breaking into a grin as Eunbi giggles and darts away. The emperor runs after her and I smile, taking a delight in this moment, this memory...

A tugging in my chest brings me pause. I turn around, scanning the trees, expecting Rui to be near. But...that isn't right. In this memory, Rui is engaged in an intense snowball battle with my sister, not lurking behind me. So why...why do I feel him?

"The soul-stitched can also visit each other's dreams." Is it

possible that Rui, my Rui from the waking world is...here? On the mountain, as his past self ducks snowballs thrown by Eunbi?

But a moment later, the feeling is gone.

Frowning slightly, I scoop up more snow, packing it tightly. Perhaps I imagined it.

Although part of me knows I did not.

A mildly annoying melody is swirling through my bedroom as I begin to wake, my head pressed into my pillow, my eyes sticky with unshed tears from a dream that I don't remember. The tune is reminiscent of the obnoxious buzzing of a mosquito. There seems to be words hidden within the song—commands. *Lina, Lina. Hop out of bed and stand on one foot. Lina, Lina. Do a handstand...*

I brush them aside and yawn, sitting up. Rubbing my eyes, I yawn again.

Good morning, Lina.

The melody halts and my eyes focus blearily on Rui, tucking Manpasikjeok into the folds of his dark purple hanbok. "Good morning, little thief," he says, leaning on the wall across from the bed and arching a brow. "Manpasikjeok doesn't work on you anymore."

I flinch. "You promised never to use that damned thing against me again." In Gyeulcheon, Rui made a vow. He broke it once, to force me away from the battle between him and Jiwoon. And now he has broken it again. "Your promises are lies, Rui. You break them when you wish it. You shatter them without a care." The Voice is outraged, pacing back and forth atop my mind. "How dare you do this? Were you expecting to wield Manpasikjeok against me? Is that why you were testing me?"

Rui shakes his head. "No."

"Does this alliance mean nothing to you?" Outraged, I slide out of bed and summon my scaled blades. "Does this wedding mean nothing to you?"

"It means—everything to me," he replies quietly, eyes on my snakeskin.

My breath rises and falls unevenly. "If this is another one of your lies, Rui, tell me now." I step toward him and my hand angles my blade to his throat. The Voice jerks my legs so I take another step, the sharp edges brushing his throat.

"Lina," Rui says, "I was only wondering." For a moment, he almost looks—fearful, and I feel a flash of apprehension through the thread. But then the moment is gone, and his visage is as smooth as ever.

"Wondering what?" I breathe, angling my head. "How much of an Imugi I am?"

His eyes flicker. "Yes. Exactly that. Manpasikjeok does not work on m—" He cuts himself off, but I know what he was going to say.

Manpasikjeok does not work on monsters.

"On Imugi," he recovers. "There are many questions about your...heritage. I went about it the wrong way, but I thought it necessary. My court will want to know. Even with the alliance, they are wary. I must be honest with them about this, so that when I assure them of your intentions to ally, they accept such as honesty as well..." He continues, but his words fade into a muted mumbling as I stare blankly at my scales. As I remember that split second of fear.

I am not a monster. I am not a monster. I am not a monster.

So why does he look at me like I am one?

Irrelevant, snarls the Voice, and tears my sadness to shreds, leaving only cold exasperation in its place.

"...now Imugi crawling all over Iseung," Rui is saying, as the Voice forces my ears to open. He sounds almost conversational, but there is a tense underlayer that I do not overlook. "Did you know? They seem to be keeping away from the mortal eyes so far—I suspect they're throwing a revel in the sewers—but already I think that they have had breakfast. I took a morning stroll and saw some interesting splatters on the cobblestones. I nearly stepped in it." He wrinkles his nose in distaste.

Why does he talk so much, so early?

"Which had me wondering," Rui continues airily, gazing out the window, "what, exactly, we're to cater at our wedding for the guests you so magnanimously invited yesterday."

"They do not need to eat at our wedding, if it disgusts you." I allow my scales to recede and lower my scaleblade from his throat. "And yes, I am aware of their presence here—since I told them to arrive today. It is the start of the new era, Rui." My head cocks as I fasten my jikdo to my waist. "Have you something against it?"

"Not at all," Rui says after a long moment. "Not at all." He smirks, razor-sharp as I frown at him.

He frowns back.

"Good." Breaking the stubborn staring contest, I stroll toward the kitchen. "With the Imugi now here, we should wed soon. The alliance is more important than ever." My fingers grab an apple pear from an earthen bowl atop the wooden counter and begin to peel the skin away from the sweet, crisp white fruit.

"For what is a wedding without an alliance?" Rui mumbles quietly, settling himself on a cushion and pouring himself a cup of steaming tea from a kettle that he must have prepared earlier. There are dark rings underneath his eyes, as if he has not slept.

My brows inch closer together as I bite into the fruit. Sweet tartness explodes on my tongue. "It's more than an alliance," I say, raising a brow. "We're soul-stitched." **Destined for wonders together.**

Rui smiles slightly, eyes gleaming. "That we are." His voice is thick with an emotion I cannot quite name, and his finger shakes around his cup of tea. He raises it to his lips and takes a sip, avoiding my eyes.

My throat clears, the Voice piling brisk words atop my tongue. "I'd like to begin planning our wedding," I continue, taking another bite of my fruit. "It would be in the best interest of the alliance for it to occur before the Night of the Red Moon." For on that night, five from now, the palace will be a bloodbath. And I do not want his kind to look down upon Iseung and decide to put an end to it out of some foolish sentiment.

"We will do as you wish," Rui promises. "I saw the happiness in your eyes as you spoke of a traditional wedding." Rui sets down his tea and manages a crooked grin. "We will purchase your fancy hanbok, jagi, and I will wear whatever is required of me even if it does not align with my trademark wardrobe. Living family I do not have, but friends I do. I—"

Oh, please. My look of distaste does not go unnoticed by Rui, who sighs.

"If this is to cement an alliance, it makes sense that both sides should be present. Besides, we need somebody to throw the chestnuts and dates."

"Sonagi could," I shoot back, even though I know it's quite impossible for her to do so.

"Doubtful. She has no fingers, merely a very long body and lots of fangs." Rui waves a ringed hand airily, the other toying with one of his many dangling silver earrings. "My court and your court will both come. It is, as you said, the beginning of a new era. No?" He cocks his head, and it feels like a challenge. The air thickens between us, crackling with tension.

Fine. We shall set our dislike aside.

My lips smooth into a bland smile. "Of course it is," I say sweetly. "Our wedding, then, should be a grand affair between both the Imugi and the Dokkaebi." My finger traces a groove in the table. "We will host it in Jeoseung. Tomorrow night. We shall spend today preparing."

Rui blinks, his mouth parting in disbelief. *"What—"*

"Jeoseung is a neutral ground, now that the Imugi prowl on Iseung and the Dokkaebi remain in Gyeulcheon. A neutral ground is what you wanted, isn't it?"

"How romantic," Rui drawls. "A world of death—" My eyes narrow warningly. He clears his throat, smiles innocently, and wisely drops the subject. "If you wish to wed in a dead realm, little thief, then we will wed in a dead realm. Will you be inviting your mortal allies as well?"

I snort at the thought of those sniveling fools braving Jeoseung. "Perhaps those brave enough to come." *Iseul, perhaps. And Seojin.* The Voice strokes its chin contemplatively. *They can bring a message back to the others, give them time to adjust to the new knowledge of a changing world.* "Song Iseul and Ryu Seojin. I will invite them today."

"We cordially invite you to the marriage of Haneul Rui and Shin Lina," Rui says drily. "Midnight, the underworld. Do not linger for too long."

Brilliant wording. The Voice nods approvingly. *We will put it on paper.* "Precisely."

The emperor goes still, his eyes darkening. "It is as if you don't understand my jokes anymore," he says quietly, and immediately looks as if he regrets it—he shakes his head and runs a hand down his face, looking so many years older.

It was a joke? The Voice fumbles for words. *How does he expect us to reply?*

Let me.

Straining, I wrestle for control and speak for myself. "I was joking as well," I say, grasping his hand across the table and squeezing reassuringly. "The invitations will be more along the lines of: *We cordially invite you to the wedding of Shin Lina and Haneul Rui. My* name first."

He smiles slightly, looking pleased and surprised. "Oh? And will you adopt my family name, or will I take yours?"

I blink, for now I am the one caught off guard. "I…"

Rui senses my hesitation. "For purposes of the alliance, we should share a common name. It presents us as a united front in an easily conveyed manner. When somebody thinks of one, they will think of the other simultaneously. So I will be Shin Rui, if you so wish it. Or you can be Haneul Lina. It matters not to me what you choose. I simply want you to be happy." He swallows hard, fingering a few of his rings. "I just want you to be happy," he repeats in a whisper.

"I am happy." My chin tilts upward as I return his steady stare. "Rui, I have everything I have ever wanted. I am on the cusp of ridding this kingdom of the Blackbloods forever. I have found family again, with the Imugi. A purpose, with the Prophecy. And I have you. I will always have you." When he says nothing, eyes shining, a shiver rolls down my spine for an inexplicable reason. The Voice stiffens in displeasure. "Won't I?" My heart suddenly feels small. Small and fragile.

Rui smiles, just slightly, glancing down at our hands. His long lashes hide the silver of his gaze, so I cannot tell if his smile reaches his eyes. "I will take your name," he says a moment later. "It will send a message, I think, to those of my kind who will regard you with contempt."

It does not escape my notice that he has not answered my question. Not really.

Uneasiness roils within me, and the Voice frowns. However, I give no outward sign of my discomfort. "Shin Rui," I say, polishing off the rest of my fruit. "It does have a certain appeal to it." Standing from the cushions, I roll my shoulders and check that my jikdo is at my hip.

Rui watches me curiously. "Where are you going?"

"To purchase dates and chestnuts," I say promptly, stalking

out of the kitchen and into my bedroom, where I don my stealth suit before grabbing my cloak and pulling the hood over my head. "And to purchase our hanboks." The Voice has made my tone businesslike and brisk, despite the excitement I feel at the prospect of the wedding. "I'd also like to speak to Sonagi and invite her and her children. Iseul and Seojin, too. And perhaps, if their master is letting them back onto the streets, I'll kill a few Blackbloods on the way for my serpents to eat. I'll toss them down into the sewers." There are only Feathers and Bills left, assuming that Wooseok has yet to strike. I've been less active the past couple of days in my killings, and suspect that Kalmin will have sent some patrols out to hunt me down. As if they could.

"As far as wedding preparations go, this is certainly the most bizarre," Rui comments drolly.

"You're welcome to accompany me."

"And I will." He joins my side. "Although it is quite early in the morning to watch corpses being eaten by Imugi."

"It will be later by the time they are eaten," I say, and belatedly the Voice realizes that it has failed to grasp yet another one of Rui's jokes. ***Shit,*** it mutters as Rui shakes his head.

We step into the summer morning. The air is thick with humidity, and the sky above hosts a blanket of thick, yellowish-gray clouds. It is going to storm again. Inhaling the smell of far-off lightning and thunder, I begin to head toward the marketplace—until I realize that there *is* no marketplace. Rui stole all the vendors. I sigh in mild exasperation, giving him a halfhearted glare from the corner of my eye. He scowls.

"I may have kidnapped them, but remember who ate them. It certainly wasn't *me*."

"I would *hope* not." I roll my eyes. "The Coin Yard has a few produce shops," I say, changing the direction of my stride. Rui easily keeps up beside me. "And a handful of garment stores that carry the hanboks we need. We'll go there." I am careful to keep my face concealed as we walk through the cobblestoned streets, as does Rui.

As we walk, I see no patrols, and wonder—with rising excitement—if Wooseok has finally struck. If the Feathers and Bills are dead in the palace, Kalmin will be surrounded by a sea of corpses. The idea is fantastically amusing that I laugh under my breath.

"What?" Rui asks, looking suspicious.

"Nothing," I reply lightly as we enter an empty, narrower street boxed in by stone fences surrounding decrepit hanoks. My boot steps in something that squelches, and I glance down in some surprise and disgust.

"See what I meant about interesting splatters?" Rui points to the large sewer grate not far off. A trail of rusty blood leads to it and vanishes. "Your friends are in there."

"We all need to eat." I stride to the sewer grate and move it aside. "If the victims supported the Blackbloods, they received an appropriate fate. Are you coming?"

"Ah." Rui shakes his head. "No, I'll wait for you up here."

Shrugging, I drop down into the sewer. The sewer is drowning in Imugi—they are on the walls, the dripping stone ceiling, on nearly every inch of the ground, and in the wastewater as well, poking their heads out with interest. When I inform them of the wedding's date, their maws twist into something that seems to be the Imugi equivalent of a smile.

A moment later, I tense. I've reined in my senses, so it is hard to tell… I think I have heard male voices, thick with violence, and a midnight soft laugh filled with danger.

Rui.

In a blink, I've launched myself toward the opening in the ceiling and ignoring the bark of protest in my leg, have pulled myself up to the street above, where Rui, looking quite amused and only slightly annoyed, is backed up against the stone wall by two burly, white-clad men pointing swords at his throat. Their faces are vaguely familiar and I recognize them as Bills, trained assassins who work for Kalmin. One of them—I think his name might be Subin. The other, I'm not sure. Perhaps Daejung? It's inconsequential. They're Bills, regardless. Their names don't particularly matter to me; they're all the same.

It seems that Wooseok still has yet to strike, after all. I feel a flash of intense impatience and abrupt annoyance with the scrawny, scared boy and wish for him to make haste.

Rui's hands are in the air, his eyes slits, his mouth quirked upward into a dangerous smirk as he meets my eye over the men's shoulders. **Who are they to threaten the life of our greatest ally?** the Voice seethes. **How dare they.**

My heart twists in anger and my fists curl at my sides, but Rui shakes his head almost imperceptibly at me with a familiar little smile.

The bastard is having *fun*.

"Come, now," Rui says wryly, turning his attention back to the blades at his throat. "How long were the lot of you following me?"

"Boss wants you dead. Heard a whisper you were here, walking the streets. Got eyes all over." The one I think is Subin spits on Rui's cheek. It runs down his skin and Rui wipes it away with distaste. "Stupid Dokkaebi."

"Stupid Dokkaebi," his companion echoes and snorts hoarsely. "With your stupid pointy ears." He barks out a rough laugh.

"Please don't stand so close to me." Rui's amusement has grown tenfold. "Your breath is truly, astoundingly bad."

"Don't tell me what to do. This is our kingdom," Subin snaps.

"And you're scum on our streets," the one who might be Daejung cuts in with a snarl. "And our Claws and Legs and Crest are dead. It's your doing, isn't it Dokkaebi? You want to take your kingdom back from us?"

"I've never killed a Dokkaebi before," Subin says with a nasty smile. "I'm excited."

"Me too." Daejung sneers. "Boss wants you gone as soon as possible. Here or at the gala, it don't matter no more. You have to pay for what you did."

Rui's eyes are glittering with clear entertainment. A distant rumble of thunder rolls through the ever-thickening air. "Holds a grudge, does he?" The emperor does not seem at all bothered by the swords at his throat. I am not surprised. He was not very bothered by my dagger in his chest not too long ago, after all. "Well. You can certainly try to kill me. It does sound like an entertaining twist to the morning. Or," he smiles, "you can run."

"*Run?*" Daejung scoffs. "You're cornered, Dokkaebi. You—"

This has gone on for long enough. We have other things to attend to. In exasperation, I clear my throat.

The Bills, highly skilled but never particularly smart, take their eyes off Rui and focus instead on me. Under my hood, I grin.

"Hello," I purr as Rui slowly, so slowly, begins to draw Manpasikjeok out of the pocket of his robes. He doesn't need it, though. Because in a blur of speed and strength, I shoot toward the gaping men, scaleblades extending from my wrists, and slit their throats. They fall in a spray of red and with two wet thumps. I frown at Rui. "I could have done that sooner," I say and nudge one of the bodies. "You really do have the oddest sense of what fun is."

He shrugs languidly. "I found them amusing. They would have made fine court jesters." Then he wrinkles his nose. "They really did reek—"

And an Imugi lunges out of the nearby sewer grate in a blur of green and closes its maw around Daejung, dragging him back down underground. I hear a chorus of pleased hisses rise from down below.

Rui blinks once. Twice. "That was certainly unexpected—"

A second Imugi shoots out and drags away Subin, winking at me as it disappears back underneath the kingdom. There is a heavy thud, a splash, and then a loud crunching.

"I can't imagine that they taste very good," Rui muses, looking faintly disgusted. "If their scent was any indication, I mean."

"Agreed." I smile fondly down at the sewers. "I would let them eat whomever they desired, of course, but an empress is nothing without worshippers."

"Worshippers," Rui repeats, arching a brow. "Subjects are for rulers. Worshippers are for deities. Do you fancy yourself a goddess?"

"Why should I not?" I spread my hands, grinning. "Look at me, Rui. At the power that flows through my veins. At what I am prophesized to do."

"I never thought you the sort to long for personal godhood," Rui replies, seeming to concentrate incredibly hard on flicking an invisible speck of dust from his hanbok. "With your worshipping of them and whatnot."

"That was before this. I needed something to worship, to believe in, when I could not believe in myself. When I was weak. But now I have power." My legs lurch into a stride once more. "The gods are gone. They left these kingdoms, these people, behind. They are unclaimed. I could claim them."

The emperor makes a noncommittal noise and a sharp surprise flares through our thread. "You shouldn't be surprised," I inform him drily. "You've heard the Prophecy. And think, Rui—with me beside you, you'll be a god in your own right."

"I've never much longed to be a god," Rui replies as we walk. "It seems boring, with responsibilities I have no interest in at all. And I don't have the patience to listen to prayers. But tell me, Lina—what do you imagine yourself to be the goddess of?"

An interesting question, muses the Voice.

"The goddess of sugar rolls, perhaps?" Rui suggests, placing a hand on the small of my back. The Voice blinks at this display of casual affection, but allows my body to lean into his touch. "Or perhaps the goddess of sharp, pointy things? I think that would suit you rather well."

"I think I'll require more time to decide," I reply, for the Voice is still deep in rumination, forming and discarding ideas for my title. **Goddess of Imugi?** It's fitting, of course, but do we have the potential to be *more*?

"Of course. More important matters are at hand," Rui says wryly. "Chestnuts. Dates."

"And a halved gourd."

"How could I forget?"

"And the hanboks, of course. What color will yours be, Rui?" Traditionally the man wears blue, and the woman wears red. But we are anything but traditional.

Rui's hand squeezes my own. "I look magnificent in every color, little thief. Perhaps we should discuss the color of the gourd instead." His tone is light, but I feel his hesitancy. His…reluctance?

Stung, I drop my hand. "Have I offended you in some way?" I demand as we near the small shop in the Coin Yard. It is little more than a wooden shack, eaves hanging with bundles of herbs set out to dry. A sloppily painted sign reads SOME FRUITS AND SOME VEGETABLES AND SOME THINGS in running black letters. "I feel your uncertainty." The Voice is glowering out through my eyes toward Rui, who sighs and shakes his head as he notices my glare.

"Forgive me." He smiles slightly but it looks forced. "Would you believe me if I said that I was nervous?"

"Nervous?" I repeat, pushing open the battered door of the shop. An uneven floor creaks underneath my feet as I step inside, glancing around at the barrels of mostly overripe fruit and vegetables. An old woman sits in the corner behind a counter carved out of a hunk of rotting wood, bent over a small loom. Her arthritic fingers are deft as they weave strands of silk, her sunken mouth tight with concentration. She does not notice as we enter, nor does she notice the flies buzzing around the softened produce, feasting to their delight.

"Nervous," Rui repeats softly. "For I have never done this before. A wedding, I mean. And when one lives as long as I do, there is not much that they have not done." He shrugs. "Although I have never been in a shop that smells as putrid as this one. You mean to buy our dates and chestnuts from here?"

Locating the barrel of nuts, I'm pleased to see that they're in fine condition, for the flies have been more drawn to the sweet stench of fruit. "We may have to purchase the gourd elsewhere," I admit, grabbing a handful of chestnuts. "You have gourds in Gyeulcheon. Tell your friends to find one." I glance at the old woman, still hunched over her weaving. "Let's go." I shove the goods into my pockets with considerable satisfaction.

"Ah, little thief. Living up to the term of endearment yet again."

"I'm sure she won't entice me into a rigged bargain if she catches me," I say out of the side of my mouth, stalking to the door.

"Mm," Rui agrees noncommittedly, flicking a golden coin from the folds of his robes toward the woman. It clatters before her, yet she gives no signs of noticing, still entirely consumed by her work. "Only a Dokkaebi emperor would do such a cruel and callous thing."

"Agreed," I reply coolly as we emerge outside. My hands tug my cloak closer around my body as a crack of thunder shakes the sky, storm clouds coalescing above until there is a grayish tint to the world. Rain will soon pound these streets. "But rest assured, I shall get my revenge on you."

He blanches.

I think I imagine it at first—the flinch. The way that his body tenses, his shoulders mounting slightly upward, his eyes widening. But I know that I have not. The Voice feels a flush of suspicion. It was only attempting to make a jest. A joke.

And my heart shivers in my chest, the thread between us suddenly cold. So cold.

"By revenge," I elaborate slowly, "I mean that we're now going to the tailor, where I'll have you try on many different hanboks. It was a joke."

The Voice seethes. ***What is this? He looks frightened. Of us.***

And he does. There is suspicion in his gaze that is like an arrow to the heart, and raw distrust that preys on all my insecurities. All of this, for some sarcasm? No. I do not think so.

With a jerk, the Voice forces me to walk closer to Rui, forces my voice to come out harsh and biting. "Do you fear me, Rui?" I step into an empty alleyway, leaning against the wall and glaring at him as he comes to stand across from me, attempting a crooked smile.

"Fear you? Certainly. But in the most romantic way possible—"

"Are you *afraid* of me?" My cadence twists, and now it is baiting, taunting. The Voice's suspicions come hard and fast, spilling from my mouth, pushed out by insistent hands. "Is that why I woke to you testing whether Manpasikjeok still works on my mind? I have half a mind to break that flute, you know."

"It's only as I've said. I've never done this before. It is why I feel uncertain. I've never wed before."

"Oh, but you would have," I breathe, for the Voice has been filled with an insatiable desire to win this argument with words as sharp as swords. "Is that it, Rui?"

He has gone very still.

"Perhaps," I whisper cruelly, delighting in the awful words loading upon my tongue like bullets in a pistol, "Perhaps your heart only ever had room for one. Perhaps you wish that I was her. But she's dead, Rui. She's gone, dead, buried, *broken*."

Rui goes white around the mouth. He draws closer to me until the space separating us is tantalizingly small. *"What did you just say to me?"*

I sneer up at him. "I said," my mouth repeats, slowly, deliberately, "that perhaps you wish she was your soul-stitched. Perfect, perfect, *dead* Achara."

No. No. I do not want to be saying this, not to him, not to Rui—
Quiet, the Voice snaps, sending a flare of pain through my head. My protests wither and die while my lips comply with the Voice's wishes. They form another ugly sentence, and I am powerless to stop them.

"Maybe," I whisper, "your heart stopped when hers did. Maybe, Rui, it's just as decayed as she is."

Thunder roars and lightning splits, brilliant and blinding. A downpour of rain, a summer squall finally released by bursting clouds, slams downward onto Sunpo, mercilessly torrential. Heavy winds blow the storm sideways, the droplets of water impossibly sharp as they slam into my skin. I glare at Rui through the sheets of water, chest heaving as I struggle to breathe through the water and anger.

"How—how *could you say that? How could you say that—*" Rui's face is tight with disbelief and rage, rivulets of water dripping into his flashing eyes. Another burst of lightning illuminates the silver of his eyes and the furious flames of blue crackling within.

"It's true, isn't it?" I shout back, thrusting my hood away from my face. "You don't trust me! You *never did!*"

My breath is knocked out of me as Rui slams me against the wall, fingers digging into my shoulders. *"I did!"* he shouts over the din of the thunder, water spraying from his lips, "I trust Shin Lina. I adore Shin Lina—ardently, desperately, passionately. But you—*YOU ARE NOT HER!"* Fire swirls in his glare. His fingers are warm, their heat seeping through my cloak. "I *see you for what you are—*"

"And what is that?" I demand. Rui hesitates, blinking rainwater out of his eyes—and I choke in pain, eyes widening. *"Who do you—"*

My shoulders are burning.

Steam rises into the air as Rui's hands, gripping my arms, glow with the faintest tinge of Dokkaebi fire. It is blisteringly hot, hot enough that it is freezingly cold, cutting into my skin and bones like a knife.

It slams into me with the force of a tidal wave—and it shoves the Voice into the very back corner of my mind.

The Voice shouts once in alarm and goes abruptly quiet.

Unconscious. Slumbering. But it will wake soon. I can feel it.

My limbs loosen, the strings holding them upward cut. My body is my own.

My thoughts are my own.

I am entirely my own, as I am in my dreams. Unwatched. Unmonitored. Independent.

I am Shin Lina.

Rui inhales sharply, a look of horror crossing his face as he stares at his hands. He makes to move away, but I shake my head, gritting my teeth against the pain.

"No," I manage to gasp. "No. Don't let go." I grab his hands with my own, choking back a groan as the fire licks at my palms and fingers, searing away skin. Somehow, the Dokkaebi fire…it has *freed* me. "Rui," I whisper, even as I feel the Voice stir within my head, dragging itself to its feet with a groan. *"Rui."*

His eyes meet mine in surprise and understanding, communicating love and grief and horror all in a fleeting moment of fire and fear that shoots down our bond.

But then it is over, and the Voice is back, and I am utterly gone.

"*—think I am?*" my mouth snarls.

Rui is staring at me with a mixture of emotions that I have no time to decipher. Blood hot with wrath, I shove him away as my shoulders sear, their flesh bubbling with burns. He staggers and sinks to his knees in the puddles. My skin begins to knit over the wounds as I glower at the Dokkaebi emperor. "I am the Prophesized, I am Shin Lina. I am your soul-stitched. Trust me and wed me, or fear me and bow."

"I do." Rui unsteadily hauls himself to his feet. "I do trust Shin

Lina," he says very quietly, his silver eyes boring into mine, as if searching for something that he cannot quite see. "I do adore Shin Lina. For I adore her as the moon does the sun, as the lightning does the thunder."

I blink, and the Voice falters, caught off guard. No longer is Rui shouting. No longer is he enraged. Instead, he kneels in the rain, looking forlorn.

"I treasure you, Lina," he whispers, gaze unbreaking. "I do."

Of all the confusing situations... "And I, you." The words taste like metal, feel mechanical, as the Voice mutters in exasperation.

Rui bows his head. His shoulders slump. The Voice thinks that he looks relieved, but I think he looks defeated.

As the summer squall finally recedes, the sun peeking out of receding clouds while a light drizzle replaces the furious storm, an old proverb slips into my mind.

"When it rains and shines, the tiger is getting married."

CHAPTER TWENTY-EIGHT

Rui does not come to bed with me tonight. Instead, he travels to Gyeulcheon.

His eyes are hollow with exhaustion and lingering upset as he summons the corridor of darkness that will take him to his realm. "It is best that I deliver the news of our alliance in person," he explains as I tilt my head questioningly at him from where I lounge on the bed. "Besides," he adds with a hint of his usual amusement, "there is still a need for a gourd." Despite having paid double for our hanboks to be prepared in time for tomorrow, we still lack the gourd for the ceremony.

Ever since our fight in the rain, Rui has been abnormally quiet—reticent through our purchasing of our hanboks, withdrawn as we sat in the Moonlit Hare to extend invitations to Seojin and Iseul, who is staying with him in his chogajip behind the jumak. Even when Seojin stared at the emperor, demanding to know if I was truly marrying the *Pied Piper*, Rui said nothing and instead stared fixedly at his hands.

Only the notion that the wedding is to take place in Jeoseung seemed to outweigh the shock of who, exactly, I'm marrying. Seojin appeared stunned, and that feeling only grew when Rui—speaking for the first time in a good half hour—informed him that my new allies would also be present...and that my new allies are giant serpents with very sharp teeth.

His lack of tact infuriated me. But Seojin has promised—albeit warily—to attend with Iseul.

"Fine. Retrieve the gourd and send your court my regards," I sigh, waving a hand. Fatigue is heavy on my bones, and I desire nothing more than a deep night's sleep. Snuggling closer to my pillow, I close my eyes. Yet Rui has not left the room—I feel his stare on me and reopen my eyes. *"Yes?"*

"It is only that..." Rui hesitates. "Shouldn't I give your love to Eunbi?"

"As you like." My hands pull the covers up to my chin and gesture impatiently. "Farewell, Rui." I do not mind that he is leaving. Although our fight lasted only as long as the brief summer storm, tensions still brew between us. I can feel them, and I'd rather they not keep me up at night.

Rui does not reply. Disappointment hangs heavy over the bedroom, although I do not understand why.

And then there is a rush of wind, and I know he is gone.

Our soul-stitched is capricious and unpredictable. The Voice sighs, nestling up against a corner of my mind, yawning. **But as long as the alliance is secured, his wily tendencies matter not. Although they truly are wearying.** Sleepily, I turn Rui's ring round and round in my fingers as dark pink moonlight sparkles through the hanji-screened window. Soon, the moonlight will turn bloody and red. The Night of the Red Moon is around the corner and is close, so close. And my wedding is even closer.

Contentedly, I close my eyes.

And I sleep.

INTERLUDE

The inner circle is enjoying a quiet, *peaceful* dinner in the observatory after a long, grueling day, when the air begins to ripple.

Sitting on her cushion, Hana raises her eyes to the glass ceiling, beyond which dozens of moons twinkle among the stars. "Here we go," she mutters as the Dokkaebi emperor emerges from his shadowed corridor, strides across the glossy black floor, observes their dinner—bulgogi with fluffy white rice and kimchi—and hauls an unsuspecting Kang to his feet.

"Rui," Kang half chokes, dropping his chopsticks as Rui steps back, looking satisfied and…triumphant. His eyes glow blue. "What—"

"Dokkaebi fire," Rui announces, breathing hard. He exerted himself to travel here quicker than even his usual swiftness. His circle watches in acute wariness as Rui begins to pace, manically, across the observatory. "I used it—I hadn't meant to, but it's enraging, I could crush it in my hands for what it makes her say to me—but I used it all the same, and for a moment it *worked,* truly worked… It was gone, completely gone…"

"Slow down," Chan says, swallowing his bite of beef. "What happened?"

"Today, in the streets. We had a fight." Rui stops pacing and abruptly turns on his heel, pointing at Kang in triumph. "Dokkaebi fire. I am telling you, Kang, that the answer could be within my Dokkaebi fire. Perhaps we're soul-stitched in love after all. Perhaps we don't need to guide the thread, but only use the fire, and the thread will follow."

"You...used your fire on Lina?" Kang asks slowly, sifting through his emperor's hasty words of excitement. He picks up his staff from the floor and leans on it heavily.

"We had a fight," Rui repeats, and his eyes are focused somewhere far, far away—on a girl in the rain, on azure fire and thunderstorms. "It...escalated. I grabbed her shoulders, and I did not realize..." He swallows hard and moves his eyes to Kang's. Anguish burns in them. The eager, cobalt flames have long since guttered out. "I didn't realize that my temper—it had escaped me, and my hands were burning with it. It was then that I thought... but maybe I imagined it. It happened so quickly, so briefly. And then it was over."

Kang inhales sharply. "You're saying," he says slowly, "that you burned her. And that the true Lina emerged?"

"Yes," Rui breathes, staring into the eyes of his friends. Chan and Hana are silent, shocked. Kang is peering toward him, equally as shocked, knowledgeable eyes narrowed. "Yes."

"And you are confident that it was her?" Kang presses, knuckles shining around his staff, "That the Prophecy was entirely absent? Think, Rui. A war could be prevented if you speak the truth."

"When we were...together, the other night, I could feel her," he answers softly, savoring the memory, holding it close. "In my arms, she was *there*. But this feeling, on the street...it was like that, tenfold. For a brief moment, it was her. Truly her."

The waters of Kang's mind begin to ripple.

Dokkaebi fire.

A power granted only to the Dokkaebi of royal blood, the Haneul line. It is a mystery where it comes from—despite years of study, Kang has yet to find the answer.

But is it possible...possible that it holds the secret of Lina's redemption. That *this* could be the key to coaxing the red thread of fate in the direction of love. If Dokkaebi fire can defeat the Prophecy, there will be nothing—*nothing* forcing Lina and Rui into a fate as mortal enemies. A fate of being true loves would be much more likely. And a war would be avoided, lives saved, Imugi dealt justice…

Library. He must go to the library. He must shift his research efforts to the mysteries of Dokkaebi fire. "Keep her as preoccupied as you can. Continue your efforts with her, Rui. Let the wedding cement the pretense of the alliance, and negotiate terms for the union." It is an important pretense. "Continue to prepare the troops, for we have until the Night of the Red Moon."

Kang breathes heavily, overcome with anticipation. If war can be avoided, if so many innocent mortal lives can be spared from the hungry maws of the Imugi, if Lina can be brought back from the clutches of the Prophecy alive, then there is hope for them all.

But Dokkaebi fire is dangerous, and he must find the perfect balance.

"I must go," Kang says. "There is a possibility—a *possibility*, Rui, not a guarantee—that there is a way to end this before it is taken too far."

"Now," Rui says, and his blood sears hot with triumph and hope. His blue fire, his most potent weapon…a cure. His fingers tremble with fear and a ravenous longing. "Can we not end this now?" There is nothing he wants more than his Lina returned to him, wholly herself. The desire for it, the need, cramps his heart in his chest.

"Do not do anything rash." His advisor moves toward the doors, heart pounding with hope. "Do not even so much as move until I have had proper time to research. Dancing with Dokkaebi fire is dangerous. One misstep will lead to death." As he pushes open the heavy doors, he breaks into a run, desperate to reach the library.

Perhaps there is hope, after all.

CHAPTER TWENTY-NINE

My gums ache, and my mouth is filled with copper. I groan as I awaken, clutching a hand to my mouth.
What—
I lean over the side of my bed and spit out two teeth and green blood. Bewildered, I gape at the fallen canines, and gingerly prod at my mouth, expecting two gummy holes. But instead, my fingers touch teeth—sharp teeth that cut through the skin of my fingers.
Mirror. The Voice steers me out of bed and marches me toward the bathroom. In front of the mirror, I open my mouth, revealing...
Fangs.
Small white fangs where my canines used to be, curved slightly inward, like those of a snake. Of an Imugi.
Shocked, I poke at them again, splitting my healed-over skin, and blink in surprise when I glance down at my bleeding finger. The blood is mixed with a different colored liquid—a shimmering black. I smudge it between my thumbs, tilting my head. I feel nothing but a slight tingle that quickly fades.
The sound of the Voice applauding fills my mind. ***Delightful. Our fangs are laced with Imugi venom.***
Imugi venom. The same poison that nearly killed me.
In the mirror, I watch as my mouth curls into a self-satisfied smile, as my new fangs gleam and glisten. My heart falters in surprise as I think I see my eyes flash gold, but then the color is gone, replaced by the usual brown. ***Our evolution continues,*** the Voice murmurs, gently pushing me closer to the mirror. ***This is***

only one of the new powers that Sonagi spoke of. **The power to kill our enemies with pain and poison.** My tongue runs over the new fangs, and with a jolt, I realize that my tongue, too, is different.

It is dark and forked. A snake's tongue.

Interesting... The Voice yanks my tongue out of my mouth for inspection. My fingers poke at it curiously, my eyes squint at it in fascination. ***How very interesting.***

Horror fills me, ice-cold and biting, and I struggle to pull away from the mirror. But the Voice holds strong, and I cannot do anything but stand still, staring, smiling. ***Both very welcome accessories for our wedding tonight.*** My tongue flicks into the air with a slight hiss. ***How beautiful we'll look, how strong and powerful.***

They will think I'm a monster— I struggle again to lurch away from the mirror, but my efforts are in vain.

Your protests grow dull. You are not supposed to fight back. As a consequence, the Voice forces me to lean even closer, gluing my eyes to my fangs. ***Look, Lina. Look at who we will become. At the wonders that are now in our reaches.***

I look. I have no choice.

My mouth continues to smile that horrible smile as the Voice dances upon the surface of my mind in glee, whirling and twirling in ecstasy to the rhythm of my frantically pounding heart.

"The gourd," Rui announces, appearing in my bedroom with a wicked smile and the gourd. I tense in surprise where I'm sitting on the bed, brushing my freshly washed hair in an attempt to rid myself of the tangles and snarls. Rui holds the large, bottle-shaped vegetable with an expression that indicates he is quite, quite pleased with himself. Gone is the sadness that clung to him like a foul-smelling cloak yesterday, replaced by the Rui that is much more familiar, smelling instead of licorice and plum blossoms. The Rui with glossy black hair, brushed to perfection, with impeccably placed silver jewelry and a dark purple hanbok that looks as if it is worth more than the entire kingdom of Sunpo.

With a magnanimous bow, he presents the gourd to me, smirking as I take it in my hands. "It is the best gourd in all of Gyeulcheon. I picked it myself."

Such cheeriness. I stare at him. "I see that you're in high spirits today." Gingerly, I place the gourd on the floor and examine him suspiciously. "Why?"

"Must I have a reason?" He cocks an eyebrow. "It is our wedding day, little thief. I expected *you* to be in higher spirits." Rui leans against the wall, idly toying with a ring. "For today I become Shin Rui. Your husband. And you become my wife."

My husband. Heart heating with joy and adoration, I stand and smile, starting toward him.

But Rui has frozen, eyes on my teeth.

I snap my mouth closed, yet the Voice forces me to open it again in a grin. "Of course I'm in high spirits," I reply, letting him stare at my fangs. I step closer to him, curving a hand around his neck and bringing my face closer to his ear. "Tonight will be a night to remember," I whisper, the words tasting like triumph on my forked tongue. I pull away and allow Rui a glimpse of it.

He stiffens slightly but quickly relaxes, as coolly amused as ever. "Are you aware, perchance, that your tongue is now black and forked?"

"Yes." My grin grows. "I am."

"And that you have fangs?"

"Most definitely. Do you like them?" I flash them again.

"They...suit you," he says slowly after a long moment, a corner of his lip pulling upward.

"Truly?" Pleased, I run my tongue over my fangs, enjoying his rapt attention.

"Truly." His eyes glint. "It allows me to see you for what you really are."

I close my eyes in pleasure as he brings his hand to my jaw, tilting my chin upward, leaning down so his lips brush against mine. "And what's that?" I whisper.

"The Prophesized." He grins against my mouth before he abruptly steps away and strides toward the door. "I find that I have a craving for danpatjuk," he says casually over his shoulder as I huff in annoyance. "Don't you?"

"Not particularly," I reply, but follow him into the kitchen anyway.

The hanok is soon filled with the sweet smell of red bean porridge as Rui feeds fire into the stove and hauls a bag of red beans out from a small cupboard. As he cooks, I run my tongue over my teeth, delighting in the pointed fangs I find there.

Eventually, Rui carries two hearty bowls to the table, and settles on the cushion across from me, already eating with enthusiasm. I scoop some onto my spoon and take a small bite, watching Rui as he glances up at me. "When I was young," he says, "Asha taught me how to cook this, and only this. It was the one meal I'd eat, and so she deemed teaching me how to make it a survival skill."

"It's nice," I say, toying absently with one of my fangs. The venom brushes against my skin and tingles in a quite pleasant way. Like cold water, refreshing to the touch.

Rui points at me with his wooden spoon. "Do you have poison on those, jagi?"

"Maybe."

"*'Maybe,'*" he repeats mirthfully. A wicked, wicked look crosses Rui's face as he rolls up his sleeve and presents me with his wrist. "Let's find out. Bite me."

My brows angle downward and I swat his wrist away. "No."

"You do," Rui murmurs, cocking his head. His earrings shimmer in the morning light. "You have venom, Shin Lina. What is next? Do you transform into an Imugi?" He smirks. "Do you *molt*?"

"I doubt it." I take another bite of porridge and make a face. "Your danpatjuk is clumpy, by the way."

"Cruel words so often spill from your lips," Rui sighs, standing. "How they wound me."

He clutches dramatically at his chest before listlessly sauntering over to the cupboard in which my drinks are stored. His elegant fingers fold over the neck of one of the many bottles of *Sallinna*, and pop open the cap with little more than a flick.

Pointing at me, he raises the wine to his lips and takes a long swig. "Mm," he drawls as he wipes his mouth with the back of his wrist. "Not very strong, but strong enough to reinforce my…prior indulgences." With an indolent smile, he leans against the wall and takes another mouthful. "Would you like some, Lina? It goes quite well with the porridge, actually, although my stomach is churning slightly. Only slightly," he assures me, raising the bottle again to his lips.

So that's what it is. The Voice hisses in annoyance and disapproval. ***He is intoxicated.***

I have noticed that there is an underlying scent to his usual fragrance. Something bitter. Faint enough that I missed it at first, but when I expand my senses… Alcohol. Just as it was the evening he proposed.

But not the smell of warm, spiced wine heated over crackling fires as snow falls with gentle flakes. It is instead the smell of stale wine. Old wine. It is hard for immortals to get drunk—and I wonder how much Rui has consumed to get him to this state. "You're drunk," I snap, setting down my spoon.

Rui rolls his eyes. "No," he says innocently. Too innocently.

"Yes. You are. Why are you drunk the day of our wedding?" I rise from the cushions and fold my arms in disbelief. "Truly, Rui. Do you require so much liquid courage?"

"It will wear off before then," says Rui, but even he does not look so sure. "And perhaps I do. Perhaps drink is the only thing able to make me feel…" He trails off, voice tightening. Pain blooms upon his expression and he quickly looks away, his chest rising and falling unevenly. "Forgive me, I did not mean—"

"Feel what?" The remnants of our fight in the rain strain between us. "You get drunk to steel yourself enough to marry me?" Tears of frustration and hurt well momentarily in my eyes; the Voice blinks them away and replaces them with hard anger. Coldly, my legs stalk toward him and my hands yank the wine from his hands.

Before he can protest, I put my own lips against it and allow a rush of *Sallinna* to pour down my throat. I savor the bitter bite of it before shoving the bottle back into Rui's arms and glaring up at him, scrubbing at my mouth with my sleeve.

"It was only for my nerves, Lina. This is—"

My voice is the lashing of a whip as I spit, "Cut your fucking hair."

Rui blanches. "What?"

"Your hair," I say slowly, enunciating each word as I brush my fingers through his long, silken locks. "Your symbol of mourning for Achara. I want it *cut* before tonight. For this is our wedding, a new chapter. Your mourning," I whisper, "has no place in it."

Rui closes his eyes and I expect him to refuse, for us to be embroiled in another fight. The Voice is ready, leering, tensing my muscles in preparation for—

"As you wish," Rui says quietly as he opens his eyes.

I blink in surprise.

The Dokkaebi emperor, lips set in a firm line, glances about the kitchen. "Do you have a pair of shears?"

Eyeing him suspiciously, I fold my arms. "They're in the bathroom." I keep them there for when I must trim my bangs. I'm close on Rui's heels as he makes his way to the bathroom, and I snatch the silver shears from where they sit on the shelf below the mirror. "Here," I say, thrusting them at him.

But Rui does not take them. Instead, he closes my fingers over the clippers. "If you want my hair shorn," he says in a low voice that is suddenly sharp, "you will be the one to cut it."

"Fine," I bite back. He turns to face the mirror and I stand behind him, twining my fingers through his locks.

The Voice is angry, imagining harsh, angry chops and uneven strands cut too short. I yank on a handful of his hair, shears poised to strike —

But it isn't right, to maul beauty like that. Rui's hair has always been one of my favorite features. Grimacing, I clench my teeth, and my hand shakes with the effort of keeping the shears closed. A bead of sweat trickles down my forehead as I try to resist the horrible urge...

The Voice is amused. ***Does this matter so much to you? Fine, then. I suppose a pretty face is more interesting to look at than an ugly one.***

And it loosens its hold over me — just enough for me to control my hands. I run them through Rui's silky hair, combing it out. He's watching me in the mirror, sharp and alert.

I take a bit of hair between my fingers and make the first cut.

It is tedious work, cutting such long hair. My fingers cramp around the shears, and my eyes strain to measure the correct lengths to cut each time. Silken strands flutter to the floor. As I work, the Voice — immensely bored — relaxes its grip enough for me to speak.

"I always loved your hair," I whisper, feeling a pang of sadness. There's a flicker of surprise through the thread, and Rui's silver gaze meets mine in the mirror. His hair now falls to his shoulders, and I'm still working.

"I'll still have hair," he says suspiciously, "won't I? You aren't going to bald me, are you, Lina? I find that I don't quite want my scalp to be visible to all."

I shake my head, cutting strands loose, watching them fall. I have little experience with this. I cut my own hair before returning to Sunpo and hadn't even thought to use shears before Rui intervened. I worry that the result will be laughable. But when I'm done, it's anything but.

Cut so short, released from its heavy weight, Rui's hair is wavy. I've cut it so that it falls into his eyes just a bit and the tousled midnight locks scrape against his sharp cheekbones.

His new hair has changed the shape of his face, somehow, too. It enhances his chiseled features, and his strong jawbone is visible in a way it wasn't before.

He looks...breathtakingly handsome.

I am reminded of the portrait I once saw of him, the portrait Achara painted. His hair was like this then, too. But he was smiling. Happy. He isn't smiling now. Instead, his face is a portrait of careful coolness.

Well, well, the Voice purrs, taking back the reins, ***nicely done.***

Rui is gazing into the mirror, but not at himself. At me. "Thank you," he says simply.

I sniff haughtily. "You should have done it a long while ago," I retort icily as I put the scissors back. "You can sweep up the floor." I leave the bathroom, shaking out my sore, stiff hands. As I pass the door, three brisk knocks sound.

Summoning my scaleblades, I yank the door open and come face-to-face with two Dokkaebi I would be perfectly content with going centuries without seeing. "What do *you* want?" I half snarl, propping my hip against the doorframe and glaring daggers at Park Hana and Kim Chan. "And where's the one with the stick?" Kang is not with them—not that I mind. I have been content with the lack of the trio's presence, but now...

Why are they here? The Voice scowls as Hana sniffs, looking offended. "Kang is nose-deep in a very important study, thank you," she says sharply. "And it's not a stick, it's a *staff*." Unconcealed dislike twists her pale face into a pout. "Move."

"No," I reply sweetly, refusing to budge. "If you're here for the wedding, you have the wrong place. And the wrong time."

"Like I give a singular flying *shit* about your wedding." Hana narrows her eyes, her hand twitching toward the slitted pockets of her shimmering green hanbok, in which I suspect there is a small dagger. "If you ask me—"

Chan clears his throat. "Rui invited us," the general explains stiltedly. "We come in good faith." But his green eyes are still warily on my scales. "Is he inside?"

He invited them? Without telling us? Annoyance sends my blood heating. "He is not," I snap. "He has gone for a very long walk—that way." I gesture pointedly to the street. "Goodbye."

The door is halfway closed when a hand reaches over my shoulder and forces it back open. My body stiffens as Rui slips an arm around my waist and takes another sip of *Sallinna*, regarding his friends with a pleased little smirk.

"Hello," he says, oblivious to my elbow jabbing into *his* waist.

There's a beat of shocked silence as the two Dokkaebi stare at their emperor. "Rui," Hana finally manages, "your hair, it's—"

"Shorter?" Rui smirks. "Thank you for pointing that out, Hana. I was entirely unaware."

Hana and Chan exchange a long, weighted look.

"Do come in. Make yourselves comfortable." Rui practically drags me out of their way, and I stomp on his foot. Hard. He winces.

"What are you doing?" I hiss as Chan and Hana enter, the latter sending me a saccharine sneer. *"This is my home—"*

"Technically," Rui points out, "I am the one who bought it. So *technically—*"

"Who is watching Eunbi?" As Hana and Chan make their way into the kitchen, I glower up at Rui, who looks slightly surprised that I've asked after my sister. The expression has me scowling.

"Asha," he replies after a brief pause. "Your little sister is eating her weight's worth of sugar rolls and bouncing around in excitement. She can hardly wait for the wedding."

"That makes one of us, then," I sneer, stepping back. Rui's eyes glitter and his smirk becomes razor-sharp. "Why are Chan and Hana here? The wedding is not for hours upon hours, and you know that there is no love lost between us. Your court does not care for me—"

"That's not true," he replies smoothly. "They're quite fond of you, actually."

"Oh, my apologies. I didn't realize. Is that why Hana looks at me like I'm a bucket full of rotten fish?"

Rui sighs. "Lina—"

"Rui," Chan calls from the kitchen, "your danpatjuk is clumpy." There is a sudden clatter. And then—"I spilled it," Chan mutters, sounding more amused than sorry. There's the sound of Hana snorting. I practically see red.

Dokkaebi, in our house, making a mess, uninvited by us— Unacceptable.

"I will call upon my Imugi," I hiss, and it really is a hiss, slithering off my forked tongue. "And I will command them to eat your friends whole, for I am sure that Sonagi will appreciate a hearty breakfast. Alliance be godsdamned."

"And that," Rui says while raising his brows pointedly, "is exactly why they're here. To speak of the alliance, the specifics of such a drastic union. They are not here to torment you, little thief. I will make sure that they remain placid."

When I fail to respond with anything more than a withering stare, Rui sighs and gathers me into his arms, pressing his chin to the crown of my head as I reluctantly accept his embrace. He strokes my back with his hand, and despite the Voice's wary mutters, my body begins to relax. Face buried in Rui's hanbok, I close my eyes, shoulders slowly lowering, fists uncurling as I hug him tightly. Suddenly I realize that I am tired, so tired. I wearily allow the scaleblades to recede.

Already, this morning has been too much for me. The stress — the worries, the tensions, the pressure, the relentless determination to fulfill the Prophecy...

"I should have told you that they were coming," Rui says quietly onto the top of my head. "But I wanted to start the morning off on a gourd foot."

I feel him physically cringe, as if ashamed of his own joke. And indeed, the pun is so terribly awful that even the Voice understands it, and groans in a mixture of disgust and bemusement.

That's quite enough, it mutters. ***We have things to get on with.*** With a forceful yank, the Voice jerks me from Rui's embrace, and sets my pace toward the kitchen as Rui's hands fall to his sides.

Danpatjuk is spilled all over the wooden floor. My lips twist into a snarl as I lean against the wall, arms folded, glowering at Chan and Hana where they sit upon the cushions with stony faces. Hana's glare, in particular, is somewhat impressive. She's seething, and I can reasonably infer she's thinking bloodthirsty thoughts about me.

I don't particularly care.

After a few moments, Rui saunters in, sighing heavily as he takes in the upset bowl. "Nicely done," he says with deep sarcasm, sipping from his bottle of wine. He leans against the wall with me, shaking his head in mourning at the clumps of porridge on the floor.

Chan smirks, confirming my suspicion that it was done on purpose. I open my mouth —

"The treaty," Rui quickly announces. "We should work out the details."

The general's green eyes turn hard with calculation. "Lina," he says carefully, "I'd first like to request that you consistently share with Gyeulcheon the records of your plans."

"Does that include what I eat for dinner, and how many times I brush my hair per day?" I examine him in boredom. "You mean, I assume, my plans concerning the conquest of the Three Kingdoms. Fine. Rui will be privy to my plots, and he will share them with you should he wish. And in exchange, you stay out of my way. No military interventions, no attempts to cease the Fulfillment of the Prophecy or my destiny."

"*'Cease the Fulfillment of the Prophecy,'*" Hana mutters under her breath. "*'My destiny.'* You sound, girl, like a witless fanatic—" She falters as I bare my teeth. "Oh. You have fangs now." She sounds rather weary and not at all surprised. "Lovely. Secondly, we would like clarification on what you expect to occur when your Imugi finally transform into Yong. For that happens when you reign over the Three Kingdoms, no? Well, that's all well and good," she adds, her voice dripping with a sickly sweet sort of condescension like I'm an incompetent child, "but have you thought about what comes after your beloved Prophecy is fulfilled? What happens to you and your Yong? Mm?"

"We will be worshipped," I reply smoothly. "This world has lacked its gods for so long. I will be a new one. The weak need to believe in something. To find strength in someone. I can offer that." My lips twist into a smile. "Shin Lina, Empress of the Three Kingdoms. Leader of Yong. Goddess of Wrath." For that is the title the Voice has decided on for us.

Goddess of Wrath.

"It's fitting, no?" I purr to Rui, who is drinking wine with particular relish while Chan and Hana gape openly.

Goddess of Wrath. It is who I am. I feel it, in my very soul. For what emotion has been my constant companion through my eighteen years of life? Anger. A deep, bubbling anger...and a thirst for revenge.

"I would have preferred Goddess of Sugar Rolls," he says after he swallows a large mouthful. "Or Goddess of Pointy Things."

Chan and Hana are still stricken where they sit.

"You say that so—*casually*," Chan finally says sharply. "Have you no thought for the extremity of such a claim? To take godhood for your own? What will you do to them if they do *not* worship you?" he half hisses. "If they do not stand by you?"

My smile is cold. "My Imugi will need to eat, won't they?" Bored, I examine my nails. "I also have my own requirements for this treaty. First, that all Dokkaebi, save for my soul-stitched, remain in Gyeulcheon as they have been. I'm aware that some of you are not so open to the idea of my reign, the two of you included. I'd like to avoid any potential inconveniences of uprisings and revolts, so...stay in Gyeulcheon. And," I add, "I want Eunbi returned to me when I reclaim Sunpo."

When she weds, and has children, the control of the Shins will grow greatly. And when the Prophecy is truly fulfilled, when we make our home in Yeomra's halls, there will still be Shins left on Iseung. Our children and hers. They will be ladies and lords and warriors, emperors and empresses. The Shin reign will never end.

Rui clears his throat. "It may be safer for your sister to remain with us," he says delicately. "Especially as you begin to conquer the Three Kingdoms. There will be those who wish her harm as you begin your...campaign. It would be of no consequence for her to remain with us. We've grown very fond of her."

I hesitate.

If something were to happen to Eunbi, if her potential were cut short...

"She would not go uncared for," Rui says quietly, and I chew on my bottom lip thoughtfully. "You'd have visits—she could be the final link that unites our courts."

"When the Three Kingdoms are conquered, I will want her back."

"And if we disagree? If we are adamant on her remaining in Gyeulcheon permanently?" Silver flashes blue as fire flares in Rui's glower. Something in me recoils at the sight of it, and my entire body stiffens. "Gyeulcheon will forever be safer for Eunbi than Iseung. You *will* have eternal human discontent on your hands, Lina—yes, that is a fact—and there is nothing more dangerous than a mortal who has lost it all and desires vengeance. Nobody is safe from them." He smiles slightly, but it is a bitter smile. "Surely you know that."

I ignore his insinuation that I know the ruin of mortal grief intimately. I am well above that now, for I am immortal and vengeful, powerful and potent. What do I care for mortal toils? "When I conquer the Three Kingdoms," I repeat, "I want my sister back. And I want her at my wedding tonight. I will not move on that stance."

"We have bigger topics to cover," Chan says gruffly, frowning at Hana. "Topics such as trade. We want tribute."

I scoff. "Of course you do."

"*If,*" Hana says tightly, "you successfully take over all three kingdoms, which you seem determined to do, we want access to Wyusan's pelts and meat from their wilderness, as well as access to Hallakgungi the Flower God's garden of Seocheonkkotbat. We want fruit from Bonseyo's famed orchards—"

"Fine," I grit out.

"As well as precious minerals, natural resources such as wood and stone, along with other commodities, paid every season's solstice." Hana settles back in her seat and arches a delicate eyebrow. "Are you willing to share your toys, Shin Lina?"

Sighing in exasperation, I pinch the bridge of my nose.

This is going to take a while, I assume. Most of my day.

And I am proven right. The danpatjuk on the floor grows cold and even more clumpy as the three Dokkaebi lay out the terms of the alliance, and as I negotiate with sharp words and sharper glances. It does not, however, escape my notice that with each request—appeals for a yearly tribute of goods, pledging to keep my Imugi away from Gyeulcheon, suggestions of consequences should the treaty be broken—it seems as if they are attempting to learn more about my future plans, gleaning what they can about what is to come via suggestive words and well-placed proposals.

It begins to feel less like a negotiation and more like an interrogation. I am cutting and quick, biting back half answers and wary rebuttals as the Voice grows restless and snappish, pacing so loudly across my mind that I get a terrible headache. By the time the Sunpo sun burns in the sky, having reached its midday peak, I am tense and drained, my muscles aching from standing motionlessly for such a long time. But the Dokkaebi seem satisfied with the terms of the alliance, Chan departing with a muttered apology to Rui about the porridge, and Hana strutting past me with a syrupy smirk and a little wink that sends my jaw clenching.

I slam the door as they step onto the street, air rippling before them, and whirl toward Rui. He stopped drinking perhaps halfway through the meeting, and has already sobered up—his eyes are clear as they take in my furious expression. "A warning," I snap, rolling my aching shoulders, "would have been nice."

Rui looks vaguely bored. "Yes, we've covered that," he replies with an even vaguer wave of his hand.

I sigh irritably. "I need to res—"

Three brisk knocks on the door.

"I am *not* entertaining any more inane conver—" I cut off a second after flinging the door open, staring at a mildly bemused-looking Iseul and a wary Seojin—who is eyeing the street behind them sharply, shielding Iseul with his body from behind.

Iseul is dressed extraordinarily fancily. Her hanbok is a deep blue and glimmering, the diamond necklace I gave her draped around her neck. Her light hair is in a very elaborate updo. Seojin, on the other hand, wears a simple gray hanbok, his dark hair falling into his face less than usual. I grimace as Iseul cheerfully waggles her fingers at me.

"Hell-*ooo*," she practically trills.

The Voice is always pleased to see the powerful Gumiho. "Iseul," I say, tension draining from my shoulders. "Hello."

"Well, you look a bit frazzled," she says jovially. "Of course, that *is* to be expected on your wedding day. I heard that there were to be giant snakes. Where are they?" She peers over my shoulder hopefully, as if expecting to see an Imugi—and instead finds Rui.

Iseul's face contorts immediately. Rage and blame and hatred flit, one after the other, in rapid procession. Her cheeks stain pink. "*You,*" she seethes. "If only I had my shovel. I find that I am in the mood to dig a *very* large hole." No humor, or wry wit, laces her tone. It trembles. It shakes. And I stare.

Rui looks at her with sudden recognition and somberness. His guilty pain stings my skin, scratches my heart. "Song Iseul," he says quietly. "The last Gumiho." The effect of his words is immediate.

As quick as a cracking whip, Iseul turns toward me and lunges into the giwajip, her teeth bared. Even in her mortal form, her speed astounds me, and her nails would rake my face if not for the armored scales I summon atop my cheekbones. *"You told him?"* she hisses, advancing once more. Seojin has lurched into the giwajip as well, slamming the door as if the flimsy wood will keep the world away from his friend and her secret.

"Lina told me nothing," Rui returns, and Iseul halts momentarily, turning to glower at the Dokkaebi. "She didn't need to. I've seen you before, Song Iseul. I might be absent from this world, but I still hear whispers. Rumors." It is nearly the same thing he told me, when I demanded to know how he was aware of the mortal assassin, the Reaper. "Luckily, those who suspected your identity were…dealt with." He withdraws Manpasikjeok for a moment, a cruel not-quite smile playing on his face. In that moment, I know what happened to those mortals. Lured away to Gyeulcheon as part of the tithe.

Iseul breathes heavily, shoulders heaving. "Do you expect me to thank you?" she spits. "After you let my kind die at the hands of hunters? You didn't even bother intervening. You, the one being who could have *stopped them—*" Her voice breaks and she draws herself up to her full height, which is not very tall at all, smaller than even my five foot three. "I would eat your soul right now," she growls, "but I sincerely doubt it would taste like anything other than *cowardice.*"

Seojin is watching this exchange tensely, tautly. The Voice is watching it through my eyes curiously.

Her hatred of him is clear. *His* feelings on the matter, however, are indiscernible.

"May I remind you," he says coolly, "that we tried?"

Iseul wavers.

"It should have been easy enough to stop," he continues. "Bloodthirsty humans. Mortal weapons. But it wasn't."

"*Why?*" Iseul snarls.

"Because of the Prophecy," the Dokkaebi says slowly. "The one given to Bonseyo's emperor by a shaman with an ear to fate."

A Prophecy. Once listened to, inevitably to be fulfilled.

Iseul flinches. "It could have been changed." But she has faltered. Seojin makes his way to her side and takes one of her hands in his. She barely stirs.

Rui holds her gaze. "Do you remember it?"

"Of course I remember it," she snaps, before taking a shaking breath.

"*A son, stolen too soon*
underneath the light of a waning moon.
His heart and his soul
in a stomach full.
A fox now sated
with an end sealed, fated.
The woods shall fill with swords that gleam,
that wipe the population of Gumiho clean."

When Iseul finishes, her voice is choked. Rui bows his head.

"There is a pattern throughout history. Prophecies will always come to fruition." His voice is raspier than even Seojin's now, and he looks at me as he speaks before quickly returning his gaze to Iseul. "The Fox Hunt's Prophecy prevented Manpasikjeok from working. My soldiers and I should have had an easy victory against the mortals, but unfortunate accidents plagued our ranks. First, it was a bout of extreme summer sickness that incapacitated half our ranks. Then it was a seemingly innocuous wrong turn in the Wyusan Wilderness that left us lost for days. Finally, it was a fatal encounter with a mortal hunting troop. Victory should have been easy, but my troops inexplicably dropped like flies, wounded by far inferior weapons. We were forced to return to Gyeulcheon. And the Prophecy was fulfilled."

"But the Gumiho population wasn't wiped clean," I say, puzzled. "You still exist, Iseul." Anxiety fills me. Are Prophecies changeable, after all? But Iseul, shoulders slumping and suddenly looking very small, shakes her head.

"For a Gumiho to be born," she says quietly, "two Gumiho must mate and bring forth a fox-child that lives for one thousand years in its animal form. When I die, Gumiho die with me." Iseul takes a shuddering breath and smears the back of her hand across her face. Seojin gently takes her into his arms, stooping slightly to murmur something into her ear.

I meet Rui's eyes over both of them. He looks away.

Iseul pulls away from Seojin, and for a moment, she looks nothing like the Iseul I know. Her expression is—chipped, almost, wrought with hairline fractures. No light dances in her eyes. But then I watch as, piece by piece, she scavenges the parts of herself back together. A smoothing of her brows here, a tilt of her chin there. Shoulders back, nose up. A brush of nonchalance across the lips, a drop of sharp wit into the eyes. Flick away the tears, fluff up the hair, don't let them see you cry again. Don't let them see how you are falling apart on the inside, bones breaking, heart shattering, blood roaring.

I see Seojin watching this, too, his hands twitching at his sides as if he wants to mend her broken parts—*truly* mend them—with his healer's hands. As if he knows that this is all an illusion.

Iseul turns away from Rui, and I know that the topic will not be discussed again. "Lina," she says, her voice only slightly hoarse, "*tell me* that you've at least started preparations. Don't take this the wrong way, but you look absolutely *awful,* darling."

CHAPTER THIRTY

Iseul pokes at my scar appreciatively while Seojin looks immensely bored in the corner of the room.

"*Hmm,*" she muses. "I don't think we should cover this up, do you? But I'll need red paint, as well—for your cheeks—" It is tradition to paint two red circles on the bride's cheeks, a detail I nearly forgot. "—and perhaps for your lips…" Iseul trails off, frowning as I open my mouth slightly to respond. But I never have the chance. "Well, that certainly is new," she says, blinking. "Are those *fangs?* I never noticed them before. And your tongue…"

Seojin, leaning against the corner's wall, blinks—coming to for the first time in a near quarter hour. The room grows cold with his shock.

"The snakes," he says. "Yesterday in the Moonlit Hare, I asked how they were under your thumb. This is the answer, then." Seojin rubs his jaw, his stare dark. "You're like them."

The Voice hesitates, detecting a flicker of fear across his face. Perhaps it is just the fear of the unknown that is human nature. Or perhaps it is something more dangerous.

If one of our two bravest allies is afraid of us, there is no telling how the others will react. He must stand by our side. If we lose his loyalty, we lose the Gumiho's as well.

Knobby fingers poke the corners of my eyes, which water with tears, and the same fingers force my lips downward into a tremulous pout. The Voice pinches the back of my throat, and the words that I speak are suddenly tight and strained with shame I do not feel, not really.

"The Imugi are my allies," I whisper. I raise my hand, allowing scales to surface on my skin, diamond-hard and glittering. Seojin goes rigid. "I have been—gifted abilities by them. Abilities that will allow me to reclaim Sunpo." Truth, but not quite.

"Imugi." Seojin looks momentarily blank.

"The giant serpents of which I have spoken. They made me their empress. You'll see them tonight. They're friendly, but I know that I look..." I break off, blinking rapidly. "Please. I know how I look."

Although my outward appearance is trembling and distressed, cold determination fills my mind with sharp cunning. I watch as Seojin continues to rub his jaw as he observes me.

"What have you offered in exchange?" His level questioning reminds me of his brother, a spymaster born and bred.

Iseul scans my face. "There's a Prophecy, isn't there?" At my expression, she nods. "I suspected it from the moment you revealed yourself. These things do tend to go hand-in-hand."

"What does it say?" Seojin.

Not too much truth. "That they have been destined to aid me in destroying Konrarnd's empire," I reply carefully. "And in return, they may return to Iseung. They are not monsters." This is the first time Seojin is hearing in detail of the Imugi, and I must set the precedent. I will not tell him of raging serpents fighting in strife against the gods. "They are merely a species that wishes to return home. Under my protection, they will do so."

Seojin leans back against the wall—this time for the support.

"You may think me a monster for my fangs, but I assure you, I am no more a monster than the man who murdered Sang. Who dumped his body into Habaek's River."

Seojin closes his eyes.

Iseul sucks in a small breath, going to him. As she places a hand on his shoulder, she looks at me. "You're not a monster."

I do my best to look dubious and small.

"Lina, I'm a Gumiho and a madame. When I was fifteen, I kidnapped a lord and held him for ransom, and used the money to found the Dove Coop. When I was sixteen, I did the same thing again, but with his wife—and used the money to wrestle a small monopoly over the halji trade. And last year, when I was seventeen, I kidnapped their child and used the ransom money to invest in a number of opportunities that have so far yielded me absolutely nothing. And then this year, I kidnapped their infant nephew for the sake of tradition, and then used the money to buy some new hanboks—that I never even wear—from Bonseyo. Now that family is penniless. I'm really in no place to judge you. Sometimes the true monsters lurk within bodies of beauty. Scales and fangs don't make you a monster."

"You did *what?*" Seojin asks a moment later, eyes flying open.

She ignores him. "I couldn't care less if you have started to look a bit like them. Neither, I'm sure, does Seojin."

Seojin hesitates, but for only a moment. Iseul is staring up at him, years' worth of friendship meeting his eyes, urging him to agree.

"Right," he says hoarsely.

"Besides." Iseul grins. "You shouldn't waste any more time. Your vows need writing, and your cheeks need paint. Seojin?" She withdraws a pouch of yeokun from her pocket and presses it into Seojin's hands. I watch him carefully as he slips out of my bedroom.

Later down the line, Ryu Seojin may become a problem. But for now, he will agree, for Iseul and the death of Konrarnd Kalmin.

N ight falls, the day having passed with surprising quickness. The yellowish sky and burning sun are replaced by a velvet darkness and a reddish moon that glows among the sparkling stars. As Iseul and Seojin assist me with the donning of my wedding hanbok, my heart flutters against my ribs like a butterfly in a cage.

Some part of me that seems to have been slumbering for quite some time is singing in joy—joy that I have found happiness, joy that Rui will today become my husband, my lover for life. I can barely breathe past the sheer excitement as Seojin, eyes politely averted and working with a detached, clinical sort of attitude he must have learned at his healing academy, helps me step into the sokchima. It is the most underneath layer of the hanbok, a corset with a light skirt attached.

Iseul grins up at me as she fastens the chima, the red skirt, around my waist, tying its band just below my breasts. "A hanbok I'd gladly take a nephew hostage for," she whispers with a wink.

"Here," Seojin says, now bringing the jeogori toward me. The jacket's sleeves are flowing and striped with the colors of the rainbow, and they are cool and silken against my skin as he ties the ribbon with deft fingers.

"You really do make a beautiful bride," Iseul murmurs, dusting off the wonsam—the hanbok's topcoat—and approaching me with it held delicately in her arms as if it is the most sacred treasure. "I hope that your Dokkaebi understands what a gem he's won. It's rare that a woman can disembowel a man in one move while also looking like a beautiful goddess. I fear that you and I are the only ones in existence who are able to do so."

As I don the golden wonsam, elaborate with scarlet embroidery of blooming flowers, my throat unexpectedly closes with emotion. The Voice is not pinching it shut this time and strokes the ridges of my mind in soothing reassurance as I fight back tears. I'm getting married.

I'm getting *married.*

The wonsam is long and elegant, and the floral-embroidered sleeves drape well past my fingertips. To hold it in place, Iseul wraps a red sash around my chest, and steps back to admire her work. I step into the beoseon that Seojin has set out for me, the cotton socks warm on my feet. The slippers are next, slightly snug on my toes, but comfortable all the same.

"Hair," Iseul declares, and with surprising strength, runs a brush through my hair, ridding the short locks of the snarls that have accumulated today. With determined yanks and a few muttered curses, she manages to coax them into a low, braided bun with a few loops, and pins my bangs back from my face. Eventually satisfied, Iseul gestures for Seojin to fasten the jokduri to my head.

The headpiece consists of a vaguely hexagonal silk-covered outer crown that becomes narrower toward the base, topped with small metal ornaments. Four arrangements of thread—red, black, yellow, and green—hang from pearled clips onto my forehead. A long hairpin is inserted next, placed through the loops in my hair, the silver metal sticking out on either side of my head. Daenggi—dark cloth pieces with elaborate golden designs—are draped across both sides, where they hang down to my chest.

"Hold still," Seojin orders as he dips a brush into the jar of red face paint. With eyes narrowing in concentration, he paints a circle on each cheek, filling both in with color. His movements are carefully measured, as if he is performing a surgical procedure. "There," he says, stepping back with a look of relief. "We're finished."

"It's nearly midnight," Iseul says suspiciously. "Where's the Dokkaebi?"

I hesitate. Rui has not yet returned from Gyeulcheon. "He may have traveled to Jeoseung already," I say, hoping that it is so and ignoring the prickling of doubt in my chest. "Perhaps we should leave now, with a few minutes left until midnight."

"Oh, *thrilling*," Iseul says jovially. "But first…don't you want to see yourself?"

Suddenly anxious, I twist my fingers together, throat suddenly aching with the familiar desire for a smoke—to let halji settle my fears and calm my nerves. *One. Two. Three.* I take deep breaths and twist my index finger with my opposite thumb. "I... I..." Sternly, the Voice halts my fidgeting. "I suppose so," I say calmly, and Seojin tilts his head at my sudden change of demeanor. Iseul doesn't notice.

"But of *course* you do," she announces, grabbing my shoulders and steering me out the door and toward the bathroom, covering my eyes just before we reach the mirror. "One," she counts, enjoying herself, "two...and *three!*"

Her fingers fly away from my eyes, allowing me to peer through the looking glass with a trembling heart that fears for what I will see. Old insecurities rise, even as the Voice attempts to squash them down—what if my nose looks too pointed underneath the powder Iseul has applied? What if my small stature makes me swim in my robes? What if I am ugly and so unlike the woman Rui had given his heart to first that he refuses to wed me? What if... What if...

The breath rushes out of me as I stare at the bride in the mirror.

We look beautiful, Lina. In my mind, I feel that the Voice seems to be standing behind me, hands as gentle as a mother's where they are placed on my shoulders, a proud smile on its lips. **We look beautiful.**

And it is so.

The hanbok fits me perfectly, the golden color of the wonsam bringing out the beautiful hue of my skin. We did not cover up the teardrop scar—instead, it stands bold and defiant against my face, a testimony of all that I have endured to finally, finally, reach this point. My angular eyes are smoky and dark, painted by Seojin's precise hands, the monolids lined with a dark powder that brings out their beautifully narrow shape. The same red that colors the circles on my cheeks rests on my lips, glossy and full, curled upward into a perpetual smirk. The pointed nose I worry about constantly, demands no attention—for I look beautiful.

I look powerful.

And Iseul was right. I look like a goddess.

As the Voice sighs in satisfaction, my mouth curls into a grin and my fangs show.

"Perfect," I breathe, still looking at myself. "Perfect." I tear my gaze away, focusing on Iseul—and Seojin, who lingers in the doorway. There is still no sign of Rui. *He had better keep true to his proposal,* the Voice mutters nervously. *He had better show. And he had better be sober.*

"So," Iseul says, cracking a broad beam, "I *do* hope I get to meet the snakes now."

"You do," I reply. "Give me your hands."

Seojin and Iseul exchange slightly confused looks before holding out their hands. *Not that way. Fools.* "Palms up," my mouth snaps impatiently, turning Seojin's hand round. Iseul frowns at me slightly but says nothing. "This might hurt," I say nonchalantly as I shake my arm out of my oversized sleeve, revealing the scaleblade I've summoned.

Seojin sucks in a breath, jerking away.

Iseul coughs. "Lina," she says slowly, although she doesn't pull away her hand, "if you don't mind me asking, what is *that?*"

"A scaleblade." The sharp blade scrapes against the palm of my hand, revealing a welling line of teal blood. "And blood," I add, curling my hand into a fist.

"Your blood is so *pretty,*" Iseul marvels, staring. "I've never seen anything like it."

"You next." And Iseul grimaces as I slice into her hand, coaxing out the liquid that, to my surprise, is a fiery orange. Some splatters to the floor below. Iseul swallows hard but does not give any other indication of her pain as she stares at me in both curiosity and bewilderment.

"Don't hurt her," Seojin growls from the doorway, furious. He looks as if he's half about to attack me, despite his claim of being a gentle man.

The Voice falters, and my eyes blink in surprise. Even Iseul looks startled. "Seojin," she says soothingly, reaching toward Sang's brother, "I'm fine. I'm assuming that this has something to do with entering Jeoseung without being dead. And if it's not..." The madame grins at me. "I'll be *very* displeased. And I'll be digging two holes, rather than one."

Seojin does not look quite reassured, but he approaches me all the same, hand held tentatively outward—palm out, this time. He sucks in a breath as I drag the blade across his skin, and Iseul moves to his side.

"See? It doesn't hurt too terribly, does it?"

The vein in his forehead jumps. "Can we move along?"

I narrow my eyes at his tone but concede. "Fine. Follow my lead." My fingers curl around the cut that has already started to heal, squeezing out droplets of blood to the floor below. *"Yeomra,"* I whisper. *"Yeomra. Yeomra."*

Exchanging hesitant looks, Seojin and Iseul follow my lead. Iseul looks, bizarrely, as if she is trying not to laugh. Seojin most definitely does not.

The dark mist swirls around us, lifting us from our feet. I throw my head back in glee as the magic transports us, the icy wind whipping strands of my hair loose. I hear Seojin scream a curse, and Iseul shriek—in joy or terror, I can't tell—as our feet land with thumps on the ground. Purple petals flutter around us. And we stand in the vast stretch of Jeoseung's flower field.

CHAPTER THIRTY-ONE

We are the only ones here. Neither the Dokkaebi nor the Imugi are anywhere in sight and I cannot help but feel a surge of fear.

"*Oh.*" Seojin is breathing hard, face pallid. The word is terse and clipped with his fear. He's leaning on Iseul, who is looking around in sheer delight.

"This is really Jeoseung?" she inquires. "How *marvelous*! It's so lovely to know that when I die, I won't burn for eternity for my multitude of sins!" Her face breaks into a wide grin, but I'm still looking around the field for a telltale glimpse of silver eyes.

What if—what if the agreement has been broken? What if I am standing here, waiting for a groom who will never come? Has he gone off somewhere, drunk out of his mind? Has he been drinking all day as he was this morning? Have I been made a fool? I suddenly feel ridiculous in my wedding attire and have the horrible urge to cry.

Scowling, the Voice sponges away the tears rising to my eyes. *If he is not here, he will pay,* it assures me.

"Where are the *snakes?*" Iseul demands loudly, also turning this way and that in scrutiny. "I was told that there would be *Imugi.*"

Almost as if in answer to her echoing demand, the sound of a flute—beautiful, lilting, as sweetly melodious as a drizzle of honey—wafts through the cherry blossom air, weaving through the field. *Rui,* I think, my hand fluttering to my throat like a nervous butterfly. *Rui.*

The Voice slaps my hand back down to my side, but I think that it's smiling too as it watches from behind my eyes and listens through my ears.

There are no words in Rui's song, no attempts at commands. There is only the melody, a song that is sparkling and as sweet as crushed sugar...yet at the same time, bittersweet, like the rind of an orange or the last smear of a sunset before nightfall. The music wraps around me, a blanket of warmth and welcome, and it is impossible not to smile while tears prick my eyes.

Rui is here. He's *here*.

Heart in my throat, I follow that saccharine thread of song through the flower field and into the skeletal forest, vaguely aware of Seojin and Iseul following behind me. As I walk, long, elegant shapes slither from the forest's shadows until I am flanked by a succession of Imugi. Iseul crows in delight, and Seojin chokes on a gasp.

"Daughter," Sonagi whispers, golden eyes wide with appreciation as she joins my side, her huge form slithering next to me as I follow Rui's song through the forest. *"Empresssss. How beautiful you look."*

"Thank you." My smile grows as she flicks her tongue toward me in affection. A moment later, we step into an expansive grove, and I gasp softly.

The grove is beautiful. Sweet-smelling flowers, the same periwinkle as Jeoseung's moon, dot the soft, moss-carpeted ground. In the center of the glade, a large, dark wooden mat has been set. On it is a table, elegantly carved out of the darkest oak, low to the ground and housing the gourd that Rui brought to my home earlier. It has been split into two halves, both carved into cups. There is also an elegant carafe of dark wine, the chestnuts, and the dates. On both the east and west sides of the mat, there are small wooden buckets of water. My breath hitches. This is exactly what I wanted, exactly what I used to dream of. So bright is my joy that the Voice allows it to shimmer within me for a few long, beautiful moments.

And standing before the marriage mat is my betrothed. Rui.

He stands with his elegant fingers curled around Manpasikjeok, with his glistening lips pursed over the enchanted flute. His music swirls around him, twisting and twirling around his hanbok—his deep blue jaryungpo, the formal robes cinched at the waist with a silver sash embroidered with silver flowers, all of which match his glittering eyes. Atop his wavy black hair is the iksunkan, a formal dark headpiece of a cylindrical shape, and his baji—silken and black—show beneath his jaryungpo, as do his moka shoes.

Through the thread, I feel a surge of anticipation and hope and perhaps a bit of fear as I smile at him; the column of his throat is as graceful as a swan's as he continues to play, his long lashes concealing his sparkling stare as he becomes lost in the music.

He is beautiful, and he is mine.

As I approach, the song swirls and sings, glittering and golden, the tune hauntingly beautiful. It climbs higher into the air, rising and falling like waves of a starlit sea, twisting and twining like heartstrings. Tears flow freely down my cheeks now, and the Voice does not bother to brush them away. They taste of salt and stars and sorrow.

The music slowly fades, Rui tucking Manpasikjeok away into the folds of his jaryungpo as the remnants of his melody linger in the air, mixing with the rushing of the Seocheongang River close by. The Imugi remain watching in the woods, a hazy, soft, golden light falling upon us from their eyes. It illuminates Rui's face as he steps closer to me, taking my hands in his. Up close, it is clear that his eyes glisten with unshed tears.

"Lina," he whispers quietly. "My little thief."

"Rui," I whisper back, and I smile, my blood so hot that I fear I will burn. "Rui."

His answering smile is soft, and it transforms his whole face. For a few moments, he seems so much younger than he truly is.

Quietly, he presses his forehead to mine. We share a moment of intimate silence, clinging to the other's warmth, until a soft voice speaks from the shadows.

"Bride and groom. Guests and allies."

The Imugi hiss in surprise as Kang appears from the forest. He holds his staff in his hands, flanked by Hana and Chan, both of whom seem to be keeping their expressions carefully blank. Eunbi—Eunbi is with them, jumping up and down and waving at me with a chubby hand, seemingly to care little for the underworld and the monstrous serpents on the other side of the forest.

My little sister has eyes only for me. "Lina!" she calls, still jumping. "Lili, Lili, *Lili!* You look like an empress!"

The Voice and I can't help but smile at Eunbi as she continues to jump, her yellow hanbok shimmering, her hands clapping in excitement.

Then her eyes finally shift to the Imugi, and her jaw drops. *"Giant snakes,"* I think I see her mouth in shock.

Kang is clad in his usual simple white robes, and as he and his companions step to the side, Rui plants a gentle kiss on my forehead.

"Let the ceremony begin."

As Eunbi washes my hands in the small bucket of cold, clear water, my fingers tremble violently. This. This is the beginning of the most powerful alliance in history, the beginning of my destiny.

Sonagi nods slowly from the forest as I meet her eyes. Seojin and Iseul sit in the glade, watching attentively—or Iseul is. Seojin is pale-faced, watching the forest behind him warily as the Imugi hiss approvingly.

Rui's hands are being washed by Chan and Kang, symbolizing

a new period of purity and change. My heart beats so wildly in my chest that it feels as if it will burst through, escaping, rolling across the mossy ground. I am doing it—I am marrying Haneul Rui. Right now. I am engaging in the same traditions that the farmer's wife did all those years ago, when I watched them wed with the wide eyes of a curious child.

"Are you nervous?" Eunbi whispers, her eyes wide. "To marry him? You're shaking like a…like a…" Eunbi frowns, unable to think of an appropriate simile. "Like Asha when the stew is left in the pot for too long," she finally finishes.

"I'm not nervous," I reply smoothly. The Voice is currently attempting to wrestle my pounding heart back to a normal pace. *Damn organ,* it hisses.

Eunbi frowns. "Lili," she says, gently turning my hands round and washing them with water, "you seem sort of…strange." I notice that one of her hands has a cut on it, no doubt from the journey here, and I marvel at her constant optimism. The child is somehow unbothered by a world of death.

"Not strange." My lips turn up in a beatific smile. "Just…happy."

"Oh," Eunbi whispers. "I see." She suddenly beams, gap-toothed and cheerful. "Good. I'm happy that you're happy, Lili." With that, she skips back toward Hana and Chan, leaving me to rise to my feet and turn. Rui stands on the opposite side, his mouth curled upward slightly crookedly. Next to him stands Kang, his ancient gaze meeting mine. A prickle of unease drifts down my spine at his suspicious glance, but then he is looking away, his words steady as he speaks next.

"Tonight we witness the final joining of two souls already stitched together, the binding of two beings—each one the holder of a kingdom, each one as powerful as the stars in our sky…and we witness it together, Imugi and Dokkaebi, brought together for the first time. Let us remember this night as the beginning of a new era, the formation of new friendships and family. For today Haneul

Rui weds Shin Lina and their lives become one, their hearts bound by the red thread of fate. Let our animosities disappear like ashes in the wind, replaced by ties of affection and loyalty."

Rui's eyes are shining as we follow the steps of the traditional wedding and make our way to our respective ends of the table. He sits on the east side while I take the west. I leave enough room to bow twice toward Rui, signifying my loyalty and devotion. He bows deeply in return, and we repeat the actions again. As Rui rises, I think I see a tear glistening on his cheek.

The Voice holds its breath in anticipation as I complete the final bows—four of them, returned twice by Rui. Perhaps it is unfair that the woman must bow more to the man than the man to her, but this is the tradition I have grown up with. And it is comforting to know that even as I bow, I hold a power just as potent as Rui's.

Perhaps more, the Voice points out smugly.

A little smirk plays on my lips as I rise from the last bow. Appearances are so deceiving.

The Imugi sway in pleasure, hissing. Hana and Chan applaud halfheartedly. Iseul whistles shrilly, and forces an ill-looking Seojin to clap by grabbing his hands.

Slowly, Kang makes his way to the table and pours the wine from the carafe into one of the gourd cups. "The first cup," Kang narrates quietly. "Vows to the heavens and earth. To treasure each other as you treasure the forests and clouds." With an almost sad smile, he slides it to Rui, who raises it to his chest with a small nod before tilting it to his lips and drinking. The cup is then handed to me, and I taste the sweet wine on my tongue.

"The second cup," Kang continues, voice soft. "A promise to each other; a promise of loyalty."

The other cup is now used. This time I am the first to drink from it, and Rui the second.

"The third and final cup…a promise to forever be joined to each other in a cherished union in the realm above and this realm below."

And for the final time, we share drinks from the first cup, with Rui drinking first and I second. Rui's lips are stained purple-red as he watches me drink with avid eyes. He is trembling as I swallow, his eyes fluttering closed, his hair lifting slightly in a wind that smells of dying roses.

"Lina," he whispers, rising to his feet and making his way to my side, where he kneels and pulls two large rings of thick jade from his pocket. Trembling, he takes my hand in one of his, sliding the new ring onto my fourth finger on the hand lacking the band he gave me upon arriving back in Sunpo. "Garakji," he whispers, sliding the next ring atop it. The Imugi hiss in soft appreciation, tongues rolling out in surprise. I think that I hear Hana choke on a scoff.

Garakji.

Two rings given to the bride, who wears them both on her fourth finger until her husband passes. Then, the woman sends her love to Jeoseung with one of the rings slid onto his finger, while she wears the other one above ground to symbolize eternal loyalty. The rings are cool against my skin, cool and smooth. I swallow an inhale of surprise. I did not tell Rui of this tradition—I thought it would be too much, too lavish—but he must have known. The Voice peers through my eyes with keen appreciation.

"They're lovely," I say with smug satisfaction, admiring how gorgeous they look on my finger.

The excited susurrations of the Imugi still as he clears his throat. "I have…longed for this day for some time now. I have— It is hard for me to believe, truly believe, that this—that—I…" He falters. Stumbles. Trips over his words.

I have never seen Rui stammer before.

Not like this, awkward and trembling, unable to look me in the eye. He shakes his head and, out of the corner of my eye, I see the other Dokkaebi tense.

"Would you believe me if I said that I was nervous?"

"Rui," I whisper, brushing a stray strand of his hair out of his face. "Rui, nae sarang. You can do this."

He must ***do this.***

But he grasps my hand in his, holding it to his cheek. Tears fall from his eyes like snowflakes on a winter's morning. "Lina," he begins again, clutching my fingers tightly, "They say that—there is a saying that has rolled off the tongues of mortals for as long as I can remember. *'A dragon rises from a small stream,'* they say. Before I met you, my heart was as cold and as still as a frozen river, unable to be thawed by even the warmest rays of sunlight. But then I met you—and my desire, my...devotion, it burst from my heart as one of the *true* Yong of old would erupt from a stream"—here, Rui shoots a quick, almost taunting look at Sonagi, who rolls her eyes, undoubtedly hating the insinuation that the Imugi are imposters—"unexpected and magnificent, a brilliance of color, stretching into the air, soaring among the clouds.

"I have never known such joy, as if every moment I am with you, Shin Lina, I am soaring through the clouds and swooping over the white-capped Yaepak Mountains. I had—*have*—never known what it is like to be so utterly infatuated. I... I adore you, Shin Lina, with every beat of my thawing heart. I do," he murmurs, and I swallow hard, struck by the sheer intensity of the words. "I adore *you,* Shin Lina. My friend. My soul-stitched. My...my wife." He holds my face in his hands, and I raise my remaining hand to cup his cheek.

"And I, you," I reply fervently, feeling the eyes of the Imugi and the Dokkaebi upon us, feeling the enormity of closing this bargain, sealing this deal. Rui's eyes widen, and a flare of his hope buries into my skin. I take a deep breath. With these words that I wrote, I will have it all.

Reign, uninterrupted by war. The Voice sounds pleased, although it had not been the one to write the speech. That task was entirely my own, the Voice not knowing what to say or how to say it.

"For you are my other half, Rui—my soul-stitched, and the part that I feel I have been missing for so long," I recite quickly, eager to finish the ceremony, to claim this alliance, to be one step closer to my destiny.

The Voice pushes the words from my mouth with haste, impatience. Some part of me wants to stop, slow down, savor the sentences. But I do not, and Rui's hope flickers as my lips work mechanically, likely taking meaning away from the words I wrote in earnest.

"You do not run from me, instead you embrace me as if running into a storm with your arms thrown open, not fearing the lightning or the wind or the thunder. And when I am with you, what I feel is dizzying and frightening and dangerous. I feel as if I am in the midst of a sword fight, a mere inch away from death, my heart and blood pumping with exhilaration and purpose and pride as I block and parry and slash. You make me feel alive, alive as only those balancing on the brink feel." I finish this long-winded declaration with hasty impatience.

Rui makes a small noise in his throat and slowly steps away from me. His eyes are so very bright, and a muscle works in his jaw.

"A kiss," Kang says quietly, "to seal the union."

Our kiss is chaste, quick. The Voice doesn't seem to mind it, is not puzzled by it as it was by our heavier, hotter joinings. Eunbi cheers in delight, squealing my name, as the Imugi hiss in elation, sounding like the rushing of waves across the sand of a beach. Hissing cheers erupt all around us, the Imugi practically dancing—the forest harboring a sea of writhing serpents—and to Eunbi scampering to the table where she grabs the dates and chestnuts. "Remember this, Lili?" she calls, cheeks flushed with excitement as she prepares to throw the food.

"I remember," I reply, unable to wipe the smug smile from my face.

The alliance is sealed. Rui and I are one.

Eunbi squeals in excitement as Rui laughs, a hand around my

waist. She draws her hand back and hurls the chestnuts and dates through the air. I am meant to catch them in my skirt to predict how many children Rui and I will one day have…

But as I hold the folds of my skirts out, preparing to dart to catch the nuts and fruit, I catch nothing. Eunbi has thrown them too low, too hard, and too fast. The chestnuts and dates scatter upon the ground before even a half second has passed, leaving Eunbi to clutch her mouth with guilty hands.

The underworld falls silent. Sonagi's hood flares in displeasure, while Hana looks vaguely delighted as she stares at the cracked shells of the nuts. Kang's eyes are dark and filled with premonition as he meets my gaze. A chill runs down my spine. Rui has stiffened next to me.

A *strange foreboding is in the air*, the Voice whispers darkly, stiffening my limbs and tightening my mouth.

"Lili, I'm sorry—" Eunbi's lower lip trembles as she rushes to pick up the fallen foods, fingers scrambling in the dark mist. "We can try again. I'm sorry, I'm sorry…" She is about to cry, red-faced with shame.

"It's fine," I finally manage to snap in a tight voice, unclenching the folds of my chima. Eunbi flinches as if slapped and bursts into tears, and retreats to Hana's side, where the other girl pats her on the head comfortingly and sends me a glower.

"It's just a silly superstition," I hear her murmur to my sister. "Think nothing of it."

"But she's angry with m-me…"

Kang clears his throat. "The union is bound," he announces, eyes on me once more. "The alliance is sealed."

The air is once again filled with choruses of triumph and pleasure, sparkling and electric with happiness. Sonagi slithers toward me, whispering congratulations in my ear.

"Thisss iss only one successs among many, daughter," she murmurs. *"More iss to come. Much more."* As she retreats back

toward her celebrating children, I look to the woods and I almost think I see four figures standing behind the towering trees, still and silent, not daring to come closer.

I almost think I see hazy flashes of blond hair and green eyes, sparkling hazel, and chestnut curls.

I almost think I see two lanky men—one older and one young, but both with somber faces—and two identical girls with looks of concern as they raise their slender hands in greeting.

And behind them...a flash of lilac eyes and a looming shadow that speaks in the tongue of death, of chaos and roaring winds, of terror and bloodstains, of peace and relief, smiling with sharp white teeth.

But then they are all gone, flickering out of existence before I can be sure I really saw them. Nothing lingers in their places.

"Lina," Rui murmurs in my ear as the Imugi circle us, their eyes glittering in golden satisfaction. "Lina. My soul-stitched. My wife."

I close my eyes and hold him tightly.

CHAPTER THIRTY-TWO

It is an odd feeling, to be wed. To be a...wife. I almost do not believe that the past few hours have happened. The rings on my fingers are the only reminders that it has not all been a dream. That I am wed, that I am Empress of the Imugi *and* Empress of the Dokkaebi... That it is all real. Truly *real*.

The kingdom is dark and silent as we reemerge on the doorstep of my giwajip, still trailing tendrils of otherworldly mist. The scent of cherry blossoms lingers on our skin like perfume as we step inside our quiet home, hand in hand. The garakji have warmed on my finger, but chills still trail up my skin. Haneul Rui—*Shin* Rui—is my husband. My heart leaps into my throat.

Eunbi and the others have returned to Gyeulcheon, and the Imugi have departed to the sewers. My husband and I are alone. Even the Voice has receded to a corner in my mind, allowing me autonomy over this. Over our wedding night. Yet it is still there, monitoring. And even with my brief reprieve from its control over my body, it is still feeding my mind the same line over and over, as it always is.

Do not question, do not question, do not question...

I do not quite understand what it is warning me not to question. But I also do not mind the noise. It's a song, a mindless tune, that fades easily into the background of my cognizance. Sometimes I barely hear it at all.

Rui turns back to me, a crooked grin curling his wine-stained lips. "Well," he says in a soft, husky tone that sends my toes curling in their slippers, "that was quite the ceremony."

"It's not over yet," I whisper throatily, sliding a hand up his chest. His eyes widen, and I watch as he swallows hard. A flare of recognition shoots from his heart to mine.

"Lina…"

"Yes?"

His cheeks are flushed, his eyes bright with—concern?—as they search mine. "Lina," he repeats quietly, "are you sure?"

"Why wouldn't I be?" I tilt my head, smiling even as inwardly, I falter. Does he not…want this?

Want *me?*

My arm falls back to my side. I fight not to let my emotions show on my face, but they must, for Rui shakes his head. His throat bobs.

"No, Lina, I—I want you very much. It's only that…" For some inexplicable reason, his eyes are on my forehead, as if he is trying to see the inner workings of my mind. I bristle, moving away, skin prickling under his stare. *Why does he scrutinize me so?*

Rui inhales shakily and rubs his mouth with his hand, blinking rapidly.

"It's only that," he begins again a few long moments later, voice low, "I want to take my time with you. We have all the time in the world to consummate this marriage, my Lina," he says gently, brushing a knuckle against my cheek as I stare at the floor in humiliation, "When Dokkaebi make love, we do it…little by little. Our courting process is long, stretching over a vast period of time. Already we have done much more than others of my kind would have. And our marriage has happened so quickly that I still want to court you. To savor you. It is important to me." Rui takes my hand in his. "Do you understand?"

"I do," I murmur, raising my gaze from the floor, embarrassment slowly receding.

A look of utter relief crosses his face.

"But," I whisper, "I want to kiss you tonight, Rui. I want to do... *something* with you, tonight."

Rui hesitates.

I look into his eyes, running my hand back up his chest and cupping his face. "Rui." My voice is hoarse even to my own ears. I lift onto my tiptoes and brush my lips against his jaw. Rui shivers, his hands moving to hold my waist. "I want to touch you," I murmur, "and for you to touch me."

Rui is searching my eyes, peering into their depths with acute intensity. His mouth lifts, only slightly, as he seems to find what he's looking for. "Lina," he breathes, and I smile as I tug him to the bedroom.

Each step has my blood heating and longing blooming in the depth of my stomach. Reddish moonlight flickers on the walls and ceiling. The glittering illumination is romantic, and I send a silent thank-you to Dalnim for painting her moon such a lovely color tonight. Perhaps she looks fondly on Rui and me tonight, for Rui's bloodline can be traced back to the lovely moon goddess. And tonight, our bloodlines have joined.

Rui softly shuts the door, and I tug him toward my bed, where I wrap a hand around his neck and guide his lips toward mine. We kiss with languid desire, for this night is ours, ours and ours alone. I run my hands down the silken material of his jaryungpo, marveling at the sharp contours of his shoulder blades and back underneath the robes. As our kissing becomes hotter, heavier, I eagerly fumble with the silver ribbon at his waist—but Rui pulls back from me ever so slightly and cups my face in his hands. His cheeks are flushed and hot, his eyes searing, and his lips glisten as he breathes...

"*Mine.*"

The word sends a shock of lightning straight to my core and a swell of emotion rising in my chest. *His.* My eyes are hot and prickling as I whisper the word back, watching how the emperor's face softens, how his throat bobs at my echo.

"Turn around, Lina," he whispers, his fingers trailing down my back. I oblige, and my eyes flutter shut as Rui presses a kiss to my neck, his fingers slowly loosening the sash along my waist. It falls to the floor as delicately as a cherry blossom.

"How many layers" — Rui's voice is slightly hoarse as his fingers slide the golden wonsam away from my shoulders to reveal the jeogori and chima underneath — "does this hanbok *have*?"

I smile, and when I speak, my voice is soft yet layered with heat. Every part of me feels warm with desire. "Enough to confuse even the Emperor of the Dokkaebi, it seems."

He laughs quietly as I step out from the wonsam. The jeogori and the chima are next, and I think Rui's fingers may be shaking as he begins to untie the chima's knot.

Finally, the chima falls to the ground, and I stand clad in only the underdress. I slowly turn to Rui and see that darkly burning admiration is flushing his face as he reaches with trembling hands toward my hair, freeing my locks from the various pins, headpieces, buns, and braids. The shiny black tresses fall in soft, short waves to my chin, which Rui brushes his knuckles against affectionately before slowly — shakingly — reaching for the thin, corset-like gown that I wear.

But I stop him.

"My turn," I whisper, enjoying how his throat bobs as I remove his iksunkan, allowing his hair to flow freely, a waterfall of silken black. He inhales sharply as I consider his beautiful jaryungpo, decide that I do not quite feel like spending too much time ridding him of it, and instead press one of my scaled blades to his chest. Rui's breath catches in his throat.

With growing satisfaction, I slice through the fabric, the sharp edge grazing the skin underneath just slightly enough that Rui's eyes widen. I smile as the jaryungpo falls to the ground in two ribbons, revealing his bare chest, lean and hard with muscle. My heart stutters at the sight of him, bathed in the reddish moonlight seeping in from the window.

Shin Rui is beautiful. He could easily be a young god, fallen from the heavens. In this moment, I think he might be.

"I suppose," Rui whispers huskily, "that you should be quite careful where you point that blade if you cut off my pants."

The blade recedes back into my skin. "You can do the rest yourself," I murmur.

Rui's stare is avid and hungry as he steps from the baji, revealing every inch of his perfectly carved body. Oh. *Oh.*

I swallow dryly as he smirks, following the trail of my eyes and looking extremely pleased with himself. Every inch of my body is taut with desire as he trails his hands up my bare arms, lighting my every nerve on fire. As he fingers the fabric of the underdress with a sly glint. As he cocks his head and slowly unlaces the back.

The sokchima falls around my feet, a pool of wrinkled white fabric. I stand bare before him, bathed only in moonlight.

And for a moment—just a moment—my insecurities set in.

Too skinny. Too small. I wonder if Rui can see the ghosts of my bruises, of my abuse at the hands of Kalmin and his Blackbloods. If he can see how I was, back then, ribs protruding from my skin, my flesh crusted with dirt. If he can smell the grime and the guilt. My confidence falters and fractures. I fight the urge to cover myself even as my eyes blur with shame. I resist the temptation to cover the puckered scar on the back of my thigh with my fingers and to duck my head, hiding my too-pointed nose. I feel the Voice frowning as it watches, wondering if it should take control of my body once more, if it should intervene—

But Rui sucks in a sharp breath as he drinks me in. I feel his hand on my waist, I feel the unsteady pounding of his heart as he places my hand on his bare chest and leans his forehead against mine.

"Beautiful," he whispers hoarsely, and tucks a strand of my hair behind my ear with his free hand. "You are so beautiful, Lina. You are—magnificent." He takes a shuddering breath and my vision clears, showing me the reverence etched on the planes of his face as he looks.

My throat tightens. He means it.

For a moment, it is hard for me to believe—but then he is kissing me in a way that leaves room for no doubts, no arguments.

I close my eyes as he runs his hands up the arch of my back, pressing his lips to the corner of my neck. My fingers knot in his short hair as he scoops me up and carries me toward the bed, our lips meeting as he lays me down atop the cool sheets. His lips are hungry as they press to mine. I kiss him ravenously and, with a finger, I trace the curvatures of his face, the sloping of his neck, the hard muscle of his chest.

I see now why Dokkaebi courtship is slow, sampling only a little at a time. The anticipation is delicious as his lips trail across my body in a blaze of fire as brightly burning as his flames of azure, kissing my neck, my breasts, my stomach...the insides of my thighs. Gently, reverently, he coaxes my legs to hook around his shoulders and runs his hands down my calves. My entire body shivers and my eyes flutter shut as his lips move closer and closer to the place where I ache, so badly, to be touched. Rui gazes up at me as he slants his lips across it.

I gasp his name. The emperor's smug satisfaction sails through our thread as I writhe underneath his mouth and his touching, teasing tongue that sends jolts of heat through my body as he tastes me. My senses expand, and I can feel every stroke, every flick of his tongue. *Oh gods.* My legs begin to shake around his shoulders and hoarse, breathy whimpers escape my lips as my back arches from the mattress. The waves finally crashing, I cry out, unable to stop tremors from wracking my body. As they begin to recede, Rui rises—looking extraordinarily pleased with himself as he lies next to me. "I would ask if you enjoyed that," he murmurs into my ear, shaking slightly against me, "but it's entirely clear that you did."

"Mm," I murmur in agreement, placing a hand on his chest. "You can feel it?" I remember what he said the other night, a look of wonder in his eyes. *"I felt you, through the thread..."*

"I can," he whispers. "But I didn't need to. The way you're still trembling, even now, is confirmation enough—" Rui breaks off with a soft gasp and stills as my hand glides down his chest, grazing his stomach...and moves even farther down. "Little thief," he groans, pleasure shooting down our thread. "What are you doing?"

I smile, quite pleased with myself for drawing such a reaction from him.

"Lina," he whispers hoarsely after some time.

"Hm?" I grin, enjoying the way his eyes have fluttered closed, savoring the hoarse hitches in his ragged breathing.

"L-Lina." He is growing tauter, his muscles tightening.

My smile grows. It's delicious to see him like this, sweat shining on his forehead, his face flushed and eyebrows slightly drawn. Rui, usually so cleverly collected, is falling apart underneath my hand. I can feel it, through the thread connecting our souls—his pleasure, his wild abandonment. His vulnerability, entirely at my mercy.

"Lina," he groans, my name little more than a hoarse breath as he arches into me, his body shuddering. I can hardly see anything past the haze of pleasure that overcomes me—his pleasure—as powerful as the pounding of waves against the shore.

When I come back to myself, Rui and I are lying tangled together. He is toying with a lock of my hair, his eyes heavy-lidded with satisfaction. "That was..." The emperor seems, for once, at a loss for words.

"I know," I whisper, kissing him gently as the pink-tinged moonlight begins to turn into a faint summer gold and illuminates motes of dust floating delicately in the air. Crawling out of bed, I return to him with a damp washcloth, which he takes with a small— slightly abashed—smile.

"Thank you," he murmurs. His eyes sparkle.

Sleepily content, I smile and nestle closer in his arms. We stay like that for what might be minutes or hours, our breathing slow and heavy and sated.

"It's nearly morning," Rui murmurs after some time, and I sigh, stretching luxuriously.

"Mm," I reply drowsily.

"Do you have any plans for today?" Rui asks casually, still toying with my hair. "Capturing kingdoms, perhaps?"

"Don't be silly," I murmur back, closing my eyes as a wave of exhaustion hits me. The Voice stirs, slowly taking back my body. "That doesn't start until three nights from this morning."

"Ah." Rui drops the lock of hair. The bed groans slightly as he shifts his weight. I feel his gaze on me. "I am quite excited for the gala—it was quite thoughtful of the scarlet-haired to extend an invitation. I only wonder what I should wear. Something fantastic, no doubt. And it must outshine Konrarnd by far."

"You're truly going?" Opening my eyes, I blink at him blearily.

Rui smirks. It is cold and narrow, razor-sharp and dangerous. "Of course I am. I'd like to see the bastard die for all that he has done to you, to the ones you've loved."

"Oh, he'll die," I reply sweetly, my fingers itching with the desire to end Konrarnd Kalmin here and now. The Voice stirs in my head. *Patience.* "They *all* will."

He is silent for a brief moment, toying with one of his many rings with his long, tapered fingers—staring up at it with silver eyes that hold centuries of cunning. "Will civilians be at the gala?" he finally asks slowly, still playing with his ring. "Has the scarlet-haired invited innocents?"

Through a haze of sleep, I remember Seojin's invitation. "Yes," I reply drowsily, nestling deeper into the blankets and closing my eyes once more. "He has."

"And are your Imugi able to differentiate between friend and foe?"

That hardly matters. Irritated, I shrug. "They will not touch my ally on the inside." My Imugi are clever and know to avoid the one remaining gray-clad Claw.

"Is that enough?" Rui whispers.

My mind falls into the realm of dreams before I can formulate a reply or feel the bed shift underneath me as my soul-stitched moves away from my silence.

INTERLUDE

In the darkness of the library, the royal advisor hunches over a monstrously large book, squinting at the yellowed pages filled with the runes of the Old Language crammed upon the pages in indigo ink. His hair is tangled and matted, his face gaunt and his brows pulled so tightly together that deep creases form in his skin.

This is his fault, he thinks grimly. His fault. His fault. *His* fault.

As the minutes tick by, the advisor shakes his head, turning the pages, the line on his forehead growing deeper and deeper. The windowpanes of the book-filled maze are splattered with rain— outside, thunder roars and crashes while silver fissures of lightning snake from the sky, cleaving apart trees and starting fires atop the rolling hills. Words swim before his tired eyes, each hinting at the mystery he must uncover.

Fire, flame, fear, fighting.

He turns the page with trembling fingers.

Crackle, courage, conscious, clarity.

His heart begins to pound.

Pure, power, pain, prison.

Lightning sets fire to the sky outside.

Blue, blood, breaking, bonds.

Rain pours from the sky like tears.

Sweat, sorrow, soul…

Salvation.

In the library, the advisor continues to read.

And he begins to hope.

CHAPTER THIRTY-THREE

I sit in the garden of the Talon's palace, listening to the burbling of the koi pond, my back leaning against one of the many drooping willow trees as soft morning mist creeps through the blades of dewy grass.

It is quiet here, in my dreams. And I remember. Remember everything. Remember that the Voice is actually the Prophecy, remember the night I hit my head.

And I can think. Really *think*.

When I am awake, I am allowed no such luxury, unable to mull over my own circumstances. I am unable to question *why* there is a Voice in my head, *why* it takes control of my body. I know it is there, but I am unable to do anything but play along, feeling nothing but the occasional prickling of confusion or stubborn resistance before even that is dissuaded.

For each time I try to question the puppet master in my mind, the thoughts are swatted away by the Prophecy's idle hand, as lethargically as if shooing away a pesky fly. But here, the Prophecy sleeps when I sleep and must dream its own dreams—no doubt of the Three Kingdoms underneath our reign, of Yong taking to the skies with roars.

But not true Yong. The Imugi are false dragons, wicked where the original Yong were gentle. What is it Sonagi said?

"The true Yong do not exisst anymore, banished by time and their meek nature. But we hold the ability to change that."

The new Yong will not be meek, nor mild.

Sighing, I set the twig down in the grass and hug my knees to my chest. So much has happened this past night. Rui has married me. No longer is he Haneul Rui—he now carries my surname. *Shin.* Shin Rui. My throat tightens with a mixture of disappointment and hope.

Surely my soul-stitched realizes that I am not myself. Surely he plans to...to stop me. I *need* him to stop me. Why hasn't he detained me, imprisoned me? Although the Prophecy knows no better, *I* know him well enough to understand that he would not forfeit a grudge so easily, especially one as ancient as the resentments he harbors against the Imugi. He did not forfeit Iseung then; he will not do so now. I know him well enough to know that there is always a separate motive behind his every move.

Rui is not the sort to watch an ages-old enemy triumph.

Rui must stop me.

For the Prophecy gives no regard to the lives of any but ourselves. I fear what may happen on the Night of the Red Moon. A bloodbath will drown the kingdom of Sunpo. It will not stop with Konrarnd Kalmin. It will not stop until Sunpo, Wyusan, and Bonseyo are all mine.

Sunpo will be mine three nights from this one.

The royal family in Bonseyo—the reigning, feuding Jeon dynasty...the current emperor and his son, the crown prince—they will all be slaughtered under my hand soon after.

The Wyusan Wilderness will burn. Its warrior-empress, Empress Moon, will draw her last breath under my blade.

All for the Fulfillment of a Prophecy that I, Shin Lina, do not want.

There was a moment...in the rain...when my cognizance was free to emerge from the iron-tight hold that the Prophecy so often harbors over it. I close my eyes, remembering the blazing burn of the Dokkaebi fire against my skin, remembering the way Rui's eyes widened in realization that I was myself. But it lasted only a moment, and the Prophecy slammed me back into the prison of my own mind, once again taking the reins as if I were a disobedient horse in need of strict reprimand.

I gnaw on my bottom lip. The Prophecy did not see what had occurred in those few moments of freedom. It forced my mouth to continue the sentence it had broken off right before the fire.

"I trust Shin Lina. I adore Shin Lina—ardently, desperately, passionately. But you—YOU ARE NOT HER!"

He knows. He *must* know. I spoke the predictions. Rui is waiting, biding his time. The wedding…is it deceit? To get close to me, flush out my plans? It must be.

I blink back tears. If only our wedding were real, if only I was never attacked in that godsdamned forest… If I hadn't been given the enhancer, if only it hadn't mixed with the venom…

No. I mustn't think of what might have been.

Perhaps Rui plans to stop me on the Night of the Red Moon. I hope he does. There's a tugging in my chest that jerks me out of my reverie, and—

"Lina?"

My back stiffens against the trunk of the tree as its curtain of foliage parts. I know that voice, I would know it anywhere. "Rui," I breathe as soul-stitched steps into my vision.

He is more than just a dream; I know he is. But unlike the memory on the mountain, he is entirely solid, unchanging in the ways that dreams sometimes are—flesh and blood and bone. I feel him, here with me—feel his presence, smell plum blossoms and licorice. A low sob escapes my lips as I stand, lurching into his arms. I have only just seen him. Mere hours ago, we explored each other's bodies with trembling hands—but not like this, not when the Prophecy is entirely gone, when I can speak and speak freely. "Gods, Rui…how are you here?"

His grip around me is tight, so tight. "We're soul-stitched, Lina," he says into my hair. "I can find you anywhere in the world. Even in dreams. It just took me some time to learn how. I didn't expect it to work tonight. Is it you? Is it really you?"

"It is," I say, pulling away from him with effort. "It is. I don't know how, but it is. How did you know…"

He smiles, but there is sadness in it. "I didn't," he whispers. "I came here out of curiosity. I didn't know you would be here, like this. But I'm glad you are."

"The Prophecy once said it could not see my dreams," I explain. "And that when I sleep, it sleeps. It won't remember this, either. But when I wake, it will be there. It always is."

"It won't always be," Rui says forcefully, holding my shoulders tightly. The weeping willow's curtain flutters slightly. "We are… trying to stop you."

Relief weakens my knees. "You *are*," I breathe. "You know that I—that this isn't what I—" What I wanted. What I am.

I am not a conqueror, no matter how much I may wish at times to control the wild world around myself and my sister. I am not—I am *not* a goddess.

For me to think such a thing, to think myself worthy of the title, goes against everything I was ever taught. The gods are either born divine or chosen by the heavenly emperor, Hwanin, to ascend to godhood. To claim to be a goddess with no endorsement from Hwanin, to parade around calling oneself the Goddess of Wrath is so utterly wrong that I feel physically sickened.

I am not worthy of being a goddess. And if the gods take notice of the imposter calling herself one of them, if they look down from Okhwang and see not the girl who loves and cherishes them, but the girl who blatantly impersonates them…I think I will die of shame.

But when I am awake, I do not feel this guilt, this horror. For I am a prisoner in my own mind. My own body.

I am not in control.

"I know," he murmurs, tucking a strand of hair behind my

ear. "You're certain that the Prophecy does not hear us?" he asks, glancing around. "That whatever knowledge you gain here, it will not remember?"

"I don't think so," I say quietly. "But I won't remember it, either, until I dream again. Until I'm alone. What is it, Rui? What do you have to tell me?"

My soul-stitched sits in the grass and I join him on weak legs. His mouth is working, and through the thread, I feel an immeasurable sadness. "Many things," he whispers. "I hardly know where to start. You may hate me, for some of them."

"I could never hate you," I reply fervently, grasping one of his hands in mine. "*Never*. We're soul-stitched. We're true loves."

A sound like a laugh and a sob escapes his lips. "That's just it," Rui says bitterly. "The truth is that soul-stitched aren't always bound together as true loves by the red thread of fate. Sometimes, they're bound as mortal enemies."

I jerk back in shock. *Mortal enemies.* The words are like a bucket of icy water dumped over my head. A horrible shiver runs through me, chilling my heart, freezing my bones. Soul-stitched as enemies? Not as lovers? "That—no. No. That doesn't make sense." Even to my own ears, my words sound weak. Pleading.

Rui's silver stare is hollow. "I had to keep it from you," he rasps. "We need to guide fate to love. If the Prophecy knew there was a possibility that you and I are enemies, it would have assumed it to be the fated path and would have dragged us down it."

"No," I say, my heart racing. Breaking in my chest. Rui and I have to be true loves. We *have* to be. "But—the thread between us. How we can feel each other. How you can come here, in my dreams. Why would enemies have those abilities?"

"To torment each other," he replies, so quiet that I can barely hear him. "To hurt each other."

My vision swims with tears and I draw a shaky breath in growing realization. We could be either, he and I. Fated for love or hate.

"The marriage, Lina…the alliance…it's all to try to coax the thread to bind us in love, and to buy ourselves time. We're trying to avoid a war. To ensure that we are not joined as mortal enemies. But you know…you know I cannot allow the Prophecy to take the Three Kingdoms."

I close my eyes. "I understand," I rasp, honesty weighing heavy on my tongue. I do. As much as I want to scream and yell and sob at what my life has become, at what *I* have become, now is not the time. Now is the time to think strategically. Practically.

The person I am while I am awake is dangerous.

She is cruel. I wanted to be kind. She sins. I wanted to atone.

I feel a sharp flash of fear as I remember how I snapped at Eunbi in Jeoseung when she mishandled the chestnuts and dates. Never have I growled at her like that. Shame burns my face as I yank a handful of grass from the ground with fervent viciousness. My sister. Eunbi. What will become of her should the Prophecy succeed? Will she be married off in a loveless partnership for my own benefit? Will she be hunted by angry mortals? Or… My throat tightens. Will she become like me? A tyrant, a greed-consumed monster?

No. Eunbi is Good.

So what will she think of me? When I begin to hurt people—truly, irreversibly hurt more people than I ever have?

"Please tell me that you have a plan," I whisper, opening my eyes.

Rui's throat bobs. "I received a dream of my own tonight," he says quietly, "from Kang. He learned how to travel dreams in the Wyusan Wildernesses. Although it's exceptionally difficult for him to do, it's how he contacts me when I am out of reach. He said…he said that he found the *Blue Book of Fires*. It's a tome of magical knowledge, given to us by Mireuk the Creator centuries upon centuries ago. A birthday present, if you will," he adds, and I can tell that he's trying so godsdamn hard to lighten his tone from the desolate whisper it's been. "In it," he continues, "are details of Dokkaebi abilities. Abilities of my family line, specifically, starting with Emperor Haneul Dakho. My grandfather."

"Go on," I urge quietly.

"My family... You know that we possess abilities that regular Dokkaebi do not. That even the Gaksi Dokkaebi, my inner court, do not. Among these abilities is my Dokkaebi fire."

My lips part.

"When I-I touched you in the rain"—he shakes his head—"I never meant to hurt you, but in a horrible way, I'm glad I did. Because—"

"Because for a brief moment it was me," I finish, remembering how the Prophecy dropped unconscious, leaving me—alone. Myself. "I know. I'm glad, too. Are you going to—can you not just blast me with flames? Wouldn't that work? If it kills the Prophecy, we would be soul-stitched in love. There would be no reason for us to be bound as enemies."

My soul-stitched snorts bitterly. "That's what I thought, too. But Kang says that there is a fine balance when it comes to the usage of Dokkaebi fire. Too much fire will kill you. Too little will be ineffective against the Prophecy. But just the right amount at just the right moment... Kang says it is possible that it could kill the Prophecy, and only the Prophecy." Rui is speaking quickly now, and I can see a hesitant hope sparkling in his eyes. "The balance is necessary, and elusive. But if anybody can find it...it's Kang.

"Yet this topic is still...new to him. He doesn't know how, or why, my fire could harbor this salvation."

"I suspect he has a theory, though," I murmur. The wise-eyed advisor does not strike me as the type to fumble for answers without theorizing some of his own. "What does he think?"

"*The Blue Book* is written in the Old Language. Some of the runes are...hard to decipher, even for him. But it seems, from his research, that Dokkaebi fire comes directly from a power source in Okhwang, tapped from the sky kingdom of the gods. It is pure, undiluted power—literal, godly power that runs in the veins of my family's line. The purity of its origin could combat the corruption of the Prophecy. But as I've said, the balance is...delicate."

"You have to find it," I urge desperately, holding his hand tight enough that my knuckles turn white, and he winces. "Rui, you need to—you need to get this godsdamned thing *out* of my *head*—"

"I will," the emperor promises, eyes flashing. "I swear it, Lina. But Kang has told me to wait until he knows more. I will not risk killing you. Kang also seems to be...forming a plan of his own." Rui's mouth is tight as he grips my fingers. "He is clever, my advisor. Almost as silver-tongued as I am. But I can tell he is withholding something from me."

My blood grows cold. "Rui," I say, very steadily, "what is he planning?"

"I intend to find out. I won't let him do anything to hurt you, Lina." Rui presses a kiss to my lips. "I promise," he whispers as the edges of the dream begin to fray, as the willow tree begins to waver.

"I'm waking up," I gasp. "Rui—" His features are growing blurry, fading faster with every passing second. "Quickly, Rui, my sister. Is she—"

I think he might shake his head. But his returned words are muted, muffled...

I wake.

Rubbing my eyes blearily, I realize that late morning light is streaming through the bedroom window. Puzzled, I raise myself to my forearms and glance to my left. Rui lies asleep, his chest rising and falling evenly. My breath is coming in pants, and I am slick with sweat, although I do not understand why. Perhaps I have had another nightmare.

Good morning, the Voice mutters, awakening with a yawn. ***There are only three nights until the Night of the Red Moon.*** Wearily, it moves my legs over the side of the bed and I stand.

While he slumbers, we will work.

Outside of Gwan Doyun's chogajip in the Coin Yard, with the stench of fish strong in my nose, I pound on the door with a fist, my jade garakji shining in the sunlight.

Where is he?

My knocks grow louder, heavier, the door shaking under my knuckles—until Doyun wrenches it open, his face deathly pale as he takes in the hooded figure standing atop his doorstep. I smile, a flash of white fangs. "Hello, Doyun."

"Reaper," he says hoarsely, and I do not like the *wariness* in his tone. I have not forgotten his initial refusal to bow at my feet. "Shin Lina. What are you doing here? At this early hour?"

My head cocks. "I come bearing a reminder, dear Doyun," I purr, dangerous grin glittering in the darkness. "Three nights from now, you will attend the gala. Afterward, you will be tasked with calming dissent among you...mortals. I expect you to sing my praise, no matter how red the streets run, no matter what monstrous beings you may see lurking in the darkness. Do so and you will be rewarded. Disobey and you'll be sorry for standing in my way, hm?" He trembles as I lean forward, my grin growing. "Can you do this, Gwan Doyun? Can you keep your promises?"

His mustache quivers but his eyes flash with the very sort of *suspicion* I cannot stand. **The insolence.** "No matter how red the streets run?" he asks. "With...with blood, you mean?"

"What else would I mean?" I whisper, pulling back. "With gochujang? Please. I don't think so." With a smirk, I turn to go.

"Wait." The man's voice, although wavering, is clear. "Wait, Reaper."

Slightly annoyed, I turn. *"What?"*

Doyun clutches the doorframe with trembling hands. "A-a coincidence, is it, that you are Sunpo's deadliest assassin... That you came to my door knowing the-the specifics of my wife's death? I-I have been thinking..." He swallows hard, and I smell his terror— but also his anger. "That you claim to know *exactly* who did it?

You come to my door a pretty maiden, but now you're—you're... You promised me death of the murderer at my own hands if I wish it—do *you* keep your promises?"

I most certainly do not. My smirk grows. "Oh, Doyun," I croon. "Hoping for a position at Sunpo's joke of an investigative bureau? I should warn you that none of the investigators meet peaceful ends. This is a dangerous kingdom. I'd thought you would have known that by now." I cluck my tongue. "Do as I say, or perhaps another lesson will need to be taught."

His rage, sharp and acidic, hits my nose and stings the back of my throat. I chuckle, departing. "Goodbye, Gwan Doyun."

Im Yejin is next. As I make my way to Haewon's Fabrics, I note, with some interest, that there are no Feather or Bill patrols today. As I slip past the wizened old woman without bothering to give a password and climb down the ladder, I wonder if Son Wooseok has finally struck.

The shipsmith looks up from her parchment as I enter. She's been sketching a geobuksun—the sturdy, wooden warship—and I'm pleased to see that she's remembered her task, that she needs no reminder. I'm even more pleased to see that Son Wooseok is standing next to her, quill in hand, jotting down what looks like measurements onto a pad of paper.

"Lina," Yejin says in gruff surprise. Wooseok jumps, glances up. "We're working on the beginning stages of your ship, as promised. I was about to send word to you about this tramp here." She elbows Wooseok's side and he winces slightly. The bruises are fading from his face, but I'm willing to bet that there are new ones hidden to the eye. "He came to me last night."

"I did it," Wooseok says, drawing himself up straight and staring at me. "The aconitum coreanum in their drinks, the vial in Lee Yoochun's room. The Feathers and Bills. They're dead. It's only the Crown now."

A slow, sharp smile twists my lips.

The Blackbloods are eradicated. Claws pulled out. Legs chopped off. Feathers plucked. Bills broken. Crest shorn. Triumph flares through me, and I taste victory on my tongue.

"And the gala?"

"Kalmin is—" Wooseok clears his throat and shakes his head. "He's g-gone entirely mad. I stayed to watch before I ran. When he found the bodies, he started crying and screaming, but then he was laughing. Hysterically. He took one of the wine bottles and I thought he was going to drink it, but he...he started waltzing around with it, laughing the entire time. He was spinning. *Twirling.*"

Laughter of my own bubbles in my throat. It's exactly how I wanted it. Kalmin, alone and suffering.

I wonder if he saw the similarities.

Finding his gang dead in the same palace I found mine.

"Then he went to his armoire. He started ripping into everything, his suits, his robes, his shirts. He tore them into shreds, piles of shreds. But he left one outfit untouched. The one he planned to wear to the gala. S-so I think that the gala must still be occurring."

"You've done well, Wooseok," I praise, coldly pleased at the boy's success. "You'll be amply rewarded." Reaching into my cloak, I pull out a handful of Gyeulcheon coins. "Here," I say, tossing them carelessly toward him. They fall to the floor with a ringing clatter. Wooseok kneels to retrieve them, and Yejin gives me a long, hard look as the boy scrabbles to shove them into his pocket.

"As you were," I command over my shoulder, and return to the shop above, humming jovially under my breath as I continue on my rounds. Everything is falling into place perfectly.

Everything will soon be mine.

If I concentrate hard enough, I can smell death, decay, and rot coming from the direction of the palace. I grin, lips stretching so wide that my cheeks ache.

And the day has only just begun.

INTERLUDE

"Manpasikjeok," the Dokkaebi emperor says in quiet threat as he leans over his advisor's book-stacked desk in the warm, candlelit library. "It's beginning to look very tempting, Jeong Kang."

The advisor sighs, gingerly marking his place in the ancient *Blue Book of Fires* with a worn leather bookmark. He's situated himself in the middle of this winding labyrinth of novels to avoid this precise conversation, but successfully hiding from the maker of the realm is difficult to accomplish, to say the least. Rui has always been extraordinarily clever, and it's impossible—truly impossible—to keep a secret from him for long.

But this secret must be kept.

For it could be the key to a war averted and the Prophecy defeated.

The shock of it, along with the Dokkaebi fire, may be enough to summon the true Lina and grant her autonomy over her own mind and body once more. Yet Rui would never agree. Never mind that the girl will not be in any true danger from him, or harmed. His emperor lacks the ability to look at strategies as strategies. His heart, which beats for Shin Lina, gets in the way.

"Manpasikjeok is forbidden to use against your own kind," Kang replies softly.

"I've made exceptions before," Rui replies coolly, "and I have no qualms about making them again. What are you keeping from me, Kang? I see it in your eyes. You're plotting something."

Kang sighs, lacing his ink-stained fingers. Rain pounds against the roof and windows—it is storming outside, a warning as to his emperor's volatile mood. "I am doing my very best to do as you have asked. To release Lina from the Prophecy without causing her irreversible harm. Tell me, Emperor. Have I ever betrayed you?"

Rui shakes his head and runs his fingers through his newly shorn hair. It's an odd feeling, to have it off his back, falling only to his cheekbones. It should feel…lighter, but he feels, in his heart, even heavier than before. "No," he admits. "You've always followed your orders."

Kang is his advisor for a reason—for his unfailing wisdom and loyalty. And his friendship, steadfast and sturdy.

"And I will not do so now. All I ask for is more time. Until the Night of the Red Moon, when your soul-stitched kills her enemy and claims Sunpo. If you want her back, Rui, this is the way."

"Fine," Rui cedes, nodding even as a muscle pulses in his jaw. "But know this, Kang, if you go back on your word, there is nowhere far enough for you to run from me."

"I know," Kang steadily replies, turning back to the *Blue Book of Fires*. "But you are wrong, Rui, in assuming that I would run." For he has always been one to admit his mistakes.

The emperor eyes his advisor for a few moments more as thunder cracks and lightning splits Gyeulcheon's many-mooned sky. Then, with effort, he departs from the library, leaving Kang to his studies—and whatever else he might be plotting.

The emperor's mind is a tempest of confusion, anger, hopelessness, and desperation. As he walks, he thinks of Lina. Lina, under the willow tree. Lina, in his arms. Lina, surrounded by Imugi, smiling a smile so different than the ones of which he has grown so fond.

A wicked smile. An evil smile.

Rui means to go to the throne room, where he has a meeting scheduled with Chan—and he nearly makes it. But as he crosses the plaza, underneath the thunderclouds rolling above the glass ceiling, his vision blurs. Belatedly, Rui realizes that his breaths are coming fast, too fast, and that his neck and back are slick with hot perspiration. He stumbles, blinking rapidly as he falls to his knees before the burbling emerald fountain spilling khana nectar. The world spins.

He's been poisoned, Rui realizes. That's what this must be. It feels as if he's dying, as if his heart is going to burst into tattered shreds of flesh. Poisoned. He gasps for breath, but he cannot find it—

A small, inquisitive face looms into vision as Eunbi frowns down at the emperor, who looks ill. "Rui?" she asks, taking in his sweaty face, his rasping breaths. "Are you sick?" She touches his forehead with a hand. It's hot, but not feverish like Lina's used to be when she was bitten by snakes in their old hut. "Should I get somebody?"

As Rui closes his eyes, gasping for breath, he hears Eunbi's small footsteps as she sprints across the plaza and pounds on the throne room door. "Chan? Chan! I think Rui is sick—"

The sound of the doors opening, and a heavier set of footsteps joining the young girl's. Chan kneels down next to Rui, cold with alarm. His emperor is breathing quickly, but each breath is shallow. His fine, dark emerald robes are soaked in sweat.

Chan glances up to the clear ceiling. The storm is shaking the palace, gusts of wind slamming against the walls. Rain pelts the glass, but it's followed by hail the size of Chan's fist, and snowflakes as well. The moons flare out from behind the clouds—yellow one moment, orange the next, then a bright blue, white, pink, purple. The clouds are rolling in, and then out, in, and then out. *Shit,* Chan thinks.

"I found him like this," Eunbi explains nervously, hovering behind Chan. "I think he fell. I think he's sick. Is he…dying?" She swallows hard. She likes Rui, with his funny jokes and big palace.

She doesn't want him to die, not now, right when he's become her brother-in-law. Eunbi has never had a brother before, and she likes it. Likes *him*, so much. And if he dies, then Lina will be sad, and Eunbi doesn't want Lina to be sad—not now, not ever, never ever *ever*.

"No. He's not dying." Chan recognizes this. It's happened to his emperor before, after Achara died. Gently he coaxes Rui into a sitting position. "Eunbi, will you fetch a glass of water from the kitchens? And another glass of ice?"

Eunbi nods fervently and scampers off. Anything to help Rui. He's so strong all the time and it feels…scary to see him on the floor like that.

"Rui," Chan says gently, "you're not dying. I know it feels like you are, but I promise that you're not. This has happened before, remember?"

The emperor is dry heaving, hardly able to breathe.

"Let's do what we did the last time." Chan wishes he could call for Kang. A general doesn't tend to have a great bedside manner. "Let's try to breathe deeply."

Rui chokes down a rattling breath. His friend's hand is sturdy on his back. He tries to focus on that, rather than the way his heart is pounding.

"Good," Chan says, rubbing circles on Rui's back. A few Dokkaebi children are peeking out from the hallway—Chan shoots them a withering glare and they quickly disappear. "Can you take another one of those?" He tries to smile encouragingly, but it turns into a bared-teeth grin of warning at the children, who have come back. This time, they scamper off for good.

Sucking down another rattling breath, Rui grips his general's other hand tight, needing the comfort. Chan squeezes back.

The hail has stopped, and the moons are steady. But the snow still remains and the clouds are moving in abrupt, absurd patterns.

"Water," Eunbi pants, bursting back into the plaza and all but shoving the cup at Chan. "And ice."

Chan takes the two cups and sets them on the floor. From the glass of ice, he takes four cubes and presses them into Rui's hand. It is what Kang used to do when these attacks were more common, in the days after Achara died. The freezing temperature gave Rui something to focus on.

The ice bites into Rui's skin. He closes his fingers around the frigid squares and takes another breath. He's not dying. He's not. He hasn't been poisoned, he tells himself sternly. He's having what Kang calls an eruption of emotion, a physical reaction to his mental state — which, admittedly, has been in a dark place as of late.

His hand grows wet as the ice melts. Breathing deeply, Rui reaches out his magic to the sky, calming the clouds and halting the snow. The storm still rages, but it's a steady storm, a normal rainstorm. Rui opens his eyes, finding that his heart is returning to its normal rhythm.

Chan hands him the glass of water. Rui takes a long sip, the water soothing his dry throat. He sits still for a few moments more before letting his vision refocus.

His general and Eunbi are watching him with identical expressions of concern. With Chan's help, Rui pulls himself to his feet. "Well," he says, taking another sip of water, "that certainly wasn't much fun." His legs are still shaky, and he leans on Chan heavily.

Eunbi's eyes are very wide. "What happened?"

Rui waves a hand dismissively. "I fell," he says smoothly. "It took the breath out of me. Thank you for the water and ice."

Eunbi eyes him speculatively but chooses not to pry. "You're welcome."

He manages a small smile. "How's the sugar roll supply?" he asks as Chan begins to help him walk to the throne room.

"Almost gone," she replies proudly.

"Almost? You'd best get to work." Rui holds his smile as Eunbi laughs and skips away, undoubtedly to steal sugar rolls from under Asha's nose. As Chan closes the doors of the throne room, and as Rui slumps in the thorned chair, he lets his smile fall.

"That was a bad one," Chan says, coming to stand before the dais, hands clasped behind his back.

"I know." Rui massages the bridge of his nose. "And the first one in years. It's just...all of this. Lina, the Prophecy, the Imugi, war preparations, the marriage... It must have caught up to me—" He breaks off, sighing. "Thank you for what you did."

"Don't mention it." Chan clears his throat. "If you want to meet later instead..."

"No. No, it's fine."

"If you're sure."

And as Chan begins to speak of the army's training progress, of who he wants to sort into cavalries, of the battle tactics he's drawn up for every possible situation...Rui closes his eyes and wishes, fervently, that this was all just a terrible dream.

CHAPTER THIRTY-FOUR

Standing before Seojin's chogajip behind the Moonlit Hare, my knuckles rap sharply against the wooden door, once, twice. I hear hushed whispers, and then an abrupt thump. A few moments later, Seojin opens the door, looking slightly disheveled.

"Oh," he says, a quick flicker in his eyes the only sign of wary surprise, "it's you. We thought it might be the Blackbloods. Iseul was preparing to behead you with her ax." His words are more clipped than usual, and there is a haunted glint in his eyes that was not there before—or at least not to this extent. I remember how ill he looked in Jeoseung, and wonder in annoyance if I've damaged him.

"I was doing nothing of the sort," Iseul says, appearing over Seojin's shoulder, hair mussed and lips red. She's hiding her ax behind her back. "And I resent that notion."

"You have nothing to worry about," I tell her. "The Feathers and Bills are dead."

Iseul blinks once, then twice. And then her lips break into a giant smile. "My, *my*," she purrs, laughter in her voice. "Well done."

"The Night of the Red Moon is three nights from now. The gala is still slated to occur."

Seojin clears his throat again. "Lina," he says stiffly. "What are you going to do?"

"I'm going to avenge your brother," I say curtly, a familiar anger and desire for revenge burning my tongue as I speak. "I'm going to avenge them all. You know that."

"I do," he replies slowly. "But I wonder if my brother is accepting of what is being done in his name. Imugi, on Iseung. You say they're harmless, but these creatures are not in the mythological texts. It makes me wonder why. Humans erase creatures they were afraid of from the books."

I grit my teeth.

Seojin and his suspicions are becoming a problem.

"And there are whispers of men and women being dragged down into the sewers. Already the streets are spotted red. The people of this city are being injured. I do not accept that. I am a healer. I don't hurt."

Those men and women deserve their ends. Supporters of the Blackbloods. I open my mouth to say so, but Iseul is quicker. The Gumiho stiffens and fixes her friend with a glare so cold that the air turns frigid.

"It's only a taste of their own medicine," she snaps with a viciousness that takes even me aback momentarily.

"These people did not kill your parents," Seojin shoots back at her.

"They're all the same. Except you." Two bright pink spots burn on the Gumiho's cheeks. "Or am I wrong, Seojin?"

Seojin swallows hard, the war inside him evident. He looks at Iseul, and I see that he is slipping from me. There is a rift.

But perhaps I can accept that.

Now that there is a divide between them, even if I lose Seojin, it's possible that Iseul will remain by my side. I see her for what she is now. She is like me. Walking vengeance. Together, we will claim what this world owes us. We are both the last of our kind. The last Talon. The last Gumiho. Iseul is *mine*.

"These creatures lived in death," Seojin finally rasps. "Now they bring it here. I won't be involved. Not anymore."

"You would prefer a Blackblood rule to mine?" I snarl, and I see his determination waver. "Sang would be ashamed of you.

You want the man who killed him on Sunpo's throne? Truly, Ryu Seojin? Your cowardice makes me sick."

He goes pale. Closes his eyes.

"Seojin." Iseul's eyes are hard, and I wonder if she would burn humanity to the ground if given the chance. "This world belongs to the Imugi as much as it does your kind. Why should the world not return to how it was meant to be? Why shouldn't humans know what it is to be powerless and weak and frightened for once?" With a harsh shove, she moves past Seojin and steps onto the street. "I'll find my own lodgings from now on, thank you."

Seojin's eyes fly open as he takes a step back, doubling over as if punched. "Iseul. Iseul, wait. It's not safe."

She turns, giving him a truly withering stare over her shoulder. "But it is now. Because Lina is here. The Imugi are here, and the Blackbloods will die. There is room for a Gumiho in this world again. Isn't that right?"

I incline my head in a nod.

Seojin looks, for a half moment, like he might run after Iseul and beg her to stay. But he only watches, his fingers white around the doorframe for support, as she stalks away onto the street.

Then he turns his gaze to me. His raspy voice is barely audible. "You've brought carnage to this kingdom. Enough that I don't know if it will ever heal. You've made me see death, and it is something nobody should ever see while they are alive. You're a monster."

"No," I reply icily, "I'm an empress."

At my words, he does not look scared. He only looks sad.

I wonder if, after I leave, Ryu Seojin will finally let himself cry.

"You're angry," Rui murmurs as I harshly scrape a comb through my damp hair. He lies on our bed, watching me through hooded eyes. His knifelike mouth curls in a smile as I turn from my seat at the end of the mattress to glower at him. Reddish moonlight spills through the window's paper screen, highlighting the contours of his face and bare chest in its glow. My mouth dries a little at the sight. "You've been in a foul mood since you returned this afternoon, little thief. Don't try to deny it."

"I'm not," I say in a voice that suggests the very opposite. The Voice grips my tongue, and when I speak again, my tone is more measured. "I'm perfectly fine."

Rui arches a brow. "During dinner, you stabbed the mandu so hard that the pork flew out and smacked you on the forehead." Although his smile has vanished, his lips twitch as I set down the comb and frown at him. "Also, Lina, I can feel it." He gestures between us, to the thread binding us. For a moment, it's almost visible—a flickering string of scarlet, emerging from my chest and disappearing into his. But then it's gone, invisible once more, although I can still feel it.

"Fine," I snap. "Fine. If you must know, I lost an ally today."

My husband straightens, immediately at attention. "Who?"

"Ryu Seojin."

It takes Rui a moment, but he eventually nods. "The Gumiho's companion. I'm not sure we were ever properly introduced." He runs a hand through his hair. "Why has he left?"

I scowl as I climb into bed. "He does not harbor fond feelings for my destiny. He prefers Kalmin's rule to mine, even though they killed Sang."

"Sang." My soul-stitched blinks, not quite making the connection. And I realize I never told him who Ryu Seojin is. I swallow hard.

"Seojin is Sang's brother."

"Sang's brother?" Rui blinks, startled. "You did not tell me." His gaze is piercing as I pull the blankets up to my chin, seething.

"It slipped my mind," I mutter.

A lie. In truth, I did not want to confront my guilt more than I had to. But that does not matter now. All I feel toward Seojin is an intense, consuming dislike.

Rui is silent for a long time before saying, quietly, "That's not like you, Lina."

"I forgot. Much has been happening." The Voice is feeding excuses into my mouth, one after the other. "It's of little importance."

"You loved Sang," he replies softly. "I only thought you would—come to me with this news. That we could…talk about it, if you wanted to."

"I don't want to," I clip out. "I didn't then, and I don't now."

Rui's jaw clenches but he says nothing, and for a few long moments, we lie in tense silence.

"How is your court?" I finally ask. Rui spent most of the day in his realm, tending to Gyeulcheon's affairs.

"It's well," he says, voice still slightly taut.

"How have the people taken the news of our marriage?"

"They are—" Rui shifts, the blankets rustling as he turns on his side so he faces me, rather than the ceiling. "They are still adjusting to the idea."

"I see," I murmur.

"It will take time."

"Of course."

Again, we fall into uneasy silence. I feel the Voice pacing, trying to think of something to say. But Rui speaks first. His voice has gentled, and the lines of his face have softened. He reaches out a finger to trace the curvature of my cheek. "Soon you will reclaim this kingdom," he says quietly. "Soon you will make the scarlet-haired suffer for what he did to you. To them. Are you ready?"

"Yes," I murmur, leaning into his touch. "Are you?"

"Oh, entirely." He kisses my forehead. "Sweet dreams, Lina."

CHAPTER THIRTY-FIVE

K onrarnd Kalmin, although he will never admit it, is afraid. I can practically taste his fear from here, standing on the roof of my hanok, enjoying a bottle of sun-warmed spiced wine in smug celebration.

The last two days dragged, undoubtedly due to my rising anticipation of this coming night. I have been tense, snappish, unable to sit still and instead channeling my energy into stalking the streets, hunting down associates of the Blackbloods, and discarding them into the sewers for my Imugi, who have been steadily gnawing through Kalmin's remaining connections. But even so, the gala is still slated to occur. Undoubtedly, Kalmin—mad with grief and fury—thinks he will achieve some sort of victory by refusing to budge, whether it be catching the perpetrator or simply appearing to be the exact opposite of what he is…

Which is *terrified*.

As I take another swig of wine, I can almost feel the Talons standing next to me on the rooftop as a dry afternoon wind lifts the strands of my hair. I can almost feel the weight of the Prophecy on my shoulders.

Everything depends on tonight.

We must not falter. The Voice, pacing atop my mind, speaks vigorously. ***We must not fail. The plan has been set in motion. We must take Sunpo tonight. We show no mercy. We show nothing but vengeance and power.***

Images flash before my eyes, guided by the Voice's words.

Sonagi and her children overtaking Sunpo, crawling atop hanoks and slithering through the streets, maws dripping with fresh blood. The gala, attendees lying dead and bloody in the halls, eyes unseeing, limbs ripped from them, the stench of gore thick and potent, the palace decorated in death.

This is—familiar. This scene is *too* familiar.

And suddenly, I am back to that night, that night where it all went so horribly wrong, that night when I walked into the same palace to find bodies and blood everywhere.

The carnage sprawled across the palace in heaps of limp, disfigured bodies seeping scarlet as they lay flat and unseeing on the bloodstained floor. Weapons rusted with crimson lay scattered on the ground. Others were embedded into still flesh with grim finality.

On the roof, the sun blazing down on my skin, I gasp. Bile rises in my throat. My sharp vision blurs into smears of nothingness.

The Voice hisses in resentment, losing control of my limbs as my kneecaps hit the hard, sunbaked tiles of my giwajip. Its resentment only grows louder as my thoughts, in my own voice, battle through to the forefront of my mind and escape the corner in which they'd been shoved.

I cannot—do to others—what was done to those I loved—not innocents—not the innocents—I cannot be like—not like Konrarnd Kalmin—No—

So difficult, the Voice seethes, digging its nails into the tender folds of my brain. A searing ache splits my head and I gag, my body going limp on the roof. **Why must you question it all? Why can you not do as you are** meant **to—why,** why **must you** think**?**

Through the pain, I cling to the memories as if clinging to the ledge of a precariously high cliff. But the Voice looms above me, teeth bared in a snarl. **Why must you** fight? it demands, and I scream through my teeth as its foot comes down heavily on my hand. My grip spasms and then I am falling away from the cliff, falling, falling, falling…

On the roof of my giwajip, my legs stand. My fingers unfurl. My chest begins to rise and fall more evenly.

Tonight is the birth of a new reign, a new era. When the moon shines a brilliant, bloody red—a sickle in a death-dark sky—that is when an empress will be born. With Sunpo under my control, I can turn my sights to Wyusan and Bonseyo. Yong will take to the skies. It will be glorious.

And there is nobody to stop me.

Nobody.

There are whispers upon the realm of Iseung.

Whispers that the insignificant kingdom of Sunpo, the Eastern Continent's dark little crevice of dirt and grime and blood and crime, teems with shadowed beasts—beasts of scales and slithers, beasts that emerge from the underground in a flash of dark green, closing their jaws around flailing limbs, dragging wailing victims to their lair.

There are whispers.

But tonight, they will become screams.

For it is finally, finally, the Night of the Red Moon.

A storm rages outside, thick and thunderous, shaking my giwajip's foundations. Although the clouds are thick, the sickle moon's purely red light still shines bright and the raindrops look like blood as they pound down on Sunpo's streets.

I smile, fangs pricking my dark lips. The gala begins in less than an hour and I am more than prepared. Clad in a silken black hanbok, my face powdered and painted to perfection, my hair coiffed and arranged to perfection, I am unrecognizable as the sickly, traumatized girl who had been ordered to steal a tapestry from the Temple of Ruin so very long ago.

I am an empress.

The Voice hums in pleasure, stroking my mind in approval.

Everything is prepared. Sonagi and her children await my signal. Konrarnd Kalmin and his invited guests await their deaths. Smiling one last time at the mirror, I go and find Rui.

My soul-stitched has indeed kept true to his promise of accepting Kalmin's invitation to the gala, evidently finding a surplus of amusement in the fact that the crime lord wishes to have him killed there. Rui has made no attempt to disguise who he is. The emperor wears his glittering silver jewelry and lavish, deep-purple hanbok with pride, Manpasikjeok hanging loosely in his grip. We will enter separately, for his entrance will be when my revenge is moments away from being taken, the finishing touch to an already elaborate painting.

Rui's silver eyes meet mine, glittering with an indecipherable emotion. "Lina," he says quietly, striding across the bedroom and pressing a kiss to my forehead. "You look beautiful."

"I would hope so," I reply, smoothing out my bangs and fluffing my hair. "Tonight is what I was made for."

Rui's throat bobs. "A night to remember."

"Precisely." I grin and stretch out my hand. My heart has begun to beat in rapid, rapid anticipation. Tonight. Tonight. The Prophecy, nearly fulfilled. I am close, so close… "Shall we?"

My husband takes my hand. His mouth smiles, but his face is pale. "We shall."

The main gate of the palace is not as flooded with chattering denizens as it would have been without my…efforts. There are only a few groups of men and women awaiting entry through the gates, clad in a variety of different garments—extravagant hanboks, simple robes, tattered clothes smeared with dirt. Parasols are lifted high against Sonagi's storm, slippers darting over deep puddles, a few unlucky guests' makeup running down their faces as the rain beats down even harder. It looks as if Kalmin has hired new guards to man the entry, replacing his old cronies. It's of no consequence to me. They'll be disposed of soon enough.

I join the short, steadily moving line with a satisfied smile, inhaling the night air. I can almost taste the bloody moon that hangs up ahead among the glowing stars and furious storm clouds—it tastes like the pulp of bloody oranges, like syrup-coated cherries and dying roses.

Behind the newly hired guards and through the main gate, the palace is mostly silent despite the festivities. Its flared roofs shine under the bloody moonlight. Konrarnd Kalmin is within.

Fresh fury overtakes me. This palace does not belong to Konrarnd Kalmin. How dare he pretend otherwise.

Focus, the Voice demands, and my heart rate steadies. Everything must go as planned tonight. I cannot afford to falter, to freeze.

Rui has not entered the palace yet—he will join at just the right moment, at precisely the right time, teleporting through his shadowed corridor with a dangerous grin.

"Lina," a familiar voice whispers from behind me, and I turn to see Iseul huddled underneath a parasol and cutting past the one guest waiting behind me, a scowling man whose grimace abruptly vanishes when she turns to give him a sweet smile that I know has absolutely no sincerity behind it. He clearly doesn't notice that her eyes are rimmed with red, or that there are dark circles bruising the skin underneath them. Seojin's loss has affected her more than I anticipated. I hope it does not distract her.

As the man blushes, Iseul turns back to me, her glossy lips stretched into a smirk, her fingers straightening the pink ribbon of her yellow hanbok. "Works every time," she explains triumphantly.

"It's *priceless*, isn't it?"

"Seojin isn't coming?" I know the answer, but I can't help asking. I'm not at all surprised when Iseul stiffens.

"No," she says sharply. "He's not. Obviously." She swallows hard, her mask of smug entertainment cracking down the middle and revealing a hurt, lonely girl. "But I stole his invitation," Iseul assures me, blinking rapidly. "We'll still gain entry."

"He's a fool to abandon you," I say, the Voice carefully measuring drops of reassurance into each word. "A fool not to see what, together, we will accomplish."

She sniffs, drawing her shoulders back and angling her chin upward. "My thoughts precisely." But she's still blinking rapidly, and two spots of color burn brightly on her cheeks.

"He'll regret his decision soon enough. Tonight will be a performance for the histories. You remember your part in this?"

"How could I forget?" she replies with an attempt at a smile that doesn't reach her eyes. "I'll cherish devouring his soul. Even if it tastes like utter shit, which it absolutely will. I'll need a chaser afterward. Juice, perhaps. Sweet pear, preferably. Although I'll take apple, if you have it."

My laughter is dark, but it fades quickly, for we've come closer to the gate and must be scanned for weapons. A guard smiles with yellow teeth as he stalks closer to me. "Weapon check," he says, voice wet and gruff all at once. "Arms out."

"Weapon check?" Iseul asks in surprise. "Why, *who* would bring *weapons* to a *gala*?"

"Arms out," he repeats, glowering at me.

Gritting my teeth, I consider gutting him here and now, but I do as he says. Rage rises in my throat as he takes his time patting me down for weapons. Not that he'll find any. My blades are hidden underneath my smooth human skin.

His hands linger on my hips, my thighs. I clench my jaw. Behind me, Iseul is undergoing the same process with dramatic, impatient sighs. I bite my tongue until I taste my own green blood to prevent myself from sinking my fangs into his neck and leaving him to fight the futile battle against Imugi venom. Finally, he steps back with a wormy smile on his lips as he points to the garakji on my finger. "Tell your husband that I'd pay good yeokun for a night with ye."

Behind me, Iseul snorts. "Yes, *do* tell him, Lina. I'd pay good money to see the damage he inflicts."

"Oh, I shall," I say sweetly, imagining Rui convincing him to fall upon his own dagger with Manpasikjeok.

The sentry sniggers and waves us on.

We cross the wide cobblestoned courtyard. I pick across the uneven stones and skip over suspicious looking puddles. Although we're still outside, the air smells stale. Rotten. I suppose it's quite hard to get rid of the stench of an entire room of bodies.

As Iseul and I ascend the weed-tangled steps, picking our way through the overgrowth toward the green and scarlet palace, the scents of the gala in their entirety reach my nose. Perspiration. Sour wine, left out too long. Stale, old halji. And most potent of all…fear. Kalmin's.

"Well," Iseul snorts, "I can already tell that this is going to be quite the depressing party."

Disgusted, I breathe in only through my mouth as we reach the large wooden doors, passing by the small scarlet columns wrapped with vines and gouged with marks of daggers. They're open, halfway, allowing us entry into Konrarnd Kalmin's final gala. The stench is even stronger here: dried blood and sickness and the faintest tinge of the poisoned wine…sickly sweet. Did Kalmin even manage to move all the bodies out?

Iseul and I exchange cruel, anticipatory glances.

"Stay out of sight until I need you," I whisper.

"Gladly," she replies, pinching her nose shut. With one final glance at each other, we slip inside.

My back straightens and my eyes narrow, looking around

the palace. The memories threaten to swarm up and swallow me whole—

The carnage—limp, disfigured—seeping scarlet—prone and unseeing—weapons rusted with crimson—embedded into still flesh—grim finality—

But the Voice stamps those out with a stern foot. I feel a surge of pleasure as I note that Iseul was right: this is truly the most depressing gala I have ever set my eyes on. There are only fifteen guests by my estimation, and they stand in awkward clusters on the black-tiled floors, plunged into semidarkness. No candles are lit, and the only light comes from the bloody moon slipping through the crack in the doorway. There is no music, no food, no dancing. Just guests whispering among themselves, and no sign of the man of honor: the Crown. The throne at the back of the room—a brilliant red, a small structure itself with hanging emerald eaves crafted of painted wood, lifted upward by a bloody dais, framed by two deep green columns—is abandoned, empty. Kalmin is nowhere in sight.

Iseul slips behind a column to wait, to stay out of sight. I walk farther into the room, my shoes clicking on the floor. In the silence, my breathing seems loud.

"Where is he?" a woman is whispering to a small cluster of other guests. "We come all this way to show our support, and we're repaid with…this? Where are the drinks? The food and the music?"

"I think the bigger question is," a heavyset man replies, "where is Kalmin?"

"Do you smell that?" This question from Gwan Doyun, standing not far away from me, looking haggard and hungry and scared. He has come, as promised, and his eyes are darting nervously around the room. "It smells like death in here."

"Interesting." My returning smile is cold. "I hadn't noticed."

Something in my voice makes him flinch. I barely notice. My attention has turned to something else.

An uneven gait coming from a nearby corridor. A raspy sort of breathing. A faint clinking, like he's holding a bottle of wine in his hand by its neck. My eyes slowly slide to the hallway to my right. The red moonlight displays a distorted shadow coming closer. Closer.

And then I see him.

Kalmin.

Konrarnd Kalmin.

The world seems to fall away beneath me as I stare, my throat too tight with fury and hatred and bloodlust to breathe. My mind goes blank with hatred and I cannot even hear the Voice. I can hear only the sound of my own scream, broken and shrieking, that night I entered this same palace to find a bloodbath awaiting me. A flame of fear, sharp and bitter, rises in my chest before the Voice blows it out and replaces it with cold rage.

His red hair has grown and is slicked back with a bitter-smelling oil. He wears a suit in the style of the Northern Continent, all black and white, the jacket slim and contained only to his torso, his pants starkly visible. His face is gaunt, sallow, with deep bruises of shadow under his eyes. Stubble lines his chin, his upper lip, and despite his fine clothing, he smells like carrion so pungently that even his sickly sweet perfume cannot cover it.

Thunder booms and shakes the walls. White-hot, hateful satisfaction lances through me like a blade. I have not seen him, truly seen him, since my time in Gyeulcheon when he was nothing but a wordless puppet under Rui's control.

This is even better.

"Guests," Kalmin slurs, spreading his arms. "Welcome to my gala." He is speaking, speaking in that mockery of my language, green eyes unfocused. The men and women have grown silent in shock. They can only watch as Kalmin staggers toward the throne, climbs up the dais, and collapses on one of the lower steps. "Isn't it just"—a terrible, bitter smile twists his lips—"wonderful?"

Silently, stealthily, I move into shadow before his glassy eyes can find me.

"You know," Kalmin continues, wiping his mouth, "there's a pile of bodies in the other room. I can't get them all out myself. Flies everywhere. Crawling on their skin."

A handful of guests are moving toward the door. Kalmin's eyes dart to them, and the fog instantly clears. Face suddenly contorting in lucid rage, he smashes his wine bottle onto the floor and stands, unsteadily pointing at the would-be escapees.

"*Stay*," he snarls, and they do—frozen with shock.

Kalmin is panting. The room rings with the echo of his command and gradually grows silent. A silence that is broken by Kalmin's rough laugh. "Good," the crime lord drawls, stepping from the dais and walking—albeit unsteadily—toward his guests. "Good." He steps close to a portly man, peering into his face. The man's eyes are wide. "Mr. Lee," Kalmin says, fixing the collar of the other man's robes. "Did you hear about my Crane? All my Blackbloods, they were... Well." The crime lord steps back and laughs again, and this time the laugh is high-pitched and wavering. "They were *killed*. And I know that one of you did it," he snarls viciously, laughter suddenly gone as he shoves Lee to the ground and—from his jacket—pulls out a pistol. "Was it you?"

Hidden in the shadows, I grin.

This is entertainment at its finest.

"No," the man pants. "N-no—"

Kalmin narrows his eyes. "I know that the killer is here," he declares, stepping away from the fallen man. "Show yourself! Is it you, Dokkaebi?" he screams, throwing his gaze up to the ceiling. "Are you here?"

A beat of silence.

A moment later, the doors slam shut with a *bang*, drowning us in pure darkness. The guests gasp, and a woman screams. I chuckle, soft enough that none of them hear. With my acute vision, I can see perfectly well as Iseul saunters back to her hiding place, dusting off her hands.

Kalmin's breath hitches.

And then he starts shooting, blindly, toward the door. *Crack. Crack.* Men and women scream, scattering, stumbling through the darkness to hide behind pillars. I hear Gwan Doyun choke in fear, whimpering as Kalmin shoots another bullet. *Crack.*

Pistols have only six bullets. He has used three by the time I am behind him, having moved through the shadows, invisible to the eye.

Standing so close to him, I can barely breathe. The stench of him is overpowering, cheap cologne mingled with odious reek and the bitter dyes from his dark suit. The rot in his back molars, the filth behind his ears, the lice scuttering across his skull.

I fight back a gag. The stench of him is inescapable, surrounding me like a wet blanket, unable to be shrugged off. It is a great comfort that he is about to die. That I am about to kill him.

That, without a soul, he will never see the peace of death.

My lips pull into a wide, wide smile as I slowly extend my scale-covered hands toward Kalmin's pale neck.

That was Yoonho, slumped against a wooden column with a bullet hole dark on his forehead.

In a moment, my hands are wrapped around his throat.

His skin is warm and sweaty and slippery, and I feel the vibration in his throat as he roars, lifting the hand with the pistol and firing twice more. The bullets only graze the sides of my face, where they futilely scrape against the scales. I squeeze, hard, and he drops the pistol. It skitters away and vanishes out of sight.

"Hello, Kalmin," I whisper in his ear as he gurgles, chokes. "Did you miss me?"

And that was Chara, sprawled across the embroidered carpet, her blond hair limp and matted with blood as it hid her face while a sword rested in her back.

He thrashes violently, but it's no use. With a cold, calculated viciousness, I slam him against a column so that he faces me. Spit froths at the sides of his lips and his green eyes widen, bulging out of their sockets. He can barely see me through the darkness, but I know he can see the flash of white fangs as my smile grows. Just as I know he recognizes my voice: low and scratchy and sly.

I watch in delight—sick, cruel delight—as Kalmin blinks, taken aback by the abrupt change. The surprise quickly morphs into suspicion and then disbelief—and finally, pure, undiluted shock. He makes to jerk away, gurgling, but I hold him tight by the neck, grinning up at him with an animalistic smile, my entire body shaking with the need to *hurt*.

"*You*," Kalmin wheezes, the word little more than a wet choke. I reluctantly loosen my hold, knowing that he is losing time and oxygen. I will not kill him. Not until he has no soul to pass into the realm where my family now resides.

"Me." All around us, the sound of whimpers fades. I am only dimly aware of the guests attempting to find their way to the door, for all I see is *him*.

The man who took everything from me, who took *everyone* from me—the man who murdered my family and stole me into slavery, the man who beat and abused me, the man who sits on the throne of the kingdom that belongs to the last Talon.

Chryse was not far from her sister, her green eyes dull and unseeing, and her pale hand curled loosely around the hilt of the dagger embedded in her chest.

My breath rises and falls evenly, but inside, my blood is boiling, burning hot—blistering the Voice's fingers as it attempts to cool it back into calmness. Nothing can still my wrath. It burbles up inside me, and I taste it—my terror and confusion that night in Unima Hisao's manor, I taste dirt and dust and grime from the beatings I took from Asina and Jisu and Kalmin. I taste the tears I wept at night while tending to the bruises and lacerations spanning my grimy skin. I taste the rotten pieces of meat and stale rice I was forced to eat every night, I taste the bile that rose in my throat every time I was summoned to obey Kalmin's wishes, I taste the heartbreak and the guilt that has hounded me ever since.

"Did you think I was dead?" I cluck my tongue, raising my other arm to brush a strand of his oily hair from his face with a scaleblade. "Foolish, foolish Crown. Death does not die, and neither will I. Surely you know that by now."

He's trying to speak, trying to wheeze something out, but even with my relaxed hold, he cannot.

"Did you think," I demand under my breath, "that I would give my life to save your disgusting, worthless one? Did you think that this kingdom, *my* kingdom, would be yours forever? Did you think," I sneer, my tongue tasting of bitter fury, "that you could kill the Talons so easily?" I laugh softly as I pick up one of his hands and toy with the fingers. *Crunch.* Kalmin screeches in pain. "Did you *think* that your dying Blackbloods had been picked off the streets like flesh picked off bones by a buzzard by anybody but me? That anybody but me could do so? That it was the work of the Pied Piper, and not the Reaper of Sunpo? Of course you did. Because you are a fool, Konrarnd Kalmin." A bolt of lightning illuminates the ballroom. It smells like fire, and it reveals my face. My scales. My fangs and forked tongue.

And Sang...

Seeing me for the first time since he sent me off to sell stolen jewels in the Fingertrap, Kalmin screams.

The spy's face was still, but contorted with pain as he stared blankly at the looming ceiling.

"Asina died screaming," I whisper, crushing his broken fingers under my grip. Sweat dribbles down his forehead and seeps into his trembling mouth. "She died screaming, just as Chara and Chryse did. Just as Yoonho did. Just as Sang did. Don't you want to know how I did it? Don't you want to know how she died?"

His body was horribly pale and bloodless, and patched with bullets.

His lips were blue.

I smile, and it is a terrible sight to see. Kalmin's entire face distorts in terror. *"Let me show you."*

The fingers of my mind reach out through the kingdom, seeking out Sonagi. It is easy to find her—like seeking a way home I have traversed thousands of times. We truly are interlinked. My will is hers. Briskly, I brush against her consciousness—a wall of smooth scale and crashing thunderstorms—before retreating back into the palace.

At last, the Voice breathes as the walls and floors of the palace tremble slightly. **Here it begins.**

Above us, the emerald rafters spill dust downward onto the floor. The guests, still scrambling to make it out the door, are discouraged by Iseul, who grimly shoves them back as she promised. For these people have associated themselves with the Blackbloods, associated themselves with the lowest of the low. They chose to come here tonight.

And now they will stay. It is only fair.

The Imugi are coming.

Kalmin's entire body shakes as he stares at me in horror. "What is this?" he rasps, but his demands hold no power over me. Not anymore.

"My wrath," I hiss, just as the doors of the palace explode inward with a deafening crack of thunder.

CHAPTER THIRTY-SIX

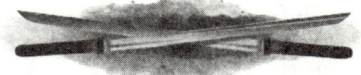

In a flash of red moonlight, monstrously large bodies of sleek black scale burst into Sunpo's palace led by Sonagi, whose hiss of triumph sends attendants screaming in horror and trampling one another in an attempt to escape. Still trapped against me, Kalmin screams—finally, screams, and it is a delicious sound. He flails, attempting to wrestle away from me, but I jerk him back up, now holding him by his neck, exerting just enough pressure that he is immobilized, save for his mouth, which continues to loosen the hoarse scream of pure terror.

Coward, the Voice and I think in unison.

I inhale the smell of fresh blood as it sprays through the air, Sonagi cutting her way through the guests toward me, her gleaming fangs a shining sickle. ***Beautiful.***

"You took everything from me," I whisper into Kalmin's ear. "And now I'll take everything from you."

As the guests fall with beautiful rapidity, gushing gore, I make sure that my prey sees every moment of it and hears every scream of agony. Every plea for mercy. Every wet, gasping last breath.

I stand in the middle of the carnage, holding Kalmin's neck with bruising fingers, grinning as I am splattered with blood. "Don't you dare close your eyes," I breathe, satisfaction filling me with cold delight. For so long I have ached for this, yearned for my revenge... And now it is finally, finally here.

Gwan Doyun, as I promised he would be, is untouched. Mind to mind, I ordered Sonagi to leave alone the sniveling, skinny man with a thin mustache and robes of lower quality than the other guests? He huddles in a corner, and I smell his terror as he mumbles incoherent words. I want to tell him to uncover his eyes. That he is witnessing the rebirth of a kingdom. That I will be his empress soon enough, his *goddess*, and he will be wise to revere me.

My kindred feast without ceasing, ripping into necks and stomachs and chests with violent satisfaction. The slippers I wear beneath my hanbok have become damp with a mixture of warm blood and cold rainwater.

And soon, only Kalmin stands amid the sea of corpses, staring down at the scraps that remain of his army. He is a pale, trembling worm in my grip as I cluck my tongue. The Imugi still, swiveling their heads toward me and the man I hold in my grasp.

And toward Song Iseul, who is delicately picking her way across the carnage, lifting her hanbok above the blood-slick floors. Her eyes are shining, but not, this time, with tears. With satisfaction. Blood has sprayed across her face and she licks a droplet from the corner of her mouth. Behind her comes Sonagi, scales sliding across the floor, teal sprayed with red.

"Daughter," she murmurs, her maw dripping blood. *"I hope we have made you proud."*

I smile, digging my nails into Kalmin's neck as he shrieks in desperate horror, straining away from the leering serpent and the now-grinning Iseul.

"The night is not yet over," I reply, and throw Kalmin to the ground. He hits the puddles of blood with a wet crack as his kneecaps shatter. He howls in pain, fingers scrabbling in the carnage, his voice shrieking in terror as he fights to escape Sonagi—but his efforts are futile. Her body has formed a circle around him where he kneels, trapping him in a cage of glittering, blood-specked scales. Lithely, Iseul jumps over Sonagi and joins him in the circle.

"Kalmin," she purrs. "Have you ever met a Gumiho before?" In a flash, a white, nine-tailed fox stands where Iseul was, muzzle pulled away from sharp, sharp teeth.

Kalmin screams, long and high and shattering. It's the scream of a little boy, not of a kingdom's crime lord. Of an abuser. Of a cold-blooded, murdering bastard.

Iseul shifts back to her human form, laughing cruelly. "I'll take that as a no, then."

"Pathetic," I sigh, shaking my head and resting a hand on Sonagi's scales as I stare down at Kalmin. "Absolutely pathetic."

Kalmin's eyes turn toward me, bloodshot and crazed. His chest heaves. "Lina," he pants. "Please. *Please.*"

"No," I reply, my voice as icy as the Yaepak Mountains. "You will suffer this, Konrarnd Kalmin."

"I will—" Kalmin is blubbering, desperately sobbing. "I will *destroy* you—"

"*Destroy me?* As I recall, you tried that already. And look where you stand now. You may have killed my family, Kalmin," I whisper as my legion of Imugi draw closer, winding around me in devotion, forked tongues flicking my arms. As Iseul bends low, readying herself to spring. My army. My power. "You may have broken me once. You may have left me scars that will gouge my skin and my heart forever. But you *never* destroyed me.

"In fact—" I chuckle, for it truly is ironic. "In fact, in attempting to do so, you delivered me into the hands of fate. Into my destiny as ruler. Empress of All. Child of the Prophecy." I step closer, staring down at him in triumph as he shakes in bewilderment. Sonagi's mouth widens into a smile as I draw the silver ring from my finger. "Truly, Kalmin. If not for your greed and insatiable gluttony, I never would have entered Gyeulcheon. I never would have met the Dokkaebi emperor. And I never," I breathe, raising my ring to my lips, "would be standing here now."

The metal brushes against my mouth, sparking against my skin. Through our thread, I feel him come before he appears. Dark shadow swirls through the palace as Rui emerges to stand beside me, his wolf's smile glittering as Kalmin's face contorts into a wail—the wail of a man who realizes that he has brought his own undoing upon himself, a man who had everything he'd ever wanted for a brief, brief moment and is now seeing it snatched away with nothing more than a flick of a wrist. A man who knows that his end has come by the hands of a Talon.

My soul-stitched moves to stand by my side, tall and imperious, waves of ancient power rolling from him. He says nothing, for he doesn't have to.

The smell of urine fills my nose.

Kalmin has wet himself.

Pathetic.

The Voice attempts to lift my finger, to signal to Iseul to end it here and now—but I still have one question for the leader of the Blackbloods. One question that burbles up from a deep, broken place inside me, low and keening with pain. One question that rises to my mouth and tastes of sickness. The Voice attempts to still my tongue, but I resist, whispering the words with a trembling voice—different, suddenly, from my tone of frosty fire.

"Do you remember them?" I ask, and time seems to freeze—Sonagi stilling mid-circle, Rui stiffening next to me, the blood barely flowing across the floor. "Their names. Do you remember their names?"

Because I do. Every single day. Every single night.

Their names are the fragments of a long-stopped song forever echoing through my head, having done so for so long that they have blended into the background of my every thought. But sometimes, if I listen closely enough, I can hear them.

Sang. Chara. Yoonho. Chryse.

Sang. Chara. Yoonho. Chryse—

Three different emotions flash across Kalmin's sweat-drenched face. Horror. Confusion. And then...spiteful resignation, as if he knows he is going to die and that nothing he says, nothing he does, will stop my wrath.

"What use have I," Kalmin replies, spittle flying through the air as he glares up at me through red, strained eyes, "for the names of the dead?"

I taste tears in the back of my throat. I taste blood.

"I remember them," I whisper.

Kalmin holds my gaze, his jaw trembling stubbornly.

"I remember them all."

I lift my finger.

Sonagi uncoils herself, moving away. I step closer, scaleblades emerging from my skin. Iseul waits for my signal.

Kalmin quakes as I haul him up by his tunic. The stench of urine and fear is thick. His snake eyes are wide. I tilt my head.

"I want you to know something," I whisper. "There is no afterlife for you, not after this. There is no peace." Iseul snarls low in agreement as I trace my blade down his neck, not drawing blood, but drawing a panicked screech from Kalmin, who attempts to writhe away. I hold fast. "There is nothing for you, Konrarnd Kalmin. Do you hear me?" I smile as I draw my scaleblade back. "Absolutely nothing."

I think he might say my name. I think he might beg. I don't care.

My blade cuts clean into his left leg first. Let him know this pain. He howls as I throw him to the ground, blood spraying into the air. His head smacks against the floor and bounces back up, but I force it down once again as I straddle him. The Imugi are hissing in delight, and Iseul is grinning with cold eagerness for what will come after I carve into Kalmin's chest. After I rip away his tunic and press a scaleblade into his pasty skin and write the names in blood.

SANG.

Kalmin lurches and screams underneath me, fingers scrabbling at my wrists. But he's weak, so weak as I write the next name.

CHARA.

His eyes are bulging out of their sockets with pain now. His lips spray spittle onto my face.

YOONHO.

The stench fills my nose. He's wet himself again.

CHRYSE.

I've never heard such screams.

I write the last name with grim finality.

LINA.

Because a part of me died with the Talons. A part I'll never get back.

My handiwork is sloppy, gushing red. I stand and crook a finger to the Gumiho.

Iseul leaps forward. Presses her lips to Kalmin's. It is not a kiss. It is a devouring. She is *eating* him, consuming him as his legs jerk and kick and finally, finally fall still. Iseul stands, delicately wiping her lips, and looks down at the body as she swallows.

The empty, vacant body.

There is nothing in there.

Nothing at all.

I thought it would feel different.

But as I sit atop the throne, staring at the sea of blood below, staring at pale-faced Doyun huddled in the corner, the twining Imugi before me, I feel hollow. Empty. There are no Blackbloods. There is no Kalmin. There is only that mutilated corpse in the corner, and…this.

And how beautiful it is, the Voice whispers, stretching my lips into a smile. **The kingdom, ours. Power, ours. The Prophecy, ours.** It jerks my chin upward imperiously as I listen to the sound of Doyun's teeth rattling as he trembles and trembles and trembles.

Iseul is drenched in blood and grinning wildly. Rui leans against a scarlet column, silver eyes indecipherable as he watches the Imugi. They swarm around me, circling the dais, nestling beside the throne. I stroke Sonagi's head absentmindedly. She is next to me, her pride palpable.

"Doyun," my voice demands, cold and clear. "Come to me." I glower at the man who cowers from me, but he does not move.

"Don't make me say it again," I warn, softly and lethally, my fingers stilling atop Sonagi's head.

Moments pass as slowly as molasses. Then he drags himself to his feet, terrified prey moving toward the sharp-toothed predator. As he moves through the carnage, he blanches.

"Bow," I say, crossing a leg and observing him coldly. "Bow before your empress." The words ring through the silent palace. "Before your goddess."

Doyun remains standing, although his scrawny knees are knocking together so loudly that I can hear them.

"Doyun," I purr, "would you like to experience what you just witnessed firsthand? *Bow*."

With one final look of wary terror, he falls to his knees, as if cut loose from strings holding him up. **Finally.** Power, icy and glorious, rolls underneath my skin as I nestle back on the throne. I've done it. The kingdom is mine, truly mine. The Prophecy is one step closer to being fulfilled.

I close my eyes, inhaling the stench of bloodshed—

"STOP."

My eyes fly open as the voice cracks through the palace like lightning across a churning black sky. As my spine stiffens, the Voice hisses in displeasure as the air quivers, and as three corridors of shadow stretch out into being, bearing with them two Dokkaebi. Hana and Chan. Their fingers shine bone white around the hilts of their woldo and dangpa, their hair braided back for combat. Chan wears armor over his hanbok—bronzed shoulder pads and chest pads—his mouth twisted into a terrible scowl. Hana wears her stealth suit and her eyes blaze black as she glares at me from across the floor. She is the one who has spoken.

"What is this?" I hiss, staring at Rui.

Rui, whose acute guilt and anticipation shoot down the thread. His jaw is tight, his skin ashen.

Another corridor of shadow. Two more figures emerge.

Kang, whose usual white robes have been replaced by robes of deep black. Dark circles line the bags under his eyes. His staff is nowhere in sight. In one hand he holds a long, slightly curved sword.

And his other arm is wrapped around Eunbi.

CHAPTER THIRTY-SEVEN

For a moment, my mind goes blank. Not even the Voice can comprehend what we are seeing.

Eunbi.

Eunbi should not be here, a part of me is screaming. *Why is she — why is she —*

Hush, snaps the Voice. **This turn of events — it is unexpected — we need to think — be quiet —**

Whyissheherewhyissheherewhyisshehere —

I said, be QUIET —

NO —

I think I hear Hana gasp, hear Chan hiss a demand, a curse, a swear. I think I hear Rui roar Kang's name in fury. But I am not sure.

Because my little sister stands in a deep puddle of gore. Her eyes are wide in horror and shock. Disgust and confusion. Disbelief and fear. Such a deep, unending fear.

Tears are beginning to roll down her cheeks. There are red ribbons in her hair. Kang holds her tight as his eyes meet mine.

I jerk to my feet, my Imugi hissing in confusion and hatred as they swivel toward the Dokkaebi. My heart pounds unsteadily in my chest. I taste bile. "Why have you *brought her here*?" This is not for a child to see. This is not... Eunbi isn't like me. She can't — she's never seen — no. She knows I kill. But knowing is different than seeing.

My breathing comes in ragged pants as I stalk down from the

throne past the still-kneeling humans, flanked by four of my Imugi, two on either side of me. Rage roils in my blood and I quicken my pace, aiming for the trio, scaleblades extending from my wrists. I will *kill* them, I will *kill* them for bringing her here—

Kang's eyes are unfathomably sad as he presses the blade of his sword against Eunbi's throat.

My sister's eyes slowly move to the sword.

And then she begins to scream, choked words surging from her lips. *"LILI? LILI? LINA!"*

In shock, my steps falter, and the Imugi still as well, unsure of how to proceed. Eunbi. Eunbi.

The Voice is gasping in panic—***Our princess***—but all I can hear is the sound of her scream, panicked and high and shrill, the scream of a little girl, my little girl, my little sister—

And I am vaguely aware that Kang is shouting a word at Rui, a word that sounds like "NOW," and that Rui is lurching from the column, making his way to stand behind me. I am vaguely aware of his voice, shouting something in furious return, but I am frozen. All the threats—all the threats Kalmin made, threats to hurt Eunbi, to kill her...they came to naught. The sight of a blade against my sister's throat is a gash across reality, and I cannot comprehend...

Kang meets Rui's eye over my shoulder, an unspoken signal passing between the two of them.

I barely have time to register it before the world goes *blue*.

Searing fire envelops Rui and me as he turns me to face him, encasing us in a ball of fire. The flames lick at my skin as Rui cups my face, a tear tracing a path down his handsome face. I hear my Imugi screaming, shrieking cries of terror for the fire, for my life. "Lina," he whispers. "Lina, my love, my little thief. Come back to me."

Eunbi. Eunbi—

I can hear her screaming, shrieking in terror, sobbing and wailing and cursing...

Rui steps away, leaving me alone within the orb of fire as the flickering blue walls finally cave inward, burning my skin, lancing my blood like hundreds of thousands of needles. I scream, falling to my knees as my skin cracks and bubbles and burns, as the Dokkaebi fire eats me alive, gnawing through my hanbok, wrapping around my limbs. Through my burning eyes, I can vaguely make out the Imugi rushing Rui, who fights them off with pillars of the same fire that I now burn in.

The flames feast upon my skin, and I retreat into a hidden part of myself, into a corner of my mind where nothing can hurt me... where it is only the Voice and me...

But the Voice is gone.

No—that's not true. I can hear it screaming as well, can feel it falling over itself in an attempt to extinguish the flames blazing around it.

And as I burn, I remember.

The Prophecy.

Kang's secret plot.

I gasp and choke on smoke and flame as I peer through the flickering blue wall at the carnage surrounding me. At Eunbi, Kang's blade pressed to her throat, his eyes burning into mine. The message is clear. Kill the Prophecy, or we kill your sister.

Don't...fall for it...don't...do this...

It's scrambling for a foothold, to reclaim my body and mind as its own. I scream in desperate denial, scream Eunbi's name, over and over and over again. I hug my blistering knees to my chest as the breath rushes out of me in the form of a hoarse scream, squeezing my eyes shut tight. *"GET OUT OF MY HEAD,"* I roar, as the Voice clings to my mind, refusing to let go. I can feel it— trying to take over, trying to worm its way into a hidden place, to hide. But I won't let it. For Eunbi. For my baby sister.

As the fire ravages my body, I cling to the memories that I—Shin Lina, the true Shin Lina—hold close to my heart. Not memories of killing or victory or Imugi...but of my baby sister.

For Eunbi.

Don't...this is your destiny...

The memories come, hard and swift, running like wild wolves across my mind and trampling the Prophecy underfoot.

She lets go of Rui's hand and runs toward me, arms outstretched. She is taller now, I realize with a small gasp. At least by two entire inches. She has grown while I was away. "Lili!" Eunbi cries, her voice ringing through the hills as she crashes into me, wrapping her arms around my waist.

She's still screaming. Eunbi. Eunbi, my family. I think I might be dying, might be burning alive. But the Prophecy is burning, too—flesh and fingers charring, cracking, crumbling.

"Here," Eunbi said through a big mouthful of kimchi, scallions, and pork. "You can have my last one, Lili."

The Prophecy cries out as it is backed into a corner of my mind, burning and blazing with blue fire. It's working—

"I love you, Lili. I love you so, so much."

But the agony is killing me. I can feel it. Even as my skin fights to reknit itself, to smooth itself over, I am dying.

And there will be no coming back.

Not this time.

"Tell me a story, Lili."

I struggle to breathe, but I inhale only fire. I try to see but all that is there is blue flame. The pain is receding now. My limbs loosen. On the floor I go slack. In my mind, the Prophecy bats weakly at the fire. It is dying, too.

"*LINA!*"

A desperate roar, muted through the fire. Rui.

"*LINA!*"

I close my eyes.

"You haven't let bad things happen to me. You'll protect me! You always have!"

And with a final crackle, the flames die.

Motionless, I cling to the floor, my skin slowly reknitting itself with excruciating difficulty. My breathing comes in rasps. I choke on smoke. I fight for each beat of my heart.

Coldness envelops me as an Imugi coils itself around me, icing my burns with its frigid scales. Sonagi. It must be. I swallow disgust and hatred as she flicks my burnt face with her tongue, urgently hissing for me to open my eyes. But I cannot move, not until minutes pass, and until red, raw burns begin to smooth over into whole flesh once more.

"Lina."

Rui's voice, but from very far away. I open my eyes and through blurred vision, I see him, Eunbi, Iseul, and the other Dokkaebi standing within an orb of Dokkaebi fire, impenetrable by the half dozen Imugi who circle it with bared fangs. Also within is Gwan Doyun, glowering with a set jaw.

Eunbi.

As my vision slowly sharpens, I see that she is sobbing violently, small shoulders wracking.

Eunbi. Little sister.

Sonagi moves to the side and I fight to rise to my feet. It takes minutes for me to stand, but I do, on shaking legs. I am naked save for a few smoking scraps of fabric. My head is bald, burned. I am barely alive.

"Eunbi," I whisper, and my voice is a mere thread. I stagger forward, but I cannot approach the fire. Pain still blisters my every bone, boils my blood. My scalp erupts in agony as my hair begins to grow back. "Baby sister, I love you—please don't cry. I-it's going to be all right." Burnt sugar on my tongue. I don't know if anything will ever be all right again.

"Shin Lina." Kang's face is stiff. "Call off your Imugi."

Iseul blinks, confused. "Lina, what is this?"

My Imugi. I raise a trembling finger, and the serpents retreat, slithering behind me. I fight down a fresh wave of terror. Imugi. On Iseung. Under my command. *"Halt."* The Serpentine Language tastes like sickness on my raw tongue. My stomach heaves and I barely refrain from vomiting.

I am myself again.

And I hate what I have done. What the gods must think of me now…

"Kang, please," I sob. "Please, *please* don't hurt her. Hurt me instead. Eunbi—she's not like this. She's not…" Tears sting my burnt skin that is fighting, desperately, to restitch itself. My eyes meet Eunbi's and she…she flinches away, horror and disgust written clearly on her face. But Kang is lowering the sword, slowly, carefully. The orb of fire disappears, and I stumble forward—but I fall before I can reach my sister. I think that she will run to me, but she doesn't. It's as if she's frozen, staring with that terrible revulsion at me…

But Rui comes. He comes, stumbling, torment in his gaze. His gait is uneven, and I feel his guilt and shock through our thread. "Lina," he breathes. "It's you. I feel it."

I swallow hard and, on trembling legs, push myself toward Rui. My left leg burns in furious pain as I walk, but I grit my teeth.

I must reach him.

And I do. Silently, I pull him hard into an embrace, burying my face in his shoulder. His hands slowly come to settle on my waist, in spots where the horrible burns have healed. "Why did you bring her here?" I cry, fisting bunches of his silken robe. "Why, Rui? Was this Kang's plan?"

"I never would have hurt her," Kang says quietly from behind me. But Eunbi is still sobbing hysterically, clinging to Chan. She didn't know. She didn't know she would be all right. She didn't know. I pull away from Rui and fix a furious glare on Kang.

Part of me wants to set Sonagi on him. Part of me wants to watch him bleed.

But Eunbi wasn't harmed. It would be different—so very, very different if she were. Yet I am back in my own body, my own mind.

And there is no need for more senseless killing, this night.

"Lina?" Iseul is shaking her head in confusion. The blood is drying on her face. "What's going on?"

I shake my head silently and turn back to Rui. My soul-stitched. "Nae sarang," I murmur, brushing a tear from his cheek, "Thank you." Taking a deep breath, I turn to the Imugi. The monsters I once believed my family. It is time for them to return to Jeoseung. There will be no more tithes. No more talk of turning to Yong, conquering the Three Kingdoms. "*Sonagi*—"

"LILI! LILI!"

Eunbi. I whirl around, stricken. Gasping wildly in panic, I sidestep Rui—and see that my little sister is no longer with Chan. Instead, Gwan Doyun has yanked her toward him and she sobs hysterically, face red and puffy. The Dokkaebi's faces are slack with shock, and Iseul meets my eyes, and the helplessness within them knocks the breath out of me. Time seems to slow.

Because Gwan Doyun is pressing Konrarnd Kalmin's abandoned pistol to my Eunbi's head.

He is *pressing a pistol to my Eunbi's head.*

His hand is shaking. His teeth are bared. His eyes are wide and wild, pupils so dilated with rage that he resembles a shark that has smelled blood.

Everything blurs except for that pistol.

He must have scooped it off the floor in the chaos, must have somehow yanked Eunbi away from where she held fast to Chan, must have pressed the revolver to her head before anybody could react. One wrong move and my baby sister is dead. There is one bullet left.

And I killed his wife.

I slit her throat, stole his ring, and lied and cheated and cajoled. *Does he know?*

He must. When the Prophecy and I last paid him a visit…we were not exactly subtle. The world falls away at my feet. *This is how Kalmin felt,* I think somewhere within the fire of panic burning in my mind. *This is how Kalmin felt when he realized he brought his own doom.*

This is how Kalmin felt before he died.

Rui makes a low sound of horror, bloodied fingers reaching within the folds of his robes, no doubt meaning to draw Manpasikjeok. But Doyun spits in warning, jabbing the pistol harder against Eunbi's head. She wails, frightened, as he spits again.

"No song is faster than a bullet," he growls. Gone is the meek, frightened man I once met. In its place is a monster, fueled by wrath and revenge. "Neither is a snake," he adds venomously as Sonagi begins to move forward. She halts.

Eunbi.

My baby sister.

My family.

"Don't do this." My hands fly to my throat, nails digging at the skin in terror as my Imugi stir restlessly, whispering in their horrible tongue, swaying back and forth as my voice breaks. My fingers split the skin and become moistened with warm green blood. Perhaps if I hurt myself enough, I will realize that this has all been a dream. A nightmare. "It wasn't—it wasn't me—the Prophecy—the Voice—"

"One year ago tonight," Doyun whispers, "my wife was murdered under the scarlet moon. Gwan Yoonji."

I swallow hard. "Yes," I manage to say, my eyes on Eunbi. Hers are squeezed shut. Anticipating a bullet. "Yes."

"Her throat was slit." His eyes burn into mine. "You promised you knew her killer. You promised I could kill them."

"I did." My throat is dry with terror. "I did. Let her go. Let Eunbi go and you can kill them." I'll die. For Eunbi, I'll die.

"It's you, Shin Lina," he spits, voice hard. "You murdered my wife. You slit her throat and left her on the floor. Do you think I'm stupid? That I wouldn't figure it out?"

"Doyun. D-Doyun. Listen to me. I'll keep m-my promise. Aim the pistol at *me*, Doyun. Shoot me. Shoot me. Kill me." My words blur, frantic. "I just . . . I wanted t-to apologize, t-to a-atone…"

"You thought," Doyun screams, his face a mottled red, "that I could ever forgive you?"

"No. No. *I* stole your ring, *I* took advantage of your grief. But Eun-Eunbi did not do any of that. She's little, don't you see? She's *a child, a baby —*"

"Don't." Iseul's voice is hoarse. "Doyun, this little girl is innocent —"

"So was my wife," Doyun hisses. "So was Yoonji." He presses the pistol harder against her skull.

"Please." Tears drip down my nose. Eunbi is staring at me through swollen eyes, her small cries ruining me. Yet there is trust in her gaze, trust that I will fix this. And I will. I will. "Eunbi is innocent. If you take her life, you are no better than me. *Please.*"

"Did she beg too?" Doyun is sobbing now as well, ugly sobs, snot running down his mouth from his nose. "Did *Yoonji beg too?*"

Next to me, Rui takes a small step forward, hands held high in submission. "That is *enough*," he says quietly. "Doyun, you do not want to do this. There are other ways —"

C R A C K

The blow of a bullet shatters the world into one thousand jagged shards.

It rips through reality as a dagger through silk, a blade through bone.

Eunbi falls, her hair trailing its red ribbons in her wake.

She falls and she does not rise.

My sister.

My sister is dead.

Eunbi is dead.

CHAPTER THIRTY-EIGHT

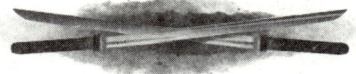

Eunbi used to have night terrors.
She would wake up from them, screaming, unable to stop until I crawled into her bed and held her tight.

Sometimes I had nightmares, too.

Eunbi's small, chubby hands would shake me awake.

But this is not a night terror.

And I will not wake up.

I see it, but I do not see it. Not in the way that I know matters. My eyes work but my heart does not. It has stopped beating in my chest. Under my ribcage is a dead organ. It will never beat again.

My eyes see.

My heart does not.

That is Eunbi's body, small and limp. And that is Chan, roaring in rage, snapping Doyun's neck in one sharp motion and throwing him to Sonagi and her children, who hiss screams of fury and shock. And that is Rui, his lips moving wordlessly as he whirls toward me, agony and rage and horror simmering off him in the form of blue flames.

This is me, sinking to my knees above her body, clutching my hands to my dead heart.

And now I see nothing. Feel nothing. Hear nothing.

Except for the Prophecy.

Small and badly burnt. Clinging to the furthermost corner of my mind. Refusing to let go. Refusing to take that final fall and leave me so utterly alone in this cruel, cold world. I feel its blistered, gnarly fingers scrabbling for purchase as it says my name.

As it says my name, and I listen.

INTERLUDE

Deep within the mind of an empress, two gnarled hands lift a dark-eyed girl with a teardrop scar to her feet.

Don't be scared, the Prophecy says quietly to Shin Lina. ***The pain can end. Let me take it from you.***

Take it from me, Shin Lina repeats, barely audible. *This agony, I do not want it. Please. Please take it from me.*

For she is broken.

Thoroughly and completely broken.

Her skin is shattered glass. Her mind crushed porcelain. Her heart a cold lump of cracking stone.

I can be enough for the both of us, the Prophecy replies gently. ***I will be enough for the both of us. Take my hand, Shin Lina. I will do the rest. You will not even notice the difference.***

Mechanically, the girl does as it says. Fingers interlink with fingers. Palms press against palms. And the Prophecy smiles as it leads Shin Lina down into the furthest crevice of her mind, through nooks and crannies, past cobwebbed memories and murky musings long ago forgotten.

The cage looms into view, a cage of dust and rusted rungs. Shin Lina does not even protest as the Prophecy nudges her inside. Her kneecaps crack on the dingy stone as she falls, bowing her head as the door of the cage screeches shut. With a grim smile, the Prophecy forces the door shut and locks it with not one, but seven, keys.

The Prophecy idly lifts a hand behind its shoulder, tossing

the keys into an abyss of nothingness. They fall away, vanishing, unbecoming, never existing at all. ***There,*** the Prophecy murmurs. ***That's better, is it not?***

The girl does not reply. She merely kneels on the ground, unmoving and silent. The Prophecy smiles to itself. The girl's stubbornness, her incessant *questioning,* has been such a problem. Now, that stubbornness is locked in a cage, unable to escape.

If she turns her head, she will see that the Prophecy's face is the same as her own—pinched and narrow, with the same teardrop scar and the same dark eyes. But the girl does not turn. The Prophecy chuckles.

Goodbye, Shin Lina, the Prophecy whispers, taking one final look at the husk of a girl before tracing its steps back to the forefront of Lina's mind.

Goodbye.

CHAPTER THIRTY-NINE

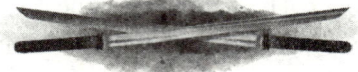

The words ring through the palace, flat and frigid, coated in icicles.

"You betrayed me," I say, rising to my feet, my hands sticky with my dead sister's blood. I run my eye coldly over the Dokkaebi where they kneel on the ground a few paces away, their heads bent in mourning. As I speak, they stiffen, horror flitting across their countenances.

"You *betrayed* me." I lift a finger, and Sonagi joins my side, followed by twenty-nine of her children. They hiss as the heads of the Dokkaebi snap upward, revealing faces of shock. Iseul moves to my side as well, shifting, her fangs bared. "How *dare* you?"

Haneul Rui is the first to rise, unsteady, his jaw slack. I feel his rising alarm. "Lina—"

"The wedding," I continue softly. "The alliance. A perfectly placed trap to ensnare an empress. A goddess. I'll admit, it was well done. Yet what an inconvenience war will be. I'd rather like to skip ahead to the Fulfillment, but I suppose that the spilling of Dokkaebi blood does not sound altogether unappealing."

"You are not Lina." It is Kang who speaks now, low and vibrating with warning. Chan and Hana level their weapons in my direction. I roll my eyes as I step away from the blade and the prongs of the trident.

"I would not say that, not precisely." How to explain in a way these simple minds may grasp my meaning? "I am Shin Lina, but I am the *Prophesized* Shin Lina. The one who will fulfill her sacred duty. The one who was reborn, the one who will release Yong to the skies."

"You speak in riddles," Chan spits.

"Perhaps I do." I curl my lips upward into a smirk. "Or perhaps you're just not very smart. I would suppose the latter." I slant my gaze toward Rui. He looks quite unwell. Through our pesky bond, I feel the world fall apart at his feet. "And you. You are a *traitor*, Haneul Rui. And I do not take kindly to traitors." My Imugi rear back, showing fangs, venom dripping down their maws. "Will you fight? Or will you flee?"

His hands burn blue with Dokkaebi fire. I hide the wariness that spikes down my spine at the sight of those awful flames, my face remaining a mask of cold calm. "Little thief—"

"***Little thief.*** *What a pitiful cry of hope.*" I snigger, coolly amused. "Surely you won't try that trick again, will you? You see it was ineffective." Clucking my tongue, scales arise on my skin. "No, Haneul Rui. You have only two choices tonight. You betrayed me, you know. If it had worked, all I have fought for would have been for naught. So, as I said, Dokkaebi..." My scaleblades shoot from my wrists. The frame of my face, the soft spots of my neck, cover themselves in scales. I smile. "Fight or flee?"

Iseul steps away from the Dokkaebi to join my side. Behind us, my Imugi writhe in anticipation, a sea of scales. My army, so eager for blood. For brutality.

For the Fulfillment.

"You are outnumbered," I breathe, watching as the infernal Dokkaebi tighten their grips on their weapons. Rui's eyes glisten with tears. ***Pathetic.*** "And you are completely and utterly outmatched in power. You know that, so I suppose you'll choose to run." I cock my head. "It's truly a shame that I don't intend for you to make it out of here alive."

"Lina." Rui's voice breaks on my name. "*Lina.*"

I sigh, entirely bored. "I've no time for pleas, nor apologies.

Goodbye, Dokkaebi. I cannot say that I will be sorry to see you gone." As I speak those last few words, I launch myself toward the Dokkaebi emperor, while my Imugi swarm the other three. My blades sing through the air as I vault over his shoulder, slicing through the skin of his shoulder, spilling golden blood. Rui groans in pain, turning to face me.

"I will not fight you," he gasps.

"More's the pity," I croon, and send him stumbling back with a rough kick to the chest. "I was looking forward to it."

"*Lina—*" He cuts off as I attack again, this time sending him crashing into a pillar. The wood dents under his impact; he drops to the ground and struggles to his feet. Manpasikjeok falls from his robes and clatters to the floor.

Farther away, Chan and Hana are battling a horde of Imugi, while Kang faces Sonagi and Iseul, in her fox form. Rui's eyes glint blue and I tense in anticipation for the agonizing flames, but they do not come. Instead, he whirls away from my next strike, leaving his flute on the ground unattended.

Slowly, I take it in my hands.

The instrument is cold. Smooth. Heavy. Manpasikjeok, the Flute to Calm Ten Thousand Waves. Dainty swirls of silver wrap around the dark length.

This flute could bring me a surplus of trouble in the future. My worshippers could be…diverted. Turned against me.

We can't have that.

"Lina," Rui pants. "*Don't.*"

But I do.

With my immortal strength and a cold leer, I snap the Pied Piper's flute in half.

Music erupts as the wood cleaves, as if it is the memory of all the songs Manpasikjeok ever played. The force of it is enough to send me stumbling back. Its sound is *visible*—a cloud of shimmering dark mist that explodes outward before falling to the floor, silent.

Rui staggers backward, eyes wide. Smirking, I toss the two pieces over my shoulder and cock my head.

"HANA!" Chan roars as the female Dokkaebi falls, pierced by fangs, poisoned by venom. The emperor chokes as he watches Chan's lover fall, hitting the tiled floor limp and nearly lifeless. Slowly, he turns back to me, and something shifts in his eyes. Realization.

And firm resolve.

But he does not attack. Instead, the air ripples, and a long stretch of darkness opens near Hana, Chan, and Kang. "RETREAT!" Rui roars, and his friends obey—Chan scooping Hana up into his arms, Kang sliding underneath Sonagi's approaching head and sprinting toward the corridor.

"Follow," I demand furiously to my Imugi—but the Dokkaebi have already disappeared, just missing Sonagi's fangs, and Rui has already opened a second portal behind him. It is just an inch away from his heel. A slight shift backward and he will be gone. Panting, I slow for a moment and meet his eye.

His gaze is dark with pathetic grief.

"If we must go to war," he says quietly as lightning flashes across the ballroom that has become a battlefield, "then we will go to war. But every blade I raise will be a knife to my own heart, and every wound you give me will be a balm upon my agonies. For I never wanted to hurt you, Lina. And it is true that I still do not." He steps backward into the portal, and as shadows close around him, he smiles—just slightly. "If you are in there, Lina—my wife, my soul-stitched—please know this. The time that we had, I will forever cherish. I loved you. I still do." He closes his eyes. A single tear glimmers on his cheek. "I always will."

"As if," I spit, "I could ever love *you.*"

It is then that the thread between us becomes fully visible—a thread of deep, sparkling scarlet twisting and winding from his chest to mine. I glare at it in undiluted disgust.

The Dokkaebi blanches, as if stricken with an injury more potent than I could ever muster. His eyes are latched onto that useless, insufferable thread with an unspeakable disappointment and terrible fear that I feel through the bond. "*No,*" he whispers. "*No…*" He staggers backward, pressing a fist to his mouth.

And a moment later, Haneul Rui is gone, the red thread vanished.

I take a deep breath, standing in the middle of the palace, my chest rising and falling unevenly. And although my useless, lying husband is gone, hiding in his realm of moons and magic, I speak the words aloud.

"*Let the war begin.*"

POSTLUDE

The Empress of Sunpo lounges upon her throne, a ship in a sea of slithering scales. Her Imugi snake across the bloodied floor, eating what is left of the night's feastings, whispering to one another in the language of darkness. Her Gumiho stands beside her, smugly triumphant. Soon, morning will come. Soon, the kingdom will bow to her.

Child of the Prophecy. Empress of All.

Goddess of Wrath.

As it should be. As it was always meant to be.

The empress's eyes are closed, and behind her eyelids she sees kingdoms burning and stars shattering, dragons dancing through velvet-dark skies. *It is beautiful,* she thinks, stroking the Mother of Imugi's bowed head. *It is so beautiful.*

"When do we begin?" the Mother of Imugi asks, hissing eagerly in her ear.

"Soon. So very, very soon." The empress opens her eyes as the first rays of morning light seep across the red-gleaming floor.

The irises flash golden, for they are snake's eyes, burning and bright, slit down the middle by a dagger of inky black.

The empress coaxes the silver ring and the garakji from her fingers and crushes the metal and stone in her grip. Their remnants sparkle as they fall into the deep puddles of thick, still-warm blood.

The Prophesized smiles, slow and sharp.

And somewhere, deep within her mind, a cage rattles.

Acknowledgments

First and foremost, my apologies to the reader for the tragedy and suspense of the ending (although I would be lying if I said this wasn't my evil plan from the start). Consider this my official recommendation to come prepared with a box of tissues for the final installment in this trilogy.

I'm so grateful, as always, to my wonderful parents who continue to support and encourage me. I am here because you cheered me on, and I love you both so much. To my brothers, who are not overly impressed that their older sister is an author and continue to mercilessly tease me about anything and everything. They will probably tease me about this acknowledgment, but that's the beauty of it. Serena Nettleton, for the steadfast friendship and sisterhood we have shared this past decade (△). Grandma and Grandpa, your excitement and pride in this series is one of the greatest gifts I could have received. I hope you skipped all the kissing scenes. Halmeoni and Haraboji, for the love you have given me, along with a hearty dosage of delicious Korean food. 사랑해요, 할머니! 사랑해요, 할아버지!

Thank you so much to my agent, Emily Forney, for the heartfelt advocacy and hours spent discussing (and crying over) our favorite romance books. A warm hug of gratitude to Kamilah Cole, who is both a wonderful friend and a talented author.

To my editor, Stacy Abrams, and the team at Entangled Publishing (Liz Pelletier, Curtis Svehlak, Viveca Shearin, Toni Kerr, Meredith Johnson, Riki Cleveland, Heather Riccio, Elizabeth

Turner Stokes, Debbie Suzuki, Hannah Guy, and Nancy Cantor): thank you for all the hard work you have put into this book from its first draft to its release. To Veronica Gonzalez at Macmillan, for distributing these books into the hands of readers.

And again, to the audience—thank you for spending time in the worlds of Sunpo and Gyeulcheon (with the occasional detour into Jeoseung). We'll be seeing each other again soon…

Wrath of the Talon is an epic, pulse-pounding adventure romance. However, the story includes elements that may not be suitable for all readers. Death of a loved one, violence, indentured servitude, physical and emotional abuse, smoking/addiction/withdrawal, orphanhood, drinking alcohol/hangovers, PTSD, and sexual situations all appear in the novel. Readers who may be sensitive to these elements, please take note.

Let's be friends!

🐦 @EntangledTeen

📷 @EntangledTeen

f @EntangledTeen

🎵 @EntangledTeen

📰 bit.ly/TeenNewsletter

entangled teen
an imprint of Entangled Publishing LLC